# LONDON

# ONE

## LUCIAN

*December 2017*

"Hold the plane!" Jane shrieks as if it's even a possibility. With a sigh, I stand and toss my paper and empty espresso cup into a nearby rubbish bin just as Jane leaps through the sliding doors of the gate in a dark purple blur. As she draws closer, I take in her dress. Geared more toward summer weather, the sleeveless, deep V-cut, knee-length dress hugs her mid-section before flaring out dramatically. The flare is completely intentional due to the sight of the lighter purple tulle beneath—which I have zero doubt was deliberately added for the *Cinderella* effect. Given our current weather and the forecast for our destination, I find her attire utterly ridiculous.

Face reddening, brows pinched due to strain, I catch sight of the reason as Jane torpedoes towards me. In one hand, she clutches a slip of a jacket and matching purple fur . . . something? Conversely, in the other hand, she drags a heavily worn, tattered suitcase—wheels seeming to spin in all directions to work against her. As my phone is scanned with my electronic ticket, I catch sight of her matching dark purple heels. As I gauge their preposterous height, she predictably fumbles, flying straight toward me, forcing me to steady her as her wayward luggage slams against my shin.

Grunts exit us both as I spot a sheepish wince through a wavy rogue lock of her shoulder-length, dark brown hair before she sputters a breathless apology for both me and the gate attendant.

Once I'm sure she's gained her bearings, I release her as she rests her things on the gate counter and starts rummaging through her oversized purse for her ticket.

"I've got it," she assures us both as she fruitlessly searches her bag. "I was just on my phone," she repeats a second before her eyes bulge, and she produces it housed in a neon yellow case, which reads *'I'll cut you'* in bold letters across the back.

The gate agent's agitation has Jane thrusting it toward the agent in proof, all but adding an enthusiastic 'ta-da!' This is a second before she loses grip, and it lands squarely on my newly polished shoes, clobbering me on the toe.

"My God, I'm so sorry," she admonishes as we bend to retrieve it. Narrowly missing a broken nose, I back off, allowing her the space we both need.

Taking another cautious step away—for my own safety—the agent gestures to Jane to scan her ticket as she begins to flip through her phone, specifically her pictures.

"There's an airline app," the agent reminds her.

"I took a screenshot to make it easier." Jane frowns when a picture of her dress appears on a hanger. The large display of her screen makes it easy for us all to see.

"Sorry, I took a few preliminary trip snaps," she offers. A blink later, we seem to be in the *before* phase as she appears in a floor-length mirror—after she's donned her dress. This is followed by at least ten more photos of Jane in different stages of makeup. A few with sparkling purple eye shadow that matched her dress—which, thankfully, she opted out of. Those pictures are followed by what looks like an indecision of hairstyle. Up, then down—which she went with. The following five are testing various shades of lipstick until finally, we're graced with our first *after* selfie, in which Jane poses with a two-pound dog.

The next few shots are pictures of a woman holding said dog. Blurry photos—unintentionally taken—follow these. The shutter is seemingly pressed as the phone is in transit to Jane's handbag.

"Almost there," Jane assures us as she frantically swipes her phone.

Selfies of Jane blur in the back of what I assume is an Uber. This is only confirmed with one last shot when Jane appears, doing an about-face in the back seat to pose with a perplexed Uber driver, his expression screaming 'what the fuck?'

A few painful swipes and photos later—the last few of the international flight sign—we are finally graced with Jane's ticket barcode.

With another inflated sigh, the exasperated agent grabs Jane's phone, scanning her ticket while looking at me with a wide-eyed 'good luck' expression. Lips threatening to lift, my answering expression should be easily interpreted as, 'There's not enough luck on the planet.'

More apologies pour from Jane as she trails me down the runway, dragging her ancient suitcase behind her while doing her best to keep up with my long strides. Though her ridiculous heels give her some height, she continues to walk in them like a newborn fawn.

"Dr. Aston, I'm sorry, *truly*, I was so excited about the trip that I lost track of time . . . and my neighbor was late in picking Poochie up and, oof," she stumbles again as I opt for *fight* over *flight*—primarily for my benefit—to once again steady her on her feet.

"Jane," I grunt as she lands awkwardly against me.

Slowly, so slowly, she lifts her apprehensive eyes to mine, sweat beading her hairline, her lipstick somehow smeared slightly across her upper lip in the seconds it took us to hike from the gate to the door of the plane.

"Yes?" She asks softly, scanning my face for a trace of apathy, or more likely expectation, due to our former run-ins.

Expectation because I've made her very aware of my aversion to her bad habits. Particularly the habit that interferes with our working relationship. Staring down at her now, I can't bring myself to scold or insult her. Mostly because her eyes beseech mine for some inkling of understanding or sympathy for the *self-induced* drama she seems to have suffered in an effort just to make it to the plane.

"Let me get your bag."

"No, no, Dr. Aston, thank you, but—"

"*Lucian* and I'm afraid I have to insist because I'd rather not suffer another injury before we embark."

Deflation clear in her posture, she releases temporary custody of her bag along with a defeated nod, adding a hushed, "I'm sorry."

"It's fine. Let's get to our seats. We were meant to board first."

Her eyes lighten, and my blatant barb is either ignored or overlooked as she announces to the flight attendants we pass—along with everyone else in earshot. "Oh, I almost forgot!" She scans the cabin, rattling with excitement. "It's my first time in first class!"

I don't bother to point out further that one of the perks of the expensive seats is that we wouldn't have had to wait to board *if* she were punctual.

One of the two flight attendants gives me a lingering gaze— along with the lift of her lips—before focusing on Jane, her eyes softening due to her abundant enthusiasm. "Welcome aboard. You're going to love it."

"Thank you," Jane says, glancing over at me, her smile lighting the whole of her heart-shaped face, her pale blue eyes twinkling.

It's unsurprising that one small act of kindness has Jane's excitement shifting back. In the time I have spent in her company, it seems an engrained trait that Jane feeds off those around her. Not that she needs a boost because she's naturally ebullient. Ebullient being an understatement.

Though sharp as a tack in the OR—I can begrudgingly admit that—Jane still possesses a childlike wonder. Her infectious, uplifting spirit made her a favorite of our surgical floor before I arrived and a patient preference for those unfortunate enough to make a return trip.

Oddly enough, Jane's innocent demeanor doesn't accurately represent her true nature. Case in point, Jane was kind enough to brand me with a nickname within a month of us working together. A name that has stuck and is consistently whispered behind my back—*Dr. Prick.*

A staff and patient favorite she may be, Jane's habitual tardiness is the core reason for the grudge I harbor against her.

Much like the airline's refusal to rearrange flight times to suit her wardrobe decisions and the tardiness of *Poochie's* minder, cutting times for life-changing surgeries wait for *no one.*

Despite the favoritism, to this day, it baffles me that Jane has managed to stay on staff.

She's been late to my OR *twice* in the six months she's been in rotation on my surgical team. Both times, I have reprimanded her—*harshly*—the second with a threat to have her removed from my staff and report her to administration, thus earning me the title of Dr. Prick.

Though we've been paired to represent St. James in our upcoming medical consults and surgery, Jane is far from the ideal choice I would have made as a representative of one of Boston's top surgical teams. Let alone a sound travel companion. A perk of being St. James' newest addition, I have yet to choose the permanent fixtures in my OR. One thing is for certain—when my six-month review comes up after the new year—I will ensure that Jane and I's professional relationship ceases when our return plane's wheels touch the ground.

Unfortunately, until then, I'm stuck with the hurricane known as Nurse Cartwright outside of the operating room. If there's any allowance for luck or miracles where Jane's concerned, I'm positive she must be circling close to her ninth life. Oddly enough, if Jane had sufficient discipline to scrub in on time, she would have the potential to be a sound candidate.

"Oh, wow!"

I jump back a fraction as Jane reacts to our accommodations, slipping into her pod seat before looking up at me as I start to work her geriatric suitcase into the overhead locker. The flight attendant joins me in the effort as Jane looks around like she's just taken her first step into Versailles. The flight attendant and I struggle for several seconds before finally securing it into the locker. After, I slip my luggage beside hers with ease and with room to spare. Unbuttoning my suit jacket, I fold it and catch Jane's curious gaze on me just before she flits her eyes away.

A trickle of sweat glides down my back as I finally take my seat, feeling as though I've just been through an ordeal of some sort rather than boarding a plane. Slightly out of breath, Jane turns to me, eyes glistening as she flashes me another full smile. "I can't believe we're going to Europe. *Six weeks*, Dr. Ast . . . er . . . Lucian," she says, testing my name out on her tongue. "Isn't it wonderful?"

Unblinking and in a far different state than the relaxed one I was in minutes prior, I stare back at Jane as more perspiration seeps into my starched shirt. "Splendid."

# TWO

## JANE

He hates me.

Charlie: Who?

Dr. Prick. He hates me . . . Loathes me entirely. *said in Grinchiest tone.

Charlie: I swear to God I heard that in Jim Carrey's voice. Did you wear the dress?

Of course!

Charlie: Well, who could ever hate you wearing that?

I know, right? Wait . . . that was sarcasm, wasn't it? I texted the wrong support group chat.

Charlie: Need I remind you that I make up the totality of your support group chat? Barrett left a month ago when you started sending photo bombs of you and Poochie in matching sweaters.

His loss. So, then, do your job. Hand Wave Emoji. Support needed!

Charlie: How is he dressed?

Like a posh, sophisticated Englishman and brilliant

surgeon . . . and yes, still disgustingly gorgeous. Jesus, I thought he was hot in scrubs. You should see him in a tailored suit. FIRE EMOJI

Charlie: Picture.

Hell no. It's all I can do to keep from staring at him. I can already tell I'm on the last of the only nerve he has.

Charlie: You have an eight-hour flight ahead of you. Extend an olive branch and make the best of it.

We have nothing in common. He just passed on champagne and ordered a single malt scotch.

Charlie: One glass! Do you hear me? ONE GLASS OF CHAMPAGNE FOR JANE.

Don't you ALL CAPS ME!

Charlie: NECESSARY. You know you can't hold your liquored tongue.

Need I remind you that I have a fear of flying, I'm on a PLANE, and the flight is NOT short. Two glasses.

Charlie: Don't do it!

Fuck it. Really, what's the point? He's allergic to me, and it's so obvious. But, to be fair, I was a little late. OOPS TEETH EMOJI

Charlie: WHAT? HOW? It's a night flight!

I was worried about the dress, hence the two dozen pictures I sent you.

Charlie: Which were pointless because I told you not to wear the Barney dress.

Well, too bad. I love it. And it's not a Barney dress. It's just dark purple!

Charlie: The exact shade of purple as the fucking dinosaur and completely inappropriate for Boston and London winter . . . but whatever, it's your nipples that will be cut glass ready, not mine.

Me and my nipples need a new support group, and I have a jacket and a muff.

Realization strikes as the flight attendant seals the plane door closed.

> Correction, had a jacket and muff.

> Charlie: What in the hell is a muff?

> It's a fur you put your hands into. It matched the dress perfectly! It kind of winterized the outfit, and I was in such a hurry that I left it and my dress jacket on the damned gate counter! CRY FACE EMOJI.

> Charlie: To that, I say good riddance.

> Now I will freeze. FROZEN FACE EMOJI

> Charlie: You were going to anyway. Focus, Jane. You need to seize this time. You still want on his surgical team, right?

> Right.

> Charlie: So, from here on out, do your absolute best to show him who you really are, and stop being all Nervous Nelly around him.

> Too late for that. I kind of tripped in my heels and faceplanted in his chest . . . before I dropped my phone on his foot.

Bubbles and more bubbles.

> Delete whatever you were going to say, and stop coming at me! I'm nervous enough as is.

> Charlie: FACEPALM EMOJI

> Charlie: Okay, damage control. Just . . . try to overcome the intimidation factor and remember he shits, and it stinks like every other human.

> Eww, you had to go there.

> Charlie: It's the truth. Bullshit aside, everybody loves you, Jane. Knowing you, if you just relax and be yourself, you'll find a way to win him over.

> Doubtful. He's a single-malt scotch man. I have absolutely nothing in common with a scotch-ordering man. Whiskey man, I can do. A light beer man, a breeze, but not a single-malt scotch man. He's so bougie that he probably starches his underwear or has a service do it.

> **Charlie: Speaking of . . . please tell me you're covered in that department.**
>
> **EYEROLL EMOJI. You don't know shit about being on the plus-size struggle bus when it comes to underwear, so keep it to yourself. This dress was my one fairy tale indulgence because, in case you've forgotten, I'll be in Europe for the next six weeks!!!**
>
> **Charlie: True. HAND CLAP EMOJI. CELEBRATION EMOJI MEDAL EMOJI MEDAL EMOJI MEDAL EMOJI**

I need no interpretation for the last three emojis. This trip brings with it a sense of accomplishment that feels a lot like crossing a finish line—not just for me but for both of us. Growing up in Triple Falls, North Carolina, where Charlie still lives, we lived hand to mouth. A trip overseas for one or either of us is nothing we could have ever dreamed of in our lifetime. With both our parents being the definition of deadbeats, we barely scraped by. That's why, as soon as we were capable, we both got jobs, Charlie at seventeen and me at only fifteen. In doing that, we ditched our parents before they could hand us off to another relative for 'a couple of months' or had a chance to fully desert us.

At the end of the day, Charlie and I raised each other, and though we don't have a happy childhood to report, it doesn't bother us in the way it probably should. It's no big mystery to either of us why. We raised ourselves despite the family we were dealt and batted away any hand they could have had in *shaping* us. It was no easy feat, but at the end of our struggle, we're proud of the fact that neither of us is anything at all like the two people we were supposed to call Mom and Dad—and to this day refer to as Kim and Allen.

> **Charlie: You've worked so hard to get to where you are, little sis. Seriously, just do your best and try to get along with him. If he remains stand-offish, then fuck it, forget about trying, and enjoy yourself. I hate that you'll miss Christmas and New Year's, but if anyone deserves a dream vacation, it's you. Just know we'll miss you.**

My heart drops at the idea of missing my nephew opening his Christmas presents. In going overseas, I'm missing out on one of the few trips I can make per year to see them. Charlie's boyfriend, Barrett—whom she refuses to marry, which may actually be her only residual baggage thanks to Kim and Allen—has his roots firmly planted in Triple Falls. The perk is that Elijah is growing up in a community with a support system we never had.

**Stop, or I'll cry and ruin my makeup. Kiss Elijah for me and tell him auntie is going to bring him presents from every store in London and France next time I see him.**

**Charlie: Don't overdo it, but text me when you get safely to your hotel and let me know how the flight went. You've got this, Jane, even when you don't.**

**K. Love you. OMG . . . we're about to take off!**

**Charlie: ENGLAND FLAG EMOJI, CLAPPY HANDS EMOJI, QUEEN EMOJI, and remember FUCK DR. PRICK.**

**Saving that for a Frenchman. WINK EMOJI**

Glancing around at those who occupy the other first-class pods, I can't find a single excited expression to match my own. Those surrounding me look bored and are either already connected to some device or are blanketed for the seven-hour flight. Maybe I should have expected it from people who can afford to take this kind of comfort for granted. Perhaps I should take note of their behavior and act accordingly, but I can't seem to find a damn to give as I familiarize myself with my pod. Unable to hold my excitement any longer as the plane begins to speed down the runway, I brave a glance over at Dr. Aston . . . Lucian, whose own expression seems just as indifferent as everyone else's.

Good God, isn't anyone happy anymore?

Though equally unimpressed as our neighbors by our accommodations, he steals my breath for a beat.

*Don't fixate, Jane.*

Managing to look away before I'm caught, I do whatever I can to not concentrate on or try to identify what mix is used to make up the heavenly cologne I got a strong whiff of when I faceplanted into his chest. Or the feel and strength of his hands as he righted me after I crash-landed into him.

In trying to look and feel my best today, I'd embarrassed myself in front of him yet again. Objectively, I can't blame him for being wary of me. Admittedly, I've made a shitty impression on him since he started at St. James six months ago. Then again, he doesn't at all have any sort of warm or welcoming air about him in the slightest.

While Lucian has the 'don't fuck with me' aura down pat, I have a keen sense there's something far deeper inside him. It's telling in his eyes at certain times, especially during patient care. It's guarded, and you have to look for it, but it was there, seemingly *for me*, just before we boarded. That should give me hope, but given the fact that he seems to loathe we're breathing the same air at the moment—and is doing a poor job of masking it—I doubt I'll ever get a layer deeper than I have.

Even so, Lucian Aston is one of the best cardiothoracic surgeons in the world. Like all the others up for and vying for the position, I want permanency on his surgical staff, if only to watch him work more miracles.

As I think it, I find my eyes drifting back toward him as he drains the last of his scotch and lifts both his chin and glass toward the buckled-in flight attendant—who's openly ogling him—that he's in no rush.

Not that I blame her. Even in my periphery, I can make out how thick his sand-colored hair is, and that's just the start. Light, honey-colored eyes, a prominent nose, along with a wide mouth, and perfect, thick lips.

The man is a fucking marvel to behold, but seemingly, and ironically, a heart doctor with no pulse.

It's unfortunate how his personality consistently deflates my loyal lady boner. Shrugging to no one, I refuse to allow Dr. Prick's ill perception of me to dampen another second, giggling giddily into my glass as the plane is caught by air and we begin our ascension.

To London.

London—the star of so many of my favorite novels. I've always been fascinated by the city's rich history and culture, seeing as how it's nothing like where I was raised. I've been daydreaming about this trip my whole adult life, and for the first time in my *adult life*, I'm in the position to live out a fantasy.

Six weeks in Europe!

All fucking aboard!!!

Gesturing to the flight attendant for another glass as she unfastens her seat belt, I shiver as goosebumps cover my arms, and the natural and slightly champagne-based high sets in.

*One life, Jane. Live it!*

# THREE

## LUCIAN

Reclining in my seat after a subpar dinner of questionable chicken, al dente rice, and cheap scotch, I close my eyes and am halfway to a decent reprieve when Jane's voice startles me awake.

"So, good doctor, where in England did you stem from?"

Looking up, I see Jane hoisted over the dual partitions meant to act as a privacy wall as she peers down directly at me, ignoring it altogether.

"Dorset early on, but mostly Richmond," I reply, signing off on getting any sleep for the time being. Adjusting my seat back into the upright position, I force Jane, her dangling wavy locks, and frosted blue gaze out of my space.

"Did you like it?"

"Growing up in Richmond? Not that I had any choice in the matter, but yes."

"Is it close to London?"

"Not far."

"How great is it that you get to visit family for the holidays?"

"I won't be."

"Oh?" She glances away briefly, "Sorry, I just assumed since we have a good amount of free time that you'd be seeing family."

I nod because I have no intention of expanding on the topic. Though it's my first trip back to London since leaving, I have no plans of revisiting my reason for it. There's no point. Jane eyes me closely, seeming to read my reservation about it while downing her third glass of champagne. Feeling as though the subject is safely dropped, I'm thankful when the lights dim, a sure cue for everyone in the cabin to settle in as the flight attendants start to hoist the rest of the carts away.

As I go to readjust my seat, Jane ditches her glass on one of the passing carts before popping back into view.

"I'll miss seeing my nephew, Elijah, come down the stairs on Christmas morning for the first time since he was a baby. He's seven now. I hate that he won't believe soon. You know . . . in Santa. There are only a few magic years left. Do you have any nieces or nephews?"

"Two. Nephews. My brother's children."

"Just one brother?"

"Tragically, yes," I relay, giving too much. Thankfully, she misinterprets.

"So, you don't get along?"

"We aren't close, no." *Fuck.* I rethink a second glass of scotch as the attendant prods me with inquisitive eyes.

"And your parents . . . ?"

"Alive and well, also living in Richmond," I say, politely declining both offers from the flight attendant, one for the drink, the second of an entirely different nature. Shifting my focus back to Jane, I exaggeratedly air out my blanket to close the discussion.

She lowers her gaze as I spread it over my lap and dips her chin slightly before disappearing over the partition.

Ten peaceful seconds later . . .

"Lucian?"

"Yes?"

"I feel like we got off on the wrong foot, and I want to apologize for being late those *two* times. It was completely unprofessional, and I won't be late to your OR, or any other OR, for that matter.

Honestly, I have never been late to surgery *once*, aside from yours, and I know there's no excuse, but it truly was a run of bad luck. That said, I am sorry."

"Understood and appreciated," I say, hearing the slight slur in her speech.

The silence beckons me as my eyes burn from overuse, a painful and familiar reminder of another long stint without sleep.

"So, why did you want to become a doctor?"

"Surgeon," I correct.

"Surgeon," she clears her throat, and I can practically see her eyes roll. But it took me eighteen grueling years to become a specialized surgeon, and I damn well deserve the proper title.

"Being a physician has interested me since I was young," I offer, "becoming a surgeon and choosing my specialty came later. You?"

"I have absolutely no issue with blood, bones . . . like *zero* gag reflex. I figured I should use it to my advantage, and I often do."

My eyes bulge as she giggles again—unseen—before a loaded, long pause ensues. "Oh . . . uh, that was completely inappropriate, Dr . . . Lucian. I did not at all mean that the way it came out."

Sure she didn't. "It's fine."

"Champagne, sorry, I'm a little loose. I don't drink much, and I'm not a big fan of flying. Sorry . . . again." *Hiccup.* "So, what are your plans while we're there?"

"None to speak of—"

"Because I have to say my plans are rather *ambitious.*"

"Oh, how so?" I ask.

When she pops up again, I snap my blanket to my chin and blink up at her.

"Well, if we're getting personal."

I shake my head. "We're no—"

"I'm going to see every tourist destination imaginable and do whatever it takes to make it memorable." She waggles her brows. "Let loose a little since I've been on my very best behavior for . . . God, it's been *way too long.* Anyway, I'm determined to have a story to tell the girlfriends back home. You know what I mean?"

"I'm quite sure I don't."

"Well," she shrugs a shoulder as if nudging me, "maybe I could help *you* in that department. I mean, after we nail the job part of it," she declares in afterthought. "That's the most important thing and why we're going after all."

I nod because, at this point, I'm terrified of the direction this is taking.

"So, what's a *scotch man* do to have a good time?"

"A scotch man?"

"What do you do for fun? Golf or something?" She asks, just as I notice her eyes get darker toward the iris. I've never seen a pair quite like them.

"Golf? Not my sport, no."

"Are you *into* sports?"

"Not especially."

"Ever played one?"

"I dabbled in both rugby and football when I was in my teens and early twenties," I fire back, arming myself for another question as I get slightly sidetracked by her return gaze. The coloring really is a spectacular blue. Stunning, actually, and only emphasized by her dark hair and pale complexion.

"Oh, rugby, that's a tough guy sport, but you aren't that far from your twenties, are you?"

"Far enough," I answer.

"I'm guessing thirty-one?"

"*Six.*"

"*Really?*" She might as well have said *that old?* "Huh, I can't picture you playing rugby."

I can't picture myself getting an ounce of sleep if this continues. Feeling like she must have read my expression she sinks a little behind the partition. For some reason, it unsettles me. Just as I go to speak, she beats me to it.

"Well, I'll let you sleep. Sorry to be all talkative, I'm just feeling the jitters, and I'm just so damned excited."

"It's natural," I offer.

"I've been dreaming of going overseas since I started college, probably longer. I never once thought I would. I guess you could say I grew up on the opposite side of town—nowhere near the tourist destination. I never thought I'd see a palace, let alone one that hosts a true Queen. And France, oh my God, don't even get me started."

*Please don't start.*

"Anyway, I hope to get to know you a little while we're over there."

"We'll be spending some time prepping, what with the meetings for the surgery."

"I mean *outside* of all that . . . though it's my priority. How lucky are we?"

"Fortune's fools," I sigh.

"Goodnight, Dr . . . Lucian."

"Goodnight, Jane."

"*'Suck,' he orders, and I gape at him. The audacity of this man.*"

My eyes pop open as a masculine chuckle echoes somewhere close in the cabin, and the sexy rasp of a woman's voice again sounds. "*His eyes are unyielding as I barter with my devil, eyeing the head, my mouth watering. Stalling, I glare up at him and squeeze him from thick base to engorged tip. He's dripping, and I find satisfaction in that.*"

Doing my best to pinpoint the source, I shoot to a sitting position and meet the mirth-filled eyes of the man in the window seat. His eyes lower to the right of me, specifically on Jane. "Got a live one there, huh?"

Springing into action, the narrative continues. "*I continue to pump him with my hand as he traces my hot-pink-stained lips with his finger before pushing one into my mouth and adding another.*"

Bending over the partition, I find Jane fast asleep, a black-out mask on, an e-reader stuck between her hip and the side of her chair.

She's covered from head to foot in multiple thin blankets, practically mummified. Laughter continues to erupt in spurts around us, and Jane remains fast asleep while the narrator reads off the following line. *"On impulse, I suck as he curses before replacing his fingers with the thick head of his cock."*

"Jane," I snap, and she barely rouses. Just as I manage to grip the edge of the e-reader and free it from its tight confines, the damned thing sings in my hands. *". . . choke on the fullness of him as my jaw burns while I furiously try to fit him in my mouth."*

"Jane!" I all but shriek as I desperately hit every button to silence the fucking thing. Wishing I had a window to toss it out of, I'm subjected to more as the laughter multiplies while I frantically tap the screen to bring it to life.

Jane rouses slightly as I finally manage to kill the sound before powering it down.

The man in the window seat muses as Jane finally lifts her sleep mask and smiles up at me. "Well, good morning, Lucian."

"Is it?" I grit out as the cabin lights come on, only to make the moment even more humiliating by spotlighting us. Jane frowns at the shade of my complexion and, no doubt, the sheen of sweat accompanying it before recognizing the e-reader I'm white-knuckling between my fingers.

"Why are you holding that?"

I thrust it toward her as she adjusts her seat up. "This was going off."

"Oh?" she winces. "Sorry, when the timer on my mask goes off, it sometimes continues to read on my Kindle. *Whoops.*"

Whoops?

*Whoops?!*

Completely unphased and painlessly unaware that the entirety of business class just got a glimpse of her reading preference and X-rated wake-up call, she grabs a small plastic bag from her purse. "I'm just going to go freshen up." She frowns. "Hope you slept well. I think I only managed a few minutes."

Feeling as though I might explode, I watch as Jane stands and stretches. Her skirt rises close to mid-thigh as the man in the window seat openly ogles her, his interest becoming more dedicated as Jane passes him. That is until he meets my hostile glare. "Sorry, man. She yours?"

Rather than answering, I give him a telling enough look, and he raises his hands, feigning innocence, though his eyes continue to follow her backside.

Watching him watch her, I recognize the *real* issue this trip will eventually present. While Jane's been doing her best to assure me that our business in London and France is a priority, she made it abundantly clear during her champagne rant that she's got an agenda.

Meanwhile, for me, the outcome of the six weeks has a crucial bearing on my future and direction as a surgeon. That alone is enough to let me know that I can't, in any capacity, allow her to 'let loose' nor create 'a story to tell the girlfriends.'

For the next six weeks, I will have to watch her like a hawk and keep her head out of the clouds—away from whatever European fantasy she's concocted and intends to see through. A sinking feeling settles over me that the only way to do that successfully would be to chaperone her in London and France—if only to keep her pacified enough to see my own agenda through.

Sadly for Jane, my updated itinerary includes making sure no fairy tale of hers comes to fruition, and worse, I'll be the scripted villain to ensure it. As Jane joins me back in her seat—filling out the form the flight attendants are passing out for non-citizens to enter the UK—I take note that the man's eyes are back on her, and he seems positively . . . captivated.

Glaring at him to get my point across, he finally turns back into his seat as Jane shifts her eyes toward me, a whisper of a smile ghosting her lips and a knowing glint in her eyes. As I scrutinize the reason for it, it dawns on me.

The e-reader was payback for brushing her off last night.

She knew damn well that it was going off. From what I've seen, she couldn't give two shits about the opinion of others, while reputation—particularly in the medical field—means everything to me.

I narrow my eyes as she focuses back on the form, a glossy curtain of hair shielding her from further examination. It's then I declare a silent war on her best-laid plans. I suspected that alongside her innocence and sincerity lay a bit of a heathen. Now, I'm positive that when crossed, said heathen comes out swinging to those unsuspecting. Sadly for her, I'm no fool.

But the way she manages to hide it . . . it's genius, really, though I'm onto her.

Embarrassingly wiser, I tilt my head back, inhale some patience—*deeply*—and hold it until I'm forced to exhale.

This may very well be the longest six weeks of my life.

# FOUR

## JANE

I blow into my hands as we wait for the next available cab while willing myself to stop shaking. If Charlie could only see me now, she'd be wagging a finger at me with a ready 'I told you so' to dispense. Regardless, at most, I'm only an hour away from warming up and thoroughly regretting the dress.

Asinine as the choice might be, it serves a few purposes—one of them being my version of a Holly Golightly "Breakfast at Tiffany's" entrance. While I'm not a diehard fan of the movie, I do love the character's free spirit. I plan to mimic it and just *go with it* in my time here.

Running my hands lovingly down the fabric—even though I'm freezing—I lift my chin slightly and remain steadfast that the temporary cold is worth it. Sadly, it's the lack of sleep and the long line getting through customs combined with Lucian giving me the brush off last night that has me feeling a little . . . well, a lot out of sorts. These things rapidly diminishing both my resolve and my mood.

"Did you not bring a jacket?" Lucian asks in his smooth English timbre.

To my detriment, my teeth choose that moment to start chattering. "I left it and my m-muff on the c-counter at the gate."

"That was hardly a jacket," he retorts, "and what is a muff?"

"It's a roll of fur that keeps your h-hands—" he quirks a brow as if he doesn't really want an in-depth explanation. "Never mind, I'll manage."

Just then, a gust of freezing air blows, and I fist my skirt against my thighs to keep it from flying up. Though the skirt is respectably knee-length, the icy breeze seems somewhat determined to make it an issue.

Lucian's wary eyes sweep my goose-pimpled flesh before jutting them down to our most recent source of friction—the three over-sized and, admittedly, overstuffed suitcases I brought along with my carry-on. All of which are piled in a heap next to me. When Lucian saw just *how* packed I was, he cursed under his breath but remained otherwise mute—though I swear I did see his left eye start to twitch.

It's not like I asked him to be my personal bellman, and I state as much. "Lucian, I have every intention of hauling my own luggage during this trip." He scoffs as I openly scowl at him and decide to make it a personal mission that he does not touch another damned piece of my luggage—especially since he's extraordinarily *prickly* this morning, pun fully intended.

Several loaded, silent seconds pass, and it's during them that I know he's doing his best not to lash out at me—as if the jerk has a right. Though I can't see why he's holding back now, he never bothered not to humiliate me in the OR. This is why I can't find an ounce of regret for turning the tables this morning by powering off my mask after cranking up to full volume on my e-reader.

I didn't sleep a wink and have the residual embarrassment of his brush-off to thank for it. Champagne buzz or not, I'm no idiot, though I can play ignorant when the occasion calls for it. Or, at the very least, feign polite interest—which he did not do. Those few minutes were humiliating, and the alcohol did little to temper the sting. The longer we stand here—predictably at odds—the more my resentment for him starts to grow.

Both anxious to get to our destination and take a breather from the other's company, I shake my head in objection when Lucian flags a black cab. "I read horror stories about black cabs in my research before the trip," I relay in a hushed tone. "Bad things sometimes happen to people in those things."

"Bad things sometimes happen to people *everywhere* on any given day," he retorts dryly.

"Listen up, Doc. I won't be subject to some deranged cabbie because you're not patient enough to wait."

Just as I finish, a man *half my size* climbs out of the cab and greets us with a warm, friendly wave.

"Looks truly dangerous," Lucian mocks before greeting the driver as he opens the back of the cab for our luggage, "but I trust you're well versed in hand-to-hand combat?"

"Hilarious," I snark before pawing his forearm. "Just . . . don't accept any champagne or anything that isn't *sealed* to drink. Having a penis doesn't make you any less of a target."

"I'll keep that in mind." He doesn't bother to conceal his eye roll as the cabbie struggles to get my luggage inside the back of the car.

It's when Lucian steps forward to help that I lift my hand.

"I've got it," I snap, giving him a pointed look before lifting the bag to the trunk. The cabbie scowls at Lucian over my shoulder, as if he's half a man for not helping, just before Lucian snatches my other bag up and deposits it. Once the doors shut, Lucian turns to me, expression smug.

Oh . . . so we're going with openly hostile already?

*Game on, prickly.*

Taking note that Lucian is not a morning man, along with his *all-day-a-dick* disposition, I climb into the back of the cab and again smooth down my dress. Lucian gives the driver an address as I take in my surroundings while we pull off, thankful for the warm air circulating in the cabin. As the back of my thighs and ass begin freezing due to the temperature of the bench seat, I truly start to rethink my dress.

All I wanted was to arrive in style—my style, my way, and make a little splash in the background. That's all.

Well, *mostly.*

It was checkbox one, and now that it's checked, I can't help but regret not digging through my suitcases while we waited, if only to grab my jacket. I probably would have, had I not felt the glare on the side of my head once I'd claimed my shit.

As if reading my thoughts—or maybe due to the chattering of my teeth—Lucian's jacket covers my shoulders. Shocked by the gesture—but feeling too damn snubbed to accept it—I shake my head. "No, thank you."

"You're freezing."

"Well, that's kind of my fault, isn't it? You've made it a point to tell me, *repeatedly.*" Shrugging off his warm, black trench coat, I wave his gesture away with the flick of my wrist. "I'll deal."

"Stubborn, I see. At least assure me that the rest of your attire is . . ." he flicks his wrist, mocking me as he collects his jacket back, "more weather appropriate."

"Not a fan of my dress?" I sneer, hackles rising.

"It's lovely," the cabbie compliments.

Lucian snaps narrowed eyes to the rearview—specifically to the driver in silent warning—while leaving the choice words that I know he's brewing up unspoken before turning back to address me. "I'm simply saying it would be best if you wore warmer clothing, something more suitable for—"

"I'll keep that in m-mind," I parrot, my delivery ruined by my damned teeth continuing to chatter as if they've been wound up. Fed up with the debacle, I briefly close my eyes in frustration and shake my head. "Jesus, I didn't mean for this to be . . . I j-just wanted to—" I cut myself off, knowing it's pointless to try and mansplain.

"To what?" Lucian asks, this time seeming somewhat interested in my answer.

"Nothing you would understand," I say, waving my hand dismissively. He's not the guy to get it or want to try and get it—or me, which he made clear last night. Just as he has in the rest of the time I've known him.

At least I can say I tried.

After loosening up with the champagne, I went all in with my attempt. Maybe it was a little sloppy and ill-timed—considering the fatigue on him—but hell, we're on a working vacation. Though the stick up Lucian's ass doesn't know any better. While his replies *seemed* cordial enough, his posture and eyes all but screamed *'fuck right off.'* And I swear I heard it loud and clear *in his accent.* Even in my champagne haze, I most definitely took the hint, but this morning, I woke up full of offense. Offense that's only ever been curbed by the *one thing* about Lucian Aston that gnaws at me most—the fact that he's drop-dead gorgeous, and I'm *stupid* attracted to him.

As in, I have not, for a single second, managed to get my shit together enough whenever Lucian is within twenty feet of me.

For months I've tried to convince myself it's just aesthetics and mostly my imagination, but that logic grows wings with every thirsty drink I take of him. No matter how small, every sip is lethal.

Every. Single. One.

Lucian is one of the few men I've seen in the flesh that is deity-molded, from the tip of his thick, slightly coiffed, sandy brown colored hair—which has that movie star type of luster—to the tips of his glossy shoes.

The only average thing about Lucian is his height, right around six feet. He's broad-shouldered, well-defined, and muscular. His confident gait and swagger alone are fucking awe-inspiring. Pair that with his damned honey eyes, chiseled features, and ultra-thick lips, and he's got an abundance of mind-boggling attributes to appreciate— let alone focus on one in particular.

Not only is Lucian blessed with the architecture, but he's also got that . . . je ne sais quoi thing, that enigmatic and unexplainable allure that makes women crazy.

I'm certain every woman on our surgical floor—married or single—has fantasized about Lucian Aston.

Then there's the accent. Jesus. The man's voice is sex.

It's his undeniable allure that turns me inside out and has had me nervous, frenzied, and fumbling like an idiot since the second our eyes met. To the point I wish I'd been forewarned before he crash-landed at St. James.

I have little doubt that bitch, Wendy, head of HR, probably watched in amusement the day he sauntered onto our floor, and we began dropping like flies.

If it seems like a bit of an exaggeration, it's not. The commotion that day was one for the books. Not even the most distinguished doctors, male or female, could keep their eyes off him.

To this day, his effect is unmatched. He still parts lips and keeps hushed whispers rolling along with the waves of wet dreams flooding our floor. Hell, until hours ago, my own fantasies were drenched with him.

So, despite the shitty, aristocratic, completely unattractive air about him—along with his clear aversion to me—Lucian is the sexiest, most intoxicating damned man I've ever laid eyes on. Which is the very reason I've been late to his OR *twice*. No matter how I reasoned that it was just his looks, I couldn't keep myself from the anxiety that came from standing across from the man for hours on end. An effect no other man, nor human has had on me, *ever*.

Lucian *was* the exception.

Now, and thankfully, Lucian himself is starting to administer the cure to the ailment with every second that passes in his company. And by the second, any lingering fantasies I have are dispersing, thanks to his recent handiwork.

Which is fine with me because I'm typically confident in my skin. Sometimes overly and overtly—like dancing naked in front of a mirror without flinching—confident. Well . . . until I laid eyes on Lucian. That's been my Achilles heel in completely detesting the man. That, combined with the fact that he's a brilliant surgeon, is why I truly want the coveted spot on his surgical team.

But as much as I've tried to dismiss his typical shit this morning, I can't seem to ignore the festering back catalog of offenses he's dealt out. Which so happens to be day one of our six-week excursion.

Despite the rough start and my rapidly souring mood, I decide to give it one last try, for both our sakes, seeing as how our trip has just begun.

*Day one, Jane. Day one.*

"I'll be dressing much warmer from here on out," I assure him through clenched teeth, summoning the will to reoffer my bent and battered olive branch.

"It's a good thing," the cabbie replies. "The weatherman has predicted one harsh winter."

"Oh," I ask, prompting Lucian. "Did you know?"

Lucian dips his chin absently, uninterested in attempting friendly conversation. As I sweep his features, my eyes instinctively lower to his overly full, lush lips, and I abruptly swat the budding thought of what being kissed by them would feel like as I tune back into the cabbie.

"—weather London hasn't seen in some time."

"Well, I'm ready for whatever. It's my first trip here," I pipe warmly as I take another peek out of the window.

"You don't say," the driver continues as I keep a polite ear on our convo while glancing outside my window just as a light dusting of snow begins falling. At the sight of it, my mood slightly lifts.

I'm here, in London.

Rough start or not, in simply being here, I've reached a milestone that seemed completely unreachable for any Cartwright—the first to graduate college and now the first overseas traveler. My newfound enthusiasm only wanes when we pull up to a building that doesn't at all, look like a hotel.

Confounded, I turn to Lucian to see his eyes brimming with satisfaction. "I guess while you were doing your research, you missed out on the itinerary I emailed a week ago."

Knowing he has me, I deflate. "I was getting around to it."

"Packing, I presume," he snarks, handing the cabbie a bill I recognize as a fifty-pound note worth about sixty-five bucks.

At least he's a generous tipper.

"Please hold the car for an hour, and I'll double the fare and tip," Lucian requests.

"Happy to, sir."

Lucian exits the car and extends a polite hand toward me. "Good, because as it seems, we're in need of temporary storage."

Glaring up at his hand, I reluctantly take it and exit the car as a merciless gust of wind crashes into me full force. Brisk air stings my arms and legs as I begin to inch my way toward the back of the cab. "I'll grab a change of clothes."

"I'm afraid we have no time for a wardrobe change, Jane. That is if we want to be *punctual.*"

"I'll just be a minute," I plea as another gust of wind welcomes me to an Icelandic sort of hell.

"Pull around, please," Lucian orders the cabbie, shutting the door on any hopes I had of saving my nipples. When he's several strides in front of me—due to an epic fight taming the lower half of my dress—Lucian stops on a dime, takes off his jacket, and hooks it in his finger in a second offering before turning back to me expectantly. Every bit of hope I mustered for a truce falls away as I stalk past him and his jacket, chin up, eyes blazing, dreading the minutes ahead.

By the time we arrive at the nurse's station to wait for our meeting with Dr. Tremblay, we've stopped conversing entirely, both our eyes averted. It's only when Dr. Tremblay approaches with a, "What a surprise, I didn't expect you until tomorrow," that my eyes snap to Lucian's, and I see the mirth dancing there.

This is when I mentally start plucking at the fingertips of the imaginary gloves I wish I were wearing and slowly begin working them off.

# FIVE

## JANE

Less than twenty-four hours ago, I was ready to, for lack of a better word, try to impress Lucian Aston—or at least alter his previous perception. Open-minded enough to attempt to get an understanding of him. All in hopes of being pleasantly surprised that I'd somehow misjudged him. Now, it's all I can do to keep from hiking up his body to rip out chunks of his shiny, thick mane by the roots.

"Dr. Aston," Dr. Tremblay dismisses in his thick and extremely sexy French lilt as we both stand opposite his large, antique desk. Anxious to flee after the longest, most uncomfortable hour of my life—in which my nipples nearly broke through the inch-thick fabric of my dress—I take the time to run my hand along the top of the dark mahogany.

"Antique?" I ask.

"*Oui*, eighteen nineteen," Dr. Tremblay rasps.

"It's so beautiful," I whisper in appreciation.

"Agreed," he says, his indicative tone prompting me to look up into his curious return gaze. "I have a few more similar pieces at my home."

"Which is where?"

"Jane, we need to get going," Lucian intercepts.

"Of course, and I have a patient to see," Dr. Tremblay says, his lips lifting as they flit to Lucian and volley between us as they have for the last hour. Dr. Tremblay, whom I found out is a close mate whom Lucian attended medical school with, was not at all oblivious to the growing friction between us, seeming amused by it, while my nipples and I were *not*. As much as I wanted to lash out every time Lucian interrupted me as he just did, I held my tongue to keep it professional. Though things have gone even further south since we arrived here, I had hoped we'd present a respectable and united front at the very least—fat chance of that.

Either way, our first meeting went as well as it could. In three weeks, Dr. Tremblay will join us in Paris and act as Lucian's second set of hands. There, we'll combine our team with Oxford's finest heart surgeons on a specialty case, which is the main reason for the trip. Heart surgeons all over the globe will be tuning in to watch the groundbreaking surgery taking place in a theatre-style operating room. Lucian, being the key cutter, will be joined by two others, as well as backup medical staff.

The pivotal factor is that Lucian will be using newly approved surgical equipment that every doctor assisting has mastered specifically for this surgery. If all goes well, it will lead to pioneer-type breakthroughs in others. The case is beyond complicated, and frankly, I'm salivating over assisting in it.

As their formal conversation comes to a close, Tremblay subtly gestures for Lucian to join him at the side of his desk. Taking my cue, I make my way toward the door, but not before noticing they've both turned their backs on me. Eyeing the expensive books on Tremblay's well-lined shelf as I pass, I hear part of the exchange as Dr. Tremblay's harsh, heavily French lilted whisper reaches me.

"—You haven't seen her . . . or Byron?" Just as he asks, he glances behind Lucian's shoulder and gives me a slow wink. I wink back.

"No," Lucian replies, eyes following Tremblay's to meet mine before narrowing.

*What. In. The. Hell?*

"You haven't spoken to *either*?" Tremblay asks, somewhat incredulously.

"We'll see you in Oxford," Lucian says, ending the questioning before Dr. Tremblay steps past him and makes a beeline for me.

"Nurse Cartwright, it was an absolute pleasure," he extends a warm hand, an even warmer smile lighting up his handsome face—a hand that I take and shake firmly, unable to help my quick comparison. Sadly, next to Lucian, Tremblay looks average, though he's anything but. Dark hair and eyes, sharply dressed, and wearing an addictive-smelling cologne, I got a heavenly whiff of when introduced. Extremely easy on the eyes, it's evident by the way his staff regards him. He's the Dr. Aston of his own floor.

As far as being well-mannered and personable, he has Lucian beaten by a country mile.

"It's been my pleasure as well, Dr. Tremblay. I look forward to working with you."

"Please do call me Matthieu, and if I may," his eyes dart briefly between Lucian and me. "I'd love it if you would accompany me to dinner," he shifts focus on Lucian, who stiffens at the invite and quickly backtracks, "that is, unless you'd like to join us, Lucian."

"Matthieu, I'd love that—"

"We'll entertain it if our schedule allows," Lucian cuts me off, his pronunciation of schedule coming out shedule the way the posh Brits say it. Hairs standing on end, I nearly lose my shit when Lucian has the audacity to snap his fingers for my attention like I'm a k-9. Gloves halfway off due to his treatment this last hour, I take a breath and bid Matthieu one final farewell before stalking out the door. Unsurprisingly, the nurse's station is twice as occupied as it was when we filed into his office. No doubt, all of them lined up to get a look at Dr. God.

If they only knew . . . Hell, *if I had*, I could have saved myself so much anxiety.

In the excruciating hour since we exited the cab, toured Tremblay's surgical floor, and met his staff, along with the last twenty we spent reviewing the details, Lucian has cut me to the quick during any response I've given. Unlike Lucian, Matthieu seems to want to get to know me and respects the opinions of extra hands in the OR. While Lucian's table-side manner leaves a lot to be desired in the personable section, until this morning, I'd always judged him as fair. At this point—and because of the way he's dismissed me—not only did he shit on my first English breakfast, but it seems he expected me to swallow every bite down with a smile.

Fuming, as they continue to converse outside the office door, I can no longer help my verbal vomit as I pass the wide-eyed nurses objectifying them both. "Just a heads-up, ladies and gents, he's given the old happy clap to *nearly every nurse* on our surgical floor. Save yourself both the *trouble and prescription*."

"Jane," Lucian hisses behind me, trailing by mere steps.

Once inside the elevator, he turns to me, complexion reddening. "And what in the hell was that?"

"One cock block deserves another, don't you think? And when the hell do you get to decide who I dine with?"

"I don't—"

"Exactly," I snarl. "You don't, so stay in your damned lane."

"We're all working together."

*"And?"* I cross my arms.

"And," he pauses as if it's obvious, "it's unprofessional to personally consort—"

"Ha!" I scoff. "As if you resembled anything close to professional back there, captain misogynistic."

"Pardon?"

"You're seriously going to look at me like you weren't aware of what you were doing back there?" When the door opens, I fly out, not bothering for a reply, fumes still wafting off me despite the chill now embedded into my bones.

As we exit the hospital and the cabbie pulls around, I make the firm decision that as much as I admire his skills as a surgeon, being a permanent part of Lucian's team will only make me uncomfortable and ultimately miserable.

Charlie urged me to use my time with him to extend the olive branch, but in truth, I already have.

One time too many.

And every single one of them, I've been brushed off.

Decision made, I mentally set my olive branch on fire and opt to spend the rest of my time here avoiding him between meetings and consults.

No good could ever come from spending personal time outside the OR with Lucian Aston—of that, I'm sure.

Though enticing as it may be to many to unravel a man like him, layer by layer—kind of like the hero of one of my romance novels— in reality, his behavior is totally off-putting. Which only makes me want to *flee* his company altogether.

It's not like I had any real expectations for us, at least on the personal side.

I knew better, have known better, and this time with him only solidified it.

Once inside the cab, my bubbling fury begins to boil over when I recall the times I've seen him consort with other members of the staff. He's nothing like the way he is when he's with me. If I'm not going to be on his team—and he can't spare a few minutes to try and at least get to know me a little—I'm *all out.*

Knowing that asking him outright what his issue is with me won't solve shit, especially if he puts a voice to it—and due to the mood I'm in, which is growing fouler by the second—I decide to ignore him altogether.

It's as we pull away from the curb on the ride to our hotel that I feel his gaze on my profile and am forced to look back at him.

Whipping my head in his direction, armed for more judgment, I don't bother to shield my tone. "What?"

"Interesting novel you were reading."

"Yeah?" I snark, reveling in the frenzied look in his eyes as he stared down at me when I woke up on the plane. "Probably not your taste."

"Definitely not, no." He gives me a pointed look. "But you knew that, didn't you, Jane?"

Scowling back at him, I fail to conceal the slight widening of my eyes when I realize our detour from the hotel and early meeting was payback.

Shit.

Somewhere between the plane and the cab, *he made me.*

In seeking retribution, the bastard purposely prolonged my discomfort by moving our first meeting up by an entire day.

At least there's an excuse for this morning, but that doesn't explain his behavior the other ninety-nine percent of the time.

Before the e-reader, though, I hadn't imagined a second of the discomfort he hadn't bothered to spare, which cements my original assessment.

Lucian is a prick—a self-righteous, pompous prick at that. That's not changing anytime soon, no matter what effort I make. Neither is his quick dismissal of me, not just as a possible candidate for his surgical team, but as a human being in general—which is something I refuse to ignore a second longer.

"Fine. Fuck it, busted," I say, squaring off, gloves on the ground. "Can't imagine what captures your interest," I mutter, "I'm guessing something along the lines of medical journals."

"Mostly, yes."

"Utterly *electrifying*," I snort derisively before dismissing him. But even as I concentrate on the passing billboards—two of which include delicious shots of David Gandy—and the fact that I'm riding on the opposite side of the highway, I again feel his gaze on my profile. As it lingers to the point that I'm feeling warmer, I continue to keep my focus elsewhere. After six months of being a blithering fool in his presence, and just as my attraction withers to nothing, the idiot is finally looking at me. I nearly burst into hysterical laughter, along with the relief at the fact that I'm back.

And have zero fucks to give about the opinion of Dr. Prick.

My confidence rightfully restored, I mentally flick him from a pedestal he never earned as each mile passes. The thought warms me, as do my insides since we landed in London.

Feeling more myself in his presence than I ever have, I resume my measured steps, intent on evading Lucian the second I can see them through.

Nothing and no one will get in the way of my dream vacation. No one.

As I test my theory and turn to him, I find him already staring in my direction. His brow pinches when he sees my expression. His eyes scour mine as I mentally pass my own test and can't, at all, help the victorious lift of my lips.

I swear a flicker of fear passes behind his light eyes, his question coming out slightly high-pitched. "What?"

I shrug in reply, my first genuine smile firmly in place as I glance back out the window.

I'm officially cured.

*Thank God it's over.*

# SIX

## LUCIAN

"I've got it, Lucian. Let me handle it!" Jane snaps, her hostility alarming as I step back. Between the hospital and hotel, I've managed not only to get under her skin past the point of niceties, but it seems my mere presence has robbed all sparkle from her eyes. Though I admit it was a bit immature to play tit for tat due to her stunt this morning, it was also important to remind Jane before she set sail on her *story quest* that we're primarily here to *work*.

I admit a bit of remorse kicked in when she began to bounce her crossed legs for the last ten minutes in Tremblay's office. Legs that Tremblay couldn't stop feasting on, as well as the moderate amount of cleavage her dress showcased, along with every other detail of her person. And Tremblay wasn't the only one. It seems every employee at the hospital scoured her from head to dark purple heel—attention to which she seemed oblivious.

Just as oblivious as her effect on our floor at St. James.

Where now, all her pre-trip optimism seems to have vanished completely. Surely she can't be that sour about an hour-long detour?

Coming up empty as to what I could've possibly done that was so detrimental to her mood, I motion for the bellman as he catches my signal and begins stalking toward us with a ready cart.

"Happy to let you handle it, Jane," I finally reply to her outburst, "but seeing as how the bellman is here—and it's literally his job to sort the luggage—maybe we should allow him to earn his wage and tip and mutually agree to sit this one out?"

Jane's shoulders slump forward slightly as I tip the driver as promised, and he gives me a clipped "thank you" before wishing Jane a sincere and warm farewell.

*Twat.*

The bellman greets Jane first, appraising her brazenly, before lifting a guarded gaze to me. "Checking in, sir?"

I nod as he focuses back on Jane. Once her obscene amount of mismatched luggage is stacked on the bell cart along with my moderately sized carry-on, we follow the bellman towards the sliding doors of the hotel lobby. Just as we hit the incline, I find myself in need of an answer. "Do you mind enlightening me on how I have so horribly offended you?"

Jane, who is surprisingly steady on her feet, trails to the left of the bellboy, I to his right, her head tilted toward me with her reply. "You know damned well how you have."

"I'll admit the stop was—"

"Cruel, at the least, demonic would be a better description." She stops on a dime and turns toward me. The bellboy pauses ahead of us but keeps his distance. "But to tick a few offenses off, let's start with last night, *Dr. Aston*—"

"I told you to call me—"

She cuts her hand in the air, and I fucking loathe the gesture, as it's one of my top peeves.

"Just so we're clear, I'm not too keen on taking orders but have an open ear for sincerely polite requests, and I don't see the point."

"Pardon?"

She practically sneers at me. "Why bother to get us on a first-name basis if you have zero intention of getting to know me?"

"We spoke last night," I reply, and she scoffs.

"You all but told me to fuck off."

I glance around. "Must you make a scene?"

"No, I mustn't," she mocks. "But *you asked*, and I'm done pussy-footing around the fact that you're an unbearable ass to try and be personable with. You talk a good game, and I'll admit you're pretty damned formidable from the jump but to the point you're insufferable to be around. It's off-putting and unattractive, and not just physically. Trust me, buddy. You've made it crystal clear that you find nothing *about me* attractive in either sense. The sound of my voice seems to be nails on a chalkboard to you. So, spare me, and I'll do the same for you. But since I'm the one that'll be forced to endure your shit behavior for the next six weeks, we're going to clear the air now, so I don't waste another second trying to get on a good side you don't seem to have."

Sighing, I nod for her to carry on, and she takes a fraction of a step in my direction. "Were you even considering me as a candidate for your surgical staff?"

I remain quiet as my updated plans go straight to shit. She'll have no part in me chaperoning her anywhere if I'm honest with my reply.

"See, me, I like to try to give people the benefit of the doubt and not assume too much because assuming makes assholes out of people. But you, sir, are every bit of the pompous jackass you come across as."

"And *Dr. Prick* is what? A compliment?" I counter.

"Guilty," she snaps, "but only because you didn't give me a chance to explain myself the first or *second time* you berated me in front of the entire surgical staff."

"Right," I say, shoving my hands in my pockets as she gives me a good once over before pressing her lips firmly together. "Carry on, Jane, don't stop now. I don't think you have the attention of every-one within a full meter."

"I think I'm good. Thanks for being upfront. I'm glad I didn't waste another minute of this vacation trying in vain."

"Lest I remind you, *this is* a working vacation, and you were chosen by administration to perform as you would at home—with-out a childminder."

She whips her head towards me as we both resume stalking toward the hotel, and the bellboy sets into quick motion just ahead of us, his back shaking from having his chuckle as Jane decides to continue handing me my arse *publicly.*

"Childminder . . . you mean babysitter? Are you serious?" Jane's eyes spark with a fire I've never seen, but I suspect she reserves expressly for times such as these. "To think I respected and admired you all this time. Well, guess what, asshole, I'll have you know that—"

It takes a mere second, maybe two, for the rogue suitcase to wipe her completely off her feet, knocking her over like a bowling pin.

"Christ!" I jerk back as Jane lands with a thwack on the freezing concrete outside the sliding doors of the hotel. Gaping down at her, I freeze when I see her eyes closed, hands covering her chest, skirt hiked around her hips just as the bellboy bypasses me, freezing his footing a mere step in front of me as we both assess the state of Jane. Jane, who is lying on her back, one leg bent . . . *fanny out.*

Unable to get my bearings from the sight of her, my greedy eyes glide up her creamy white thighs and further to her perfectly trimmed pussy.

Her perfectly trimmed, *bare* pussy.

The fire threatening to siege me is quickly snuffed out by an icy tidal wave of awareness as Jane's eyes pop open, and she gapes back at me. The pain in her pale blue return stare gives way to shock as she realizes that both the bellman and I are staring at her, half naked, and neither of us is moving.

Panicked, Jane yelps my name, snapping me out of my stupor before I burst into motion. Quickly kneeling where she's literally spread out, I immediately lower her dress and tuck it between her thighs to free my hands as the doctor I bred inside takes over.

"Don't move," I bark as I stare down at her, remembering the sickening thud that accompanied her nasty spill. "Did you hit your head?"

"Yes," she croaks, her eyes watering from pain or humiliation—most likely both.

Gently cupping and lifting her head, with my free hand, I run the pads of my fingers carefully along the expanse of her neck. "How badly does it hurt?"

"Throbbing, but I think my upper back got the most of it," she whispers.

The bellboy kneels next to me, apologies pouring from his lips as I absently palm him away.

"I'm so very sorry," he stutters out.

"Your job is pretty simple," I grit out. "Secure the *luggage and guests*—"

"Lucian," Jane snaps in scold.

". . . and escort them *safely* into the hotel," I finish through gritted teeth.

"Sir, my sincerest apologies. One of her bags got away from me. I can call for a doctor."

"I *am* a doctor," I relay, glancing around the bustling hotel while feeling secure that the two of us were the only ones to see her fall.

"Lucian," Jane whispers, utter devastation etched in her features.

"Turn your neck," I instruct, "slowly, to the right." She does, and I find relief when the task is easily carried out. "Now the left."

She does as I request, and I nod with each completed task, confidence growing that she's done no real damage.

"What were we arguing about?" I prompt.

"I don't remember," she lies.

I can't help lifting my lips. "Don't go sheepish on me now, Jane."

She opts for delivering facts instead. "Today is December 18th. Your name is Lucian Aston. We're here for a consult with a team from Oxford who will be assisting you in the layout for a groundbreaking surgery in Paris . . . and before I busted my ass—which is freezing solid by the second—I was berating you in front of a five-star hotel."

"Good," I say. "Can you try and sit up?"

"I don't want to," she croaks.

While assessing Jane's injuries, I've completely forgotten the bellboy is still kneeling next to me until he speaks up. "Sir, would you like me to—"

"Go inside and check us in, please—reservation under Dr.

Lucian Aston, adjoining rooms. Please see to it that our luggage is delivered along with some paracetamol, six hundred milligrams minimum, along with whatever apology the hotel deems fitting. I do *not* want to see a manager out here, nor does she."

"Yes, sir," he replies, scurrying back toward the cart.

"Lucian," Jane repeats, my name sounding like both a prayer and question coming from her lips. A question I know she needs an answer to.

"We were the only two to see, I assure you, Jane. Follow my finger."

She does, and I see that she's as clear as she can be considering the whipping wind and the fight against her watering eyes.

"Tell me about your pain."

"My head is pounding and my back is on fire . . . and I'm going to need a minimum of six hours in therapy."

Only able to give her a whisper of a smile, I grip the back of her head for full support. "On three, ready?"

"No, but let's do it," she whispers, a thin tear slicing down her cheek and pooling at the corner of her lip. The sight of it stretches my chest and has me clearing my throat. Remorse has its way with me completely in that moment because I am guilty of every single offense she's named and probably more.

After the countdown—and once I manage to get her sitting—she clings to me, her arms wrapping firmly around me, our fight seemingly forgotten at present.

"Tighter," I whisper to her, struggling to keep her in my hold.

"Just leave me here," she croaks, "so I can find a bus to step in front of. Isn't that a common accident here for Americans since the sidewalks are marked *look left* or something?"

"Jane," I utter low, clearing my throat to hide the threatening laugh. "Stop fighting me."

She sags in my arms before tightening her hold and glaring up at me. "Leave it to me to have the most embarrassing moment of my fucking existence in front of *you* of all people."

Instead of examining the meaning behind that statement, I

concentrate on what my inner doctor needs to do while battling the images my subconscious took snapshots of—which are continually threatening to break through. "One step at a time, Jane," I manage in an even tone.

Still plastered to me, she nods into my chest as I slowly let her onto her feet and walk her into the hotel. Once she's moving, I tick off more assessment questions. "Ankles?"

"Fine," she whispers.

"Legs?"

"Not working well for me for the last twenty-four, but that's an operator error."

She keeps her face buried as we pass through the lobby, and our bellboy spots us from check-in and rushes toward us, keycard in hand.

"Penthouse, Sir," he offers the card, and I nod in satisfaction before taking the proffered key. "I'll deliver your bags shortly, along with the paracetamol," he keeps his focus strictly on me as he speaks. Smart man. "I just want to again offer my apologies."

"It's fine," Jane says, keeping her gaze on our collective steps as I shake my head in refusal before glancing at the name embroidered on his uniform.

"Max, I'll see to it your job remains secure, but please understand you're being dismissed," I relay, while keeping Jane firmly in my grip, "and do make yourself *scarce* during our stay."

"Yes, and . . . *understood*, sir."

Feeling Jane stiffen in my hold, I know it's her bleeding heart, for the bellboy who ogled her, causing the objection in her posture. If she only knew that he would be wanking like a madman within minutes of his dismissal to the very images I'm currently fighting like hell to erase, said bleeding heart would dry up. Even in the state she was in, the sight of her was . . . it was as if the heaven's fucking parted with the way—

*Lucian!*

My inner doctor screams in disruption for the second time, jerking me back to the here and now. Once inside the lift, she pulls away from me, finding no more use for me as a human shield. "Easy, Jane, don't let your distaste for me injure you further."

"I didn't mean all of that," she offers in a clipped tone.

"You most certainly did."

"Yeah, I did," she scoffs, "and like it or not, you definitely know me more intimately now."

That one has me biting both lips while swiping the keycard for the penthouse. Instantly, the lift springs to life, hoisting us to the top of the hotel. Feeling the tension brewing inside her, I can't help but speak. "Jane, I assure you the bellboy and I were the only—"

"Don't, okay, just don't. I'm going to try and believe you."

When the lift door opens, Jane pops her head out covertly as I fight another chuckle, trailing behind her as she stalks down the short hallway leading to the penthouse door.

"Three things," she says on a pained exhale before turning and blocking the doorway.

I nod, leaning against the doorjam. "Fire away."

"One, thank you for handling that, the way you did. It was . . . impressive," she relays, the compliment seeming to pain her.

"You're welcome. And the second?" I prod.

"Please forget what you saw."

"Need I remind you that I'm a doctor?"

*A lying doctor at the moment, Aston.*

"And the third?" I prompt.

She cuts her eyes up at me with a look of a woman scorned and ready to get back to battle. "As of this moment, *you're dismissed* because I find you a vile human being. So do us both a favor and don't bother to utter another bullshit, obligatory nicety to me beyond being cordial and not cutting me off in front of our peers. I say our peers, Dr., because while I might not have a doctorate, you need grunts like me to assist you, and you should respect that. If I weren't necessary, the fucking job wouldn't have been created. We can't all be kings, or there would be no hierarchy. I will never again be dismissed or belittled by you, ever, in front of other staff again, or you'll find yourself on the receiving end of one rabid bitch. Until we are on opposite ends of the table or in a meeting that has to do with surgery, you make *yourself scarce*, and I'll reward you by doing the same."

"Jane," I exhale as she steps back, refusing to look at me. "I apologize for earlier, for the flight, truly."

"Too late," she drops her hostile gaze to our feet, "open the door, Dr. Aston."

Sighing, I do, and she shoots past me like a bullet, pulling off and tossing her heels into the trashcan before slamming a door somewhere further into the suite.

*Fuck.*

# SEVEN

## JANE

Plastered to the back of the bathroom door, eyes watering, chest heaving, I pull in deep gulps of air, still shivering from head to now bare feet.

That did not fucking happen!

*Day one: London-1 Jane-0*

Pulling my cell phone from my purse, I frantically compose and shoot out a text to Charlie.

**Mayday! Mayday! Call me!**

But if I'm keeping an honest score, the actual point goes to Lucian.

Lucian, who just saw me at my most vulnerable—half naked and whimpering on the freezing sidewalk. Lucian, who took close to immediate action and care of me, handling the situation with seemingly superhuman speed. I'd meant the compliment. It was impressive the way he handled it. But just because he *acted* human for five minutes after I went splat doesn't earn him back in my good graces at all.

He doesn't get a pardon.

Nope.

I meant what I said after, as well. I want nothing further to do with him outside of the operating room. Even then, I'll be hard-pressed not to bare my teeth at him again.

Walking up to the oblique, gold-trimmed mirror, I'm utterly stunned at my appearance. Despite the throb in my upper back and neck and inner turmoil, my hair and makeup is close to how it was when I boarded—I'm nowhere in the physical state I expected. Aside from my red-splotched cheeks to which I credit the combination of humiliation and cold.

After a hot shower, a meal, some sleep, and about a thousand hours of isolation, I should be good to go.

It's then I realize my most recent screwup. I started my isolation period without my luggage, and right now, I'd rather slide through a field of razor blades during a saltwater rain shower than lay eyes on Lucian again to collect it.

"Shit!" I screech in frustration, smacking the pristine gold faucet handle to get the water scalding before I dial Charlie. It goes straight to voicemail. Mentally, I calculate the time difference and conclude she's probably about to wake up and get Barrett to work since Elijah is out of school for winter break.

Washing my hands under the hot water because I can't think of a single damn thing better to do, I debate whether to collect my bags.

God knows Lucian's made it clear what an imposition I've been to him. Maybe I made my point clear, and he'll have the decency to make himself scarce.

Dialing Charlie again, I get no answer and curse.

Staring at my reflection, I catch the emotional overflow as twin tears streak down my cheeks. Three hours in London, and I'm freaking crying? This is so far from the plan.

"Suck it up, Jane," I snap, running my hands under the scalding water, "this is just embarrassment with a side of bruised ego." I wince at the pain radiating through my back when I reach for a towel to dry my hands. "You've handled much worse."

The pep talk does shit to erase the memory of the look on Lucian's face as he gaped at me—which would have been comical if he hadn't looked like *he* was the one in pain. Shaking my head, another tear I loathe the sight of falls, followed by another. I've been feeling all sorts of screwed up since we landed and can't seem to find a way to reel it in. So, I comfort my reflection again, as I have many times before—one of the perks of being a parentless child. "It was just a nasty spill and a bad first day. It will pass. You've got this, even when you don't."

As I go to repeat it, a nauseating wave comes over me that has nothing at all to do with the fall. My emotions begin to overwhelm me, my mind turning on me, screaming *you so do not have this* as anxiety spikes.

Karma got me good, the wretched bitch.

I was spewing so much venom before I hit the pavement that she saw fit to send a tidal wave to take me out.

That's karma for me, and maybe I deserved it, but . . . "why bitch why, did you have to serve it with a spoonful of vagina out?"

Does karma have an enemy? If so, I'd like to speed-dial whomever or whatever that may be and get her back—just this once.

All I wanted was a chance to make a decent impression on a doctor I admired and, okay, had a major crush on. Instead, I assed-out on *day one* and came out pussy blazing.

Stripping off a dress I now despise, I turn to examine myself in the mirror while trying to imagine what Lucian saw.

The fifteen pounds I fought off in preparation for the trip have me down from a size eighteen to a prouder, more comfortable sixteen.

Naked, I run my hand soothingly over the curves that took years to accept after being nearly half my current size for most of my life. I've made peace with the bits of cellulite on my ass and thighs, along with my muffin top.

To be fair to myself, I was too skinny, and I actually look a lot better with the added weight—even if it's due to a bit of overindulgence. But in high school, I was fucking miserable and starved a lot just to be in the running for some male attention. My die-hard crush on Lucian kind of put me back in that headspace, and I'm pissed at myself for it.

Nope. Nope, not going there.

Dr. Prick's view this morning isn't going to have me regressing years of progress. I've been comfortable in my skin since I was twenty, and that's not changing on the edge of twenty-seven for *anyone*. It's not so much the weight or battle scars that bother me, but the fact that in the thousands of ways I've cooked up in daydreams on baring myself to him, wiping out was nowhere on the menu.

Because given the chance, and the *right* set of circumstances, I would have easily presented all parts to Dr. Prick without a hint of reservation. Body image issues are in my past, and I kill any more internal conversation on the subject before it has more of a chance to fester. On the way to the airport, I felt beautiful, and taking one last glance in the mirror, I decide I still do. It's my pride that's battered, and that's not so easy to get over. For the third time, I call for backup, tears still spilling from me, my anxiety only ramping up. I can't for the life of me get it under control, nor the shivering as the biting cold remains bone deep. This time, when it goes to voicemail, I text a desperate message.

**What kind of sister doesn't answer the phone when you need them most!? MAYDAY ASSHOLE! MAYDAY! Call me right now. THE PUSSY IS OUT OF THE BAG!**

With a huff, I toss my phone on the counter as a sharp knock on the bathroom door sounds, which has me yelping in fear.

"Sorry, Jane, I didn't mean to frighten you. I just wanted you to know your bags are outside your door."

Not bothering with a reply or a thank you, I wait a full five minutes before cracking the door and dragging all three inside.

Tears I deny continue to make their way down my cheeks again as I unzip one of them in search of my favorite pajamas. Once I retrieve them, a sob bursts out of me before I muffle it into the fabric.

*What in the actual fuck, Jane?*

Completely confused about why I'm so devastated and feeling like the sky is falling, I pull out some underwear and start the water for the shower.

"Feel the way you feel, let it run its course, and then let it go," I mumble as I test the water and scan the massive shower with multiple heads. "So, you tripped, and Lucian saw you half-naked. Big deal," I assure myself. "He's a professional who's seen all body types. Don't let this affect you so much and ruin your trip. Correction, you won't let this ruin your trip." That order comes out as a half sob. Just as I go to step into the steaming stream, my phone lights up on the counter.

*Charlie is requesting FaceTime.*

Lifting my phone to hide my nudity in case Elijah's in the background, I swipe it with a desperate, "Charlie?"

"Ello Guvna!" she shouts in a terrible mock British accent.

"Charlie . . ." I sniff, the anxiety inside me spiking to a nuclear level as I full-on start to melt down.

"Who else would it be? Jane? Why are you crying? And what do you mean the pussy is out of the bag?

"I . . ." I shudder. "I f-fell."

"You told me."

"Ah no, Charlie," I draw out in a pained cry. "I f-fell *again*."

"Jane. Lower the phone. You totally look like a snotty, nostrils only, Blair Witch cast member right now."

"*Who?*"

"Old movie. Scared the shit out of me until I found out it was a hoax. Not important. Lower the phone and let me see you."

"I can't," I sniff, "I'm naked."

"What? Why?"

"I fell in front of the hotel."

"Okay, hate to point it out, but it's not that uncommon for you. You're a lazy walker and shuffle your feet," she drawls out, "which is why heels should be banned in your wardrobe," she drones. "And that doesn't explain why you're naked. Where are you?"

"A bathroom," I croak.

"Okay, that's better, we're getting somewhere."

"I . . . didn't, I—oh God, Charlie, it was *public*."

Her eyes bulge. "Oh my God, do you mean *pubic?* Please tell me you had underwear on!"

"I told you I didn't want it to ride up, and I didn't want panty lines!"

"Kind of hard to see when you're in a tutu, gah, little sister. You told me you had that sorted! Did Dr. Prick see?"

"Yesss," I hiss. "And I was in the midst of telling him off."

"What happened?"

I spend a few minutes summarizing most of the details from the time I took off to the second I'm in—still naked and shivering. After a few silent seconds, I lower the phone enough to gauge her expression. Charlie and I look a lot alike, aside from the fact that she's more petite, has elvish ears, and crops her hair short around her chin. Our fair complexion is also the same pale shade, but differing by the second due to her as she reddens in an attempt to keep from laughing.

"I hate you," I croak, fighting off another sob.

"I'm sorry, but we will laugh about this later."

"I don't see that happening," I say mournfully. "This trip is already a disaster, and I've been here, what, nearly four hours?"

"I get it," she says, "but it's salvageable. This isn't like you. I can't believe you're crying so hard. It's breaking my heart because it's so rare for you."

"I know! I feel completely irrational right now and can't find my chill at all. I don't know what's happening."

"Hmmmmm," she draws out. "Can you maybe think of why that might be?"

I draw my brows and cut the shower before snatching one of the provided terrycloth robes. "Because I'm humiliated, in p-pain, and freezing?"

"Nurse Cartwright," she sighs, "can you think of any additional reason *why* you'd be feeling so out of sorts?"

"Out with it, Charlie. I'm all out of patience today," I warn.

"You haven't slept at all or eaten in hours, and you're now five of them ahead," she points out simply.

"No," I whisper hoarsely, "*this* is *jet lag*?" I shake my head. "It can't be . . . not this soon, and not this bad."

"Your brain and body are at odds, and we both know you're a nightmare when you're sleep-deprived. So, I'm thinking, yeah, a lot of your symptoms scream jet lag."

"Oh," I say, feeling better because there's an explanation, while a little embarrassed that I didn't think of it myself. "Maybe *that's why* I burst into tears when I saw the pajamas you gave me. Damn, that makes sense."

"You're still wearing those damned pajamas? They're ancient."

"They're still my favorites . . . Charlie, I'm so far from home."

"Yep, it's jet lag, and you've got a nasty case of it. Deep breaths, sis," she orders in a maternal tone. A tone that she often uses with me, and I only identified as motherly when Elijah came. "I'm so sorry day one was shit, Jane. You've been looking forward to this trip for so long. And from what you've told me, I don't blame you for finally blowing a gasket and telling him what's what. He's pretty irredeemable at this point. But never forget who the hell you are, Jane. You're Teflon. Hell, you're titanium. So, it's not him, it's jet lag that's got you a little twisted."

"I'm pretty sure baring myself to the bellman, and Lucian is most of it."

"Fuck it, Jane, people fall. Sounds like he was cool about it, even if he's mostly a jerk. Chin up, little sister. Take your bruises and lumps, and remember, you've got this, even if you don't."

"Right. I've got this," I repeat, disbelieving my own words.

"How about a few doctor's orders from the person who loves you?" she asks as my eyes spill over again.

"Listening."

"You need to shower, eat, and sleep."

"Okk-kay, but Charlie?"

"Yeah?"

"Can you stay on the phone with me a little bit longer? I've never had an anxiety attack like *this*. Talk me down for a little while?"

She grins. "Only if we can talk shit about Dr. Prick and how he's probably a dick because he has no girth."

"Suits me."

Ten minutes later, face blistering red, my sister's laughter echoes throughout the massive bathroom as I relay more details about my recent drama with Lucian.

"I swear to God," she heaves, "I'm . . . you're my fucking hero. I have not lived enough life to hold a candle to yours. Excellent work with the Kindle stunt. I'm so proud to be your sister, you vindictive little minx."

"Yeah, well, it backfired. You were right about everything—the dress, my nipples, all of it."

"I'm serious. You're halfway around the world with a fine ass man, and not only do you tell him off, but you flash your shit at him just after."

"Hysterical," I rasp dryly. "And too soon."

"I can't even. Are you groomed?"

"Freshly waxed, asshole. Need I remind you I have plans of se-ducing a Frenchman?"

"That's plan *B* now, right?"

"Are you insane? Did you not hear a word I said? Why in the hell would you think him a candidate?"

"Only because you've been pining for him since he hit your floor."

"Have not."

"Who do you think you're lying to? I've never seen you so damn hard up for a man."

"That was before I got to know him."

"Yeah, yeah."

"Just because he was decent to me *after the fact* doesn't mean he wants to pet the kitty."

"Have you asked him if he wants to pet the kitty?"

"What are you, five? Shut the hell up. I'm humiliated."

"Meh, he's a doctor. He's seen it all."

"You would think, but he hasn't—"

A sharp knock sounds on the door.

"Yes," I call out.

"Jane, I've tried, truly, I have. I even froze on the balcony for a good five minutes, but I'm afraid I'm going to have to relay at this point that I have heard nearly every word of your exchange with your sister." He hikes his voice, "my apologies, Charlie."

Charlie's laughter echoes just before I drop my phone in the toilet. A toilet I hadn't flushed yet.

*Fuck this trip.*

# EIGHT

## JANE

A bsently flipping another page on my Kindle while still not re-
taining much of the book, another sharp knock sounds on the
other side of the door as I check the time. He's been at it every
hour on the nose. "Jane?"

"Still awake, Dr.," I bellow from where I soak in the massive tub.

"It's been three hours. Do you plan on coming out of hiding
anytime soon?"

Lifting my hand from the recently refreshed scalding water, I
see my fingers are pruned beyond recognition. "Short answer, no,
and I told you to leave me alone."

"Well, this is the part where I tell you we have something in
common in that we both aren't keen on taking orders. At the least,
you must be hungry."

"Negative," I clip out.

"Your painkillers are out here."

"I'll survive."

"Jane, don't be ridiculous—"

"I'm good, Dr. Aston, really."

"Lucian."

"Nope," I rebuke.

"At least allow me to administer the pain medication and run a more thorough physical check."

"Negative."

"Please be reasonable. You can't hide in there forever."

"I'm fine here. Is there not a bathroom in your room?" Guilt threatens until he speaks up.

"There's one in your suite, which I borrowed."

"Oh," I say, "Well, I'll make myself at home there soon enough. I'll see you tomorrow."

He clips out my name in warning.

"I'm fine, just go, do whatever it is you do."

"There's no need to be embarrassed."

"Says you," I snort, unplugging the tub, knowing he's not going to let this go.

"These things happen."

"Sure they do," I snark, standing and pulling on the robe. "Anything similar happen to you recently?"

"Well, no, but—"

"Exactly," I quip, noting my skin is unbelievably silky and fragrant due to the fancy bath milk I'd poured in liberally.

"You do realize you'll have to face me at some point."

Not a question, a statement, and I wince in the mirror because of it. "So . . . you really," I pause mid-bra fastening, not sure if I want the answer, but finish anyway, "heard *everything*?"

"I'm afraid so, yes."

"As in?"

"As in, you fancied me, and now you loathe me."

"Right," I exhale. "You do realize you could have left the hotel room?"

"I could have, but after coming back from the freezing balcony and closing my room door, the conversation echoed in. Honestly, I didn't expect things to get *worse*."

"That's Charlie for you. She's my person, and much like you—in times of peril—she has an uncanny knack for making things progressively worse. Like admitting you overheard a conversation that you had no right tuning into. But *unlike you*, Charlie is *family*, and I wouldn't take a bullet or train for you."

"While you might feed me to both. Understood, and in hindsight, I do apologize for invading your privacy."

"Well, some of that was unintentional, huh?" I jest, and neither of us laughs.

"Though I must relay, the thought of you two properly plotting against any wrongdoer that brings harm to either of you is utterly terrifying."

I can't help but smile at that while dolloping a handful of the matching scented lotion and generously lathering my skin. "Does that mean you'll be sleeping with one eye open?"

"Doubtful at the moment, seeing as how you are intentionally preventing me from having the option. Are you really going to make me apologize *again*?"

"Couldn't hurt. And are you really going to camp out there all night?"

"I'm trying to avoid it, hence the irritating communication behind a closed door."

"Fine," I huff. "Then you're going to have to give me something," I tell him while running a brush through my wet hair.

"Pardon?"

"Why don't you and your brother get along?" I ask.

Even through the thick and seemingly useless door, I can sense his hesitation. "It's a long story."

"I've got ti—" I start.

"—and not a subject that interests me."

"Imagine that. Look, Doc—"

"Lucian."

"Right, you've seen me naked and heard just about every humiliating thing I could relay. So, if you want me to open that door, you're going to have to give me *something* to work with."

"Christ," I hear him utter under his breath.

"Heard that," I say.

"Fair enough," He expels another sigh, this one traveling as he slides down to sit on the other side of the door. Another small bout of silence passes as I wince to get into the same position, sitting opposite him, my back inches from his. A few beats pass, and just when I think he's not going to come out with it, he speaks up.

"In summary, I guess you could say I'm a disappointment to my brother . . . to my whole family, really."

"How so?"

"I didn't live up to expectations. Ironically, I'm the one *who set* those expectations."

He doesn't want to give the details, so I don't press him for them. "I'm sorry."

"Well, that's life now, isn't it?" He mutters ironically.

"Though, I really don't see how being a brilliant surgeon could be disappointing to anyone," I point out.

"It's not so much my career path as it was my ambition. That alone affected my family . . . heavily."

"You still haven't given me anything real," I point out, "I'm going to need some secondhand embarrassment."

"Fine . . . let me think. Ahh, I have one. When I was in primary school, we were given an assignment to make a scientific display using household goods. You know the one?"

"The old overflowing volcano and baking soda project. I'm with you."

"Precisely. So, naturally, I went snooping, opening every drawer, and just so happened to find the perfect item to help with my space travel display. It even had a rocket rider on the side of it in bright, colorful orange—"

"It was your mom's vibrator, wasn't it?"

"Yes. Needless to say, my parents had quite the time explaining to me why I couldn't use the perfectly suited, vibrating phallus in my display."

I wrinkle my nose. "You were a kid. Give me something worthy for *adult Lucian* and *make it juicy.*"

"All right . . . ah, I tried Viagra once, out of curiosity."

"And?"

"To put it bluntly, when the fun was over, the nightmare began. I was one of those few who had an adverse reaction, and the drug wouldn't wear off. Opting out of the humiliation of seeking medical assistance—which I know seems ridiculous considering—I decided to let it work itself out naturally. The drug took two full days to finally release me from its confines, and let me tell you, I had several consults I couldn't reschedule."

"Meh, that's pretty textbook, but it'll do."

"Tough company to impress."

"Not much is going to beat what went down today," I mutter, rolling my eyes up to the ceiling.

"Agreed, but Jane, it truly was just me and the bellboy."

"I said I'll take your word for it."

"I think that's enough sharing. What do you say you open the door, get something to eat, and I'll monitor you while you get some much-needed sleep?"

"Still not ready yet."

"Jane," he says, this time his tone a little different, a little more imploring. "I know I'm not the company you want for this trip and that I can come off as a bit of a—"

"Self-important, arrogant, douchey bag of dicks?" I chime in.

"I was going to say abrasive, but sure."

"Why? Is it because you don't like me? Give it to me straight, and don't bullshit me."

"Firstly, I rarely, if ever, get personal with staff as a general rule."

"Oh, I believe that, but I've seen you with other surgical nurses and surgeons. I've even watched you cut up with them a time or two. What is it specifically about me that rubs you so badly?"

"First of all, let me clarify that I don't find you unattractive."

I wait, my breath becoming bated, but he doesn't expand on it.

"So, what is it?"

"We're very different in certain ways, and I'm sure you've noticed a few of them. You're very blunt and sometimes crude in public, to name one."

"How? By being open? At least I do my best to get to know a person before deciding if I want to invest any time and grow a relationship with them instead of staring at them with blatant judgment. And yeah, maybe I do ask a lot of questions before I think about how it might embarrass a person, but that's how I learn—by asking questions. Maybe it's something I can work on, and I do admit I can be a little blunt."

"Understatement."

"Fine, I'm overtly blunt, a lot less refined, and I get that's not your type of company."

"That's the sum of it, yes."

"Fair enough, and honestly, I assumed as much."

A beat passes before he speaks again. "Tell me about me."

"What?" I ask, shocked by the question. "Really?"

"Yes, I'd like to know, not that your recent summary wasn't pretty telling."

I screw my lips up as I try to think of the right way to convey my perception of him. "You're not just stand-offish, but the general air about you is cutthroat. Not that it's too far off par with some of the other surgeons, but the thing about that is anyone can be an asshole. *Anyone.* It's lazy and easy. Being a good, authentic human being is a lot riskier and sometimes taxing, but it is far more rewarding. Hell, the day I offered to share my homemade egg salad, you looked at the container as if it was full of shit."

"I apologize for that."

"Accepted, but maybe give a person a chance before you write them off so easily. If I had known you preferred conversational delivery less blunt, maybe I would've worked around it a bit to try and make you more comfortable. I did it deliberately last night when you wouldn't give me an inch."

"I'm aware . . . now."

"You see, the way I am . . ." I search for the right words.

"Yes?"

"My no-bullshit stance has a lot to do with the way my sister and I grew up. Not that I can't play the part. You know, do the curtsy in front of the right lineup or speak more eloquently. But when outside those confines, I prefer to be . . . me—especially with the people I really want to get to know. So, last night was me trying to get to know you outside of the OR and . . . well, and policing of my verbal vomit. My candor takes a nosedive when I drink more than two. Last night, I overindulged a little. I told you that."

"Understood. From here on out, I'll do my best to take that into consideration."

"You can do better, Lucian. Like the way you were today for five minutes."

"How so?"

I shrug against the door even though he can't see it. "Doesn't matter if you don't want to *be* better."

"Humor me, Jane."

I turn to stare at the door, knowing he's just a few inches on the other side. "No bullshit?"

There is a slight hesitation before. "Yes."

"Why?"

"I guess you could say my own breeding has much to do with the way I, too, express myself and react. Also, because my apology was sincere, more so now after hearing your recollection of my behavior to your sister."

"And?" I prompt, my gut telling me there is more.

"I don't want our surgical floor to think of or refer to me as Dr. Prick. You have quite a sway with them as you are, and maybe if you told me where I'm fumbling, it could help me get better acquainted with them and regarded differently."

"You're asking me? A woman you find crass and irritating?"

"I wouldn't say altogether irritating, just some of the things you do."

"The staff's opinion truly matters to you?"

"Contrary to what you think, I cut you short today because you were freezing, and it was my fault. I was also expediting my conversation because of your discomfort, but I feel maybe, at that point, you were too upset to notice. Ultimately, I respect your position and profession immensely, and if I didn't care, I wouldn't be asking."

Absorbing his words, I take them to heart. Maybe he was tired and irritable and jetlagged like me. It's his sincere interest in getting my advice that has me baffled. "You truly don't know how to just be . . . nice?"

"I'm positive I failed with you in that respect, and you seem to get along with everyone, so maybe I need to make more of a concerted effort."

Thinking on my toes, I turn to face the door as if I'm talking to him face to face. "Then I propose we do a little experiment instead."

"What's that?"

"Outside of our professional relationship, out of consults and the hospital."

"I'm listening."

"From now until we leave London, you have to *say exactly* what you're thinking. Be *brutally honest*, at least with *me*, no holding back whatsoever. That way, I can better show you in the moment."

A tense beat passes, then two. Just as I think he's going to refuse my proposal, he speaks up. "And what exactly is in this for me?"

"Spiritual growth for starters. Let's be honest. Now, more than ever, we need to see the *human* side of doctors. You could be *that doctor*, Lucian. You could be an exception to the asshole doctor rule."

"There's an asshole doctor rule?"

"It's mostly unspoken, but do you know how many people searching for answers for their loved ones tell me about how hellacious their process was in finding the right surgeon . . . and by the time they get to you, well, to be frank—"

"By all means, don't stop now."

"Well, after consulting with you, they have expectations and a laundry list of do's and don'ts, but their eyes still lack the hope they should have the second they landed in the right surgeon's hands . . . So yeah, you could be the exception to the asshole doctor rule. Who knows, maybe by the end of it, we'll figure out how to wiggle out the gigantic stick lodged up your ass."

A loud bark resembling a laugh sounds on the other side of the door, and I smile at its arrival. The lingering silence after tells me he's entertaining my proposal. Maybe the Prick part is his coat of armor— and somewhere deep inside him, he's salvageable.

"So, what do you say? Do we have a deal?" I ask, moving to stand, resting my hand tentatively on the knob.

Slight shuffling on the other side tells me he's moved to stand, too.

"I'm afraid you'll have to open the door for your answer, Jane."

# NINE

## LUCIAN

J ane opens the door, dressed in what I assume are the coveted pajamas she and Charlie discussed, her hair wet. Though the material is a bit thin for the weather, she seems comfortable enough as
I take her in. Her flawless face is now completely free of any makeup.
Her lips gradually lift in a shy smile, the vulnerability in her expression stunning me a bit.

"So, let's test this," she lifts her chin slightly in a prompt. "What
are you thinking *right now*?"

"That you hide natural beauty you shouldn't with too much
makeup. I have conditions."

She barely has time to register my reply. "Which are?"

"One, if there's a subject you broach that I'm not interested in
discussing, I have a right to pass."

She wrinkles her lightly freckled nose. "That puts a bit of a damper
on things."

"That's one," I state. "The other is you have to be just as brutally honest."

"Not a problem for me," she gives me a confident wink more suited to her, "and I get to pass, too."

I nod.

"So, you think I'm pretty without makeup, huh?" Her wary return stare tells me she's not expecting a reply. "That's nice to hear, but you don't have to butter me up now, Lucian. We're past that." She lets out a low whistle, scanning the penthouse as I go to object that I'm not starting our honesty truce with a lie. "Nice place."

It truly is, as I've been exploring it for hours now. The tapestries are a regal blend of gold, white, and scarlet red. The rest of the penthouse is accented with holiday décor of the same color. The furnishings are just as grand, from the monstrous four-post bed centered in her king suite to the great room filled with plush furniture and the adjacent dining area. Surrounding us are floor-to-ceiling windows with a spectacular view of the London skyline. A view that is only partially obstructed by a large Christmas tree—littered with gold baubles—and a marble hearth, which currently hosts a roaring fire.

"Very posh," I agree, as she steps further into the room and scans it. "The king is yours," I gesture toward the suite to our collective left. "I'm in the second room." I point to the door on the other side of the bathroom, where she's just stepped out of hiding.

"Thank you," she rasps wistfully, her spirits visibly lifting as she takes in the atmosphere and warmth of the large penthouse.

"Don't thank me," I say, unable to help the lift of my lips. "Thank your lack of knickers."

She turns abruptly and winces due to her injury. "Still too soon . . . *for you* and lesson learned on that front." She tilts her head when I don't respond. "You really are so hard to read. Even your eyes aren't that telling."

"Years of practice," I confess honestly.

"Hmmm, so what are you thinking right now?"

"That I'm exhausted, my patience is thinning because of it, and I would really like for you to eat and lie down so I can eventually get some sleep myself."

"Right, I'm sorry, I'm fine." She lifts her hand and crosses her heart with a finger. "Promise."

"I'm the attending, and I'll be the judge."

"Lucian, please stop coddling me. Go to bed."

"I will, but," I palm my neck, "I would like to examine you a little more thoroughly, okay?" The sickening thud from hours ago still haunts me. She landed so hard I swear I heard a crack.

"I'm certain," she squeaks out nervously.

"Jane," I point to her, then myself. "Doctor."

"Surgeon," she spouts sarcastically. "And it's not necessary."

"Completely necessary, and I promise to remain objective and detached."

"Okay, fine. But as you well know, all bodies aren't created equal."

"They certainly aren't," I allow the implication to pass through her return gaze before I speak again, "but this is a non-issue."

*Is it now, Lucian?*

"Truth is, I want to spare you—us both—seeing how our collective day has gone, but you went down very hard. Just a few minutes of my fingers, and I'll release you for the night."

Her cheeks redden slightly at my comment as I realize my turn of phrase was a bit much. As she brushes past me, a fresh scent invades my nose, reminding me of a similar scent in my mother's garden. She turns back to me, wearing a cheeky grin. "And just so you know, I did pack *knickers*."

I lift a brow. "And are you wearing them?"

She lifts her shirt to reveal the tips of them peeking out, tiny, satin red bows dotting each hip. Before I can inspect them more thoroughly, she pulls her shirt off, leaving herself in a matching red satin bra and her pajama bottoms before speaking up. "Where do you want me?"

I don't flinch in keeping my word and take a nearby seat at the large dining table before gently pulling her hand so she's standing in front of me. Turning her, I inch along her skin with my fingers, which is silky to the touch. Ignoring that bit of information, I note the faint bruise forming atop her shoulder blades and apply slight pressure along it. She hisses through her teeth in reaction.

"How is your pain?"

"Low four."

"Head?" I prompt, keeping my fingers working as I retrace my steps from hours ago, after her initial fall.

"Still pounding, but less than it was five minutes ago."

"Good. Six hundred milligrams of paracetamol should be enough to manage the pain and get you to sleep. Turn." I apply more pressure, and she stiffens slightly and shudders. "And here?" I prompt, careful of the placement and pressure of my fingers.

"Not too bad," she rasps, goose flesh erupting over her skin as I note the curve of her hips is what's keeping her thin pajama bottoms in place.

"Good," I swallow. "I'm going to lower your bottoms a bit to assess your lower back."

"Okay," she agrees easily enough, giving me her trust—trust which I'm currently undeserving of and plan to remedy.

Pulling the hem of her bottoms down, I'm graced with the sight of her lower back and the top of her arse. "You hit the ground extremely hard," I remark, glancing up to see her staring directly down at me over her shoulder before she averts her gaze. After a few more seconds of gentle exploration, I find no more injury. Pulling her pants up, I pat her gently on the hip to let her know I'm done. "Let me know if you want me to call in a prescription if the paracetamol doesn't suit."

"I'll be fine," she assures, making quick work of getting her shirt back on.

"You'll be incredibly sore tomorrow and tired. I'll need to monitor you until I'm sure you're not mildly concussed."

"Seriously?" She asks, deflating.

"Every hour for the first twenty-four. Just because you're not showing symptoms doesn't mean it isn't a possibility, and you know it."

"But I'll lose another day."

"We were set to meet Tremblay tomorrow, so, technically, it bought you half a day."

"A half day I can't use if I'm stuck here under your microscope."

She shakes her head adamantly. "No freaking way. I'm not losing more time here."

My mouth moves of its own accord. "Fine, third condition, you allow me to accompany you. As a physician, I would feel better if you let me monitor you for at least a few days."

She blinks. "You want to tour London?"

"Absolutely fucking not," I blurt, surprising us both.

She tosses her head back and laughs. "Going right in with the full honesty thing, huh?" She squints at me. "So, not excited to see Big Ben and the London Eye?"

"Not at all, and they're not far from the other," I inform her.

"I didn't know that." She bites her lip and peers down at me. "And you'll eat fish 'n' chips and mushy peas, and ride the double-decker bus?"

"Sounds delightful," I utter.

"You're being sarcastic."

"As long as that's transparent, then it's honesty, right?"

"Guess so. Seriously, Lucian, what *does a man like you* do for fun?"

"I can't show all my cards in one night. You have three weeks to find out, do you not?"

"Sure do," she fires back, her smile widening as my suspicions rise.

"Why do I have a feeling this may backfire?"

She leans toward me slightly, and that magnificent smell briefly takes over my senses. "I have no ill intent, Doc, unless you cross me."

"I've become wise to that, Jane. So, it's settled then."

"Right," she draws out.

"Which means you'll be under my medical supervision, which in turn translates to if I say 'no,' you don't. And my first no is alcohol."

"Come on, man! That's fun police shit!"

"That's the rule," I offer harshly.

"Fine, no drinking. Two days. I told you, it's not really my thing, anyway."

"Your painkillers are here," I point to the table. "And I'll order some soup to warm you further."

"I don't think I'm going to make the wait. I'm beat."

"You need to eat. You were shivering during my examination. On top of a possible head injury, you could have a touch of hypothermia, which you know you weren't supposed to soak in hot water to remedy."

"How did you know I was—"

I grip her hand, and her lips part as I pull her wrinkled fingers up for her inspection.

"You don't miss anything, do you?"

"Nothing," I say definitively. A brief silence thickens the air before I add. "Particularly when it comes to a *patient.*"

"Don't get all power-hungry on me, Doc. Your reign over me is temporary."

"Lucian," I correct.

"Lucian," she relents. "It was just a nasty spill, you know, you don't have to do," she waves her hand, "all of this."

"I'm aware, Jane."

"I'm sorry I kept you from sleeping with my pity party."

"I was taught to keep my own needs silent when it inconveniences others."

She draws her brows at that. "Well then, I'll make this easy for you. I'm happy to eat my soup and go to bed to end your shift, but I'm pretty sure we're out of any dangerous territory."

"I can still hear the thud," I utter, and her features pinch as if she can as well. Not only that, but the picture in my head is still crystal clear. She replies as if she's reading my thoughts.

"I don't suppose you can really forget what you saw?"

"Not a chance," I counter, "but only because we shared trauma."

She visibly swallows. "See? Even if it's uncomfortable, we can do this . . . honesty thing."

I dip my chin, my eyes drying painfully by the second. She seems to catch onto my discomfort and goes to speak, but I shake my head. "I know what you're about to suggest, and I'm not budging."

"Fine, but if I'm good in two hours after shuteye, you'll go to bed too."

"Three," I state.

"Two and a half," she counters.

"You've won in the only barter you'll win tonight. Take that victory, Jane, because you won't win this round. The room service menu is on the table. I'll get your luggage into your room."

When she goes to object, I give her a stern look of warning, and to my surprise, she slowly nods. As she passes me to collect the menu, I inhale another strong whiff of her heavenly scent. After gathering her bags and depositing them in her room, I stop short of the table as she peruses the room service menu. As I watch her, I unsuccessfully battle another conjured image of her—thankful for the victory over my last one.

I hadn't lied.

I gave her a doctor's examination. I was objective and in no way inappropriate or overly thorough. I hadn't let my eyes linger longer than suitable on any of the skin she exposed to me, and still, my body reacted as a man would when attracted to a woman.

But Jane?

At the least, the woman is overly animated, slightly annoying, and, at times, tactless. But on the cab ride today, as I studied her profile, I couldn't ignore the perfection of her features, or the curve of her breast before it disappeared beneath her dress, nor the urge to rub a lock of her hair between my fingers.

But attraction to Jane? I never would have thought it possible.

Typically, and often, when I hear her voice on my floor, I practically flee from her.

Now, it's all I can do to block the sight of her gorgeous pussy and the feel of her silky bare skin beneath my fingers as I examined her.

I was completely honest when I relayed to Jane that she is not, at all, my type. She's loud, boisterous, and a walking, talking, bleeding heart. We couldn't make heads or tails of each other to save *both* our lives.

In fact, I'm certain that if we were faced together with a life-or-death situation, we'd die fighting about life-saving tactics. Mere hours ago, and in my mind, there was absolutely no possibility of Jane and I getting intimate.

But as it seems—and at this precise moment—I can't pry my eyes away from her. Just as I finish that thought, Jane chooses that precise moment to look up and over at me as I maintain my expression. One I've spent a lifetime mastering.

*Please don't ask me what I'm thinking.*

"Are you going to join me?"

I manage a sharp nod.

I'm hard.

Hard in a way I haven't been in years . . . and disgusted with myself for it.

Standing in the pitch dark, at the threshold of Jane's king suite, my mind continues racing with scenarios, much like a teenage boy who's just seen his first pussy. Even with my entire being aching from lack of sufficient rest and my eyes screaming for relief, I cannot, at all, seem to rip them away from Jane's sleeping form. Turned on her side and facing me where I'm perched, she's still dressed the same as she was when she exited the bathroom—in well-worn, thin, light blue pajamas—which I admit are appealing to me for reasons far less sentimental than her own. The bottoms fit her like a second skin, hugging her shapely legs and showcasing the abundant curve of her hip. There's just enough light filtering in through the floor-to-ceiling windows of the master suite to spot the goddamned bow peeking out of the top of them—which feels as if it's taunting me. Then there's the matching top to envy as it clings to her ample chest as it rises and falls in circadian rhythm. Stalking toward the bed, I catch myself a few steps in and still, remembering myself and my place with her.

*Just what in the hell do you think you're doing, Lucian?*

Maybe it was her confession that she'd fancied me that has me thinking I have some misplaced right to get closer, but she quashed that with her comments after to her sister.

She'd been honest with Charlie in her dismissal and hadn't at all acted or shown signs of attraction when I examined her—despite the goosebumps, harsh breaths, and shudders, which could easily be attributed to pain.

In my time knowing her, I haven't once taken a second look at Jane nor spent any time thinking of her in a sexual or physical sense. However, what I'm experiencing right now feels a lot like a thirst I haven't fueled or fed in years—which includes the innate need to both mark and possess her in a claiming way. Maybe it was the dangling of the apple so close to me today and the prolonged abstinence from sex.

For me, this woman is completely off limits—at least in my way of thinking—but my cock is entirely ignoring that, to the point I'm almost entertaining relieving the throb.

*No.*

Mentally, I snap the door shut on that. It will get no reward for its depravity tonight.

Getting lost in the part of her lips, I decide to try and be as brutally honest with *myself* during these weeks as I agreed to be with her. In doing so, my first realization is that for the first time in my nearly three-year self-induced stint of celibacy, I'm recognizing attraction. It's not at all by choice. It's simply that . . . at the moment, my current draw to Jane is refusing to be ignored. Perhaps it's her confessions or that it's been that long since I've cohabitated with the fairer sex, but either way, it's alarming just how strong it is.

Where it's been a task for the last thirty-four months for me to concentrate on *anything other* than cutting and repairing hearts, I suddenly find myself fascinated by all *physical things* Jane Cartwright.

This sudden hunger can't be attributed to her berating me earlier nor her stance on my behavior. No matter how intimidating I may seem to her, I've been confronted more than once in that regard. The difference is that tonight—during our through-the-door conversation—I found myself wanting to earn her approval somehow. That, along with every other truthful reason I gave her.

Or maybe, and more simply, I want to redeem myself after today's sparring match, her nasty spill, and her tearful confession.

A spill I can still physically feel to my bones, adding an ache to the rest of me. My guilt—combined with the memory of her fall—has had me staring at her for long minutes in lieu of a check-in on the hour.

*This is Jane, Lucian, wise up.*

Cock angry and throbbing the more I stare, I continue to remind myself and my prick that, on any other given day, this is the very woman I have a strong aversion to. The things that make her a force to be reckoned with do not, at all, coincide with how I conduct myself. Which is probably the very reason I entertained her proposal. Rarely have I ever stepped outside the lines of my upbringing and breeding. What she's asked of me might seem easy for some, but will be completely out of my comfort zone.

What in the hell was I thinking agreeing to three weeks of being forthcoming when it's entirely against my nature other than in the operating room?

In truth, I haven't much cared about what my peers think of me personally but rather craved, if not demanded their respect professionally. But after hearing Jane's cries today, I've since realized I don't want to be Dr. Prick—especially if the pain in Jane's voice can be duplicated by another member of staff because of my carelessness and cruelty. Credit to where it's due, Jane has, for months, been trying to elicit some sort of friendly professional relationship with me, and I have been every bit the bastard she's accused me of. At the least, I owe it to her to try and get along for the betterment of our time here and our working relationship. But as of now, that's the furthest thing from the forefront of my thoughts.

Eyes greedily traveling from her bright pink painted toes to her full hip, I feast freely on her form again, settling briefly on the delicate hand resting on the pillow she's cradling.

"Lucian."

I nearly jump at the soft, raspy, sleep-filled call of my name as my eyes dart to hers, wondering how long they've been open . . . and staring back at me. Has she been watching me openly lust after her?

Christ.

Can she fucking see how hard I am for her right now?

"I'm fine, Lucian. Please, go get some rest."

Relief shoots through me as I realize she's mistaken my border-line stalking for over-concern. Suddenly more fatigued than I can ever remember being, I back away from a door I had no business darkening and bat away any lingering delusions my cock and I were just entertaining. "Sleep well, Jane."

"Night," she replies, and I freeze when I hear the shake in her tone before stalking toward my room. I hold in my curse until I'm behind my door. There's a strong possibility that I didn't play it off well enough, and if she confronts me about it in the morning—even in jest—the rules of our agreement ensure I have to be honest, bru-tally so.

Absolutely not happening.

If she does question me, I'll pass. If she presses in, for both our sakes, I'll lie.

I shut the door of my room, and hastily open my suitcase be-fore stopping altogether to sit at the edge of the mattress. Pressing the heels of my palms to my eyes for a brief reprieve from the burn, I try again to dismiss the images threatening to ruin me. The most current is the mere sight of her expansive curves against the back-drop of the street-lit curtains.

*Get ahold of yourself, Lucian.*

A man of routine, I find myself tossing away my nightly ritual and deciding not to bother undressing, falling face-first into the plush mattress as one last image of Jane burns itself into memory.

If this sudden affliction continues tomorrow, I'll reclaim my discipline and focus.

Even now, my brain is telling me this is a farce because there's no way I'm *this* attracted to Jane Cartwright.

*Absolutely no way.*

# TEN

## LUCIAN

"Good morning," I greet Jane as she exits her suite in her pajamas, the hotel robe tied loosely around her waist, her complexion having regained some color. "Did you sleep well?"

"Morning," she smiles brightly, taking a seat at the table, "surprisingly, very well. *You?*"

"Soundly, thank you." Admittedly and only after a much-needed wank. Despite my inner condemnation, after an hour of a restless attempt to sleep, it took an embarrassing minute to massage my frustration out—my groan stifled as I bit my lip and released what felt like months of pent-up tension. As I suspected this morning, I came back to my senses where Jane is concerned. "How is your pain?"

"I'll admit I'm sore, but it's nothing I can't work around. I already took a few of the tablets when I woke up, so that should do it."

Somewhat satisfied, I dip my chin as she eyes the freshly delivered cart. "I ordered a little of everything. I wasn't sure of what you might like."

"I'm partial to eggs and bacon."

"Ah," I say, pointing toward a cloche-topped plate. When she lifts it, her eyes lighten, and oddly, I find satisfaction in it. "Coffee?" I ask.

"Please," she replies, unfolding her napkin and tucking it in her lap.

Lifting the piping hot, silver carafe, I pour for her as she takes a small bite of bacon and I sense her lingering gaze on me. "Quick question, Doctor. When was the last time you had sex?"

Tensing, I manage to stop pouring just short of overfilling her cup. "Christ, Jane, can we manage a bite of breakfast first?'

"Look," she rests her forearms on the table, "I know you, and I don't mesh in that department on account of lack of chemistry. So, for us, it's a safe topic. *But* I'm thinking part of your hairy eyeball issue might have to do with a shortage of physical contact."

I furrow my brows. "Hairy eyeball issue?"

"You know, your stink eye along with the rest of the expression that makes up your resting bastard face."

"I see. I'll pass on the sexual history."

"Really?" She pops more of the bacon into her mouth and chews slowly, still appraising me.

Stirring a splash of cream into my coffee, I ignore her blatant scrutiny. I dreaded that she might bring up the fact that I was lingering in her doorway last night but hadn't expected it to lead to questions about my sexual status. "Pass," I repeat, "those are the rules."

"Fine. We'll leave sex off the table for now. Have you ever been in love?"

"Next subject," I dismiss, beginning to dread the hours ahead.

"You promised to try, Lucian."

"Can we not attempt to ease into this, or at the least, can I have my first sip of coffee?"

"Rethinking your decision?" A mischievous, feline smile lifts her lips.

I blink at her. "Maybe it's not so difficult for you to read me. That said, why are you interested?"

She taps the side of her cup, considering my question. "I've probably been around a half dozen guys like you in my life, and in the spirit of full disclosure, your kind specifically fascinates me."

"My kind?"

"Oh, come on," she waves a hand, forking a bite of eggs with the other, "you know you're a type."

"Is that so?"

"Immaculately groomed and dressed, upper crust, Ivy League educated, broody, enigmatic, and nearly impossible to get *any* animation from. Sorry to be the one to break this to you, but you're a type, Aston."

"Lucian."

"Lucian," she mimics. "Anyway, most of the other surgeons on our floor are boring, like Dr. Abbott. All he eats for lunch is carrots, and all he ever talks about is building plane models. Besides, I was told it's always the quiet ones that have the most to tell."

"I was taught the quiet ones are the most powerful in the room."

"Who says the two don't go hand in hand?" She lifts a brow.

"You're incorrigible."

"Thank you," she takes that as a compliment before pressing her lips together.

"To answer question two, yes, Jane, I've been in love," I admit, hoping to appease her.

"Really?" Jane leans in. "She shatter your heart? Is that why you're icy and bitter?"

I pinch the bridge of my nose. "Jesus."

"No holds barred, right?" She giggles behind her mug.

"Right, but do we have to dive right into—"

"I bet you were a lady killer back in your day," she remarks, pausing her cup before taking a sip.

This has me pausing my cup halfway to my mouth. "Am I to assume *my day* is over?"

"Scientifically, yeah, if we're talking about when you're at your most virile, your day is *long over*."

"You've got me there, Jane. It's true," I sigh exaggeratedly, "I do spend many a night crying over my tiny, girthless cock."

She cringes. "You really did hear everything."

"I certainly did, yes."

"For the record, I didn't comment on that."

"I'm aware."

"You know," Jane offers, "she was just insulting you to make me happy."

"Glad my personal expense could be of service, and it seems it's not stopping at your conversation with your sister. Do you plan on insulting me by being ageist all day? Because I can tell you firsthand that you're not very mature for your age. I'm assuming you're somewhere in your late twenties?"

"Ouch," she chuckles, "back killer, back! Okay then, I'll lay off temporarily, and yes, I'm getting closer to the downside of my twenties. But just so you know, I pay my bills on time without fail, am raising a dog alone, and brush my teeth regularly."

"Cheers," I say, having no other reply for that.

"Though I must admit I'm not a fan of the saying 'act your age.' How freaking *boring*."

"I'm afraid I might disappoint you on that front, Jane."

"Really? I guess my question is *why* when the alternative is so much more rewarding. It's just . . . there's a certain freedom in it." She tables her coffee. "I mean, sure, we grow up. We let childish behaviors go, especially when things are serious and need to be addressed with an adult lens, but . . ." she twists her lips briefly. "Name one good time you've had where you were completely age-appropriate. I bet you can't. I'm willing to bet the best times of your life have been and always will be when you cut up a little and *skirt the edge* of age-appropriate."

"Why do you think that?"

"Because regressing back to more carefree times is what we all do when we let loose. Ignoring our adult troubles and responsibilities is the only way to do that."

"Interesting theory," I table my empty cup.

"You disagree?"

"Not necessarily, no."

"Well, it's carefree moments like those—especially with a job as intense as ours—that I truly live for."

"I see."

"Anyway, the only real way to grow is to ask questions and discover," she leans forward. "Yes, maybe I am a bit immature at *twenty-six*, but I have a better excuse for some of my lingering childishness than most people. Well, other than it's just plain fun." She gives me an exaggerated wink.

"And what's that?"

"Pass on that answer for now," she averts her gaze.

*Interesting.* "So, you think you have something to learn from me?"

"Of course. I have something to learn from *everyone*, and so do you," she points out, leaving no room for argument. A lock of dark, glossy hair falls from the messy knot atop her head as she glances out of the large windows spanning the living area. When she flits her focus back to me, a reignited spark flames in her eyes. "Speaking of good times, where are we headed to first?"

"That's your call, as I'm sure you have an itinerary?"

She grins. "Right."

"Get dressed, and I'll meet you back here in half an hour?"

"You're really going to escort me?"

"I negotiated this as a condition of our deal, remember?"

"It was last night, Lucian. I didn't hit my head *that hard*. Question is," she tilts her head. "Why?"

"Mainly to keep you pacified and in one piece until I trust you to venture out on your own."

"Huh, and you think I'll go missing or something?"

"Or something. Let's just say in traveling here with you, you've scared me a bit in that regard."

"My own personal childminder," she muses. "Okay, well, whatever floats your boat. Let's go rock London Town."

When she stands, I frown at her plate. "You've hardly eaten three bites."

"I'm still stuffed from the soup."

"You didn't come close to finishing that, either. Are you nauseous, Jane?"

"Stop hovering, *helicopter Doc*. I'll eat a huge lunch. Promise. See you in thirty."

*Thirty-nine* minutes later, Jane walks out of the master suite looking fit in jeans and a thick red jumper. In addition, she's donned winter boots and a proper jacket. This one heavily insulated, ribbed, and stark white.

"So, I know I'm late, again," she gazes up at me through thick, freshly painted black lashes, "but can I get points for weather appropriate?"

"Perhaps a few," I utter, annoyance waning as her eyes trace my face carefully for any sign of resting bastard face—which I make an effort to shield.

"You look nice . . . in casual clothes," she adds, her eyes trailing from my hair to my thick, shawl-collar sweater, dark jeans, and short, leather wellies.

"You as well. Shall we?"

"Am I ready to tour London with my own personal guide while getting to know *the real Lucian Aston*? Sounds good to me."

She's back. The Jane that our surgical floor adores. If she harbors any remaining grudge for me today, it's not showing, and I find myself thankful for it.

As we wait for the lift, I study her profile as her comment about our lack of chemistry draws a bit of interest from me.

With her declaration lingering, I conclude that the goose flesh and breathlessness must have been due to her pain. Filing any further examination back, I instead concentrate on her other admitted mission of getting to know *the real* Lucian Aston.

Who in the hell does she expect me to be exactly?

Other than the man I was groomed and raised to be and the surgeon she's already acquainted with due to long hours in the operating room.

Put simply, I'm a man of strict morals, principles, and discipline.

Even as I think it, I can't help but wonder what I could possibly give her outside of that.

Have I become another Dr. Abbott? *Am I* downright boring?

Chances are, I have little to offer that will surprise her. In fact, I can safely say I haven't done a remarkable thing in nearly half a decade. Nothing that I can recall.

My life wholly revolves around being a surgeon. When I was a dozen or so years younger, closer to her age, I wasn't that much different from what I am now—though I admit I was less laser-focused and could be distracted more easily, especially by women.

As of now, boring could be an accurate word to describe me, but my life hasn't always been so lackluster. I've lived—taken part in plenty of expeditions, traveled a few off-the-grid roads, and made questionable choices now and again. I've had my share of sexual trysts, but a majority of those things reside well in my past.

Any attempt for me to pinpoint when I stopped caring about anything other than being a surgeon would be in vain.

I know exactly when all my ambitions and personal desires for my life ceased to exist. The truth rings clear in my head and heart as I confront myself with this admission in particular—I haven't taken a full breath of life nor wanted to since Alexander took his last.

Whatever life I had—eventful or not—*I abandoned.*

That's the truth of the matter.

A truth I will not share easily with Jane. But what I can give her are parts of the Lucian I once was. Even then, I'll be hard-pressed to find anything she may deem entertaining. I'm not a man with an extended library of anecdotes and war stories to tell. Whatever I do have as far as admissions go won't be a lie. It just won't be an accurate representation of who *the real Lucian Aston* is *now.*

Sinking further into that line of thought, I mull over her statement about my *type*. It wasn't that long ago that I could animate without effort—I acted more instinctively and indulged a little more selfishly.

Pondering her questions at breakfast as the lift opens, a memory surfaces, and without thinking much about it, I bend and whisper my confession to her mere inches from her ear. "My first love was a fair-haired menace by the name of Paxley Buxton."

Jane turns to me, icy-blue eyes wide due to my proximity as goose flesh *again* erupts along the skin at her collar and neck.

*Interesting.*

Baited, she keeps her focus on me as we both step in. "I'm listening."

Hitting the button for the lobby, I glance down at her. "She was six, and I loved pulling her pigtails. It was our thing until one day she let Billy Swells pull them." Crossing my arms, I stare up at the ticking floor count. "I guess you could say I've been jaded ever since."

She rolls her eyes exaggeratedly as a smile blooms across her face. "Like I said, Dr. *Full of Shit*, twenty questions is over *for now*. Take me to the nearest tube."

As her smile lingers, and she rattles with excitement about the day ahead, I think back to the last time I felt anywhere near as alive as Jane is now and continually try to answer her question for myself.

*Who in the hell are you anymore, Lucian Aston?*

"Left! Left! *Left,* Jane! *Christ almighty!*" I shout as Jane, once again, threatens to abandon her life to get another share-worthy photo. Gripping her jacket—just as the driver lays on his horn—I snatch her out of harm's way in time to save her from a day two disaster neither of us will come back from.

"Oh, shit, sorry," she squeaks, eyeing the car that very well could've taken her out far worse than a piece of stray luggage.

Just after, when the enormity of what had transpired truly hit her, she pocketed her cell phone. Eyes zeroed in on me, she steps up to me resting her palm over my skyrocketing heartbeat. "I'm so sorry, Lucian. That most definitely isn't the way I hoped to get you animated."

It's then I realize I've broken into a cold sweat as my pulse sounds in my ears, partially muting her ramblings in combination with the bustling street noise surrounding us. "... truly sorry, I'm done with the cellphone for today, and I definitely won't be joking about look left again."

She continues to stare at me for several long beats before bursting into laughter. "I'm not laughing. I mean, I am, but," she holds up a finger as she tries to gain her composure. "It's not funny, really, but I can tell you're pissed and trying so hard not to level me. The effort is appreciated, as is the fact you just saved my ass for the second time, but I have to ask, how irritated are you now?"

"On a scale of one to what?" I snap.

Laughter slowing, expression riddled with guilt, she flashes all her teeth in apology. "I'm guessing we're at the extreme opposite end of *one?*"

"Closing in," I exhale steadily in an attempt to calm myself and regulate my heartbeat. A heart Jane is still covering with her palm.

My pulse evens out as she continues to run a soothing hand along my chest, and for some reason, I allow it as her words start to register more clearly. "Phone is gone, *promise.*"

When she releases me from her touch, I finally inhale a full breath and use it to scold her. "As it should be, seeing as how you can't truly experience being here through a phone camera lens. Otherwise, why not save yourself the expense and just look at some damned online photos of London?"

"Point made and taken," she says, biting her lip in a shit attempt to hide her amusement. "Tell you what, I'll strike another deal with you. From here on out, I'll only bring it out for the most *memorable* moments."

"I'll take that deal if only to keep you safe from yourself, Nurse Cartwright."

"*And* I'm paying for lunch," she tosses in.

"Not necessary."

"It's the least I can do."

I don't argue with her as we begin to cross Westminster Bridge, the London Eye to our right. Jane pauses as we pass a man in a kilt playing bagpipes, and she immediately digs into her pocket in search of her phone. Eyeing me, her shoulders drop as we bypass him and instead continue to cross. It's been years since I've been anywhere near the more tourist-laden areas of London, and ironically, I'm not anywhere near as uninterested as I thought I would be.

"Parliament is over there," I say, pointing out the long part of the massive building which faces the river Thames. "On the other side is Elizabeth Tower, which you Yanks call Big Ben."

"Oh," her eyes light as I deflate, dreading the fact we must cross a heavily trafficked street to get to it. I've never been so terrified of doing such a simple task in my existence. Jane laughs when I hesitate at the crossing and reach out to grip her marshmallow coat. In turn, I give her 'the hairy eyeball.'

As we manage to cross the street safely, taking the short trek to get to the iconic clock, Jane speaks up in disappointment as we draw closer. "Is that scaffolding?"

"I'm afraid so."

"It's surrounding the whole damn thing! Seriously?" she cries.

"It's been there for quite some time," I relay, leaving out the part of just how long, which was well before I left London.

"Well, shit," she curses. "It's not like I was going to get a picture anyway."

I smirk. "I might have allowed it."

"Lucky me." She blows out a labored breath. "Okay, so the clock is a bust. Now what?"

"I can tell you what's close. Let me review your list."

"It's on my phone," she explains, pulling hair from her mouth again due to the unrelenting, whipping wind.

"Go ahead then."

As she pulls it out, she continually fights for sight due to her unruly hair.

"Jane?"

"Hmm?"

"Why haven't you pinned your hair back? It's been assaulting you all day."

"I wear it up so much at work, figured I'd give it some freedom," she says absently, still going through her notes on her phone. When she remains unsuccessful in her progress due to her rebellious mane, I step forward, crowding her to shield her before gathering her hair securely in my fist. Stiffening, eyes bulging, she glances up, gawking at me.

"What?" I ask, puzzled by her parted lips and wide eyes.

"It's . . . well, you're fisting my hair, Lucian."

"I'm aware," I draw out. "Would you rather I not?"

"It's totally a 'your type' thing to do."

"Nonsense," I scoff.

"You're a naughty, naughty boy, aren't you?" she prompts, eyes glinting.

In that instant, I decide that if my one-word description is *boring*, then Jane's one-word assessment is *cheeky*.

"I'm simply helping you so we can see to your list."

"Uh-huh," she goads as she scrolls along her screen.

A minute later, with patience thinning, I glance around. "Jane?"

"Hmmm?"

"I know London rather well. How about I conduct the rest of today's tour?"

She regards me suspiciously. "What's the catch?"

"No catch or deal amendment. It's simply an offer."

She narrows her eyes. "And you won't accidentally reroute us back to the hotel? No funny business?"

"I'm the boring one, remember?"

She angles her head, considering me. "Maybe not so boring."

"No? Have I remedied that somehow?"

"Not exactly, you're just easy on the eyes," she says matter of fact.

"In other words, you're objectifying me."

"Not purposefully," she shrugs. "You can pay me back by ogling my arse if you want."

"Your jacket is covering it," I state plainly.

"So, you looked." She grins.

*Cheeky indeed.*

Keeping my grip on her hair, I step forward and bend so we're at eye level and her lips part.

Lack of sexual chemistry, *my arse.*

"You know, Jane, my sexual status and past have absolutely nothing to do with being more personable with the employees on our hospital floor. I can't help but to wonder if *your* curiosity is what's prompting the questions."

"Got me there," she grins unabashedly.

"Well, I hate to disappoint you," I say, releasing her hair and positioning us by taking her right side so I'm closer to the street, "but I don't openly talk about my sex life and wouldn't even if I had a more extroverted personality. Some things are meant to be and remain *private.*"

"Message received," she concedes easily as we resume our walk. "Or maybe you want me to pin my hair up so you can pull *my pigtails.*"

"Nonsense."

"If you say so," she teases, "back to the tube?"

I nod as I guide us toward the train station. Jane insisted we use the tube as a means of transport for the day, seeing as how she pre-ordered a credited Oyster card full of fare money. As we hit the crosswalk, she nudges me. "One question, good Doctor Aston."

"Fire away," I say.

"Are you having a good time *at all*?"

"As opposed to—"

"Argh. Never mind. You can keep that honest answer to *yourself,*" she tosses over her shoulder as she blindly steps forward.

"LEFT, JANE! LEFT! *Fucking hell!*"

# ELEVEN

## JANE

A s the seconds tick by while Lucian idles next to me in wait for
our tube, I recognize I might have been delusional in believing
my attraction for him had diminished. I talked out my ass this
morning when I assured him we had no chemistry.

Because from the minute he examined me last night to this very
moment, Lucian's *lone* chemistry is making one big fat liar out of me.

When I walked out of my suite to see him waiting this morning,
I damn near salivated at the sight of him sleep-rumpled, his thick,
sandy hair tousled. Though he was fully dressed, the look of him deliciously unkempt did things to me. My imagination went into overdrive from the second my gaze landed on him. If that wasn't enough
of a mind screw, when we met up in the penthouse to start our day
together, I damn near gawked when I drank him in—the way he was
dressed electrocuting my libido while kickstarting more fantasies.

Lucian Aston in scrubs—*delectable*.

Lucian Aston in a suit—*mouthwatering*.

Lucian Aston in designer casual—*Jesus by the river.*

His scent alone is fucking lethal. Pair that with his surreal, light brown eyes, high cut cheekbones, square jaw, and the most luscious lips ever gifted, and I'm in deep, deep, thigh-high booted shit.

Or, I would be if there was a chance for me to act on any attraction I have for him, which boomeranged back with a vengeance last night when he examined me.

As of now, and because of our blunt conversation, any chances of acting on anything are slimmer than none.

Though I admit, it has been a lot easier to converse with him since we had our come to Jesus and struck our deal. Slightly more at ease, I'm no longer vigilantly guarding myself or my tongue as closely and am comfortable speaking my mind. It's just that every time I lock eyes with the man, I lose my bearings a little.

Combine that with the fact that he just fisted my hair in the middle of a busy London street, and *Fuck. Me. Dead.*

Which technically, I would be if he hadn't saved me from idiotic self-destruction—death by cell phone.

*Only you, Jane.*

The more we spend time together, the more my fumbling idiocy threatens to return. If only he hadn't chained us together for the next two days. If only I hadn't agreed to it. He's not bad company at the moment and seems to grow more comfortable in mine. I want, no, I *need* to gain my freedom. If only to save myself from, well, *me*, or at least who I am when I'm around him.

Though I'm flirting purposefully to conceal my true attraction, I'm not sure how long I can hold out. If only he'd give me a bit of the Lucian I landed in London with, I could get back on track. As it is today, he's saved my damned life and looked hella good doing it. Not exactly reason enough to stop the mid-day daydreams, where he fists my hair for another reason entirely.

"Jane?" Lucian says as I fixate on the tiny light-blue snowflakes on the tips of my boots.

"Mmm?"

"We're boarding," he relays as I glance up to see the doors of the train open.

"Oh, sorry." Following him inside, I avert my gaze to anywhere but him as he takes one of two available seats and ushers me toward the vacant seat next to him. Once seated, I purposely begin taking notice of the other men in the near vicinity and . . . What. In. The. Hell?

Everywhere I look, every male in close proximity is both groomed and dressed to the nines. Most shockingly, even the older gentlemen are in top-tier designer suits, trench coats, leather gloves, and carrying stylish umbrellas as an accessory. "Good God," I utter, mystified.

"What's that?" Lucian asks.

"I haven't seen a single man who doesn't look catalog-worthy since we got on this train." Scouring every corner, I make a thorough sweep, and sure enough, there's not a slob in sight.

"Makes sense," Lucian says, "this is the time of the morning commute."

"Really?" I ask, "I don't think I've even checked the time today."

"We roused pretty early, considering we went to bed mere hours after sundown."

"Huh . . . so do you all take a class or something to look that GQ?"

"Not exactly," he muses.

"Well, Boston, hell, the US as a whole needs to take notes and step up their game," I declare, ogling the fit of the tailored threads of a man who has to be pushing his late sixties, looking better than he has a right to. "Unreal. You Brits really have your ways, don't you? With words as well."

"As do you Americans, specifically you Southerners. Half the time, I think myself daft due to some of your colloquialisms."

He smiles, and I don't, which confuses him as I work it out. "What, not impressed by my humor?"

Biting my lip, I decide to keep to the terms of our deal. "I'm assuming colloquialism means a saying?"

"More or less," he nods, drawing his brows. "What are you thinking?"

"I'm not really." *Be honest, Jane.* "I'm mostly embarrassed."

"How so?"

I bite my lip. This was a bad deal. A stupid deal. My cheeks heat as he prods me again. "Is it because you were unsure of the meaning?"

"Uh, I don't think I've ever heard it used in context, is all." I dart my eyes away but feel his remain on me.

Humiliated *again*, in front of Doctor God, *again*.

Will this shit ever end?

"Okay, I kind of lied a second ago," I admit, "it brought up a memory."

"Which is?"

"God, I really don't want to confess this to you." I palm my cheeks and can feel them blazing.

"So then pass," he offers.

"Brutal honesty," I remind us both before lifting my eyes to his and WHAM. Jesus, why does he have to be so fucking beautiful?

*His shit stinks. His shit stinks.*

"Jane?"

"I learned a lot of my vocabulary by reading, I guess like anyone else, but I mispronounced a word once, in front of you . . . and you corrected me."

"Ominous," he says, his lips tilting up slightly in amusement.

"Yeah," I confirm on exhale.

"I remember you pronounced it omnious."

"I wish I could forget," I mutter.

He tenses. "And I shouldn't have corrected you?"

"No, you should have. Learn and grow, right? But . . . maybe not in front of *other people*?" I lift my shoulders with my admission.

"Ah, I see," he nods, his eyes scouring me as they have the past twenty-four hours. As if I'm *his mystery* to solve instead of the other way around.

"It was really embarrassing, is all." Clamping my mouth shut, I shrug as if to play it off and again take in our surroundings.

"Jane," he prompts, waiting until I lift my gaze back to his stupefying return stare. "As useless as this may sound since I've been repeating it by the hour as of late, I'm sorry for that. It was a knee-jerk reaction to correct you and not meant to embarrass you."

"No," I dig in, self-consciousness taking a back seat. "I'm glad I confessed because that's my first tip."

He perks at this. "Which is?"

"I'm positive you're aware of it but try to remember the majority doesn't have your linguistic skills and distinguished vocabulary. You're one of the lucky ones, and that's not a bad thing, Lucian, but it does make *you* a bit harder to relate to. A lot of our staff made it to our floor on a wing and a prayer and are still up to their ears in student loans. Just, maybe, be more mindful of that."

"Understood," he says, lowering his stare to the hands resting on his thighs.

"Shit, I'm not trying to make *you* feel bad about yourself, Lucian. I really want you to feel more accepted on the floor, and if we're exchanging apologies, I owe you one for that, er, Dr. Prick thing."

"No, you don't," he dismisses. "So don't apologize."

"Well, I am, and while we're at it, I want to thank you."

"For?"

"Because you *really* saved my life back there, no bullshit. But then again," I grin, "you save lives every single day. I can't begin to imagine how that must feel."

His answering expression is not one of pride, and I can't at all read what's there in its place aside from . . . fear? But that can't be right. Lucian is nothing but confident in the operating room. He's never lost a patient on my watch, other than the hopeless cases, and that's always been post-op. Still, something inside me aches at his expression, and I quickly search for a way to drop it.

"When my number is called, I definitely wouldn't want to go *that way*. Even if I joked about it yesterday, it's not funny anymore. Which reminds me . . . I wonder how many people actually lose their lives per year for not looking left." I pull out my phone.

"You're not seriously—"

"Yep," I confirm. "I'm Googling it."

"And?" Lucian asks, leaning in to gauge the results.

I tap him with my elbow in jest, "Glad I'm not alone in my sickness."

"You've got me curious now."

"Well, sorry to disappoint. It's pretty anticlimactic," I say, scanning the text. "There's not a specific number or average of casualties, and according to this, a vast majority remain safe." I turn my phone for his inspection. "Leave it to me to be one of the very few who almost went out like that," I utter, rolling my eyes up.

"You deprecate yourself often," he points out, which has me pausing.

"Do I?" I shrug. "Well then, I'm declaring it part of a well-rounded and balanced personality. We've all got to be able to make fun of ourselves sometimes. Hell, just you wait until whoop-ass Jane kicks in. She's incurable."

"There's an even more animated version of you?" Lucian twists his thick lips, sarcasm dripping as he continues, "I'll be on pins and needles until that debut."

"Oh, she's saucy," I warn, "and at times, she can walk on water. She's anything but *plain old Jane.*"

"Ah, so I'm detecting some of your more radical behavior is simply to contradict your namesake?"

"Haven't really thought about it," I admit, "so no, God might have done the heavy lifting, but I hand sculpted the rest." A man chuckles next to us, his eyes lingering on me for a beat before he stands to exit the train. "She's entertaining, is she not?"

"Utterly," Lucian muses, honey eyes twinkling as they land back on me. The train car refills by a fraction at the stop, and with less bodies surrounding us, I become more aware of just how little space is between us. Lucian lessens it more as he leans in. "So, what way would you want to go out, Jane? If you had a say in the matter?"

"That's a morbid topic."

"Says the woman who was researching casualty rates."

"Touché, Doc." I pinch my brows. "Hell, I don't know. I guess peacefully, hopefully not in too much pain, and preferably not alone. What about you?"

"What do you picture for me?" He asks.

"Hmmm . . . Oh, I've got it. You die an old man in your study, wearing a smoking jacket while reading in one of those fancy wing-back chairs."

"Really?" He draws out thoughtfully, a sort of glint brewing in his eyes. "Now *that's* boring."

"Not what you picture?"

He leans in even further, wearing an expression I've never glimpsed or thought him capable of, and it's nothing short of sinful. "Not even close, Jane."

"Okay so—"

"If I had my way, I'd go out snorting a line off the perfect arse, but only after I've *fucked* it."

My jaw unhinges completely as I gape at him a, "whaaa," escapes me in a rush of breath as I palm my chest. Disbelief fills me, and it takes me several inhales before I'm able to utter a coherent sentence. "Pardon Moi?"

"Wrong country, Nurse Cartwright." His grin blossoms into a full-blown smile—a devilish one at that—as he takes noticeable satisfaction in my reaction.

"There you go, correcting me again," I rasp out, glancing around the car where we're safely away from prying ears and back to him. His eyes seem to darken while he surveys me.

"Did you really just say that?"

*Please say yes. Please say yes.*

He lifts his pointer an inch from his lips as he speaks, "Say *what*, Jane?"

I swallow. "G-good sir, even with all my crassness, I can't possibly bring myself to repeat it."

"That's a good thing, and I hope you don't," he whispers roughly but with a sort of commanding lilt behind it—so much so, chills skitter up my spine.

"That's your honest answer?"

"Yes," he says simply. "Don't look so shocked, Jane, I'm human. Doctors are just as human as nurses, and we live much the same way as everyone else."

"I guess I'm shocked because *doctors* especially aren't supposed to say or *do* things like that." I narrow my eyes. "Are you putting me on? You are, aren't you? You've probably never done anything close to that in your life," I harrumph. "You almost had me."

"Believe what you will, but it's not some random idea I schemed up for shock value. Quite the contrary. It's more like a wish for a *repeat* before I climb into my deathbed."

My jaw couldn't drop any lower if it were unhinged. "A repeat, as in—"

"As in, I tried cocaine in college to help keep me up to study for finals. I was in a gorgeous coed's apartment, and her flatmate was doing lines. I was curious, and she was willing. We took a little into the bedroom. It was a good night, a really good night, hence, the desire to repeat it when I'm old and have nothing to lose."

I can't at all help my gradual and victorious smile as the train slows to our stop. "I frickin' *knew* you were a naughty boy."

"Yes, well, don't get too excited. That's all the sexual history you're getting, and if that ever circles back to me," he stands and bends so we're eye level, robbing me of breath entirely. "I'll deny it vehemently, Jane, while wearing my *most convincing* resting bastard face without so much as flinching."

My lips form an O before I formulate a response, the same dark look in his eyes keeping me transfixed. "And you think *I* have a deviant side."

"We all do," he assures me as I stand to follow him out of the car. "Some of us are a lot more skilled in hiding it, to the point it seems impossible it exists."

"But I had you pegged," I boast. "Admit it, I did."

"Did you?" His accompanying smirk can only be described as delicious.

"Wow, you must teach me your ways, Obi-Wan."

"It's too late for you. You're far too outspoken and cheeky to try to master the art."

A thought occurs to me, and I speak up. "Did you only admit that to temper the sting of my embarrassment?"

"Tit for tat, Jane. Brutal honesty. That was our deal, and don't go ruining your set opinion of me, I'm not that nice." With that, he grants me another shot of the devil within, and I can't help my utter fascination as it disappears from his expression just as quickly.

"Gotta admit, you have me reeling, Doctor."

He steps off the train, watching my footing as I follow to ensure I join him in one piece. "Don't let your imagination get too far ahead of you. That confession makes up the vast majority of my skeleton collection."

"W-well," I clear my throat, my mouth dry as the Sahara, "well then, cocaine cowboy, not to worry, I'm good for the foreseeable future with that admission." When he turns his back—and his natural swagger kicks in as he confidently strides towards the exit—I follow, biting my fist as my mind races. My imagination defying his order and going haywire.

I'm so screwed.

"Off with her head!" I spout, stepping up next to Lucian, both of us staring at the displayed guillotine behind the glass—our latest stop in our self-guided tour of The Tower of London.

"Not exactly, but not far off, either," Lucian corrects.

"That's not how it went down, huh?"

"You are partially right, but you just quoted Lewis Carroll," he muses, "more specifically, The Queen of Hearts from *Alice in Wonderland*."

"Oh."

"Historically, 'off with his head' became most notable in Shakespeare's play Henry the Sixth, Act Three—an order given by Queen Margaret in the play. But that famous quote most likely originated from an order spoken by a king. Namely, one who resided here and commanded the death of *two* of his wives for treason."

"You're kidding."

"I'm not. King Henry the Eighth. He ordered the execution of his second wife, Anne Boleyn, along with his fifth—Catherine Howard."

"He had five wives?"

"Six. Divorced, beheaded, and died, divorced, beheaded, survived," he chimes off, "a rhyme I learned in primary school."

"You learned that in grade school? Brutal."

"As you said, we have our ways."

"I'll say. He actually *ordered* them to be beheaded?"

"More or less. He conspired the charges leading up to their executions."

"What an asshole," I say, glancing back at the monster-sized blade and shuddering.

"Many would agree with your assessment," he continues. "Murder does seem a bit more sinful than divorce, doesn't it?"

"Some King," I harumph. "He probably gave them the axe because of his own insecurities. Probably couldn't get it up one night and didn't want the word spread amongst the handmaidens."

Laughter bursts from a man as he walks past us, his gaze on me when Lucian and I both turn, and Lucian sighs in response. Shaking his head, he bites his top lip before eyeing me pointedly.

"Sorry," I grimace, wrinkling my nose, "but damn, that's some cold, ruthless shit."

"What's even colder about it," he says, glancing back at the display, "is it's not so much that they were suspected of adultery, but it's believed by many they were executed because neither produced male heirs. And because the king didn't want to wait for an annulment . . ." he runs his finger across his throat.

"Ruthless," I say, stepping in file with Lucian, who has made his long strides easier for me to match since we arrived here.

Exiting the exhibit, we collectively stop in the middle of a connecting bridge to admire the view.

"And here I thought I was just going to see some fancy jewelry."

"There's an abundance of history here," he says thoughtfully. "Probably far more than what's in the history books, and that is a lot."

"If these walls could talk, huh?"

"Agreed."

I turn to Lucian, allowing myself to appreciate his profile and, more so, *him*. "You know, you're one hell of a tour guide, and you give no five-cent tour. I know you probably hate being stuck as my temporary *minder*, but I'm thankful."

He turns his golden gaze toward me, his eyes sweeping my face. "Not hating it, Jane."

Before I get a chance to register his expression, a loud horn sounds somewhere close, and Lucian grips my elbow to guide me. "Come on," he says, hurrying his steps. "It's starting."

I find myself not giving a damn what *it* is, distracted enough by the interest in his posture and the renewed twinkle in his eyes.

Hours later, after an in-room dinner, Lucian and I rest our aching feet. A heavily trafficked popcorn bucket, open sodas, and assorted candies surround us where we crowd on the swanky couch. A low fire roars adjacent to us as the credits roll on *The Other Boleyn Girl*—a movie about the murdering bastard of a king, his cruelty, and his individual affairs with Anne Boleyn and her sister, Mary.

Lucian turns to me, seemingly relaxed. "Well?"

"It was good. Do you think it was an accurate representation?"

"Definitely not. There are many unknowns about the Boleyn women. No birthdates were recorded because they weren't of noble blood, and because it was half a century ago, no one is sure what either truly looked like or who was the eldest. There is still too much mystery for an accurate representation, and as always, Hollywood has its way of amplifying or exaggerating a story for dramatics."

"I suspected as much. But the fact that it happened at all is pretty damned dramatic as is," I say, glancing back briefly at the screen before focusing on Lucian. We'd both changed into more comfortable clothes, me in my blue pajamas—both my *knickers* and bra *on*—and Lucian in thick men's joggers and a form-fitting long-sleeve shirt. Clothes that would look average on any other man but are accentuated heavily by the curved line of his biceps and defined chest.

When he reached for his drink earlier, his shirt rode up just enough that I managed a glimpse of his toned torso. It was that preview that had me deducing that the man would be hellfire if he wore an adult diaper.

I'd bet my battery-operated boyfriend on it, and I'm fond of that generous fella. Even with his ridiculous appeal in boring clothes, watching the movie with him felt comfortable enough. So much so I finally relaxed enough to gorge on junk food without giving a damn about my spillage. I have a knack for catching what I don't with my mouth in between my ta-tas and have ruined many a shirt in the process. "So, would you do it?" I ask. "Execute your wife or wives for the sake of succession?"

"Considering I took an oath to heal? I would think it would be obvious. But those were different times. The pressure for a successor always threatened the king's position."

I gawk at him. "So you would?"

He shakes his head. "I would like to think I wouldn't, but we all have no idea what we would do in such a dire situation. There was always immense pressure on the monarchy. Still is, but I hope I would remain a man of decent morals in that situation."

His eyes go slightly distant before refocusing, and I know there's something there, but I don't press him or ask him where he went.

"As trifling as they were, I wonder if he loved either of them. It's so sad."

"A tragedy," he muses at my reaction.

"How do you in any way think that's funny? You know, station is still important to this day, and misogyny isn't extinct, either. Why do you all do that shit? And don't you dare blame it on your neanderthal instincts."

"So, I'm to answer for all men's behavior, Jane? You're setting me up for failure here. Definite *pass*."

"Of course you pass," I snark playfully before shaking my head. "I can't imagine living back then and keeping my mouth shut. My head would have been first on the chopping block. There's no way in hell I could have held my tongue back then. Charlie would have had to cut it out to keep me breathing."

"From what I've gathered, Charlie would have to have hers cut out as well."

"Oh, you're not wrong about that."

"If I were a gambling man—which I'm not—because I have to keep it boring," he grants me a gorgeous flash of teeth and upturned lips, "but if I were, I'd be willing to bet that you and Charlie would not only wear the king down in presence alone, but together, the two of you would formulate a plan to take his head before he got anywhere near yours."

His residual smile has my stomach fluttering and surprises me, and I don't dare draw attention to it, but Lucian has become significantly more animated today. It's done nothing but make my stomach flutter the way it is now, as well as speed up my pulse.

"You know I'm taking that as a compliment, right?" I drawl, plucking some of the remaining popcorn from the tub and cupping a little into my mouth.

"As long as you know it was meant as one," he counters, watching me as I push off the soft blanket I was huddled under and stand.

"I'm beat," I announce, glancing down at him where he sits on the couch, staring back at me. "Thank you for today. Really, it was awesome. So awesome, in fact, I'm declaring this day my first official day in London," I wrinkle my nose, "and forgetting yesterday happened."

"As you should. Sleep well, Jane."

"You too, Lucian."

Once behind my suite door, cheeks heated and smarting, it's then I know I'm again wearing a smile—because I've been doing it all day.

At the moment, I'm completely blaming chemistry. Whether it's my imagination—though it doesn't feel that way—it feels good just to be on the receiving end of a man's attention. Especially Lucians'. It's been a long time since I allowed that indulgence.

Pulling my phone from the charger, I unlock it and go to shoot out a text to Charlie. Knowing it might go unanswered due to the hour, I see five texts waiting for me.

**Charlie: Checking in. How's your ass today, buttercup?**

> **Charlie:** HELLO. Worried sister here. I need an update.
>
> **Charlie:** What in the hell? You were in tears last night. Call me!
>
> **Charlie:** ANGRY FACE EMOJI ANGRY CURSE EMOJI
>
> **Charlie:** YOU BETTER HAVE DROWNED IN THAT RIVER BECAUSE THERE IS NO EXCUSE FOR THIS.

"Oops," I wince as I quickly begin typing. I would murder Charlie if the situation were reversed.

> **Sorry! I almost got hit by a sedan by being on my phone today and had to put it up. The best part? Dr. Prick saved me from a possible last day on earth. But we had the best day! Or at least I did. I'm still not sure if he's bored and playing nice, but he's being pretty honest with me. Oh, I forgot to tell you about our deal! I'll call you ASAP.**

Unable to stop my report there—while discovering I'd only taken a few more photos today and none too upset about it—I find myself typing again.

*You've sent five photos to Charlie.*

> **Okay, don't brow beat me, but . . . I'm totally crushing on Dr. Prick again. It's worse than before. OOPS TEETH EMOJI. He's actually got a personality. God, he's so smart and sneaky, and he's got this gorgeous beauty mark to the right of his top lip that you can only see up close, and fuck me if I didn't get close enough today to see it. I'm not FaceTiming you to admit this because he'll hear, but the thing is, I think I might have been wrong, sis. I don't think he's a prick like I thought. I think he's just really, really guarded. We watched a movie tonight, and I swear he was looking at me, like really looking at me. Well, hell, this is turning into a novel-size text. Just know I'm okay and I'll call you when I can. We're going out again tomorrow, and I can't wait, and shit, that scares me a little. KISS LIPS EMOJI.**

# TWELVE

## JANE

L ucian trails me into Harrod's, the sulk evident in his posture,
and I glance back at him, pressing my lips together to ward off
the threatening smile. I know he's still miffed about my decision
to head here instead of his suggestion to walk Hyde Park. He had no
issue telling me shopping was his worst nightmare as we exited the
tube. His blunt objection had me deciding this honesty thing cuts
both ways, especially since he made it clear he'd rather be anywhere
but here. Possibly with me, which I can't decipher since he's in one
of his unreadable states.

My worry about his mood comes to a grinding halt as I shift my
focus forward when we step through the door. I take in the multi-
level store and our newly opulent surroundings—as far as I can see
above us and down to the highly polished floor we're standing on.
It's a sight to behold—especially because of the Christmas décor.

Within seconds, my heart lights with warmth as I'm enveloped
by the magical atmosphere, taken aback slightly by the emotion
threatening. The emotion that only comes with the season. A feeling easily pinpointed by those who embrace it—*Christmas*.

Though we've seen a fair amount of décor in the London streets—and it's been impressive—we haven't ventured out at night to appreciate the lights yet. But it's here, in this place, and even in broad daylight, that Christmas feels present. The luxury department store is world famous for a reason, or at least London famous, having made more than a few of my 'Must See and Do' London stop lists. A few steps into the store—it's easy to understand why.

Just ahead—to the left of an escalator—sits huge, gorgeous marble columns that disappear into the next floor up. No doubt running the length of the store. In every corner and seemingly every service, lights are strewn, occupying all possible space. Mere feet ahead to the right, behind a glass display, sits a set of crystal Nutcrackers around two feet tall. Standing as sentries, they're surrounded by lush, dark green garland, covered in iridescent lights that shift the color of the twin crystal guards, making them even more surreal.

And that's just the start of it.

"I'm not much of a shopper," I say, hating the fact that he's acting like a brat, and I'm still trying to appease him, "but I am a sucker for scenery, and this is just my jam. So, bear with me. I just want to look around for a bit." Glancing over at Lucian for a response, I see him scanning the store, completely disinterested.

Dipping his chin, he doesn't look back at me, which has me bristling a little. He's been in a bit of a mood since he got a text this morning, and I haven't at all been able to get him out of whatever funk it's put him in since. I found myself missing his smiles today, and sadly, it seems Dr. Prick is more present than the Lucian I hoped would make a reappearance. As we both get on the escalator, I glance over at him, and it's clear he's brooding. "You know, you can talk to me if something's bothering you. I can be a friend and lend an ear."

He squares his shoulders at that and jerks his chin so subtly that I almost miss it.

Giving up, I shrug in response, deciding it was both his idea and his insistence that he continue chaperoning me while knowing damn well I'm no more than sore from my fall at this point. No further medical observation is necessary. Deciding not to let him dampen another minute, I make my way toward the escalator, Lucian behind me as I marvel at my surroundings. When I step off the top, I'm stopped short by the sight before me. Well over a dozen feet tall, branches laden, it's the array of gorgeous gold ornaments littering the tree that captivate me and draw me in.

"Oh, wow," I rasp, stalking toward it. "These are so beautiful," I proclaim, hesitating briefly before running my finger along a few of them.

As I appreciate the fine details of each, one ornament in particular has me pausing. "This one is . . . beautiful. Different." I run my finger along the shiny gold Moroccan-looking pattern along the ball and stop at the solid gold plate in the center of it, the ornament's title winning me fully over.

"Oh, this is so mine," I declare, checking the price tag, which has me halting plucking it fully from the tree. I quickly dismiss the impulse purchase with a laugh, "or *not*."

I bulge my eyes toward Lucian briefly as I re-secure the ornament back on the branch, realizing he probably has no knowledge of what that eye bulge meant. I doubt he's ever spoken a syllable of "Hard Knock" in his life.

"If it's a purchase you'll treasure, it's worth the price," Lucian prompts softly from next to me. Turning to him, I see his eyes focused on me, the contact . . . intimate as he lightly brushes my features with a startlingly tender return stare. It's a look I haven't seen, well, ever. I hadn't noticed him watching me so intently, and with that awareness, my stomach begins to flutter as my heart follows. Chest thudding steadily and nearing pounding, I take him in against the steady glow of soft lights as the world starts to blur behind him. For a few heavy seconds, it's as if we're in a bubble, the sounds muffling around me as I get lost in his intoxicating return gaze. After a few heart rendering seconds, I manage to catch myself. "It's a want, not a *need*, and I taught myself in my early twenties to only charge *needs*."

Lucian nods, our eye exchange far more personal than our current conversation before he slams his eyes shut, seemingly in frustration. Confused, I'm made aware the source isn't me when he lifts his buzzing cell phone in his hand.

"If you need to take that, I can meet you downstairs."

"I don't," he replies in exhale before tilting his head back and pinching the bridge of his nose.

"You have a headache," I state as I reach out and touch his arm. He jerks back slightly at the contact.

"I'm sorry, I didn't realize it," I whisper, turning back toward the tree and snapping a picture of "The Love Ball" for lack of anything better to do. His current anger and frustration—though thankfully and seemingly not geared toward me—makes me anxious and fidgety. From the way he's acting, he seems inconsolable. As uncomfortable as I feel and am—and unsure of what to do—all I really want at the moment is to try to figure out a way to console him.

Glancing around the store, I quickly realize the ornament won't be the only thing I can't afford here and decide not to expose my lack of a healthy bank account further by window shopping in front of Lucian. I have no issue admitting I'm in the working-class category and struggle at times to make ends meet. Hell, it's obvious and not something I'm ashamed of. But for my own sake, I remind myself that Christmas is the shittiest time of year to remind yourself that you're broke.

*Broke in London.*

With that whisper piping up in my psyche, my smile returns. I glance back over to Lucian, unsure if my headache diagnosis was on point or if *I'm* the source of his headache.

"Come on, let's get you out of here. I never did get you your promised lunch yesterday. I owe you, so let's eat."

Turning on my heel, I head out of the store, not bothering to look back. There's no need to. Because I can feel him, his presence, and the dark cloud looming over him from a step behind me. That is until he eclipses my steps to get the door before ushering me safely out into the street.

Tossing my napkin on my plate, I glance over at Lucian. "That was delicious. Thank you for indulging me on the lunch decision."

"Another check off your list," he deduces, eyeing my plate. "You didn't eat much."

"I ate plenty. Fish and chips, and mushy peas, and ironically at a place named *Fishers*." I roll my shoulders back, and Lucian watches the movement.

"You've been fidgeting for the better part of the meal, Jane. That hasn't escaped me."

That surprises me, seeing as the eye contact ceased completely after our heavy exchange at the store. "I'll admit, I'm in a little bit of pain. I'm just sore at this point."

"You need more medication."

"I forgot it," I say, frowning at the growing throb in my upper back.

"I didn't," he says, pulling some of the tablets from his pocket.

"What an amazing doctor," I exclaim as he pops the tablets out of the package and into my waiting hand. "You know, if you ever start making house calls, I'll be the first to give you five stars in a Yelp review."

He shakes his head, lips simpering but refusing to fully lift. He's been mostly silent during lunch, and from what I'm gathering at this point, it's probably out of boredom. I can't imagine what entertains a guy like him or keeps his interest for long. It sure as hell isn't me.

Deciding not to punish him or myself any longer after the day we had, I decide to cut him loose for decent behavior. I reckon our relationship is as good as it's probably going to get at this point. "You're officially off the hook for the rest of the day and after. No more minder needed."

He stills and snaps his attention to me. "Pardon?"

"I think we both know you're bored out of your mind, and I'm sore but completely on the mend. This is your downtime, too, Lucian, and I really don't want to deprive you of spending it how you want to. Also, I'm not interested in trying to figure out how to keep you entertained because, honestly, it will only stress me out. So, you're off the hook. You're free."

I lift my hand to request the check from our waitress—who introduced herself as Kimberly—and she nods in my direction as I glance back over at Lucian. I note the twitch of his jaw before he draws the prongs of his fork with precision down his untouched mushy peas. "Have I offended you somehow?"

"Of course not. You were the perfect escort, tour guide, gentleman, and literal lifesaver," I laugh. "Why do you ask?"

"I'm curious as to why you're so intent on ridding yourself of me."

I bite my lip and see his demeanor changing before my eyes as he presses in, his expression starting to reek of rejection. "Well, Jane?"

"I thought you'd be happy about it."

"I was having a fine day," he flicks his eyes to mine, "until you told me I was boring you."

"Fine day? You've been in some mood for most of it and have hardly spoken a word, too. So I figured—"

"Wrong, you assumed wrong. I was debating where to take you next to keep *you* entertained. It seems I have truly wasted my time," he bites out, resting bastard face sliding firmly back into place.

"Well, we wouldn't want you to waste a second more, but that was kind of my whole point," I clap back.

"Suits me fine," he mutters, rolling his now lifeless eyes forward and, more importantly, in dismissal. The sight of it, knowing he's aware of exactly what he's doing, sparks my anger.

"You know, you're pretty childish when you're butthurt."

"Beats being the *former* most of the time," he quips.

"You dick," I blurt as he turns and leers back at me.

"I should have known yesterday was all an act and that you couldn't help but revert to, well, *you*."

"I'll have you know that I'm the one sticking to our arrangement while you seem to be going all willy-nilly."

"Willy-nilly?" I laugh. "Choice words, Doc, considering you're the one who just flipped his shit due to a misunderstanding."

"Lucian," he grits out. "My fucking name is Lucian. Not Aston, not Doc, or any other ridiculous replacement you muster up."

"Funny, I've mustered up about twenty of them while you were jacking your jaws and spewing your venom. Do you want me to name them alphabetically? Asshat, Assho—"

Kimberly chooses that exact moment to approach and grab my card. "All set and thank you. By the way, you two have been looking cozy back here. Are you on a special date?"

"Certainly not," Lucian snarks, as if the idea disgusts him.

"*Rude*," I snap at him before turning to Kimberly. "We're co-workers and here on a work trip. He's a *brilliant* surgeon, and I'm one of his staff nurses."

"Really," Kimberly says, eyes lingering a little on Lucian. "What kind?"

"Heart," we say in unison.

"Matter of fact," I add, laying it on a little thicker. "He's taking the lead on a groundbreaking surgery in Paris in a few weeks. It's going to be something to behold."

"That's amazing," Kimberly says, and Lucian nods, glancing between us, seeming unsure of what's happening.

"He is quite a catch, single too," I relay.

"Jane," he grits out as I lay a hand on his arm.

"Don't be so modest, Lucian," I turn back to Kimberly and fake a hushed whisper, cupping the side of my mouth, "he's a bit rusty in the dating department and *very tense*."

Kimberly grins as we both turn to Lucian, who's beginning to sweat as I hold in my cackle.

"Well, it's a pleasure to meet you, doctor," Kimberly says, lingering a beat before taking my card and sauntering away.

"What in the hell do you think you're doing?" Lucian bites out.

"Playing wing woman."

"Stop. Immediately."

"Why? She's beautiful. Is she not up to your standards or something?"

"This is ridiculous," he spouts in aggravation before focusing his scowl on me. "What is your game now?"

"I'm not playing games," I say, running the pad of my finger around the rim of my water glass.

"Bullshit," he tosses at me, the curse sounding odd from him.

"You need to relax, seriously. You're wound up tighter than a drum. Especially if you're going to go straight for the throat so easily."

"I'm only responding to your behavior."

"Right, it's on me," I sigh. "Well, it was a good run," I mutter dryly, "while it lasted. Let's go back to the hotel and get some needed space."

"As I said, it suits me perfectly."

When we both abruptly stand, I wobble a little on my feet. In a flash, Lucian surrounds me, his harsh gaze softening substantially as he stares down at me. "Tell me," he urges, his lips not far from mine because of the way he's cradling me to him. "Are you dizzy?"

"A little," I whisper back, but it has nothing at all to do with anything medically related. His lips. God, his lips, as thick as they are, look so soft. "Do you use a lot of Chapstick?" I ask, my whisper hoarse.

"What?" He retorts, features twisting in confusion as Kimberly approaches.

"Is everything all right over here?"

"Fine," I say as Lucian chimes in.

"She had a little bit of a dizzy spell. She took a nasty spill a few days ago."

"I'm fine," I assure her.

"Actually, she landed so hard her knickers flew right off," Lucian tosses out.

Kimberly and I both gape at him due to his bold delivery as he gently releases me and pulls out his wallet, tabling a large bill for her.

"The service was incredible. Please excuse me," Lucian's lifeless eyes find mine as he addresses her. "Apparently, I'm in need of some better company to relax."

Lucian leaves the table along with Kimberly and me as we collectively stare after him.

"All I can see is those lips," she says, just as mystified.

"Right? They're like face pillows, but . . . really *sexy* face pillows. Too bad he's a total prick."

"I don't think I would care. Jesus, he's fit," she continues.

"Does that translate to hot?"

"Yes, and dear God, if that man gave me an ounce of attention, my husband would just have to miss me." She turns to me, "but it's apparent he fancies you."

"Oh, no, he doesn't," I say, waving her off. "I bore him."

"He seemed pretty fascinated from what I gathered. Every time you weren't watching him, he was staring at you." I turn to her, my expression no doubt stunned because she nods to me in assurance that I heard her correctly. Her smile only grows. "And how long is this work trip?"

"Six weeks," I utter, tracing Lucian's retreat as he stalks toward the door.

"And today is?"

"Day three," I answer on autopilot.

"You two won't last the week," she predicts confidently.

"No," I shake my head adamantly. "He's not attracted to me. If you saw anything, you misread it."

I glance back over at her just as she holds up two fingers. "How many?"

"Two?" I say, unsure of where she's headed with it.

"So, no issue with your vision then, which tells me that he may not be the only one who is *rusty* in the dating department. Have fun," she sniggers, collecting her tip and leaving me there. I continue to stare after Lucian just as he pushes his way out of the door.

Fancies me? I can't deny I've caught him staring at me a few times—well, more than a few—some with an intense look in his eyes, but he's an intense man. His expressions are always pretty brutal and indecipherable. Still, I swear I saw some heat in them a few times. And then there was the exchange in the department store. What exactly was that?

Hell, if he does fancy me—even a little—then why the attitude and silent treatment today? Why the whiplash-inducing mood shifts?

I clearly hurt his feelings by releasing him, but why be so cutthroat about it? Is he not used to any sort of rejection?

Argh! The man is infuriating, and I've only just started trying to understand him. Knowing the window is closing for a quick truce, I make my way out of the restaurant to catch up with him.

"Lucian," I call as I hit the street. Looking left and right, I catch sight of him as he takes long strides away from the restaurant.

"Lucian, stop!" My command falls on deaf ears as he continues stalking away as if he didn't hear me. "If you don't stop, I won't look left!" I call after him as a few heads turn my way. It's a stupid play, but he's making too much headway for me to catch him. "I'm not looking left!" I screech after him in threat until he finally stops his footing. He turns back to me, his eyes clouded as I haul ass to catch up with him.

Breathless by the time I get to him, I start in on an exhale. "I'm sorry if I misread the situation. I genuinely thought you would be relieved."

"You stated that," he replies, not impressed by, well, anything I'm saying.

"Please don't be hurt—"

"That would insinuate you have that ability, Jane, which you do not. What we both have is an important meeting tomorrow, so it's just as well we cut our day short. I have notes to review."

"Seriously? You're going to shut down on me like that?"

"I'm simply saying—"

"No, you're not," I scold, crossing my arms. "You've regressed back to that fake, polite bullshit thing you do."

"Fine, then let me be clear." He stares down at me, his expression the same as the man who berated me in front of the surgical staff. "I have no interest in participating in your little social experiment nor pursuing any more of a friendship with you. Is that honest enough?"

I swallow, the sting of his admission biting more than I could have imagined. His eyes soften ever so slightly when, no doubt, my face gives that hurt away before he turns and stalks toward the curb, hailing an approaching taxi.

"What are you doing?" I ask, even if the answer is obvious as he opens the door when the cab stops, staring at me expectantly. "Getting you safely back to the hotel," he states, his tone completely void of any trace of the man I'd gotten to know in the last couple of days.

"I'm not your fucking job or your obligation," I snap, "I can look after myself. So you can see *yourself* safely back to the hotel."

His eyes scan me briefly, his expression reeking of boredom as he gives me a sharp, indifferent dip of his chin and enters the cab.

"Don't wait up, Doc!" I snap just before his door does. Turning on my booted feet, I stalk in the opposite direction from the cab pulling away from the curb. My chest grows heavy with each step as I retreat due to his own withdrawal. As the sting sets in, I check myself for thinking the situation could have gone differently.

Hours later, feet and back aching, I enter the dark penthouse on edge, annoyed by the fact that Lucian's somehow managed to shift our dynamic to where I feel accountable to him. Having spent hours walking around just to spite him, I didn't at all absorb my surroundings as his words circulated through my head. Resentment brewing—but too tired to duel it out with him on the off chance I disturb his sleep—I power on my cell light and tread lightly down the short hall toward the large kitchenette adjacent to the living room. Just as I step in, I catch a soft light emitting from a small table lamp perched next to an oversized chair just as Lucian stands.

Dressed in form-fitting thermal pajamas, a tablet in one hand, his eyes scour me briefly before he cuts the light off with his other. A tense beat passes, and without a word, I make out his silhouette as he stalks to his room and softly shuts the door behind him. My heart thunders as I stand in the pitch dark, the look he left me with etching itself into my memory as an added twinge of hurt pangs in my chest.

Whether he's aware of it or not, Lucian Aston was a born heartbreaker. I decide at that moment that I can no longer run the fool's errand of trying to get closer to him or give him a chance to wield any more power to hurt me. Because he's already capable, and he already has.

# THIRTEEN

## JANE

Receiving his summons via text the next morning, I meet Lucian in the hotel lobby. Exiting the elevator, I approach him where he stands just inside the door before dipping his chin with a subdued "Good Morning." A greeting I parrot in a similar tone, striding past him as he opens the door for me, shadowing me closely before leading me to a sleek, black sedan. A driver waits as we approach, holding the back passenger door, and greets us both warmly as we get in.

Once inside, I avert my eyes out the window, but not before catching Lucian tapping his leg with his fingers in my periphery. After several blocks of tense silence—which the driver clearly feels as he eyes us in the rearview—Lucian breaks it, addressing me in a hushed tone. "Were you able to make much progress on your itinerary?"

"Not as much as I would have liked."

"I see. Then what is it that kept you?"

I give him my best side eye roll. "Doesn't matter, Dr. Aston."

"That again," he utters dryly.

"I'm just following your lead, *Lucian*," I counter, deciding to stop the childish antic.

"Jane—"

"So, what's your name," I cut Lucian off, my question for the driver, who looks to be in his mid-thirties and is easy on the eyes in the rugged sense. His features are boldly masculine, his hair and eyes dark brown. Ink peaks out of the cuff of his jacket, which I'm fairly certain leads to a sleeve of tattoos.

"Mike," he replies, his accent distinctly different.

"Hi Mike, I'm Jane," I introduce myself.

"A pleasure, Jane."

"Mine as well. Scottish?"

"Aye," he jests, which earns him a grin from me. "Glasgow. And where exactly in the states are you from?"

"I was raised in the south, a little town in North Carolina to be specific, but I've been told I don't have too thick of an accent."

Lucian bursts out in a sarcastic chuckle from next to me, an equally ironic smile on Mike's face before he replies, "ah, yes, I see."

"Well," I say, running my hands down my sweater dress, "it's nice to meet you, Mike. Thank you for driving us today."

"It's my pleasure, ma'am."

"Jane," I correct him.

His brown eyes meet mine in the rearview as he nods with an answering, *"Jane."*

Lucian bristles next to me as a few more silent minutes tick by, and the discomfort sets in. Just as I'm about to ask Mike for some music to disrupt the increasingly uncomfortable silence, Lucian prompts me again with the soft call of my name.

"I thoroughly poured over the notes last night at a gastropub," I say, hating the consoling lilt in his tone, as if he's about to let me down gently and rebuke it as I continue. "I'm prepared."

Glancing over, I see his eyes already tracing my dress. Today, I paired a black, long-sleeved, scooped-neck sweater dress with calf boots of the same color. My form-fitting coat is the same length as my dress, which rests a respectable few inches above my knees. Leaving my hair down, I applied minimal makeup, the only real pop of color on my lips, which I shaded a matte, dark rose red. Lucian's eyes trace

every detail of my appearance before flitting back to mine. I swear I
see a trace of apprehension in them, unsure of why it's there.

*You don't care, Jane. You do not care.*

"It's a complicated case," I continue, not bothering to try and
decipher if he deems my outfit appropriate enough, "but I understand the significance of what you're trying to accomplish and how
instrumental it will be if it's a success. I've memorized the creden-
tials of each member of the Oxford team and am aware they have a
surgical staff far more experienced to lead on this one. I'm fine with
riding passenger and being a team player, so I won't utter a word at
the meeting today unless you ask me to weigh in, but I'm prepped
enough to answer *anything*," I reiterate.

"Jane," Lucian says, this time more insistently.

"There's no coming back from what you said to me yesterday," I
whisper low enough for only him to hear. "And I honestly don't give
a shit if you're sorry. So, let's go back to where we should have started
in the first place and keep it professional because, you know, fool me
twice," I sigh. I can feel his frustration from where he sits next to me,
but I don't want him getting a word in. He doesn't deserve it.

"We still have five weeks and change ahead of us," I continue,
"and you have a groundbreaking surgery you need to concentrate
on. A surgery that—believe it or not—I truly want you to succeed
in executing. I have no interest in doing anything with you outside
of assisting with it. That is if you still want me on your team." I meet
his eyes. "This is a big deal professionally for *both* of us, Lucian, and
I'm behind you one hundred percent. I'm more than confident you'll
be able to pull it off, so let's concentrate on that."

His swallow is visible due to his pronounced Adam's apple as
he palms his suit pants. In the few seconds we maintain eye contact,
I note a visible shift in his demeanor. His own decision made, he
slowly rolls his gaze toward his own window and nods.

Band-Aid freshly ripped, I decide we're both better off, especially
with the ache I'm feeling because of it. It seems he's also fine with it
because neither of us utters another word the entire ride to Oxford.

Three hours later, after taking Mike's offered hand, I step into a different world entirely. Oxford Medical School, arguably the best in the world in reputation and standing, has a matching campus that is nothing short of regal.

Knowing we're running low on time, Lucian wastes not as second of it. I wordlessly follow his lead as he strides away from the car. With me in tow, he makes a beeline for a building, the campus easy for him to navigate because Oxford is where Lucian gained his medical education.

As I trail him, I take in every detail of the sand-colored, gothic-looking buildings littered with A-framed windows and iron trimming. Buildings very Harry Potterish in look, which are surrounded by immaculately kept grounds. Though the weather isn't cooperating today as it's freezing and overcast, I can visually imagine a part in the clouds, sunrays beaming through the break of them while highlighting how green the grass is during warmer months. Silencing every question budding on my tongue, I marvel at our surroundings while becoming increasingly envious of those who get to attend such a prestigious school. Though Boston University isn't in any way a school to snub—my master's degree remaining the thing I'm most proud of—this campus puts it to shame.

Seconds after Lucian and I enter a building he navigated us to within minutes, we begin striding toward an elevator, bypassing a grand staircase. I'm determined to remain wordless. But, when he glances over at me and stops me with a hand on my arm, I can feel what's coming before he speaks it. "Jane, enough is enough."

"Lucian," I hiss, glancing around us. "Now's not the time. We have minutes to spare if we want to be *punctual.*"

His eyes flare at my barb as he smashes the elevator button. "Then you'll grant me the time until the lift arrives."

"Fine," I say, permitting myself to give him a thorough once over, his immaculate black suit tailored perfectly to fit his equally immaculate build and, more specifically, his charred *soul.*

"I do apologize for my behavior yesterday, but it truly is for the best."

"I agree," I counter amicably, which does not bode well due to the shift in his expression.

Tough shit, Doc.

"You have your reasons," he says, "and I know I'm to blame for most of them, but I'd like the chance to state my own."

"Time's up," I say as the door opens, and he curses beneath his breath and steps inside. Just as the elevator begins to ascend, I notice the flex of his fingers at his sides.

He's nervous.

Extremely nervous, and for the first time since we've met, doing a horrible job of masking his emotion.

It's even more evident with the way his eyes are darting back and forth as he watches the first floor tick off as if he's waiting for a countdown to an explosion.

"Lucian?" I ask, as sweat visibly breaks along his hairline, and he loses a bit of color right before my eyes. Tossing my pride in the back seat as our floor approaches, I turn and step in front of him. His eyes immediately collide with mine and begin to search before they hold.

"Listen to me. I don't know what has you so rattled, but I'm telling you right now," I grip his hands in mine. "These hands are some of the most skilled surgical hands in the medical field, hell—in the fucking world. You are one of the best—if not *the best*—cardiothoracic surgeon breathing. I should know. I've clocked over a hundred hours with you in the last six months, so I have the authority to say there's nothing or no one on any floor of any hospital in the world that you can't hold your own with. Command the respect you deserve just like any other day, Lucian. You've got this, even if you feel like you don't."

Lowering my eyes, I squeeze his hands and go to release them when he returns my grasp, refusing me. My eyes shoot back up to his as I realize just how close we are or how close he's gotten. Sliding his thumbs along the skin of my hands, he parts his full lips and whispers my name in a way that has the hairs on my neck standing on end. We're so close now that I can feel his exhale on my parted lips, a drawn moth to the ignited flame in his eyes as what breath I have left catches in my throat. When the elevator stops, I gently pull from his hold and step back in line beside him, reeling from the contact.

What just transpired between us took only a matter of seconds as I replay every one of them within a few of the sledgehammering beats currently battering my chest.

It's when the doors open, and his eyes connect with one of three surgeons speaking just outside of it, that I pinpoint why Lucian is nervous. Within the next beat, I realize the pep talk I gave was in vain because the reason for his anxiety has absolutely nothing to do with our upcoming surgery.

Three hours into a rapidly heating discussion on surgical approach, we break for lunch. The intricate diagrams by all three surgeons set to participate in the surgery on a lit backboard, which is currently the focal point of the stadium-seat-styled, old-world classroom. As things stand now, we'll be here for every allotted hour of our first two-day prep meeting because two out of the three surgeons on the Oxford team are still debating about the preliminary approach using the Razor—the cutting-edge surgical tool being utilized for the first time in this procedure. The tool itself is slightly bigger than a ballpoint pen. I've watched Lucian practice with it a couple of times—fascinated by its capabilities.

Before the meeting, I was only able to exchange a few words with Margarete, a whip-smart surgical nurse originally from Spain with an impressive and spotless resume. During our short time conversing, she and I got along famously, and as it turns out, she read up a little on me, too, which is flattering considering. Next to her was Brian, who didn't so much as bother to introduce himself when given the window, nor look my way once. This instantly let me know which side of mine he would reside on. The anesthesiology team and the rest of the assisting surgical staff seemed nice enough, but it would take a little time to get to know them. Time we most likely won't have due to utilizing every second in preparation for the surgery. It hasn't escaped me that I'm one of the most inexperienced in the room despite the rapidly lengthening time of my clocked hours in the OR, nor how fortunate I am to be here, repping our hospital. For whatever part they allow me to play, I find myself thankful.

As we break, Lucian exits the room, and to no surprise of mine, the brunette we came face to face with upon arriving, follows him out. I don't bother going after Lucian, as I'm not at all ignorant that there's a history there. It was made evident to us all in the shared eye exchange during the meeting—mostly hers—that there was a reckoning coming. Making my way to the bathroom, Margarete directed me to, I'm stopped at the door by Matthieu. Lucian and I hadn't had a chance to greet him because he came in a little late due to a long-running surgery.

"Afternoon, Dr. Tremblay," I greet, noting his post-op look is almost as impressive as Lucian's. No doubt dressed in some fancy label, I can't help but allow myself a whiff of his expensive, spicy cologne and note the nearly purple hue of his thick, onyx hair.

"Please call me Matthieu."

"Not here," I whisper conspiratorially.

"Let that pompous ass make you call him by his surgical surname," he expels in thickly French-accented but flawless English.

I can't help my light laugh. "He doesn't, honestly. He's rather insistent that I don't."

"That's surprising," he says. "Join me for lunch?" He asks with a grin as staff rolls in a catered cart full of mouthwatering sandwiches.

"Absolutely, just let me go wash up?"

"I'll be waiting, Jane."

His not-so-subtle words linger with promise as I grin back at him. The man truly is gorgeous, French, and clearly looking for a no-frills hook-up, which is exactly what I put on my wish list for this trip. Sadly, I couldn't be less interested at present, and it's no mystery why.

*Damn you, Dr. Prick.*

"I'll be right back."

Making my way down a series of hallways, I find myself a little turned around and, in correcting my direction, pass a few doors. It's as I pass one office in particular that my suspicions are confirmed.

"I'm thankful for the opportunity, Lucian, but you should have rang me well before we met today," a female voice I recognize now belongs to Dr. Gwendolyn Cavendish scolds Lucian as I stop my walk.

"I didn't insist upon you because of our personal history, Gwen, or out of guilt. The BMA agreed that you and Matthieu are perfectly suited to assist in this and take the lead if necessary. Therefore, it's deserved recognition and has nothing to do with anything else."

"I'm aware of how good I am," she claps back confidently. And from what I gathered, she has every right to be. From the tip of her head to expensive heels, she's polished perfection and a brilliant surgeon to boot. From what I read last night, she and Lucian are close in age, and no doubt attended Oxford together. College sweethearts would be my guess.

As their heated whispers reach me, I was dead on in gathering there's history between them, and from her accusatory tone, a history in which Lucian wronged her.

"It's been three years, Lucian. Honestly, what did you expect?"

"Nothing, which is deserved. I wish you every—"

"Don't you dare," she hisses, "I'll hate you for it."

His tone changes then to one I'm becoming familiar with—*detachment*.

"You have every reason to resent me, Gwendolyn, to hate me if that's what you feel."

"I should. Maybe I do, but if you can think of any reason why I shouldn't—"

"I have none," he replies instantly, cutting her short.

"Of course you don't. You never fight for anything, do you? Never fight at *all* or raise your voice an octave higher than appropriate. You've never bothered, not once, to fight for anything, or anyone, well aside from Alex—"

"Don't," Lucian intercepts her rant, his tone level but somehow ringing clear with warning. "I understand you're upset, but that's beneath you."

"You're right. Lucian, you're right. I'm sorry. Truly." Her mournful tone indicates the ache of a woman in love with a man who's not giving her the words she so desperately wants to hear.

I know that ache.

I'm familiar with it and decide to respect her enough to give her the privacy their conversation warrants.

I'm of the firm belief that every woman reserves the right and chance to express their love for a man, whether returned or unrequited. Vice versa of a man to a woman.

We only fall so many times, if ever in life, and from personal experience, I know missing the chance to convey those feelings is tragic—and criminal.

Unexpressed love is a sneaky poison in a way that it can sometimes hurt worse than actual heartbreak itself.

The kicker?

It's not a fast-acting pain that gets easier to manage over time but a regret-fueled poison that worsens the more time passes. If unexpressed, the question each is left with is whether the object of their affection ever loved them—and for those familiar with it—it's one of the most painful things for a heart ever to have to endure.

I loved a man once and never told him because he made the opportunity impossible by the way he regarded our relationship. I regretted it for years until I decided he wasn't much to let go of. But during that time in between, I'll never forget that ache of feeling I missed out on a right denied to me—which made and keeps him a bastard—and now consider it a lesson learned. A mistake I won't repeat ever again. Whether the man is worthy of my love and reciprocates it or not, it's my right to be able to express it and seek satisfaction for whatever answer it gets. So, if my heart ever again decides it wants to let those words fly, even blindly, they're flying.

Pulling out my phone to text Charlie, I feel the newly familiar weight of a gaze on my back just as I finally locate and push through the restroom door.

# FOURTEEN

## JANE

Seven long hours later, we're done for the day, and as we all shake hands and bid farewell, excitement is thick in the air. However, it's nowhere to be found in Lucian as I scan him. The physical toll in his posture is easily detected by me—even if it's imperceptible to everyone else. It's the same fatigue he shows after a long surgery.

Just before he exits the room, he stops and searches it, finding me before gesturing he'll meet me downstairs. I nod, indicating I'll see him there. Gathering my purse, I spot his phone on the table and conclude he fled in an attempt to keep from rehashing anymore with Gwendolyn. Glancing over at her as she shakes hands with Margarete, I see her eyes lingering in the direction Lucian left, and from her expression, I feel the second-hand break happening inside her.

Just as I retrieve it, Lucian's phone rattles in my hand with an incoming message.

> **Byron: you owe it to me, your nephews, and Mum to show. It's one dinner. Can't you manage that, Lucian? It's Christmas.**

My heart tugs in my chest when I realize whatever Lucian was trying to relay to me this morning probably wasn't about our stupid spat on the street. It's painfully obvious he's battling something far bigger, and maybe he was trying to tell me. I should've listened. Anxious to give him the chance, I make my way up the ascending steps and am just shy of the door when a warning rings at my back from feet away.

"If you're falling for him, save yourself the trouble and *don't*."

Fuck.

Glancing back, I see Gwendolyn and I are the only two left in the classroom, aside from Matthieu and Brian, who are a respectable distance away and having a hushed conversation at the board. Gwen eyes me expectantly for a response as she tosses the rest of her things into a sleek, stylish messenger bag.

"Pardon?"

"Please don't insult me by playing ignorant. He was staring at you as often as he was me. More so, if I'm honest. I'm assuming you're sleeping together already?"

"Not that it's your business, but no."

"Ah," she says. Shouldering her bag, she begins to take a few steps toward me, more so the door behind me. "Then it's only a matter of time. A word of advice."

"I'm not a fan of unsolicited advice," I run my eyes down her refined, lithe frame just as she stops and squares up to me. Reaching deep, I summon much-needed patience, knowing she's speaking from a place of pain.

"Maybe you should heed some warning from the woman who was set to *marry* him."

This information stuns me. "Have your say, but you have the wrong idea."

"No, I don't," she challenges through perfectly painted lips, "and we both know it."

To that, I keep my mouth shut because she's right, and I feel that truth sinking in. I knew it yesterday by how much it stung when Lucian lashed out before he withdrew. I already have budding feelings I shouldn't for a man I hardly know—a man who seems to have trust issues and appears to come with more tattered baggage than I brought with me to Europe.

"Trust me on this. He's not worth the effort of committing to, but only because he won't love you back. The thing that will hurt the most," she rasps out, "is that he's entirely capable of it." Hurt leaks from her as she takes the last step that separates us, her eyes dropping to my booted feet and blazing a judgmental trail up as I brace myself for what's coming.

My bet? She's going to go for the jugular, and it will either be about my appearance or lack of significant social status.

The mystery is solved when she covers both with a blanket statement.

"You don't look his type *at all.*"

"I'm not," I admit. "At *all.*"

"Still, he fancies you. That's evident," she says as I note the large diamond on her ring finger and add two and two. From what I heard, she wanted Lucian to stop her from marrying whoever put that ring there.

*This is messy, Jane. Run!*

But I stay planted and ready myself as she continues to scrutinize me. "You're in for quite the surprise. He's incredible in bed. That should be some consolation if you decide he's worth making a fool of yourself for."

"Please stop insulting me on account of being hurt. He hurt you. I didn't. I'm sorry for that, but I don't deserve the wrath because he refused you. I'll make it a point to let him know, but to him, I'm a friend."

"Lucian doesn't have friends," she scoffs, "he doesn't have *anyone* anymore, and he made sure of that."

With those parting last words—which I allow her to have—she stalks out of the room. The urge to go to him grows stronger as I'm left slightly singed in the wake of a fire Lucian clearly started and left blazing at some point before I met him. Irritated, I battle to shake Gwen's words but can't manage to take away their power for the moment.

Even so, I begin to ignore every red flag as I collect myself enough to go to him, including the flags *I'm waving* my damned self. Charging out of the door in search of him, I hear my name called. Turning, I see Matthieu stalking toward me with my forgotten coat, and I muster a smile I don't feel before meeting him to retrieve it.

When I reach him, I slide my arms in where he holds it for me and thank him. He pulls it up to my shoulders, his hands lingering on them briefly as he speaks. "If you seek him out, I'm afraid you're not going to find him in a good way."

"I'm aware. I was just accosted by his jilted bride. Any pointers for how to deal with this?"

"Give him his space. That's what he typically demands."

I turn and mull over his advice, tilting my head. "I don't know. Maybe he's had too much space in the past, and that's why he's so guarded now."

"Trust me," he steps forward while maintaining a respectable space between us. "Let him simmer out. He'll probably take a long walk. It usually does him good."

A walk.

Hyde Park.

He wanted to walk yesterday, probably to try and sort whatever he had going on inside him. But he didn't want to do it alone. He wanted to walk *with me.*

"I'll take that advice," I say as he furrows his brows in confusion when I wish him a good night.

"You're going after him?"

"He is the man I came with," I wink.

"I see. Well, I'm back in London tonight and won't be able to attend tomorrow, but if you're available, my offer for dinner stands—Lucian's excluded."

Insinuation clear, I consider him and decide to keep my options open, not that I think Lucian is one.

Or is he?

*Had* he almost kissed me?

It sure as hell seemed like it, but I like my men decisive, and the man standing in front of me isn't playing Scrabble with my head nor mincing words.

"I'd like that," I say, backing away while facing him, "let's do it."

"Plans for Christmas dinner?"

"None, but I wouldn't mind having one," I turn and make my way toward the elevator.

"I'll ring the hotel," he chimes behind me as I hit the button, turning back to see Matthieu where I left him. Eyeing me unabashedly, he slides his hands into his suit pants, his gaze relaying his brewing plans for the two of us.

Still incredibly good-looking and, sadly, unappealing for the moment for only one reason.

"Damn you, Lucian," I utter under my breath as Matthieu's rapidly heating gaze is cut off by the slow closing of the elevator doors. Panicking, I text my voice of reason as the floors start to tick off.

**Why are women, and when I say women, I mean me, so damned foolish and always opt for the complicated ones?**

Thankfully, the bubbles immediately start.

**Charlie: What happened?**

**Nothing. Well, not nothing. Lucian's gorgeous, brilliant, but bitter, jilted fiancée just inadvertently told me how inadequate I am before wishing me well because she could tell he wanted to fuck me. And she just so happens to be one of the doctors on the Oxford team.**

**Charlie: OPEN MOUTH EMOJI. MIND EXPLODING EMOJI. I'm not sure which reaction to have first. Dr. Prick sooooo wants to PET your KITTY!**

GIPHY of MAN-HAND STROKING CAT HEAD

**And ha ha to Ms. Wannabe Prick! You already won that battle with her reaction alone. Bitch. Please tell me you finished her?**

**It was too sad. I bowed out because I felt sorry for her.**

**Charlie: You're a better woman than me. So what's happening?**

I sigh as my fingers start to fly over the screen.

> Well, Jane has a hot as hell FRENCH doctor who definitely wants to pet the kitty and asked her on a date. A hot French doctor who probably would have made Oxford more memorable for her if she hadn't bailed, but noooo, what does Jane do? Jane cuts the convo short to go after the moody, emotionally unavailable Englishman who's going through some sort of serious shit. Shit that if he decides he needs a distraction from, will probably lead to Jane getting hurt.

> Charlie: Sounds about right, but stop texting about yourself in the third. All I can hear is Tarzan saying it. Jane need a Tarzan. Jane need a Tarzan meat stick more.

Barrett has entered the group chat.

> Barrett: Sup little sister, has London fallen yet? And why does Jane need Tarzan's meat stick?

> What. The. Hell. Charlie?!

> Charlie: What? I told him to jump on because we need man advice.

> Since when has that EVER been a good idea?!

> Barrett: EYE ROLL EMOJI ALREADY OFFENDED within seconds back in the group chat. Did you forget I landed your sister?

> Truth. That's some miracle shit. FIST BUMP EMOJI

> Barrett: FIST BUMP EMOJI

> Charlie: I wasn't that bad.

Our replies appear in the same second.

> LAUGH TEARS EMOJI

> Barrett: LAUGH TEARS EMOJI

> Charlie: Screw you guys. So, no need to get him up to speed. We're sitting side by side.

> YOU TOLD HIM ABOUT THE FALL? ANGRY RED CURSE EMOJI

> Barrett: Sorry little sister, but when she couldn't stop

bursting into laughter for a day straight, I forced her to fess up. By the way, props! Way to make an entrance!

I am going to find a better support group if it's the last thing I do. I'll report back. In the meantime, kiss my nephew, who happens to be the only one of you three I like right now.

**Charlie: Please be careful, Jane. I don't want you getting hurt.**

**It's already too**

I stop and back-space my text.

Is it already too late? If I go after him now, I have a good idea of what will happen. He's vulnerable—which is evident from his behavior the last few days—and it's apparent he needs someone. I could be that someone, or he could tell me to kick rocks. But if I am that someone, that's different from being someone he *wants* rather than a distraction he might think he *needs*.

And that almost kiss . . . if things take a turn and get physical, and it's a tenth of how good I imagine it would be, I'll be screwed, and then what?

Nope. I can't get physical with him—like at all.

If Lucian needs a friend, then I'll be that friend to him and nothing more.

If I have an itch I need scratching, there's a French post standing by without a hostile ex-fiancée lurking around, just waiting for the chance to belittle me.

Oh, for fuck's sake! How is this complicated already?

"Shit," I mutter, typing out my reply as the elevator doors open, and I ready myself for what's ahead.

**Keep your phones on.**

# FIFTEEN

## JANE

Not ten minutes later, I find Lucian loitering outside our building, scanning the vacant campus—the alums already having migrated home for Christmas break. Stare vacant and standing in his black trench coat, a dark gray scarf, and matching gloves, puffs of icy breath erupt from him as I approach, shivering in my own jacket.

As I near, his posture stiffens in awareness, but I don't let it deter me.

"I can't imagine attending such an incredible school. I'm envious," I finally allow myself to say. "I can only assume you've got a hundred memories flooding you right now."

He looks over to me, impenetrable resting bastard face firmly in place, and I grimace, wishing I could put my foot in my mouth. "Sorry, I wasn't thinking."

"It's not in your nature to be callous without reason," he says, surprising me with the compliment while tightening his gloves between his fingers. After a tense silence, he finally speaks up. "I'm assuming you heard."

"Some, but I walked away, Lucian, and am sorry for what I did allow myself to hear."

"I suppose it's fair," he utters on exhale.

"No, that was different."

"Not entirely," he offers before a long silence lingers, the air especially still and growing numbingly colder by the second.

"I can call the car for us both," I offer. "I can leave you here to sort yourself out if that's what you truly want, or you can walk with me and try to tell me what's eating you alive, Lucian. While I might not fully know the man you are, I know the *doctor,* and he wasn't as on point as he typically is today. So, those are your options, and I'm okay with all three."

When he doesn't reply, I snake my hand up his arm and palm his bicep. "Fine, my call, we're walking."

Lucian gives me no argument as we start toward the parking lot. Once there, I walk over to where Mike is parked as he hurriedly exits the driver's side to open the sedan's back door.

"Thanks, Mike, but we'll probably walk to our hotel. Can I get your number?"

"Sure," he takes my phone to program it in while eyeing Lucian behind me, where he rattles idly by.

"Is everything all right, Jane?" Mike utters in a low tone meant for me, concern clear for us both as he again glances over my shoulder.

"Fine, we've been couped up in that room, and we need some exercise."

Mike's return expression relays he doesn't fully buy my excuse, but he hands me back my phone with his offer, knowing it's not his place. "Ring me anytime. I'll be driving for you and Dr. Aston for the remainder of your London stay."

"Oh? Well, great. Thank you," I say as a large bill appears in my periphery when Lucian extends it toward Mike.

"Thank you, Dr. Aston. Cheers," Mike says before getting into the driver's seat and taking off as the sun threatens to set.

"That was nice of you," I tell Lucian, who absently nods. We set off walking and, once off campus, remain wordless for several blocks.

With each step, I become thankful my boots are warm and have low heels. With a thousand questions budding on my tongue, I remain silent, hoping my patience will pay off.

The sun starts to set on Oxford, which is as equally enchanting to me as the school campus. Lucian's posture finally relaxes, and he glances over at me, pausing his footing. "As I've told you before, I'm not the type of man who speaks of his issues. I was taught this way, and it's never been easy for me to reveal such things freely."

"I know," I say as I take the lead, and he follows in step, "and I won't force you to, but your way isn't working out for you, and I swear to you now that anything you tell me will be kept in confidence." I glance over at him so he can see I'm sincere, "it will go straight into my vault, but that requires a bit of trust."

The unrelenting wind bites my nose and cheeks as I urge him to pick up the pace. When we're a few more quiet blocks in, he stops and hesitates.

Reluctantly halting my footing because I'm freezing, I look over at him. Lucian opens his mouth but falls silent as if the words are stuck in his throat, and I give him a gentle nudge. "Speak it, Lucian, it's crippling you not to."

Expression riddled with guilt, he dips his chin, his voice haunted. "Years ago, I told a lie that destroyed my family and shattered their hearts. It was more of a promise I swore to uphold, that I couldn't, and it turned into my worst imaginable failure, and . . . I can't, in any capacity, seem to heal from it."

Without pressing him on what the promise was, I follow his lead as he takes off, his hesitance palpable. After a few more bated, in-sync steps—he finally continues.

"I noticed my family differed from my mate's families when I was around seven or eight. The time spent with my friends' parents and siblings had me pinpointing a dynamic that was so painfully absent in my own. Even knowing that something was off in the way we regarded one another and treated one another with so much formality, it felt wrong. I never put a voice to it. I never questioned my Mum, who I was somewhat close to. Despite knowing and *feeling* it, I allowed my father to instill the characteristics of an Aston man in me from an early age. In doing so, I joined generations of Aston men who've conducted themselves in the same manner. Never getting emotional nor overly sentimental. It was mostly unspoken but heavily implied that I was always to remain guarded and to speak clearly, eloquently, and intelligently, but only with purpose. I was to command respect and attention under every imaginable circumstance and never to show weakness." We walk a few steps more. "It remained that way up until the day I left for Uni—until one day it didn't."

He glances around as we hit a crosswalk before flitting his gaze to mine.

"Byron isn't my only brother. My mother had her last child at age forty-six. My father didn't want the baby due to the risk and possible complications, but my mother stood firm. I was already well toward earning my doctorate when she gave birth to Alexander, who was born with a heart defect."

"Which is why you chose heart specialty," I conclude.

He dips his chin as my heart breaks, already knowing exactly where this is headed.

"Alexander changed everything, both with his arrival and as he grew. Going home on break wasn't such a chore anymore and became something I looked forward to. Ironically—and though he was reluctant to have him due to the risk—my father adored my younger brother, and he could do no wrong in his eyes. What was most surprising was that Father's affection for Alexander didn't change as he grew up and refused to take part in becoming another living definition of an Aston man. Something I greatly admired Alexander for. I couldn't even find myself resenting him for so easily discarding it. He was impossible not to love. Not only did he bring life to an otherwise sterile home, but my father and I got along a lot better because he played buffer—unintentionally at first—and later very *purposefully*."

Lucian exhales, his tone full of affection as he continues. "My brother brought peace to our house for the nearly fifteen short years he lived. But when he died, he took that peace with him and then some. When he passed, it was expected that I maintain the veneer of an Aston man. No exceptions. Not for that heartbreak, nor any other. So, when I lost the ability to mask my pain, I left," he exhales. "Oddly enough, even when I did leave, I still maintained as an Aston, and whatever I've become since he died is the man you met six months ago." He gives a self-deprecating laugh. "Dr. Prick."

"Lucian," I croak in apology as his grief seeps into me.

He stops abruptly, eyes arresting, as my own water.

"So, if you've ever wondered why I don't defend myself from your observations about me, it's because I'm agreeable to them, Jane. I don't parade around as a happy man because I'm not. I'm exactly as you described because when he died, I didn't . . . I couldn't maintain, and in turn, I deserted my family, my fiancée, my life."

"I'm so sorry, Lucian," I repeat while hating that better words refuse to come to me.

"You have nothing to apologize for, but I do. It was a coward's move, and they have every right to hate me," he utters on the wind, eyes cast down.

"I'm sure they don't, but can I ask . . . what was the lie?"

"That I would save him, of course," he swallows. "They believed me. Alexander believed me, and fuck," he runs both gloved hands through his whipping hair before holding them atop his head, "I stupidly believed myself." He swallows again, his pain visceral as we resume walking.

"By the time Alexander was in primary school, the clock had already started ticking, and *I* was the time bomb. But we were all desperate. It's then I promised to save him, even though I knew he had a heart I couldn't fix. No matter how . . . how hard I tried, what doctors I consulted with, and God help me, did I go through them like water," he expels, voice gravelly, as he rattles next to me, his pain so close to the surface it feels like he's on the verge of explosion.

"I tried everything. There were no lengths I wouldn't go to," he turns to me, his eyes shining with emotion. "He was my miracle, but no matter how hard I searched, I couldn't find his, or be *his miracle* . . . and to this day, almost every day nearly four years later, I still rack my brain trying to figure out what I could have done differently."

"Lucian, that's . . ." I shake my head. ". . . ridiculous, they can't *seriously* hold that against you."

"Can't they?" He scoffs. "Well, *they* might be a bit of a stretch, but I assure you *William Aston* does." He clears his throat. "He made certain I was aware of it in the months after Alexander's passing."

"Please tell me," I grip his arm again and walk as close as I can alongside him, "I mean . . . you have to know it's just his pain talking."

"I'm not sure I believe that, or you would either if you had witnessed the way he's spoken to me since. It would hurt more if I hadn't come to hate the bastard and all he represents. Truly. His surname feels like a curse rather than privilege—always has. He wouldn't even allow Mum and I to speak the first year after I left. He would intercept my calls to make certain of it. It's as if he wanted me to lose everyone else as punishment."

"Well, that's bullshit and just plain cruel, as well as unacceptable, no matter what his pain level. What about your other brother, Byron?"

"Furious with me, but only for leaving. Still is. He can't forgive me because of the pressure he's been under since I left."

"To become the quintessential Aston man?"

"Precisely."

"You have to know your father is too blinded by the loss to see what an incredible surgeon you are."

"I'm not."

"Now that's some bullshit," I argue.

He shakes his head and pins me with his pained stare. "Most days, I feel like a statue because I was molded to be one. Trying to live in any capacity since his loss is like being forced to move in that mold. It's fucking painful and feels unnatural, and when others look to me for guidance, I feel like a fraud. Because as a highly trained surgeon by some of the best teachers in the world, I failed to do the thing that meant most to me—keeping that promise."

"Was it congenital?" I ask, knowing the answer.

His eyes float over to mine. "Yes."

We stare off, and I can already hear his protest as we both speak at once.

"I know the logic," Lucian starts as I cut in.

"You aren't God, Lucian, and next to being that powerful, we both know you couldn't have saved him. You made a promise you couldn't keep."

"Breakthroughs happen every day," he gives in a weak argument as I shake my head, refuting his logic.

"I wanted it to be true," his voice is filled with so much ache that my eyes again threaten to water, "so much, Jane. My younger b-brother was—even with our age d-difference—the closest person in the world to me. He was so full of life, yet his heart wouldn't let him live one. So damn deviant, defiant, yet so full of love and wisdom far beyond his years."

"I get that," I whisper, doing my best to tamp down my tears due to the agony in his voice as a shiver courses through me. He reacts instantly by gripping his scarf and lifting it to secure it around my neck. Unsatisfied with the offering alone, he begins to situate the scarf as his scent surrounds me. A heady mix I can't place invades my senses as I bat away the urge to get lost in it and focus on his pain. But even as I try, I can't help but trace his handsome features under what little light we have as he tucks the scarf carefully around me while he speaks.

"I think the reason that I had an aversion to you straight away," he says, his gloved hands pausing at the nape of my neck, golden gaze lifting to meet mine, "is because you r-remind me so much of him."

"Of Alexander?"

"Yes. Christ, Jane, I know that's the reason," he says on a beaten exhale, "the similarities are uncanny. The way you fill a room with your presence alone and absolutely everyone takes notice. And as a witness, I've felt the anticipation in them, too, as if they expect to laugh or be uplifted when you're close. Whether you're aware of it or not, you're the brightest light in every room you grace. I've watched it happen with the staff and patients in our hospital. I've also seen your effect here in my oldest Uni mate, who fancies you, and already our driver is smitten. That was Alexander, and that too, Jane, is also you."

Swallowing, I can't at all help the spill of tears. "That was the best compliment of my life, Lucian."

"It's simply the truth, Jane, because your effect on me is much the same. I've been too much of a bastard to admit it until this moment."

"You're forgiven, for everything, even past today when you piss me off—which is likely," I squeeze his bicep as we share a sad smile, and he lowers his hands with his question.

"Warmer?"

"Much, thank you," I relay, enjoying the added warmth of his scarf and the additional comfort it brings as we cross a little bridge. Dozens of row boats are abandoned on the shore beneath us as we collectively stop and admire the view. I turn to him, seeing him a little clearer for the man he is. "I'm so sorry I said you were a type, it was shitty, and I had no right to assume anything."

"I haven't given you much to change your impression."

"Maybe, but assuming really does make assholes out of people, and trust me, you have been one, but so have I in that respect. Anyway, I completely understand why you're so buttoned up and hard to talk to—and why it's hard to talk about."

"That's just it, Jane. There is some truth to your assumptions because my father and his mates and colleagues are so much the same. People who trade true living for some ridiculous sort of prestige while acting like breathing statues, when in truth, it's all a fucking farce. A lie. No life at all."

"Because his shit stinks," I blurt as Lucian's brows draw, and I shake my head.

*Not the right time, Jane.*

"Just forget I said that," I sputter, "go on."

He hesitates a second before continuing. "I've tried so hard to get on with it," he relays. "For the most part, my family has moved on since we buried him—or resembles the effort to attempt to—but I haven't. I tried to continue to care about my life, my fiancée and to plan my wedding—to thrive in my career. I tried to care about anything but couldn't face my failure or the fact that he was gone—so I left them. All of them. Seven months after Alexander died, I left the people who needed me, depended on me, and a woman who loved me despite the miserable fuck I was becoming. I left because I didn't want to see their disappointment anymore by my inability to move on."

A bell sounds in the distance as we head closer to town, and more people loiter the streets as Christmas lights come into view.

"I've been managing alone to keep from hurting anyone further and pray to a God I'm not sure I believe in that I'm healing enough hearts to account for those I've broken. Despite knowing it wasn't possible, no amount of logical reasoning ever sticks or lessens this pain. It's like I'm frozen, stuck head and heart in a perpetual 'what if.' So, that's why I don't argue with your assessment of me. Sadly, it's not a mask I wear but my own persona that easily dissuades anyone from being near me. Facing Gwen today was very much a knife to the chest, not because of the love I once felt for her, but jealousy because she was able to move on, and I can't."

"So don't," I speak up.

"What?"

"Don't move on. Stop trying to force some new reality where you're okay and hurt for as long as it takes for it to happen *naturally*. If that's four more years, it's four more years. I'm sorry. I'm so sorry I made you feel bad for grieving because that's what it is—grief—and it's different for everyone. I can't imagine a day without Charlie. Not a single day because she's the closest person in the world to me and the only family I have, so if you want my take," I pause, and he nods.

"I won't sugarcoat it because you just admitted half the issue aloud. Pushing your family and your fiancée away was a huge mistake and set you back further. It wasn't freeing because whether you know it or not, you're grieving them too, and they're alive and breathing. You shut down on them, Lucian, because you can't handle feeling more than you do for Alexander's loss. But once you do, it's going to hurt a hell of a lot worse before you get an ounce of relief. And that's only if you take back what you haven't lost yet."

"I have. Trust me, Jane, I have."

"But you don't know for certain." Retrieving his phone—which is still in my jacket pocket—I extend it to him, the message banner on the screen when I light it up. "Byron extended a dinner invitation for Christmas Eve."

I hold up my free hand in a plea of innocence before he gets the chance to accuse me of snooping.

"It happened the second I picked up your phone, so please don't think I was prying, but I am now. This invitation isn't a plea from a brother who doesn't want to see or know you. Who can't forgive you. He's asking for himself, his sons, and your mother."

He studies the message as trepidation skitters across his features, and my heart speaks for me. "If you need a friend, I'll come with you, Lucian—and trust me, you do, desperately. I think that's the true heart of why your grief is so abundant and won't let you 'get on with it.' You need to talk about it. To remember Alexander, along with the forgiveness of your family, and you won't allow yourself the chance to ask for it. You're doing all of it completely alone when you shouldn't have to be."

Pocketing his phone, he fists his gloved hands at his sides.

"Come on, you miserable Prick, let's take a walk so you can tell me all about Alexander, and the day after tomorrow, we're going to your home for Christmas Eve dinner."

"Jane," he shakes his head, "It's not going to resolve anything."

"It's a start, and you do owe them an apology, but not for promising you could save Alexander—a promise they had no right to hold you to—but for believing they only cared about the doctor you promised to be and not the son, brother, or uncle you took away." Gripping his bicep, I nudge him forward. "Now, walk with me and tell me all about Alexander."

We walk for hours, lost in conversation as he tells me of his person, his own Charlie. Fully animated, I can't help but admire his beauty as he speaks about a boy who never got to be a man—but didn't, at all, live in vain. He brought joy to his brother and kindled a warmth in a lifeless household. A few antic-filled stories later, I burst into laughter.

"God, this was a fourteen-year-old kid?" I ask, completely enamored with Alexander.

"Exactly," Lucian turns, his smile matching mine and reaching his eyes before it slowly disappears, and his expression turns earnest.

"I don't want you to think so poorly of me. Please understand that I tried to make up for my lie. I worked twice as hard to appease William Aston. Every day felt like hell on earth. Before I finally gave up, I tried to make Gwen understand why I couldn't move forward from how paralyzed I felt inside. She couldn't understand me because I'd been *acting* like it. It was then that I realized we were not a true match. She couldn't recognize *me* the way Alexander could. But two days ago, when we made our deal," he says as he keeps my eyes hostage. "For the first time in a very long time, I wanted to try again. I can't explain it."

"You just did, Lucian. You wanted to try."

"Much of that had to do with the pain in your voice when you were on the phone with Charlie. The disappointment you felt for something you had been so looking forward to. I heard my own pain inside yours. It mirrored much the same as how my father made me feel in the past. I hated myself for being the cause of any of it." His eyes go distant as he makes his declaration. "I don't want to resemble him, Jane. In any way. Maybe that's why I truly left."

"That makes a lot of sense," I say. "But in knowing that, I'm sorry I hurt your feelings yesterday, considering."

He shakes his head gently and stares back at me. "I don't deserve your kindness. I haven't been a kind man."

"Bright side, you're not an *unkind* man, a little prickly, but you're working on it. That counts."

"I don't know who I am anymore. I have no idea who the real Lucian Aston is. I'm a surgeon. I exist as a surgeon, a vessel, a healthcare provider, and not much else. I truly am *that boring*."

"That's ironic because I was pretty fascinated by the stories of a younger Lucian and his much younger brother, who—I have to say—totally one-ups you on the personality front even from his grave."

He gapes at me. "How incredibly rude."

"See," I chuckle. "Animation, you're still in there."

I step up to him and force his eyes on me. "I'm no angel, Lucian, so I can't heal you. But what I can be is your ghost of Christmas, past, present, and *future*. What you did can't be undone and is only being exacerbated by what you're doing here and now in the present—actively avoiding the past that plagues you and is stunting and disrupting any future you could have. You're a bred family man no matter the dynamic, and now, with *no family*, by your own doing. Whether you get along or not, you need them like you need your million-dollar hands."

"Billion," he states before biting his smirk away.

"Always correcting me," I say before we share a tiny smile. "Anyway, they're a part of you. Even if you had zero plans to deal with this in your time here, you're already dealing, and admittedly, you know it's the wrong way. So, I propose this," I take his billion-dollar hands, and he grips mine in return. "You take *me* as a buffer to Christmas dinner to start to sort out the mess you made, and I'll be the friend you need before and after."

The run of his gloved fingers over the skin of my hands has me pausing for a heartbeat.

"I won't bullshit you. It will be hard. It will be highly uncomfortable. It may even lead to an argument or twenty. From what you've confessed about your family, it most likely will. But it's not just what you need to do—it's what you have to. And . . . at some point," I step closer. "The woman you deserted—whose heart is still beating *for you*—deserves at least part of the explanation you just gave me. She still loves you, Lucian. She lashed out at me good for it because she thinks we're sleeping together. Which we definitely aren't," I say, implicating that as fact for both present and future—for myself—having no idea if it's even a factor for him.

"On account of lack of chemistry," he mimics my statement from days ago, running his leather-covered fingers over my bare hands as he draws me in further, temptation breathing just in front of me.

"So, it's a nonissue, right?" He prompts further, his return stare intent enough to have me swallowing.

"Right," I lie, as I quickly redirect. "So, that's the plan I have since yours is shit. You in?"

"It's only fair that I warn you, Jane, it will be all those things you stated. William Aston won't hold his tongue or wrath simply because you're there."

I palm his jaw. "But I'll be there, Lucian."

"Jesus," he flinches. "Your hands are fucking freezing."

He bites off the tips of each of his leather gloves before quickly pocketing them to warm my hands between his.

"I'm fine," I protest, loving his coaxing touch along with the feel of his full attention. Being the center of his focus continues to heat my insides as his rare, tender stare sweeps me.

"Christ, we need to get you somewhere and warmed," he says, concern in his expression as he continues to vigorously run my hands between his.

"Stop avoiding the proposition, Lucian. Are you in or out?"

"I should do this alone. This is my mess to sort."

"But you don't have to, and this situation is exactly what friends are for. Besides," I shrug, "I have a way with parents."

That earns me a half-grin. "Do you, now?"

"Not really," I grin back. "I said that to help, but it's a total lie."

I feel a renewed zing in my chest when laughter bursts out of him.

"So, do we have a deal?" I prod.

"Your funeral," he warns with an exaggerated exhale.

"Poor choice of words, Lucian."

"Alexander would have loved it," he says, his smile beaming and again reaching his eyes. In them, I see renewed hope, and it's then that I pinpoint it's precisely what I saw during the time he let his guard down with me—*hope*.

Releasing my warming hands, he lifts his wrist to check the time, and his eyes bulge.

"Christ, it's five am. Have we really been walking so long?"

"Seems the case," I say, just as shocked by how long we've been ignoring time, the city, and the world around us.

"Okay, so, since sleep isn't on the table, I think it's time I had a proper English breakfast. The eggs, the beans, sausages, and the weird tomato, and this time, you're buying."

"Happy to, Jane," he says, retrieving his pocketed gloves before sliding each onto my hands, "and thank you."

"Don't thank me," I say, batting away the feeling of the loss of his touch and its lingering effect. I fail, but I still manage to speak around it and keep my tone even. "The hard part isn't over, but instead of thanking me, maybe you can return the favor sometime in the future and be a friend to me."

"I'll do my best."

"Your best will do, *Doc*," I add to test the waters.

"Fine then . . . *Cheeky*," he says with a playful sigh, eyes lit.

My own heart lights in my chest, warmth spreading through me. "Lucian, did you just give *me* a *nickname*?"

"I most certainly did."

I beam at him. "I like it. A *lot*."

"As you should, seeing that it's a completely fitting, one-word summation of your character."

"Well, you should know you're more than just a billion-dollar set of surgical hands."

"If that's true," he whispers, glancing over my shoulder briefly and then back to me, his golden gaze probing. The intimacy of the moment is not lost on me as he crowds in closer with his question, "Who am I then, Jane?"

"I don't know, but I plan on finding out in the next couple of weeks."

His grin reappears. "So, am I to assume our deal is back on?"

"Assume away, Doc. Now come on, I'm starving, and we need to shower and change first, or your ex might claw my eyes out."

He winces. "She truly came for you?"

"Nothing I couldn't handle, but make time for her, Lucian," I urge him. "You're the ghost of her past that's getting in the way of her future."

He nods, his guilt evident. "I'm aware."

When I can no longer hold in my yawn, I release it as he quickly ushers me forward. "Come. The hotel isn't far, and we're set to be back at the hospital by eight."

"Though the training was painful, it sure does come in handy that we're both ninjas when it comes to sleep deprivation," I point out.

"Too right." He pauses his walk, turning to me again, and shakes his head. "I truly don't deserve your kindness. Thank you, Jane."

"I'm being a friend, Lucian. I realize you're out of practice in that department, but that's what having a friend is like."

"Then I shall do my best when it comes time to return the favor and be the same friend to you."

"Can never have too many of those," I tell him as the rest of my hopes of any personal entanglement with him—albeit a messy one— float away on my daydream cloud just before it bursts.

# SIXTEEN

## JANE

Forty-five minutes later, I'm showered, dressed, and re-packed in record time. After shooting a text to Mike that we'll meet him downstairs in twenty, I roll my bag into our shared living space. Walking toward the kitchenette for some coffee, as I peruse our suite, I call out to Lucian and get no reply.

After figuring out the fancy all-frills machine, I not so patiently wait for my cup to brew as I call out to him again. "Doc, I'm making some coffee. How do you take yours?"

Our accommodations so far have been top-notch, no doubt set by Lucian's snooty dude standards. As my Nespresso starts to fill my cup, I glance back longingly at the untouched, made bed I hadn't utilized, dreading the long hours ahead. However, I can't help but be grateful for my come-to-Jesus chat with Lucian and the truth behind what I thought he felt about me versus what he admitted. That, mixed with the compliment he gave me, honestly set my heart alight and still has me reeling.

Lucian Aston doesn't have an aversion to me, nor does he really find my boisterousness and quirks as off-putting as I thought. From what he said, he distanced himself from me due to my commonalities with his brother.

A brother he declared was the closest person to him in the world. In truth, he admitted he likes me, even if it isn't in the sense I foolishly hoped for.

But during that talk, he did bring up our chemistry again. During which, he called me out for bullshitting in a roundabout way, which has me thinking that the comments made by those around us—including those by his ex-fiancé—might have some merit to them. The air seemed to spark between us again in those tense seconds, much the same way it happened in the elevator when I swear he nearly kissed me.

It's not really rocket science, or it wouldn't be if he still wasn't so hard to read. But he is, and admittedly has trained himself to be. His emotions still aren't clearly detectable, aside from certain, rare looks that flit through his eyes. Even those are hard to read. So, unless Lucian actually voices his feelings aloud, which, according to him, is rare, the continual guessing game keeps him the living definition of an enigmatic man.

Sadly for me, something I find sexy as hell. Which may be a direct result of too many damned romance books. Maybe they've warped my sexual imagination and upped my expectations of the common man.

Oh frickin' well, I'll give up breathing before I give up my spicy romance.

Or maybe it's just my wishful thinking that has me reading so hard into everything. I have been shamelessly lusting after the man since I laid eyes on him.

God, what if Lucian does want to get physical and makes it known?

*What would you do, Jane?*

Could I be that selfish?

Shaking those thoughts away—still freshly rattled from the ache of his admissions and the lingering intimacy just after—I decide to stick to my guns and stop entertaining it, at least for today.

After downing my first espresso, I decide to give what's left of my sleep-deprived brain a rest and walk over to Lucian's parted door. I pause when I hear a repeated tap on the hardwoods, followed by a grunt and then another.

"The hell?" I lean in, listening like a stalker before picking up the faint sound of . . . hip hop music? Which seems to be blaring from some small speakers.

The repetitive, rhythmic tap continues to sound as I make out hints of the song and finally place it as "Can I Get A . . .," which has my lips lifting. At least we have hip hop in common, though his taste seems to stem a bit further back. This is no big surprise, seeing as how there's a ten-year age gap between us.

Another grunt has me jerking out of my musings as the tap, tap, tap continues, piquing my interest at just what in the hell is happening on the other side of that door.

Thinking my dirty worst and deciding I can't possibly miss this opportunity, I knock faintly, so faintly, before opening the door and . . .

"Holy fuck," I blurt as I gaze over to where Lucian is, his upper body on display while his lower body tortures nothing but black boxer briefs. I say torture because it's the only way to describe how his insane physique is manipulating the fabric as it strains against what he's packing—which is *a lot.*

From where I stand, I've got the perfect side view and take mental notes—hair disheveled, from his thick-lipped profile to his upper body, which is covered in a thick sheen of sweat, droplets rolling between his muscled pecs down to his defined abs—abs I can't count due to his continuous movement. Though he's got a runner's build, he's made the most *of everything* our good God gifted him—from his glowing skin to his sculpted arms, ripped chest, and abs, down to his drool-worthy bubble butt, which in current time has just converted me into an official *ass woman.*

Everything about him is far more alluring than I gave him credit for in any damned daydream I could conjure, and my imagination is pretty spectacular.

Soft grunts come out every few seconds with every flex of his muscles. His wrist movement is startlingly precise with every flick as my eyes consume him, and my body lights a fire in response.

He tops it with every stroke, and my mouth dries as I memorize the look of him, burning his perfection into my memory as another of his strained grunts cuts through the air.

It's the deciding factor and one I'm terrified will ruin me that fills me with fear and has painfully disappointed me in the past. Though, from what I can see, no matter how he's hanging, his hang time alone is mighty impressive.

Fear starts to set in fast that *if* he has the cock to match the rest of him, I'm going to have a hard time thinking of anything else.

Ever.

I decide I would rather not know.

"Lucian," I call, elevating my voice and waving my hand to get his attention, the music blaring from his earbuds—which I must say is obnoxiously loud—as he continues to fill the room with the tap of his jump rope and accompanying grunts. When I still get no response, I take a step in and wave again just as a smirk spreads along his perfect lips.

Not stopping his rope, or . . . roping? He easily shifts toward me, not missing a single swing of it as he practically wields it like a damned sword, hacking into my libido's sanity. His deep-set smirk remains as he keeps perfect flow. "Yes, Jane. I see you and have seen you since you knocked *five minutes* ago."

With that, my face flushes as his rare, more devilish smile takes his smug smirk's place, and he finally stops the rope before pulling his earbuds out.

"We've been here for close to an hour, *Doc*, and you're nowhere near ready." I try to scold, but it sounds like a newly-born baritone instead.

Grabbing a nearby water bottle with the hotel's logo, he takes a hearty sip before speaking. "My apologies, I was just waking myself up some."

"I can see that. You look," I bite my lip, "awake. Just wanted to tell you that I texted Mike to pick us up in twenty, but if you need more time . . ." I allow my eyes to roll down his frame briefly. "Do *you* need more time?"

His effect on me is evident in my delivery, hell, probably in my expression as my lower half clenches at the golden man standing feet away. That's the only way to describe him, surrounded by the rapidly filtering early morning light, skin glistening, eyes just as gilded as the rays highlighting his body.

"I can be dressed in ten," he offers, downing the rest of his bottle, his eyes remaining on me as he gulps it.

"Good, because I'm *starving*," I expel in a rushed breath as my stupid eyes choose that moment to finally lower. The pronounced bulge in his shorts stares back, declaring it has the divine right to be there and to be rightfully recognized.

*Oh, Mother of all fucks!*

I deflate as I realize I chose the *right man* to fixate on months ago, knowing he just gave me clitoral stimulation ammo for . . . forever, and the mental snapshots I just uploaded will taunt me for years to come.

"Is there something else you need from me?" He taunts as I shake my head, completely flustered, which he visibly feeds on.

Narrowing my eyes—instead of shying away—I relax my posture and grip the door handle. I'm a grown woman, for crying out loud, not a teenage girl. I can rope 'em and ride 'em just like any other girl with her own damn enticing bits to dangle.

"Yeah, you can remedy it by getting that gorgeous bubble butt of yours showered and covered and meet me downstairs in twenty so I can eat. I'm owed breakfast." I shut the door on his spry grin as I try to shake off the image that will consume me for the rest of my day—or life, praying for the former.

Flawless skin, bulging muscles, and an ass to bounce a quarter—hell, a tire off. Not only that, but I'm pretty sure he's packing and hasn't spent a second of his adult life crying over any lack of girth.

Pissed that he just bested me and got off on it. I crack the door to toss him some snarky afterthought and finally get my question answered and am instead met by Lucian's cock.

Because Lucian is naked.

Totally naked.

He straightens immediately once he sees me, his newly discarded boxers in his hand as my mouth drops, and the silence in the room blares in my ears. I maybe had the door closed for four seconds.

FOUR SECONDS!

How in the hell did this happen?

"I suppose this is only fair as well," Lucian says, his body on full display for my viewing pleasure.

My kitty explodes into open flames as I gape at the man standing before me, along with what's between his thighs. Even more so at the fact that it's not even hard and could bitch slap all of my combined ex-lovers with only half of what's hanging and still come out some seriously victorious *inches* ahead.

"Oh, for fuck's sake," I cry out in complaint to him and to the fate that's laughing at me. I completely fake recovery and manage to stop my rant and address him in an even tone. "Well, *good*. At one point, I was worried about the lack of girth jabs hitting close to home. Nice dick, Doc, how do you take your coffee?"

"Splash of cream," he replies from his disgustingly gorgeous face before I shut myself outside his door and shake my head furiously back and forth.

What would it be like to have a lover so perfect hovering over me while fucking me into oblivion?

A dream. A living dream.

And don't I *deserve* to have that dream fulfilled just like any other girl?

From the way he just stood there, I could have roped and ridden or left him, and it wouldn't have mattered to him *either way*— which won't do.

In no fantasy I've had or have ever had is that appealing to me in the least.

I'm no dick beggar.

I want to be *wanted*, and I want it evident. I'm not settling for convenience penis, even if it's by the *heavenly dicked doc or not*, that's for damn sure.

I have pride—an abundance of it—and I'm not letting some gorgeous God of a man, especially *this one*, have a heaving helping more of my pride than he's already gotten.

Mentally hanging up my rope, I gather what's left of my view and tuck it away for a desert-dry day. Even if we never get physical, he's the most beautiful man I've ever seen, dressed or naked. But I decide moving forward not to feed his ego. It's obvious he's already been well-fed in *that* department.

Twenty minutes later, we're seated in a small eatery I didn't catch the name of because I was too distracted in figuring out how Lucian fits so much ass into his dress slacks.

Once seated, knowing my order, I broach the safest subject as my mind finally settles down. I start batting naked images of him away, along with the constant recall of his admission of how he wants to check out when his time comes. Drawing a fast conclusion, I'd require a needle full of local anesthetic to take that thing in the *regular way*.

"Your coffee is properly stirred, Jane," Lucian says, his grin disappearing behind his menu as I narrow my eyes at him.

"You have a beautiful body, Lucian, and you know I find you attractive—which isn't news," I compliment him, not seeing any reason why I shouldn't at this point. I've already made an ass out of myself. Brutal honesty was our deal, and he's getting it.

"Likewise, Jane."

"Thanks," I dismiss, "but you didn't exactly get the same view."

"View enough," he says, lowering his menu, his eyes sweeping my face and upper body, "I assure you."

"You assure me," I parrot as he gives me nothing more than the impenetrable brick wall he is. But we still have a deal, and I plan on making good use of it.

Reaching over, he covers my hand, stopping my stirring and spoon as I give him a pointed look. "It's been a long time since I've seen a naked man," I admit freely, "that's all."

"So you informed me during your champagne rant."

"What about you?"

He grins. "Seen a naked man, aside from a patient? A good while."

"You know what I'm asking," I utter dryly.

"I recall telling you I don't freely discuss that," he says in a hushed tone as our breakfasts are set before us by our waitress, and we both give thanks.

Mouth now watering for an entirely different reason, I stare at the plate of eggs, ham, beans, and sausages garnished with sliced tomato and toast.

"This one is proper," he assures me, "I used to dine here often when I was at Uni."

"Thank you," I say, peppering my eggs with a smile. "God, I'm so hungry that I'm not even hungry anymore."

"Eat, Jane, that's something you definitely don't do enough of."

"Can't te—don't have to tell me twice," I redirect, cutting myself off as he lifts a quizzical brow. Straightening slightly, I take a hearty bite of my breakfast as a mixture of baked beans and eggs hits my tongue.

"Not bad," I shrug. "I can't make sense of the combination of food, but it doesn't mean it's wrong."

He grins and forks his own bite, his order the same.

"Tastes like home," he comments after swallowing a mouthful, which has my heart softening. England is home to Lucian, and I'm sure there are things about it he misses daily. But it's too early to rehash anything further, especially while both our moods are light. We have quite a day ahead of us—him again facing his ex-fiancée and we're too sleep deprived to have any more of that conversation, so I opt to give him a break.

"So, really, how long has it been in the women department?"

"Jane, for the last time, I don't talk about my intimate life unless it's with a new or long-term partner."

"Is that before or after you unleash Dr. DirtyPrick?" I grin.

He sips his coffee and quirks a brow as his answer.

"Fine. I'm over caring now that I've seen the goods, and we're even," I mutter, shoveling in a forkful of eggs. "So, tell me this," I implore a little wistfully, "How was it, really? Attending Oxford?"

"A lot like you might imagine the first month or so. The feeling of accomplishment in getting in, marveling at attending a school with such a rich history, and that of those who walked the halls before you. It's a bit surreal for everyone, and any Oxford alumni who say otherwise is lying." He sips his coffee. "You truly feel like you're a part of it all, but then the pressure to excel is added, and it dampens a lot of the initial excitement."

"I get that," I say, sipping my own coffee, my eyes bulging. "Damn, this is amazing," I lift my cup.

"That is the number one reason why I love coming here. Breakfast is good, but the coffee is exceptional."

"Hell yes, it is," I wave my hand through the air to cut the coffee talk in lieu of more details, and his eyes flare, "but keep going."

"Not much more to add other than it was some of the best years of my life. Being away from my father was liberating. Some say you explore who you are in your university days, and I can honestly say that was the case for me in the sense of freedom. The best part was the autonomy because no one gave a damn about an Aston man when there were so many more influential and important names amongst other fellows attending. You may think that would be a hard pill for me to swallow, but it was quite the opposite. I was relieved."

"I get that, too," I say.

"I spent the first six months getting serious, taking it all so seriously. The latter half of my first year," his eyes darken, "I had a bit of *fun*."

"Right, cocaine cowboy," I whisper with a smile, knowing exactly what he's referring to. "So, when did Gwen come into the picture?"

"Sophomore year. She started a year behind me," he says, doing that sexy dabbing of his mouth with the tip of his napkin thing.

Wait . . . when did *that* become *sexy* or a *thing?*

"Ah. Did things get serious then?" I prod, downing the rest of my cup and gesturing politely to our waitress for another.

"Personal, Jane," he reminds me.

"Horse shit," I protest. "That's not a 'have to be naked to answer' question, so your protest is overruled."

"Is it?" He bites his full lower lip and glances around as the waitress heads our way. "Well, could you be so kind as to lower your voice so the cooks aren't privy? The front house staff already seems invested."

"Shit, sorry," I glance around, seeing a few pairs of eyes on us, including those of our approaching waitress, and grimace. "Please know I'm not intentionally loud, it's just—"

"Your nature. I'm aware, Jane. As I told you last night, Alexander was much the same, and I loved it about him. I simply want to have a conversation with you. *Solely* with *you*."

I smile. "Well, that was a super nice way of putting it, Doc. Your people skills are improving."

"Yes, well, you're owed some niceties."

This time, I cover his hand, and he stills. "Not anymore, Lucian. Please, just be yourself." Taking my hand back, I scoop some eggs on my toast. "Like I said, I like you, and I don't want you to think you have to change a single thing about yourself to suit me. Let me be *the one person* in your life where you don't have to twist yourself into something different to please. Besides, that's kind of our deal."

Pausing his chewing, he stares off at me for long seconds as our waitress refills our cups before replying. "I'll agree to that."

"Good. And I propose we do an amendment to our deal."

"Which is?"

"Outside of the office, we keep this up our entire trip. You give it all to me straight and point blank. Don't spare my feelings, no matter what, and I'll do the same for you."

"Agreed," he says.

"Perfect. Now that that's out of the way, I think we're going to have fun," I lift my cup toward his, and he lifts his in return before we clink them together. We share a small smile while taking a sip.

"Now, let's go kick some surgical ass and show 'em why we're Boston's finest," I boast.

Tossing his napkin after I do the same, he lifts his hand to call our waitress back. "I'm all for that plan as well, but if I may, I'd like to take you somewhere first."

"Seriously?" I beam at Lucian before glancing back up at the bright red sign that reads *Alice's Shop*. "Alice in Wonderland was written *here*, in Oxford?"

He dips his chin. "Lewis Carroll was a mathematician at Oxford. In fact, many well-known writers have chosen Oxford as their stomping grounds over the centuries. If we have time on our next trip here, I'll take you to another place I think might be of interest to you."

"It's so awesome you brought me here, thank you," I say, taking a quick picture of the sign before wrinkling my nose, "even if it's closed."

"Not for long," a man sounds behind us, and Lucian and I both turn to see an older man approaching, sorting the keys in his hands before inserting one into the antique-looking lock of the shop door.

"Thank you so much for agreeing to allow us in early," Lucian says to him.

"My pleasure. I was coming in early to deal with the books today anyway," the man says as he unlocks the store, opening it, and taking a step in.

"I'll see you inside," he says with a warm smile before disappearing behind the door. Stunned, I look back over to Lucian, who's already gazing back at me, and step up to him.

"You called him to open it up for me?"

His eyes soften as they trace my face. "I wish I had that much sway, but I simply rang the store number on the off chance they might open earlier than what was listed online, and he answered."

My heart thunders that he did this at all, seeing as he was thinking of me when the last hours have been so emotionally taxing for him.

"Even so, this was so thoughtful, Lucian, really," I lift on my toes, palming his face before pressing a kiss to his freshly shaved jaw. As I do, I feel the faint pressure of his hand on the small of my back and miss it just as suddenly when I pull away before we turn to step inside.

# SEVENTEEN

## LUCIAN

Staring over at Gwen as she converses with her assistant, Brian—who clearly has an attraction for her, whether it be her brilliance or physical—I can't help but remember our beginning. Our first few exchanges, our courting, the laughs, along with the first time we kissed, fucked, and eventually declared our affection for one another.

At one point in time, I genuinely loved her, but the more I watch her today, the more I become convinced I did the right thing by breaking our engagement and leaving—even if I did it in the cruelest of ways.

In a way, I will forever remain ashamed, even if I pleaded with her before I left to try and understand.

When I asked her to be my wife, I knew we got on well enough to go the distance and that we would probably be productive together.

A rightful match in my father's eyes—which made things easier—though it held no weight nor bearing on the start of our relationship nor my affection or attraction to her. Not even my proposal.

Simply put, we were suited—a good match at the time.

The progression was natural and, if I believed in it, perhaps fated.

Now, I can clearly see how incredibly predictable our lives would have been, down to the fights we would have had if we had married.

Have I changed so much by being frozen in time since losing Alexander?

Have my tastes changed along with my way of thinking?

As of this moment, it seems they have. Then again, I was starting to resist everything about my life before Alexander died.

The mere threat of his imminent loss had started a resentment in me that I couldn't ignore. I began to see things for what they were—dismissing so much importance I had placed on certain things, things seemingly meaningless to me now.

It was his death that had me breaking away, apart from what I most despised about my life choices. At thirty-two, I had far too many I didn't agree with.

My musings end as our day is finally called to one as well. My exhausted eyes search for and find Jane just as she stands and stretches, her posture weary.

Despite the sleep deprivation—which I can feel in every fiber of my being—we've made significant progress today in some final decisions on technique and only veered slightly from my original plans for the procedure. Though most of it is my call, I still respect the opinions of my peers. Tremblay, especially, is noticeably absent today due to demand, as he's a maestro at the table. A maestro who hasn't once stopped looking at Jane whenever she's near, which I should probably call him on.

But to what end and to serve what purpose?

I have no claim on her, and she again made it clear last night that we wouldn't be getting physical in any capacity. Her remark had irritated me that time, but her reaction to me this morning was unmistakable.

How I wanted to close the space and take her parted, lying lips.

But I didn't because she's right in many respects that she's voiced but hasn't in others. The main one being that, personally, I'm an unsorted mess.

I have absolutely nothing to offer for the moment to any

woman—especially one of Jane's character, with a heart that matches hers. Despite my shit behavior, she's been nothing but good to me and deserves the respect of a proper suitor.

At the same time, she has been vocal about her need for a story to tell the girlfriends and repeatedly mentioned letting loose. Nothing about that says meaningful relationship.

What would I want from Jane if I was given the choice?

And if she is determined to set herself free, then who better to unleash her than the man destined to room with her for our five remaining weeks?

Perhaps a man who is growing more attracted to her by the second. A man who also grows harder for her every time she's in close proximity.

I had almost shown my cards this morning. Or rather, my cock had tried to do that heavy lifting, but I've never been much of a man to give chase and should have no plans of starting—especially with how delicate this situation is.

We're work colleagues, and if this ends badly, with the way we get on, it could cause issues further down the road.

Chemistry is a non-issue. Despite her constant denial and obvious lies, would she consider me? She seems intent on keeping firm and not blurring any lines.

Aside from that, having Jane physically will break my own rule and could get incredibly messy. Even so, my eyes wander back to her, and greedily drink her in as she puts on her coat while talking to one of Gwen's staff.

She is so truly beautiful, and I'm a fucking fool not to have noticed sooner, but again, to what end? Still, there's no denying that letting my guard down temporarily for her has proven a good decision thus far—at least for me.

Today, though I'm knackered—because of our long walk and my confession—I feel a sort of relief after having spent so many hours talking about Alexander. About my family. After admitting my worst crime as a man, she'd listened, seemingly without any harsh judgment, to someone who had only and always been a bastard to her.

As I both appreciate and mull over the nurse currently occupying most of my waking thoughts, Gwen abruptly cuts off my view, her eyes daggering into mine before she flits her focus to Jane and back.

Guilt sets in that I am a proper bastard for making my attraction for Jane apparent—though Jane seems clueless or is playing immune to it. Though Gwen has promised herself to another, she's made it clear her heart still lies with me, and my wandering eyes are hurting her.

*Christ Lucian, remember yourself and where you are.*

But therein lies the problem.

If I could again become Gwen's recollection of who I was, then I could so easily reclaim my life in London. I could selfishly have Gwen break off her engagement, wipe the dust off the furniture in my abandoned flat, and ease back into my abandoned life.

None of which appeals to me.

Knowing that is the truth of it and that it won't change, I lift my chin to Gwen to motion her over. She comes to me, a hesitation in her posture, hurt and anger shining in her eyes.

"You're tired," she remarks, her tone surprisingly warm, resembling the same tone of the attentive woman I spent years of my life with.

Remorse has its way as I reply. "Exhausted, actually."

"Long night?" She asks, her tone polite but accusing enough.

"Not in the respect you're presuming, and I would appreciate it if you wouldn't take your personal grievances with me out on my staff. That, too, is beneath you, Gwen," I say, reminding her of her behavior yesterday. Though I might deserve every venomous bite, it's so unlike her to be so malicious.

Her eyes immediately cloud with hurt, and she nods. "I'll apologize to her, Lucian."

"Don't. It will only embarrass her further, and I realize I do owe you far more than a few minutes in a closed room and wish to speak with you privately. Possibly when we return to Oxford next week?" I stand and pull on my trench coat as I survey her. "Would you be so good as to give me time I don't deserve? Dinner, maybe?"

She studies me for a long moment, considering me and my proposal. "No."

I frown. "No?"

"No, because I don't think . . . no, I'm certain you do not want to have a conversation with me," she says, offense clear in her eyes. "*At all*, and that really fucking hurts, Lucian."

"Gwen—" I start as she shakes her head, cutting me to the quick.

"You approach me when you're sincere, and only then. I deserve that respect if you have any left for me at all."

I give her a nod before she stalks off just as Jane looks over to me, her eyes prodding, expression hopeful. I subtly jerk my chin in reply before watching Gwen retreat from the room. The sad truth is, Gwen knows me well enough to know she's right, and what a fucking bastard I am for it.

Jane rests on my chest, sleeping soundly, as I spot her carefully wrapped "Off With Her Head" coffee mug peeking out of the shop bag in the passenger floorboard, alongside the added gifts she purchased for her nephew, Elijah.

I can't help smiling at the memory of Jane marveling over every little thing in the store.

Looking back, I can't remember another in my life who has ever been much impressed with such simple things. But with Jane, so many things seem to fascinate her, which, in turn, fascinates me.

As much as her face does now, as I take in what I can as the sun begins to lower on our long day, her breathing steady as she practically sleeps on top of me. After leaving Oxford, we'd both dozed off within minutes of entering the sedan. Mere miles into the ride, I lost consciousness and roused minutes ago to awaken to her tucked into me. One of her hands is now splayed on my chest, the other tucked between us, hanging limply between my shirt and suit jacket.

The top of her head rests just below my chin, and the smell of her shampoo—which I've noted has a hint of orange blossoms—scents my every inhale.

Instead of gently laying her down when I woke, I'd adjusted her to the point I could gaze upon her face when the notion struck. Which, as the minutes tick by, I admit is a mistake as I've been hard for most of the time I've been conscious.

Mike has caught my gaze twice thus far and given me shit for it with his return expression alone. I haven't found an ounce of a damn to give that he's aware I, too, have found myself somewhat smitten with her.

Jane's beauty is both conventional and unconventional. From her hairline to her high cheekbones to her perfectly plump lips that I could spend every minute tracing the outline of. I pinpoint that it's the fairness of her skin—which can sometimes look translucent in contrast to her surreal light blue eyes—a combination that makes her look ethereal up close. A view I had glimpsed when she had fallen, and again, in the restaurant when she'd stumbled, and today only briefly before she kissed my jaw.

Taking my time to drink her in, I find myself a bit mystified at how much my thirst has grown and continues to, trying to place the reasoning for it.

Is it her resistance to me?

That must be a part of it.

Is it her beauty as a whole? That certainly plays a large part in my attraction.

Where I have a certain knack for placing others, their intentions, and drive, this woman is somewhat of a mystery to me. Half of me believes she is a mystery to herself as well. Maybe, as I get re-acquainted with myself in the coming weeks, she will reveal this to me.

Or maybe she does know who she is, and I simply want to as well at this point.

In deciding to be honest with myself when we struck our deal, I allow my most recent truth to set in—I want her physically, and it's becoming hard to ignore.

But in simply staring at her—and knowing I'll lose contact if she rouses—I still will her to awaken, if only to see what she might say or what observations she'll make.

I decide then that most of my draw now is being engaged by her and challenged—which she does quite often.

But to have her beneath me, I'm almost certain that would absorb me entirely.

It's clear to me now, I want that.

But does she? Or rather, would she?

All signs previous to today—including this morning—say yes.

But women like Jane aren't a commonality, of that much I'm certain. No other woman in my life has dared seek to care for me so quickly in the way she has with an offer of friendship. Do I truly want to risk losing that in exchange for something physical?

The not knowing is becoming maddening, and though she's very matter-of-fact about most things, she's been evasive about this. Purposefully.

Lost in my thoughts as I study her, Mike's curse jars me as I glance up just as a wayward pedestrian runs dead center into the road, and Mike presses the brakes for an emergency stop.

Gripping Jane tightly to me, I brace myself for impact. Jane rouses instantly in my arms as I keep her tightly gripped, just as Mike manages to get us stopped within inches of the pedestrian.

"Lucian," Jane says in protest, her voice raspy with sleep where she struggles against my hold.

"My apologies, Dr. Aston . . . Jane," Mike sputters out, exasperated. I release Jane, who lifts in time to see the irate woman who put herself in harm's way, slam her palms on the car's hood.

"No apology necessary," I say as we all study the woman, "I saw the whole thing, Mike. She ran right out into the street."

"Christ," Mike mutters as the woman continues to bang on the hood, and Jane and I watch the spectacle. It's then that she realizes her position on me and pulls completely from my arms.

It's when I miss her warmth instantly that an internal warning rings clear for me—as I am now—it could be the mistake of all mistakes to act on my attraction for her.

The thought settles inside me as the woman gives us her farewell by gesture before finally moving on, as Mike sounds the horn to assist her in doing so.

"What's that?" Jane asks through a laugh. "Is that the English version of the bird?" Jane asks again as the woman makes it a point to thrust her V-d fingers toward us one last time before disappearing entirely from view and straight into traffic.

Mike chuckles and glances at me from the rearview. "Want to take this one, *Dr. Aston?*"

I give him a pointed look and nod, turning to Jane as she adjusts herself in her seat, wiping her face of any sleep debris that isn't there. Looking deliciously sleep-rumpled, her brilliant blue eyes alight as she seems completely unphased by the woman's erratic behavior.

Which, as a fellow Bostonian, is not so uncommon.

"As the story goes," I start, "'the bird,' as you Americans call it, is rumored to have originated with the hundred-year war."

"There was a hundred-year frickin' war? Between who?"

"Between the French and the English," I explain. "A hundred and sixteen years, to be precise."

"Shit, really? So, do y'all hate each other still?"

Mike full-on laughs as I glare at him suggestively before his chuckle slows. As he drops his eyes reading the situation, Jane drops her own, her embarrassment evident as I tip her chin up with my finger. "No doubt it wasn't heavy in your curriculum, seeing as it's our history."

She nods, seeming stunned by the finger I have holding her chin to me, which I withdraw.

"To be honest, Doc, I didn't pay much attention in any history class, so no worries. I've only just recently become interested in how the world works around me, if I'm honest."

I nod.

"So, tell me, what's with the two-finger salute?

"The origination story stems from an 'old wives' tale," I say, "but a lot of it aligns so well, it may have some merit to it."

"Well, now I *have* to hear it," she beckons me, her lips slightly swollen from sleep. "But first," she leans in, "what do you have for your nephews?"

"Have?" I ask.

"It's Christmas, Lucian. Did it not occur to go home bearing gifts?" She lowers her tone to a hushed whisper. "Like the 'I've been kind of a shit uncle lately, so let me make it up to you by spending a pretty penny' gifts?"

"Right," I say. "Good point."

"Don't beat yourself up about it. We've had one hell of a twenty-four hours, but as a Southerner, we have a general rule—we don't show up to any house empty-handed, especially on Christmas." She lifts her voice, "Hey, Mike?"

"Yes, Jane?" He muses, having heard her every word.

"Would you mind taking us to the biggest and *best* toy store in London, *please*?"

"Easily done," he says, changing lanes and signaling as we hit another stop light. Jane turns her focus back to me. "Okay, so let's hear the history of the English bird."

Resenting my empty arms, I lean in as an excuse to get closer to her. Her eyes widen a fraction, and I stop so as not to be so obvious. "So, over the years, the details may have changed—"

"Yeah, yeah, get to the goods," she cuts her hand through the air, and I can't help my snap.

"I loathe that."

Her eyes bulge. "Loathe what?"

"Being cut off from speaking with the wave of a hand. I find it utterly rude. It's one of my biggest pet peeves, my biggest one if I'm entirely honest."

"Oh, really?" She says, reddening for the second time in minutes, which makes me instantly remorseful.

"It's fine," I dismiss.

"No, no take-backs. This is good . . . Let me think of one of my own." There is a brief pause as she bites her full lower lip, and my eyes follow. "I loathe unsolicited advice—not from *everyone* but from strangers. Like, if you want to cook in my damned kitchen, and change my recipe, then I better be the one to hand you an apron first . . . and you better know how to cook better than I do. You know what I mean?"

The urge to kiss her overwhelms me in a way it rarely has. "I think I understand."

"We're doing good, Doc. This is progress." Her smile slams into me as she waits patiently for me to continue, the hand gesture absent. "Okay, I'm all ears."

"So, as it goes, the gesture stems from the hundred-year war, where generations of Englishmen trained for war with a bow and arrow to fight the Parisians. The bows themselves were rumored to be made from the *U-tree*. The arrows were then crafted for precision with the accent of pheasant feathers and the fingers used to launch them," I lift my pointer and middle, and her eyes glide down to them as I imitate the pluck of an arrow.

"Gotcha, I'm following."

"So, when the French would capture the English during wartime, they would cut one or both fingers used to pluck the arrows used against them during battle."

"Brutal," she says.

"It is," I agree, as does Mike and his accompanying smile unseen by her in the rearview.

"So, out of spite as the battles went on, the Englishmen would," I 'V' my fingers in demonstration as the woman did minutes ago.

"As in, I still have my arrow-plucking fingers," Jane says.

"As in, I still have my *pheasant fingers meant to pluck arrows from the U-Tree*. But as we have very different languages, over time, it's rumored to have morphed from that to—"

"Pheasant, U-tree, U, Phuck, you tree, U. Oh my God, that's so cool! I mean, if it's true."

"Even if it isn't, it's an entertaining theory."

"I'll say," she says, her smile lighting up the now-darkened car.

"Another rumored fact involving the holiday?" I offer.

"Hit me, Doc."

"Christmas ornaments and baubles are a replacement for the Pagan rituals involving hanging human heads from trees centuries ago."

"Really?" Jane asks, laying a dramatic hand on her chest.

"Really," I bulge my eyes at her, which earns me a smile. "Our world has always been pretty barbaric in nature, so it's not so hard to believe, is it?"

"Guess not, but *damn*, we went from heads to ornaments?"

"It's all speculation," I say, admiring the light in her eyes. "But that does help add to the meaning of *civil*ization—which, to me, is still a farce."

To that, Mike laughs, and Jane smiles and says, "At the end of the day, we've all been a bunch of pissed-off ladies screaming at cars at one point or another, huh?"

"Precisely," I say.

"Well, it's good to have someone to be in the shit show with, isn't it?"

"Cheers to that," Mike says as I nod.

"And," Jane adds. "'You learn something new every day' happens to be the favorite part of my day. At least it has been since I graduated and finally joined the land of the living," she says, to which I frown.

"Why is that, Jane?"

"Long story, so let me make sure I nail this," she says, thrusting her fingers up.

"Mastered it," I say with a laugh as I grip her fingers and stroke them purposefully while lowering them. Her eyes snap to mine due to my deliberate touch as I gently close her parted fingers.

"Hate to dampen your enthusiasm, Jane, but let's not go waving that around," I say, leaning in with a wicked whisper, "especially if you aren't willing to back it up."

I make it clear in my return gaze that she didn't misunderstand me as Mike announces our arrival at Hamley's.

Jane's attention is stolen the second I release her fingers, and she catches sight of the massive toy store. The blinking lights dancing outside her window glide along her porcelain profile as the car comes to a stop.

"Holy shit, Mike, this is perfect! Thanks so much."

"Most welcome, Jane," he says, "apologies for not getting your door." He eyes the traffic currently being stalled behind us and turns back to the two of us. "I'll drive round the block until you text me, and I'll pick you both back up here."

"Perfect," Jane says, her excitement palpable as she turns to me. "Ready, Doc?"

"Ready, Cheeky," I say, the rest of my fatigue fading with her budding excitement as I exit the cab and trail her into the store.

# EIGHTEEN

## LUCIAN

Quickly enraptured once inside, Jane bounced from aisle to aisle, her excitement infectious as she chatted up the employees and other shoppers—seemingly never having met a stranger. The festive décor and ambiance ramped up her motivation and utterly captivated her—her expression displaying the same childlike wonder when we shopped at Harrod's, which, in turn, charmed me.

She dizzied me with various facts and knowledge about Elijah and his likes while adding toys, puzzles, and games without reservation to our exponentially growing trolley—especially after learning that my nephews, Jasper and Ben, are six-year-old twins close to Elijah's age.

At some point, I lost track of her completely, feeling misplaced in the massive store, whose offerings seem endless.

As much as Jane's help is appreciated, I currently find myself wanting to make my own personal contribution in getting something Jasper and Ben would enjoy, but I find I'm lacking when it comes to *what*.

Perusing the endless aisles of the massive toy store, I scan for

Jane as well, who's now been missing for the better part of twenty minutes, and come up empty. Staring at the wall of toys, I search for something age-appropriate as guilt sets in that I'm not familiar enough with either of my nephews to know what they would genuinely want. Then, an odd sensation of being watched comes over me just as a giant, clay-red blur fills my periphery. Turning, I see someone at the end of the aisle dressed in an eight-foot T-Rex costume and nod toward them in greeting as beady, reptilian eyes peer back at me.

"Good evening," I greet, finding it odd when I get none in return. An instant later, realization strikes, and I become fully aware of precisely who's inside the silly costume. Just as I go to tell her as much, Jane lifts her plastic-covered, taloned foot before she begins running it slowly and purposefully along the tiled floor. The action mimicking what a bull would do just before . . . my eyes widen as I realize her intent.

She means to . . . *charge me.*

"Jane," I draw out her name in warning, which goes utterly ignored as she torpedoes toward me, dinosaur head bobbling as I try to think of a way to dodge her without either of us being injured and find no resolution. An instant later, I'm knocked off my wingtips as she tackles me to the floor in the center of the aisle, and I land with a thud.

Wind knocked out of me, I roll onto my back to catch my breath, body aching and exasperated. Eyes fixed on the ceiling as I try to regain my bearings, a dinosaur head pops into view, where Jane now sits partially atop me, laughing maniacally. Following the sound, I lower my narrowed eyes to see her face through the circle of mesh beneath the mammoth head as she finally gives me my return greeting. "What's up, Doc?"

"Are you fucking mad?!" I wheeze.

"Quite the opposite. I just thought I would model your nephews' favorite Christmas present."

"You can't be serious."

"As a heart attack, badun-dun, chiii," she spouts while imitating the hit of a drum and cymbal to emphasize her joke.

"I see we're healed from our first fall," I grunt, giving her my 'hairy eyeball' as she lifts from me, and I make quick work of getting back on my feet.

"Fit as a fiddle and feeling no pain," she declares enthusiastically.

"That's obvious," I brush my jacket and slacks while examining the costume. "And you believe *this* will be the gift of gifts to win them over?"

"I'll bet you everything in my piggy bank," she says, planting her gloved, talon-covered hands on her hips, the arms of the costume accurate in that they're short in proportion to her T-Rex body.

"No bet necessary. All right," I acquiesce, "if you think this will do it," I gesture toward her costume before nodding toward the stacked trolley behind her.

"Glad you agree because I bought one in your size too."

I immediately jerk my chin. "Absolutely not."

"Hear me out, Doc."

"Your efforts will be futile, Jane, I assure you."

"Come on, Lucian," she says, and something in her tone lets me know she's been planning this argument. "Think of it as an experiment in pulling you out of your shell a bit. One we can *both* take part in."

"I see. In that case, it's most definitely a *no,* and I cannot take you seriously while you're wearing that."

"That, exactly that!" She all but shouts, pointing at me as though I'm a suspect, as I flinch slightly before looking around.

"That's the whole point. In this get-up," she says, running eager gloves over the costume in presentation, "you'll be covered. Not a soul in existence will have a clue that Dr. McSnobby is parading around in a T-Rex costume."

"Parading around?" I gape at her in horror. "You mean outside of the store? You're serious?"

"Oh, Doc, that I am," she bobs her head, and I fail to hide my smile at the costume's animation and know that Ben and Jasper will, in fact, love it.

"Ah!" she says, pointing a taloned glove at me, "you're coming around to it."

"I absolutely am not."

She sighs exaggeratedly before rubbing her talons together. "Then I propose we make an amendment to our deal."

"I'm not entertaining it in the least. Give up now, or continue to plead your case. Either way, Mike is waiting, and I think we're done here."

"But you'll listen to my argument?" She asks, plucking a deluxe Lego set from the shelf and tossing it in the cart without so much as glancing at it.

"Fine," I eye her warily, "but I assure you, you'll be wasting your time."

Mike's laughter spills from the back of the car and into the street as he loads the last of our purchases. Glaring at him, I lace up the trainers I'd retrieved and exchanged from my suitcase in preparation for the long hour ahead. As he snaps the door of the car closed and turns to bid us farewell, he loses another battle as a burst of obnoxious laughter leaves him.

"Laugh it up, *wanker*," I mutter loud enough to ensure he hears me, which only increases his amusement before he bids us both a good night.

"Night, Mike, and thank you," Jane pipes as Mike turns to me, giving me an unmistakable, telling smirk that he's certain Jane's somehow procured my bollocks in a vice.

Annoyed, though my lips are slightly upturned, and feeling every bit the wanker I accused Mike of being, I head toward Jane, where she waits idly by rattling with excitement due to her newly-claimed verbal spar victory.

"I feel fucking ridiculous," I grumble, as the whirring of the small, battery-operated fan now clipped to my suit pants—which keeps the costume inflated—fills my ears along with the street noise.

"Anonymity while *not acting your age.* This is the perfect way to go about it," Jane says, wiggling her wrists in a Ta-Da motion before turning and strutting down the street, proudly taking the lead. "You can't argue that point."

"Doesn't mean I have to like it," I counter, trailing her closely and picking up speed.

"Oh, stop your bitchin' and give me some Dino swagger," she instructs as some arsehole passerby snarks their commentary from feet away.

"Wrong holiday, mates!"

Not a second later, Jane rips off one of her taloned gloves, fingers in a V. She lifts them in position to launch her new favorite gesture, and I lower her hand with a scorn-filled "*no.*"

"Bite us, Tosser," she shouts in a dreadful mock accent as I mentally brace myself for the long walk ahead. I promised an hour of submission in which I'd do her bidding, and in return, I would be allowed to claim the same in the future—at the time of my choosing. An easy enough deal and one I plan to take full advantage of once the right opportunity presents itself.

"Jane," I call out over the whirring and street noise as heads collectively turn our way from every imaginable angle, and Jane makes every effort to aid in her presentation, waggling her arse so her tail follows.

"Yes, Lucian?" She pipes, a smile evident in her tone.

"Please try your best not to get us arrested."

"No promises. Also, are you aware that when you say fuck, it sounds like fack?"

"Perhaps it does when I'm *irritated*, and you're exceptional at drawing that particular reaction out of me as of late."

"Go with it, Lucian, and try to *be one* with your *inner* dinosaur."

She makes an absurd hula motion with her tiny arms as I practically growl at her in reply.

"Atta boy," she says, patting my bicep as I begin to sweat despite the rapidly dropping temperature.

As we pass more unsuspecting Londoners, cameras begin to lift, and I cover my face to shield myself from the onslaught.

"Oh, let's pose!" Jane suggests, thrusting one leg out and waving her hands for a snap or two.

"Absolutely not!" I counter, speeding up my walk while thankful we're safely under the cover of night. While it's in no way easy to see through the cheap veil of mesh, it isn't impossible, and I demonstrate that by navigating us through the heavy pedestrian traffic.

"My hour," Jane reminds me, speeding to catch up with me, "my decision," she taunts as we reach a crossing, and in a sudden twist, those already gathered start to cheer at our arrival.

Jane instantly animates—a people pleaser to her core—rocking back and forth on her taloned feet while doing some sort of T-Rex boxing move.

A movement that looks utterly misplaced in keeping with the theme of the costume, and I tell her as much.

"You know when you said you wish you were more outgoing?" she shouts, leaning into me. The top of her inflated head dips and blocks my view of her, along with the street signal. Eager to see the signal and make more progress on our walk back to the hotel, I quickly bat her inflated head out of the way.

"I don't remember stating that, no," I reply, still pushing her head out of my view while keeping her close to ensure she doesn't step blindly into the street.

"Whatever. Here's your chance, Doc."

"Chance to what?" I argue. "Make a bloody fool of myself? I declare mission accomplished."

"Lucian, *please* don't be *that guy* right now," she lifts her voice, folding her hands in prayer. The plea doesn't at all feel like it's for her, but seemingly more for *me*. This has me pausing and looking over to catch the hopeful glint in her eyes.

"Fine," I sigh. "What is your suggestion?"

"Well . . .," she pauses to wave at a car that slows and sounds before turning back to me, eyes alight, "do you know the dance the macarena?"

"No," I clip.

"The cupid shuffle?"

"No."

"Oh, bullshit, everyone knows that one. That dance is universal."

"Not in my wheelhouse," I lie, but only partially—I'm not well-versed enough to execute it. "Also, I don't dance," I add, glancing around as even more people gather, specifically around the two of us, as expectation thickens the air.

"Okay, well, what dance *do* you know?"

"Jane, again, I don't dance," I say as more cameras lift and anxiety starts to have its way with me. "I'm not a performer. I don't perform."

"Tonight you do," she informs me as even more people begin to crowd around us. "Because according to the terms of our deal, I have an hour, and we aren't even a quarter in."

"Fuck."

"Fack," she mocks through a laugh.

"Hilarious," I grumble as two people approach us, mobile phones raised. Jane immediately pounces, roaring at them, to which they quickly scream out before laughing.

"Look," she says, turning back to me, T-rex hands planted firmly on her hips, not budging in her mission, "I'm not expecting miracles here, but you know *one damned dance*, so fess up because we aren't leaving this crosswalk until we've given them *something*."

"You're infuriating, Jane Cartwright."

"Thank you."

"Not everything is a compliment."

"Guess that depends on which T-Rex you're talking to."

"Christ, you'll be the death of me."

"Come on, Lucian. How many chances like this do you get in a lifetime?"

"Optimistically, *one*, if God's taking requests."

She laughs, and the melodic sound strikes me square in the chest. I can't help my return smile.

"Give me one song, Doc, and it's straight back to the hotel, I promise," she assures, having already somehow produced her mobile phone from inside her costume as she lifts it.

"One song, nothing more? No more addendums or misleading treachery?"

She crosses her taloned hand over her heart as I gesture for her to come closer and utter the dance I do know.

"What's that?" She asks as I mumble the name again.

"Huh, 'fraid I don't know that one, Doc, so, unfortunately, you'll be flying solo." She removes one of her gloves and begins tapping and scrolling furiously.

"Jane, no," I implore, the desperation evident in my voice as she fully ensnares me in yet another laid trap.

"You're on, Doc," she says, lifting her phone in threat as I narrow my eyes.

Weighing the challenge she just presented me with, I take a step back and mentally square off with her just as she presses play.

*Fuck it.*

# NINETEEN

## JANE

"OH. MY. FRICKIN'. GOD!" I screech in disbelief as Lucian works the T-Rex costume—or rather, his body—like he's been preparing for this moment his entire life.

One second, he was full of protest. In the next, it was as if he flipped a switch inside himself.

The instant I hit play on Biggie's *Hypnotize*, Lucian came to life along with the crowd, dazzling and dazing every single soul gathered around him.

Unmoving in my own suit, all I can do is gawk, providing no entertainment whatsoever to any of his onlookers who seem just as stunned and excited by the talent he's displaying—his dancing both mind-blowing and top-tier.

The more he dances, the more it becomes crystal clear that Doc can keep rhythm far beyond his jump roping skills, and he lied through his teeth about the fact that he doesn't dance because said skills are a step above next level.

The kick-ass, universally loved, coveted beat echoes through the freezing air from my phone as Lucian pulls another trick out of his hat—bouncing from one foot as if from a diving board and landing on top of a nearby bench. Hands tucked into his armpits, swaying rhythmically, my prickly doctor brings an entire London city block to their knees . . . while doing the fucking wedding chicken dance.

I wouldn't believe it my damned self if I wasn't seeing it with my own eyes.

Instead of using the dance's fast switch and rehearsed movements, he's slowed them way down to match Biggie's beat and made it all hip hop. A crowd has gathered around him now—rightfully leaving me forgotten—as Lucian dances his perfect ass off.

"You're killing it!" I scream as he completely animates the bulky costume, exaggerating his movements tenfold as he bounces his Rex elbows to the beat. As I watch him set his ninja dance moves free, I feel the inevitable tug in my chest—which, in truth, feels more like a yank. A yank I take seriously as I try to rope myself back to earth.

*Nope. Nope. Nope. Back, heart, back!*

Phone camera up to capture every second to serve multiple purposes—for playback later, along with future blackmail—I shake my head in astonishment as my insides threaten to imprint on him.

Now more than ever, it's vital that I'm the friend he needs me to be. As if he can hear my inner turmoil, he gains ground, drawing closer to me without missing a step. It's then he finishes us all by flattening his palm in front of him with one hand, mimicking the spank of an upturned ass with the other while utilizing his feet in a flawless mix of breakdance and moonwalk, pulling it off effortlessly.

When the song comes to an end, I crash into him, and he embraces me right back as the crowd gives him a well-deserved perfect ten in both volume and applause. He responds by releasing me and taking a rightful bow.

To both our surprise, bills are stuffed into Lucian's gloved hand as cheers continue to surround him. Oddly enough, he accepts the cash, lifting a fist full of it toward me as he's drug away for a picture—his words echoing over the obstructive heads gathered around him. "Dinner is on me, Cheeky!"

The sound of my newly given nickname strikes solidly like an arrow straight to my chest, thudding exaggeratedly as I inwardly swoon—what I wouldn't give to see his face right now, his smile. For a minute or two, he poses for his new fans, his tone friendly even as he holds his hand over the mesh to shield his identity.

Once he's back in front of me, I playfully slug him in the arm. "You liar, you said you can't dance!"

"I said I don't dance. And I haven't much since primary school."

"Well, you must have been a beast back then because that was the most epic thing I've seen in forever. I bet you ten bucks to a bucket of piss that footage goes viral."

"Ten bucks to a bucket of urine?" He asks through a chuckle. "Help me to understand, Jane."

"Ya know," I frown, "I never have fully understood that one myself, Doc, and you're changing the subject," I scold playfully as we gather amongst the waiting crowd for the crosswalk light. "That was some Channing Tatum "Step Up" jaw-dropping debut shit right there."

"What?" He asks.

"Pop culture reference, not important. You murdered that assignment, Lucian. That was unreal!"

"Glad to have pleased you, Jane," he croons, seeming sincere.

Without thought, Lucian grabs my hand as the light summons us to cross, and he switches our positions so he's closer to the passing traffic as we set off.

"But seriously, where did you learn to move like *that*?" I keep in time with his strides along with the new pep in his step, his dino swagger in full effect. "That footwork alone reeked of *pro*."

"I wasn't always so boring, Jane," he says, his tone reflective. "I rather enjoyed dancing in my formative years."

"Well, feel free anytime to admit you had fun."

"I did," he imparts quickly, squeezing my hand. "Thank you, Jane."

"Don't thank me, but just so you know, you probably started a Tok trend."

"I have no idea what that is, but it couldn't have been so memorable."

"Bullshit. I have footage right here in my pocket that says otherwise, and to show off at the nurse's station once we get back home," I taunt.

"Of course you do." I can't see his smile, even with the lights surrounding us, but I know it's there.

"The second they see it, your dance card will be forever filled, not that they aren't already eager to do some sheet-dancing with you." His hand stiffens in mine with that. As he glances over, I squeeze it to let him know it's all in jest as someone raises their cell phone and takes a quick snap of us.

Just two dinosaurs holding hands on a busy London street.

I glance over at him, feeling all the warm and fuzzies, my face hurting from smiling so much. "I hope it's okay to say that I'm proud of you. You did something completely out of your comfort zone and did it well."

"As if you gave me any choice," he muses.

"Lucian," I say in the most serious tone I can muster, dressed as a pre-historic reptile, "we both know no one can make you do anything."

"I'm thinking that might no longer be the case in keeping you for company."

"I'll take that as a compliment."

"That was meant as one."

"So," I ask, gripping his hand more firmly. "Are you ready for tomorrow night?"

"As ready as I can be," he says, his tone losing some enthusiasm.

"Sorry, I didn't mean to spoil your good mood."

"It's fine," fatigue rings clear in his words as he voices it. "To be honest, I'm a bit knackered. Would you mind if we save this money for another dinner and dine in our room while watching another film instead?"

"I wouldn't be opposed to sharing a pterodactyl sandwich and movie with you. Sounds kind of perfect."

The rest of our walk remains harmonious, albeit tiring, as we tread a dozen blocks or more toward our hotel, holding hands most of the way until we're stopped for an impromptu photo. Our costume hits paydirt with everyone we encounter, and it's driven home when Lucian admits as much himself as we near the hotel, his praise warming my insides.

My smile never lessens, even as my body grows tired from the long trek.

It's when we're finally feet away from the entrance that Lucian ushers me to the side of an adjacent, gated courtyard.

"Would you?" Lucian asks, leaning into me so I can grip the zipper at his neck. I tug it down, and he reaches back, producing his wallet from his suit pants.

"You cleaned up," I chuckle, eyeing the cash as he quickly counts it.

"Forty quid and change, not bad," he muses, tucking away the card and cash before swiping his room card to gain entrance and holding the gate open for me.

"Thank you, kind sir," I shimmy past him as his whisper reaches me.

"My pleasure, Cheeky."

I pause slightly due to the inflection in his tone, one I'm sure I've never heard, as the gate clangs closed behind us, and he again takes my hand.

"Afraid I won't look left in here?" I ask with a nervous chuckle.

Lucian doesn't answer as he ushers me into a different world altogether, far more tranquil than the street chaos we just escaped. Though the manicured garden is made up mostly of tall hedges—which have been battered by winter—they're accented heavily by expertly trimmed topiaries of all shapes and sizes.

A canopy of low-lying, lit tree branches encapsulates strung lights hovering mere feet above us, adding to the magic of the street-side garden while guiding our path. Lucian keeps a grip on my hand, steering us deeper into the captivating grounds, only stopping when we hit a dead end, enclosed by a half square of hedges.

"This is beautiful," I say, *and romantic*—which I *don't say*—as I glance over at a nearby three-tiered fountain. It is littered with little cement cherubs hoisting buckets over their heads. I glance back up to Lucian and grin as he peers back down at me inches away. "After all that show-stopping badassery, you really couldn't just own your Big Dino energy enough to make it to our suite in your get-up?"

"Get-up," he mimics, "You do realize that you are the definition of a true Yank to me, and even I'm aware of how *Southern* you really are, though you do often stifle your accent."

"Hey, I'm proud of it. Know that, matey," I drawl out, laying it on thick.

"Of that, I have no doubt," he says, reaching for me, more specifically, for my zipper, slowly releasing the front of my costume as I duck beneath the seam at the neck and finally pop free. A chilly breeze sweeps over me, but this time, it's welcome as it cools the sweat gathered on my brow.

"There you are," Lucian whispers in a way that has me snapping my eyes to his as if the sight of me is something he had missed.

"Let's get *you* found," I grip his zipper, and he covers my newly ungloved hand with his, stopping me.

"Are you sure you want to release me, Jane?"

He uses that tone again, and it's deep and . . . coaxing.

"According to section 1A of our deal amendment," he continues, "you still have around ten minutes to order me to do your bidding."

"Good point," I flash him a grin. "Whatever should I *make you do*?"

Pulling his zipper down anyway, it's when I help him push his dino head off and see his waiting expression that I'm fully taken aback—the heat in his eyes penetrating. My nipples draw up against the fabric of my bra and shirt as his eyes dip and sweep, pausing on my lips before slamming into mine.

BAM.

I feel the connection *everywhere,* along with the aftershocks that follow. He's never looked at me like *this* before, of that, I'm sure.

"Such a change in you from only last night," I rasp out hoarsely, completely stunned by the lack of filter in his face and tone.

"Seems I have you to thank, and to be honest, I wouldn't at all mind doing so," he relays, his voice heating with every word as his return stare pins me. "But rules are rules, so my ability to thank you *properly* would be entirely your call."

Guard completely absent, there is absolutely no mistaking his expression, which, in a word, is *smoldering*—or his words, and it's startling just how easily and purposefully he's able to make the switch.

"D-don't give me credit, Lucian, it's who you are. You've just been dormant for a bit."

"Have I fucking ever," he replies, barely above a whisper as I bite my lip, and his eyes follow.

Just short of clearing my throat, I redirect. "I'm looking forward to discovering what else you're hiding, but you should really make those dance skills part of your ongoing repertoire. I'll be honest, I'm pretty fond of this version of you. Much less doom and gloom."

"Are you now?" His tone caresses me as his eyes trail from my sweaty brow to my midsection. Both of us are still dressed from the waist down in our costumes as the bulk of them rest loosely around our hips, threatening to give with just the slightest movement.

Knowing my neck is heating and probably as obvious as my heaving chest, I take a long pull of the air between us and lower my gaze. Lucian immediately bends to recapture it, refusing to free me or let me retreat in any way.

"Lucian," I protest feebly as he makes his intent clear for a pregnant pause without uttering a single word. He's waiting for verbal permission that my body is already giving him. When I simply stare back, he breaks the silence.

"Are we still sticking to lack of chemistry as an excuse, Jane?"

Shit.

He's full-on fronting me out now as he leans into me, purposefully in my space. Slowly lifting a single finger, he begins to brush the pad of it beneath my lower lip. My body reacts instantly as my mind races.

Dr. Prick is about to kiss me.

*Again.*

And I want him to.

*Again.*

Just as he receives the signal—my nipples spiked and pointed straight at him—he bends to deliver, his golden eyes dipping to my targeted lips as I spew my verbal vomit. "You need me!"

He jerks back in confusion as I try to make it make sense.

"What I meant to say is," I shake my head, absolutely loathing my resolve to be the friend he needs, "is that you j-just need someone right now. A friend. It wouldn't be right or fair to you to get physical."

"Fair to me?" A gradual, devilish smile lifts his lips as he crowds me, the hungry look in his eyes mirroring that of the predator's costume he's wearing. "Are you insinuating that if we do, in fact, have chemistry and act on it, you would be taking advantage of me?"

His thumb takes the place of his pointer finger as he sweeps it gently beneath my mouth before brushing it across my lower lip. Temptation seizing me, the urge to suck it into my mouth is damn near debilitating.

"You're going through a hard time right now," I all but whimper.

"You aren't wrong at present," he rakes his full lower lip with his teeth, insinuation clear, "and you didn't answer my question, Jane."

This time, when he sweeps his thumb, he gently presses it just inside my parted lips, running it the full length between them before repeating the movement.

Fuck. Me.

"What was it, again?" I squeak.

"There's the question of chemistry." But he doesn't say it like a question. At all. More like a statement that my body currently agrees with as my mind attempts to bitch slap me back down from orbit.

"Right now doesn't count," I offer in a weak reply.

"My cock would argue otherwise."

"Your . . . cock," I swallow, my heart pounding out of my chest as a devil—who looks a lot like me—lands squarely on my shoulder and whispers into my ear.

*"Bitch if you don't let him pet your kitty, I will haunt you until your last breath."*

"Jane?" Lucian prompts heatedly, in both offer and promise, his honey eyes pouring suggestively down my frame. I shudder as he presses in further, his thumb continually running a light brush along my lips. His touch is so sensual, so intimate. I lean into it, my

Dino costume dropping like I imagine my panties would if we were in a different setting.

Libido raging, my body reminds me that I want this man more than any other man in the history of ever. With each slow stroke of his finger, I gravitate toward him.

My mouth refuses to move as my fantasies come flying at me a thousand miles an hour, the top-tier fantasy playing out before me in real life. This is happening.

Lucian wants to pet my kitty.

And my kitty is purring like a mother—

"Jane?"

"Hmm?"

"Are you going to blame the cold for the fact that your nipples are hard and your beautiful pussy is weeping?"

"You don't know that," I croak out my lie. I could probably power the entire city block from the heat building below. Hell, anyone close might already be aware that I'm about to explode, and all he's giving me is the slow sweep of his finger.

Jesus Christ, this man is fire even without his come *fuck me eyes* and *come-hither* tone, which, honestly, could scorch earth.

"So, if I tuck my fingers into your knickers and sweep my thumb across your clit like I am your lips, I won't find you wet for me?"

"Ye-ou need me to be your f-friend," I stutter out as he ruins my life by being exactly who I dreamed he would be in this department.

"We aren't friends already?" He coaxes, taking care to only trace the outline of my lips with the side of his thumb. Closing my eyes, I lose myself in the feel, imagining him brushing it along my clit the exact same way as my panties flood.

He is so close now that I can feel his exhale as he continually traces my lips, this time adding more pressure to his sweep, to the point I let out a light moan.

*Say yes, you idiot! Say kiss me! Say anything!*

I open my mouth to do just that, and my body betrays me. "I don't think it's a good idea."

"For whom?"

"For us both, Lucian," I sigh in disappointment as the devil on my shoulder starts to fade in a cloud of utter disbelief, but not before shaking a fist at me with a promise of retribution.

Lucian closes the space, his lips lightly, so lightly brushing mine as my entire being vibrates in response. His scent, which I now place as a slightly woodsy, citrus mix, intoxicates me, along with the tone of his voice that matches the intent in his eyes. I become that scorched earth as my body hums and my heart beats in warning that I might very well die right here, in a London courtyard, with an inflatable T-Rex costume pooled at my feet. Despite my attempt to stay grounded, I'm in deep space now and fumbling toward delirium.

But this is real life, and in real life, my fantasy man wants me.

"Lucian," I whisper in an attempt to shake it away and fail, my words managing past the rattle happening inside me. "If we give in tonight and it goes south, our new friendship will suffer, and I *want* to be there for you. Tomorrow especially."

That's the truth.

"All right," he utters on exhale, taking away his touch before slowly backing away.

"Besides, I want to be wanted, not needed," I declare in afterthought, standing my ground. Within the same breath, he circles my waist and yanks me flush to him, golden eyes full of fire.

Hard, so incredibly *hard*.

All of him and what I feel pressed against my stomach feels like the *motherload* of girth. His hot whisper hits my ear as I go lax in his arms. If he were to kiss me again right now, I wouldn't, couldn't stop him, and his next words have me damn near orgasming as he utters them. "Just so you are aware, what you think I'm *needy for* right now is most definitely a fucking *want*."

He presses the evidence against me briefly as I burn, paralyzed only by my own need to keep my promise to him.

To be a friend.

It's then I realized I've just friend-zoned *myself* with my own fantasy man.

Ain't that a bitch!

Desperate to touch him and so close to skirting the line that my fingers itch at my sides and my hands start to move, I'm denied when he abruptly releases me before stripping the rest of his costume.

Still shaken by what just transpired, I stand there, soaked, throbbing, and stupefied. My entire body is alive and aching, lips still tingling in remembrance of his featherlight touch and faint but perfect kiss.

Why? Why, God? Why did I just deny a man I'm so attracted to the right to touch me? A man I've spent an embarrassing number of hours fantasizing about?

But even as I ask it, the answer rings clear—to be a friend—a real friend, which is what he needs more than a willing woman beneath him.

Could I be both? Possibly.

Do I want to take that chance?

As tempting as it is, as *he is*, no. I've seen and felt his pain, and it's too much to just chuck aside for a night of sex. No doubt the best sex of my life, considering what he's packing and the expertise of his dance moves, but sex no less.

If things got weird tomorrow morning after the smoke cleared, he'd probably make an excuse for me not to come with him.

That can't happen because if my suspicions are correct—whether he knows it or not—he hasn't hit bottom yet.

Not fully, and not yet.

But none of that reasoning changes the fact that he just told me he wanted me. Outright. He didn't mince his words.

And I just turned him down.

As we silently roll up our costumes and make our way back to the hotel entrance, all I can think about is if I'll ever get the chance again. From the way he seems to have so easily recovered compared to me, my inner Magic Eight Ball tells me the outlook isn't so good.

# TWENTY

## JANE

After dinner—during which I forced Lucian to watch a playback of his epic and impromptu busking debut—we gradually came back to some semblance of our new normal after our heavy interlude in the courtyard. An interlude I'll be hard-pressed to forget anytime soon. Thankfully, the moment seemed to have passed enough for us to gather comfortably on the couch for a movie without me worrying too much about our proximity or my hand placement.

The truth of that is further brought home as I'm jarred awake thanks to the obnoxious volume of the rolling movie credits, only to realize I'm entwined with him. Glancing down from where I lay on my side, I study Lucian where he sleeps, his upper half resting on my legs, his head cocked at an odd angle between my thigh and hip. One of my palms is stretched below me, sandwiched between his bare chest and his partially unbuttoned dress shirt.

With the way we're positioned, it's as if we gravitated toward the other once we fell asleep, and I subconsciously gave into what I denied myself during waking hours.

Hesitant to move—but knowing he can't be comfortable—I

manage to work around him enough to reach the remote and click off the TV. Grabbing a nearby throw pillow, I gently lift his head and move to sit before positioning him back on my lap. Scrutinizing him for any sign I've disturbed his sleep, I'm relieved to see his chest continually rise and fall in a steady rhythm.

Unable to help myself, I trace his features as firelight licks along his profile. Fingers itching, I'm all too tempted to thread them through his thick, dark-blond hair laced with whispers of spun gold highlights.

Fuck it.

Gently raking my fingers through his thick strands, I revel in the silky feel while soaking in the look of him up close. Within seconds, I've memorized the length of his dark blond lashes, the slope and strength of his nose, the angles of his face, along with thick lips I could spend hours or years worshipping.

"They broke the fucking mold when they made you," I whisper to the comatose man resting in my lap as I continually run my fingers through his hair. And wishing on a damned star that I could selfishly take his lips and, in doing so, change my earlier answer. Wishing I was the girl greedy enough to take what I want without worrying about anyone else's needs or feelings but my own. Because all doing the opposite has ever gotten me in the past is a place back at the starting line.

Ripping my eyes away due to the temptation of kissing him awake, I tilt my head up to rest on the back of the couch and remind myself of why I'm so damned needy.

It's been nearly two years since my last disastrous long-term relationship ended and a little over a year since I've had any real physical contact. The length of abstinence is a hard-won feat for someone who craves both touch and sex in conjunction with her daily bread.

The solution for the lack of it all seeming so close—literally at my fingertips—but mentally too far out of reach.

*Be his friend, Jane.*

Resigned to continue to do the right thing, I exhale my regret and try to move myself from beneath him, freezing when his eyes open—and not at all gradually. He's awake and has been playing possum, which is only proven as he begins to stroke the tender skin of my forearm, the arm attached to the hand that's been caressing him.

"Sorry," I whisper, "you were sleeping at an odd angle, and I didn't want you to catch a crick."

*Which doesn't at all explain why you're currently stroking his hair like a stalker!*

Cheeks heating in embarrassment, I stop my fingers. The instant I do, he lifts his chin, nudging me to resume. Laughing lightly, I can't help my smile as I pick back up at his insistence, weaving my hand through his inches-long strands. My smile fades as he lengthens his caress with the pads of his fingers, his touch intoxicating.

Eyes bolted to mine, he pins me from below. Pinning and searching, as if he's trying to understand me, along with something else I can't quite place.

Vulnerability seeps from him as my heart threatens to beat right out of my chest, the crackle of the fire feet away matching the energy starting to overpower me as we just stare at one another, stroking the other's skin.

*Because this is perfectly normal friend behavior, Jane.*

Ignoring the cock blocking voice of reason continually chiming in to ruin my life, I give in temporarily to my wants, massaging his scalp as he gazes up at me, fueling our increasing connection. It's then I pinpoint the haunted glint in his eyes and pause my fingers.

"Hey . . . you okay?"

He gives me the soft dip of his chin, but the pain is there, telling me otherwise. He's struggling with something—that much is clear—but doesn't seem to want to put a voice to it right now. Not only that but he's also dropped his guard again for the second time today. He's starting to trust me, and my heart only lurches in his direction more due to the weight and truth of it.

When I rake his scalp lightly with my nails, his eyelids flutter and lower, staying half-mast as he further elongates the hypnotizing sweep of his own skilled fingers, seducing me thoroughly with the simple act.

Butterflies swarm as temptation threatens to override me for the second time tonight. The draw I feel to him is so damned magnetic and becoming so strong that it's starting to scare the shit out of me.

The thing is, I'm not so easily spooked by this type of connection. In fact, I'm just the type of gal prone to seek it out—and worse—easily give in to it.

"Are you going to sleep out here?" I ask breathlessly.

His nod is almost imperceptible as his fingers glide further up the skin of my forearm when I again glimpse the shadows in his expression.

He's hurting, and I'm lusting over him.

I'm being a creep.

Was he dreaming before I woke him up?

Is that why he looks so haunted?

I can't be a friend enough right now to ask. Not with the thread I'm hanging by threatening to snap. Feeling the need to flee, to break his hold, along with the invisible line that's binding and drawing me to him, I stop my fingers.

"Well . . . goodnight," I say as I take my touch away, and he runs the pads of his fingers down my arm one last time before releasing both my eyes and his hold. He lifts his head and pillow so I can easily move from beneath him.

"Sleep well, Cheeky," he whispers, closing his eyes as I stand, repeating his soft sentiment before pulling the blanket resting on his thighs to his shoulder.

Aching everywhere, heart heavy because of the longing and pain I felt emanating from him, I skulk back to my room. After exchanging my clothes for my comfort pajamas, I climb into bed and am thankful when sleep quickly takes me.

The next morning, I rouse, knowing the suite is empty. I feel Lucian's absence before it's confirmed when I check my phone to find a waiting text.

**Lucian: Spending the day at the lab with Matthieu. I'll be back to pick you up at five.**

I deflate due to his purposeful absence—though I know he's utilizing the time to fine-tune his skills with the Razor—I can't help but wonder if his decision to work today is due to nerves about facing his family or about distancing himself from me.

"Or maybe he's simply being the dedicated surgeon he is while you're being a self-important asshole," I scold myself before sending my reply.

**Kick some ass, Doc!**

After spending the morning doing some last-minute shopping—the whole time feeling ill at ease—I decide to mull it over with my voice of reason.

I unload half a dozen bags on the huge dining room table and prop my phone on a nearby fruit bowl. I take a seat at the head of it and hit FaceTime, thankful when Charlie appears within a few rings.

A minute into updating her, I start to regret making the call.

"You what?!"

"I turned him down," I say as my sister shouts at me while I wince under her browbeating. "I'm trying to be a friend," I state, adding to my case.

"Be a friend to *your vagina*, Jane!"

"You weren't there. You didn't hear his pain that night," I say, pulling the plastic from a roll of wrapping paper.

"I get it. I do, but you've all but prayed for this."

"I have not," I deny, averting my eyes from the screen to avoid the call-of-bullshit expression I know she's giving me. She remains mute, forcing me to meet her pointed stare.

"Fine, I have, but that doesn't mean I have to take advantage of him."

"You just said he all but laughed in your face for thinking as much. Clearly he's down for a hookup."

"Yeah, about that," I grimace, knowing I need to come clean. "Thing is, I could fall for him. Easily, if things keep going the way they are, and he's not at all in the place to return feelings. Hell, he's barely remembering he's capable of having them right now."

Her eyes bulge. "You're falling for him already?"

"I'm not in love with him," I state, knowing I'm still teetering, "but I could, and honestly, at this point, it wouldn't take much."

"You've been there for a week."

"I know, okay. I know how insane it sounds, but . . . he's been showing me more of him in bits and pieces, and I like *all of it*. Not only is he beautiful, but he's also brilliant. He has a decent sense of humor, and we get along well when he drops his guard. We have this connection brewing . . . and let me tell you, it's mighty. God, if you could only see the way he looks at me sometimes, especially last night. So, if we get physical and it's as good as I think it will be—"

"He'll make your kitty purrrrr?"

"I'm being serious," I roll my eyes, plucking one of a dozen presents from the pile the bellman brought up before sizing it against the wrapping paper.

"So am I."

"Stop with the kitty crap, okay?" Just as I start to cut into the paper, I pause the scissors. "So . . . I can't go there, then. Decision made, right?"

"Right, but what about the French doctor?"

"Matthieu. I'm supposed to have dinner with him tomorrow night."

"On Christmas?"

"Yeah, and I already feel weird about it," I frown, "like I'll be doing something wrong if I do go. That's jacked, isn't it?"

"*Hi-jacked* is more like it. Because that's what Lucian's doing, or should I say what you're allowing him to do by inviting his personal shit into your heart and headspace."

"I like spending time with him," I admit, taping one side of the box.

"I like spending time with a lot of people. Doesn't mean they get dibs on how I vacay or who I bone on vacay."

"Right," I say, measuring some ribbon against the package.

"What are you doing?" Charlie cuts in, her tone accusatory.

"Huh?"

"Don't huh me, what are you wrapping?"

I shrug. "Just a few gifts we picked up for Lucian's nephews."

"And why are we wrapping gifts for Lucian's nephews?"

"Because I'm sure he forgot or hasn't thought of it. I'm just helping him out."

"*Jane,*" she drawls out, using my name to scold me.

"What? He's at the hospital right now practicing a groundbreaking technique that could save hundreds, if not thousands of lives in the future, and I have nothing better to do."

A long pause ensues as I avoid her expression for the second time.

"I love you so much, little sister," she says, forcing me to look back at the screen. "But you're heading toward a slippery slope."

"It's no big deal. Geesh, I would wrap presents for you if you needed me to."

"I know, but that's different. You do too much for people who don't deserve it."

"Do not," I say, ducking another of her dead-eyed stares.

"You spent your damned Christmas bonus giving your neighbor's out of work son a handyman job you cooked up just to be able to help out. Meanwhile, you're still tending bar to pay off your student loans."

"That banister was loose! It was dangerous!"

"Two hundred dollars dangerous? You're too selfless, and we both know this trip is about a lot more than just surgery for you. So, instead of wrapping someone else's nephew's presents, you should be trying to make one of those royal guards lose their shit, or riding the red bus, or one of a dozen other things on your itinerary."

"Okay, okay, you've made your point."

"Good. Have dinner with the parents tonight, and be there for him if shit goes south, and then do what *Jane* wants to do from then on out. That is all you promised him. Right?"

"Correct," I nod, grabbing another present from the stack.

"Okay, then it's settled. Stick to the plan, but if we're keeping it one hundred, my money is still on Doctor Prick being the one to tear your panties off."

"Why did I call you again?" I groan.

"Because you're lying to yourself. You're already in *something* with him."

"I'm not, which is the whole point of this conversation."

"Wrong. The whole point of this conversation is that you want your sister to recklessly agree to allow you to cater to Doc and his dick and get nothing out of it. To that, I say *no, ma'am*. You deserve to come back with pictures and good memories, not a bruised or broken heart. Which, from the way your heart-splaining, already sounds like the case."

"You know," I say, pausing my hand on the tape, "you're being kind of coldhearted. He opened up to me and hasn't opened up to anyone in a long time."

"And I get that, I do, but you asked for it. In doing that, you're asking him to hijack your vacation and time, and according to you, it can't go anywhere. Which would be fine if you weren't inclined to fall and didn't have to work with him afterward. If it was a hookup without feelings, that's one thing, but the dick's too risky now. So, permission denied. I'll happily *be the asshole* because I'm the one who's watched my baby sister get her heart broken time and time again by the same kind of narcissistic, unworthy men who take your awesome heart and time for granted and hand you the receipt after to pay the fucking bill."

"You didn't have to go *there*. Damn, Charlie, give me some credit. I'm wiser now."

"No one is truly wise in love, Jane. Need some proof? I might have told Barrett we could try and give Elijah a brother or sister."

"Really?" My eyes instantly water.

"See," she points to me through the screen. "You're getting gooey already, which is why you can't let Doctor Prick bogart your vacation after tonight."

"Technically, we are here to work, not vacation," I point out. "So, I can't venture too far."

"Stop giving me bullshit excuses to spend time with the doctor you're becoming infatuated with and go with your gut. Your gut is saying don't do it. Your gut told you to call me to warn you not to do it, so don't do it!"

"Fine!" I snap.

"Fine!" she mimics, her reply far more comical.

"And by the way, Charlie," I point the scissors at her, "you are an asshole."

"When it comes to protecting you, I always will be. But I'll give you credit enough to make the decision on how and when Dr. Prick's time is up. And if he's not treating you right, or you get the vibe again, *his time is up*, Jane."

"Well, thanks for the permission," I grumble.

"Call it faith that you'll use the life raft for yourself when you need to, and you're welcome." She smirks. "Report back. Love you."

"Yeah, yeah, bye," I mutter and swipe to end the call.

Though I'm always thankful for my sister and her unrelenting voice of reason, there's nothing worse than when that voice forces you to uphold honesty with yourself when you don't want to hear it. But I do heed this type of warning because I've spent too much time on the other side *after* ignoring it.

A text pops up a few seconds later.

**Charlie: You deserve to be a man's everything. I love you, and I know your worth.**

Sighing, I temporarily stop wrapping to text her back.

**Thank you. You're right. Love you too.**

Swallowing her truth down as my own, I exhale and pull up my pep-in-my-step playlist on my music app. A second later, "Fly" by Nicki Minaj begins to filter through the room.

# TWENTY-ONE

## JANE

"Jane?" Lucian calls as I exit the bathroom after walking through a spritz of perfume. "Hey, Doc," I call back, taking one last look in the mirror, "how was your day?"

Tonight, I paired black dress slacks, short boots, and a form-fitting, wine-red sweater. I curled my hair in soft waves and kept my makeup minimal by heavily coating my lashes with mascara, lightly blushing my cheeks, and finishing the rest of my look with matte burgundy lipstick.

Satisfied, I click off the bathroom light and exit my room to find Lucian standing at the end of the dining room table looking unfairly gorgeous in dark blue scrubs. The cuffs of the fitted white undershirt he's wearing beneath pushed up his muscular forearms, his scarf and coat discarded nearby.

"What have you done?" he bellows, unaware that I'm walking straight toward him, and I laugh because of it. His eyes snap up and sweep me, his words instant. "You're fucking stunning."

His compliment warms me from head to toe as he grips the top of the dining room chair in front of him with both hands, his cheeks puffing with air before he expels it in a loaded exhale.

"Thank you, and you didn't answer me. Was it not a good day?" I ask.

"It was fine," he replies absently, scanning the table, his eyes drifting from the mountain of wrapped presents to the large gift basket I picked up this morning.

"Is that okay for your mom?" I ask. "Mike said it's a well-known shop, but we can stop for wine if you—"

"Jane," his whisper cuts me off as he cups his neck. "It's entirely too much but truly appreciated," he says, bringing his eyes to mine. "I can't even imagine how long this took you," he runs his finger appreciatively over the velvet ribbon wrapped around one of the presents, reminding me of a similar touch last night. I bat the image away as he speaks. "I hadn't even thought to wrap them."

"Well, don't beat yourself up about it. You've had a lot on your mind. Mike is coming up with the bellman in a few to pack them in the car."

Lucian continues to stare at me, seeming overwhelmed. "I don't know how to thank you for this," he sweeps me again as my lower half responds this time, and it's all I can do not to squirm beneath his weighted stare, "but I will be thanking you properly."

"Stop, it's not a big deal."

"It is to me," he says, swallowing. "What you're doing for me tonight is as well."

"Good God, has no one ever done something nice or been a friend to you?"

"It's a rarity," he utters, eyes continually scanning the table as my heart stutters through a beat.

*Stick to the plan, Jane.*

"You better get showered and dressed if you want to be on time."

He nods and rakes his lower lip with his teeth while giving me one last lingering look before turning abruptly, stalking to his room, and softly closing his door.

Half an hour later, Lucian emerges from his side of our suite looking devastating in dark boots, jeans, and a thick cream sweater, smelling edible. Hints of his cologne waft through the cabin of the car as Lucian steers us toward his family home, having relieved Mike from driving us. Though I wanted to question why, I didn't due to his current state.

Glancing over—even with his resting bastard face firmly in place—I can feel the rattle building inside of him. Posture stiff and stoic, expression hard and determined—he's armored up. I absolutely hate it and am already missing the glimpses of the man I've gotten to know this past week.

Has it only been a week?

It feels so much longer at this point, and the progress we've made feels substantial in comparison to the brief time.

Just as I mull over words for a pep talk, we're pulling up to a set of massive gates surrounded by stone mason walls that seem to stretch indefinitely in both directions. Large lanterns hang on either side of the heavy metal doors, flames dancing steadily behind the glass.

*Damn.*

If the entrance is any indication of what's on the other side, I have completely underestimated the Aston familial wealth.

I don't have to wait long to gauge the size of the property because the trees lining the drive are seasonally lit with strings of lights and multiply by the dozen as far as I can see. The same view continues for a good thirty seconds or more before a massive house, or rather, mansion, comes into view.

"Okay, I tried, really, I did. But holy shit, Doc, this is . . . wow," I exclaim as Lucian pulls into a massive square driveway, parking next to an expensive-looking SUV, which also faces the house.

The house is U-shaped, the main building facing us, wings of the same size to the right and left extended out and opposite the other while enclosing most of the parking lot.

"What kind of architecture is this?" I ask.

"Georgian. It was built in the early eighteen hundreds and for-merly owned by a Duke."

"And would you be related to this Duke?" I prod, awestricken.

He nods, staring at his massive childhood home as if he's just as much a stranger to it as I am.

"To be honest," I continue, my nerves getting the best of me as we collectively focus on the massive double doors of the entrance, both adorned with grandiose, brightly lit wreaths. "It's kind of what I expected of an affluent family, but still, it's intimidating as all get out. I can't believe you grew up in a house like this. For a girl like me, it's kind of hard to believe *anyone* does. But to be even more blunt," I run my hands down my slacks and let out a nervous chuckle, "all I can really think when I see a place like this is that the light bill must be frickin' ridiculous."

This earns me a faint smile as Lucian turns to me. "I wouldn't know. We're not to talk about money, ever. We're only supposed to have it and earn it in abundance."

"Well, I would pity you for being rich, Doc, but the alternative is no picnic," I nudge him. "That's why when I clock out at the hospital, I clock back in and sling beer on my off days and weekends. So, you'll be hard-pressed to get pity from me in that respect."

He turns to me, seeming stunned. "You have a second job?"

"Student loans. Not to worry, I should have them paid off by the time I'm forty and paid *twice* as much for my tuition." I shrug. "Gotta love capitalism."

"Christ, Jane, when do you sleep?"

"Plan on getting a lot of it on this trip," I relay, "though I'm still catching up from college."

He stares at me for a long beat before looking back at the doors, and my eyes follow.

"You know, as beautiful and inviting as it may seem, I get that ill feeling too—or maybe it's coming from you." I lay a hand on his bicep, ready to face whatever is behind that door with him, knowing he's dreading this.

"I'm sorry, Lucian. I wanted a real home more than anything when I was young and never had anything close to this, but it's not the outside that makes a home. It's about what's inside it, or rather *who*," I swallow. "And we don't get a choice in that . . . but it does become a choice later, which is why I chose my own." I squeeze his arm and release it. "So, just know going in there tonight that we have that in common."

"What kind of home did you grow up in?" he prompts, ripping his eyes from the door and shifting his focus back to me.

"Pass," I palm the door handle. "We should go. We've already been sitting in this car for a suspicious amount of time."

"No," he barks, palming my thigh to stop me from opening my door. "You're not passing."

"Uh, that's not how this works," I laugh, but it's lifeless. "Come on, we don't want to keep them waiting," I nod toward the house.

"They can wait. I want this answer, Jane. I've been extremely forthcoming with you about my childhood—about everything really—and in this area in particular, you've been more than vague."

"I wouldn't say vague. I think I've made it pretty obvious to you what my childhood was like. Can we not wait on this on account of timing?"

"No," he answers simply.

"Wow," I bulge my eyes at him, but he doesn't budge.

"Lucian, seriously, we don't have time for this."

"I'm making time," he says adamantly, "so let's hear it." He flips off the headlights and cuts the engine, turning to me, brow lifted in expectation.

"You can be a stubborn shit sometimes, you know that?"

"Likewise, and I'm due, Jane, so stop stalling."

"Fine, hell. Okay," I turn to him, "well, I'm sure you've heard the description 'poor white trash?'"

He dips his chin.

"Well, that's what I was raised by, if you could call raising what they did with Charlie and me. They more or less drug us through their nightmarish lives as collateral damage."

He waits, unmoving, a silent demand for more.

"Kim and Allen Cartwright were narcissists to their core—people who didn't give a damn about anyone but themselves, ever. If they took an interest in anyone or treated them with any sort of kindness, it was obvious it came with the mindset of eventually gaining something in return. They were leeches who never wanted to work but always had their hands out for anything they could get. All the while griping about someone else's fortune and luck when they never did shit to change or make their own."

I tuck a stray hair behind my ear.

"Neither finished high school nor bothered to try to change their circumstances—even for our sakes. With the way they treated Charlie and me, it was obvious they didn't want or plan for children but were too lazy to take precautions in that department to prevent either pregnancy. Charlie and I were just side effects of that particular laziness and were treated as such. We were severely neglected, and it showed with the way they dragged us around in public unbathed, wearing ill-fitting clothes and rat's nest hair. Every chance they got, they passed us off to whatever family would take us in for *months* at a time without checking in on us in between."

I pause in short reflection of those days as his eyes remain glued to mine, knowing he's taking in every word.

"So, as we grew up, instead of just settling for the hand we were dealt and participating in or mimicking the same shitty behavior, Charlie and I rejected our parents and all they stood for. When we were old enough to do something about it, we emancipated ourselves—without the legalities—by running away. And the legalities weren't necessary because, as far as we know, they never once looked for us. From then on, we hustled. Both of us worked underage from that point on to care for ourselves. So, I really can't answer your question on what type of home I grew up in because we never really had one." His eyes soften substantially as I glance back at the front door. "I think that's enough for now. We're officially late."

"Absolutely not," he says.

I can't help the nervous flash of my teeth. "You really are a bit demanding tonight."

"I don't give a fuck. Tell me, Jane," he says. "Where did you go when you left?"

My shoulders slump as he refuses to release me from the

conversation. "We slept on the street for a few weeks until some of our friends stumbled upon us. One of them helped us by stowing us away in an old labor house on his family's apple farm. That's when Charlie and Barrett met, or I should say *collided*," I grin, "and that was all they wrote for her. But she fought it for years before she gave in. She wasn't too keen on men back then and *still isn't*, poor Barrett," I joke. "Anyway, when she turned eighteen a few months later and could legally rent an apartment, we learned we hadn't quite escaped our parents. Through the application process, we discovered they'd used our social security numbers and had already ruined our credit."

Lucian's eyes flare, as do his nostrils. "Isn't that fucking illegal?"

"I mean, yeah. But sadly, it's done all the time by dead-beat parents."

He grabs my hand. "How did you manage after?"

"We hustled. We worked twice as hard and managed to find some good people to rent from. It took us years to pay off debts we didn't owe, but we did. We both graduated. After I got my diploma, Charlie finally gave in to how she felt about Barrett and got pregnant with Elijah shortly after. So, Triple Falls became Charlie's permanent home, which turned into a really good thing. Barrett is crazy for her, and he has the greatest family."

"And you?"

"I left Triple Falls after my first few years of community college and transferred to Boston when I got accepted. I wanted out of North Carolina and Triple Falls—at least for a while. I thought about going back home after graduating, but Charlie was practically married by then. I loved it there, so I stayed. I got my master's, and after clocking enough operating hours, I earned my way to your operating table. That's pretty much the sum of it."

"That's far from the sum of it," Lucian replies, his tone calling bullshit.

"True. There was a hell of a lot of hurdles in between before I put on my first pair of surgical gloves, but I'll spare you those details."

"But you weren't spared, Jane," he utters, his hand now firmly wrapped around mine.

"No, I wasn't, but apparently neither were you," I say, nodding towards the house. "So, let's—shit," my phone lights up, thwarting my attempt to get us toward the door, and I glance over to Lucian. "Speaking of family, Charlie's trying to FaceTime so I can see Elijah before he goes to bed. Is it okay if I take this?"

"Of course," he says, opening the car door, "I'll give you some privacy."

"No," I stop him by pulling the hand he's trying to release. "I want my family to meet my new best friend."

"All right," he agrees, lips lifting slightly as I slide the phone to answer. Elijah appears and immediately starts talking. "Hey, Auntie Jane! We made cookies without you. I miss you."

"Hey, little buddy," I say, voice shaking due to my admissions to Lucian and the truth of how far we've come. The consolation of the hell we went through stares back at me as I rest in the fact that Elijah will never go without like Charlie and I did. I feel Lucian's eyes on me due to the slight rattle in my voice. "Miss you, too. You ready for Santa?"

"Yep, Daddy's going to chop the carrots for Rudolph."

"Sounds good," I say as his eyes dart to Lucian, and he pipes up. "Who are you?"

"Rude," I scold through a laugh. "Elijah, this is my friend, Lucian. Lucian, this is my nephew."

"Ah, Elijah, I'm pleased to make your acquaintance finally. Your aunt has told me much about you, and I do hope you're sneaking a cookie in for yourself."

"You talk funny," he chirps, and Lucian and I both chuckle.

"He's British," I tell him. "And mind your manners because *you talk funny* to him, too."

"What's British?"

"Meaning from Britain, which is England, and clearly we need to work on your geography a bit," I say, scanning his face. "You know, you're starting to look more and more like your daddy every day, buddy."

"Which means he's only getting better looking!" Barrett calls from close by. "Merry Christmas, little sister!"

"Merry Christmas," I holler back. "Love you!"

"You too!" he shouts.

"Auntie Jane," Elijah groans, "you're talking to *me*, not Daddy."

"Someone is cranky," I say. "And you know I love you most, little buddy, but I don't want to keep you from your cookies. Make sure you get tucked in early tonight so Santa can drop off the goods."

"Yes, ma'am."

"I'm sorry I won't be there in the morning. Will you save me a Christmas hug?"

"There's no such thing," he says, "you're making that up."

"There *so is* such a thing. Christmas hugs are much longer than normal hugs. Ask your mama."

"Momma says you used to play the butt race game."

Lucian quirks a brow as I burst into laughter. "When we were little, yeah."

"She played it with me last night, and it's dumb," he informs me.

"Hey, not nice, and we were bored and had to use our imaginations because we didn't have fancy toys like you."

"All right, little man," Charlie chimes in, "tell Auntie Merry Christmas and go wash up for lunch."

Elijah's face fills the screen again. "Merry Christmas, Auntie Jane. I love you."

"Love you too, my heart." Lucian squeezes my hand, clearly hearing the ache in my voice. "I'll call you tomorrow so you can show me what Santa brought."

"K. Merry Christmas Lusen."

"It's Lucian," I correct him.

"Gah, that's what I said," Elijah groans.

Charlie appears on screen, scorning him. "That smart tongue is going to be tasting soap for lunch if you keep this 'tude up, punk." Charlie eyes me, shaking her head. "I don't know exactly when it happened, but it seems we're getting into our smart-ass phase. God help us all."

"I can't believe you remembered the butt game," I muse.

"Desperate times, he wouldn't go to sleep last night, so I tried to tire him out." Charlie's attention darts to Lucian when she finally notices him on screen, and her eyes bulge slightly. "Hey, Lucian, it's nice to finally put a face with a name."

"Nice to meet you as well, Charlie," he says, seeming amused by our exchange.

"Where are you two?" She asks. "You both look nice."

"We're just about to have dinner with my family," Lucian relays, "which should be an utter disaster."

His candor surprises me as Charlie grins before firing back. "I get that. Our family was a nightmare, too. That's why we evicted most of them."

"Jane just relayed as much, and I must say I admire you both for it."

I glance over at him as the sentiment hits deep. "Well... thanks," she says, just as taken aback. "And do yourself a favor, Doc, and make sure Jane doesn't drink more than one."

"I'll take that under advisement. I've already seen her on champagne, but the odds may be in our favor tonight because at least she's wearing knickers."

Barrett laughs somewhere in the background, and Charlie tosses her head back, doing the same as I narrow my eyes at Lucian.

"You shit," I grumble.

"Ha, little sis," Charlie eggs him on, "he's busting your balls already. Love it."

Lucian grins at me as I turn to Charlie. "Don't let his gentleman aura fool you. He's got a little devil inside him."

"Says the kettle," Lucian claps back without missing a beat.

"Uh huh," Charlie says, her eyes darting between us where we're crowded on screen. "I see a storm brewing."

"Well, that's because it's supposed to *snow*," I grit out in an attempt to stop Charlie's sniffing, which she's making too damned obvious. A second later, an arm wraps around Charlie's throat from behind, where she sits perched on her couch.

"Son," Charlie wheezes, "I need my windpipe to breathe."

Lucian and I laugh as Elijah jumps on her back, and Charlie grumbles.

"Whoever thought of Christmas Eve cookies obviously didn't have kids," Charlie groans as Elijah continues to pounce on her. "Thanks for suggesting he sneak a cookie, Lucian. You've probably cost me a few more hours of sanity."

"Only fair, Charlie," Lucian interjects. "I myself lost sleep the night you decided to talk *girth*."

Charlie bursts into laughter as I gawk at Lucian and bulge my eyes, "little ears."

Lucian and Charlie share a grin, and she speaks up. "Well, you two have fun. I'm going to go wrestle this little guy into eating something other than chicken tenders. Merry Christmas."

"Merry Christmas," we say collectively as I take a candid screenshot of the four of us, all smiling and looking in different directions before I end the call.

Lucian studies the picture contemplatively before turning to me. "So that's the family you chose."

"Yeah, and they're all I need," I tell him honestly. "Quality over quantity, you know?"

His eyes shine with appreciation as he looks over to me. "I meant what I said, I respect you both immensely for what you've endured and accomplished, and I want the rest of those details, along with those of the butt race game?" He grins before glancing back at the house, his expression dampening. "Shall we get this over with?"

I nod. "Let's do it."

"Shall I warn you again?" He asks, his concern seeming for *me*.

"No, but know I've got your back," I squeeze and release his hand. "And whatever happens in there, you've got this—"

"Even if I don't," he finishes, having momentarily adopted my motto as we exit the car.

"Exactly," I beam at him over the top of the car. Feeling optimistic, I grab the basket from the back seat before we head toward the front doors. How bad could this possibly be?

# TWENTY-TWO

## JANE

**M**ere seconds on the other side of the front door, a dread-filled premonition floods me with the answer.

Bad.

Really bad.

Sweat starts to gather at my back and temple as our coats are taken by one of the house staff who greets us formally, rather than warmly, before we're guided from a massive foyer into a great room.

Taking in what I can over the height of the gift basket I refused to allow Lucian to relieve me of, I'm quickly swept up in the enormity of what was referred to as a 'sitting room.' The tall ceilings alone soak up seconds of my attention, along with the massive windows and rich, luxurious draperies framing them.

The focal point is a colossal woodburning hearth currently housing a roaring fire. The mantle above is made of thick, intricately carved wood smothered in real garland and accented with oversized ornaments, along with the crystal twin nutcrackers I saw at Harrods days ago.

Rich, expensive furniture is spread throughout the room, and towering in one corner is the most beautifully decorated Christmas tree I've ever laid eyes on. All of this is taken in within the time it takes for Lucian and me to reach the two men sitting in wait next to the fire. They are both in high wingback chairs, holding crystal tumblers housing fingers worth of what I know is steps above top-shelf booze.

Not a breath later, I'm standing in front of a wall of Aston men. Men who stood as we approached, my view of them disturbed by the obnoxiously large basket I regret purchasing as Lucian greets his father and brother—formally and without affection—before making introductions.

"Jane, this is my father, William Aston the third. Jane is my colleague and works at St. James as a surgical nurse."

William is slightly older than I thought he'd be. My guestimate is somewhere in his late sixties. Though he's handsome enough for a man his age, it's his eyes, which are shrewd and detached—the same color as Lucian's—that mercilessly siege me.

There's not a trace of that golden warmth Lucian's capable of in them as they sweep me in blatant disapproval—I decide to avoid them as much as possible tonight before he can ruin the color for me.

"A pleasure to meet you, Jane," William clips out dryly, making it evident it's anything but. His return stare is equivalent to one of a man who sees a mangy mutt, who, at any minute, might lift a leg and take a piss on his overpriced oriental rug.

Within the span of my introduction, I've been weighed and measured, and I'm nowhere near the length of acceptable.

Byron being next, Lucian makes the quick introduction while sweeping his brother curiously, no doubt noting the difference in appearance due to the length of time they last saw one another. "And this is my brother, Byron. Byron, this is Jane Cartwright."

Byron gives me nothing but a curt nod before barking out a commanding "Ben, Jasper!"

Though Lucian is the better looking of the two, Byron is just as startingly handsome, though his makeup is darker—his eyes navy blue and just as frigid. He scrutinizes me as though I'm the woman in Lucian's life—something I hadn't considered initially. Though Lucian just introduced us as friends, from the way I'm being regarded, the title is not at all believed.

"Ah, finally," a feminine voice sounds as we all turn to see a woman—much smaller in stature than any of us—gliding gracefully into the room. As she nears, Lucian's eyes soften as I note the similarities and differences. It's easy to place that his high cheekbones and lips were gifted by his mother. His build, hair color, and eyes passed to him from his father. "I was beginning to worry you weren't going to make it."

"Which would be a fair assumption, considering," William expels with ease. His cutting comment felt by all but going unaddressed as Lily stops short of us, eyes soaking in the sight of Lucian with relief.

"My apologies for your worry, mother," Lucian says as she shakes her head, eyes close to glistening as she lays a hand in greeting on his arm. "No need."

Perfectly put together in a form-fitting but modest black dress, hair in a sleek chignon bun, they share a brief, silent exchange before they turn to me.

"Jane, this is my mother, Lily," Lucian continues. Lily's greeting was far more sincere, though just as reserved.

"It's a pleasure to meet you, Jane."

"You as well," I say, "and this is yours, Mrs. Aston," I add, thrusting the basket toward her as her eyes bulge slightly before warming.

"Oh, this is lovely," Lily says, taking it from me with a soft, "thank you."

The damned basket takes up all of my view of her as she speaks behind it. "I'll just go sort this . . . Byron," she prompts, and he turns to her, "pour them a drink, would you?"

"Whiskey," I say before he gets a chance to ask. "Neat, please."

"Nothing for me, I'm driving," Lucian says, eyeing me, the hint of a smile simmering on his lips, putting me somewhat more at ease even as William blasts the side of my face with his appraisal.

"Thank you for having me," I call after Lily, hearing the nerves in my voice as she pauses and turns back.

"Happy to have you," her eyes drift to Lucian. "Both of you."

"Jasper! Ben!" Byron snaps, seeming irritated that his first summons went unanswered. Within seconds, the room is filled with the tell-tale pounding of little feet. They come into view in little blurs before halting to line up in front of Byron, who rests one of his hands on each of their shoulders. "These are my children, Jasper and Ben."

I immediately step forward and bend to get a good look at the two of them. "Which one of you is Ben?"

A gorgeous little boy with navy blue eyes—I now know match Lily's—who inherited Lucian's hair steps forward, pointing to himself. "I'm Ben."

"Hi, Ben, I'm Jane. Merry Christmas."

Before Ben can answer, Jasper steps forward, wanting his share of my attention. "I'm Jasper. We're twins," he boasts in his adorable British accent.

"I know," I say through a light laugh. "That's why we got *two* of everything," I glance up at Lucian. "Isn't that right, Lucian?"

Lucian nods, his eyes lighting slightly as he stares down at his nephews with evident affection. Ignoring his father and brother's prodding, icy twin stares, I pose my question to Lucian. "Want me to help load up?" I wink at him. "Unless you know anyone who wants to help unload all those presents."

"We can help, can't we, father?" Ben says as Jasper agrees, his verbiage in near-perfect synchronicity with his brother.

"Fine," Byron says, and immediately, the boys run toward the front door. Lucian drops his guard for a millisecond to allow me to see the 'thank you' in his eyes as he starts to follow the boys out of the room.

"You can't possibly expect to earn or buy their affection back with such a simplistic ploy after missing half their lives?" William snaps at Lucian's back when he's only a step away. Lucian's answering pause is almost imperceptible before he carries on after the boys, and I glance over to William to see he's openly leering at me. "Or maybe he is that simple-minded."

Jesus Christ.

Openly hostile seems to be the theme for tonight as I inhale a breath of patience and realize there's a lot more going on in the house than grieving. The feeling alone matches one of a war zone, and it's clear this battle has been going on for some time.

Knowing this is Lucian's fight, I take the high road and dart my focus to Byron.

"He wasn't sure what to get them," I tell his brother, who politely nods in reply. "So, he got 'em a lot." I wink and get absolutely no reaction in return. Lucian's statue comment rings true in that moment as I stand off with a set of them, hoping Byron hasn't forgotten my drink order.

"Dinner isn't quite ready," Lily says, rejoining us, and I damn near audibly sigh in relief. The passive-aggressive environment starts to weigh heavily on me as Lily scolds Byron.

"Son, why is Jane still without her drink?"

"Apologies, Mother," Byron says, going over to the drink cart.

A drink cart.

This one is full of decanters of every shape and color, and I bet that the cost of one of them could pay a few months of my rent.

That is further brought home as William takes his seat, and I walk a few steps over to take in the look of the tree. No less than sixteen feet in height and real—the balsam smell hits me, and I inhale deep. From top to bottom, it's lit magically to showcase every branch. Thick green velvet ribbon is draped around it and cinched with gold clasps, while an array of gold ornaments litters the rest of the strategically laden branches. And on every other hangs an ornament I recognize—a very expensive ornament I couldn't afford to buy *one* of. Perusing the branches, I realize there are no less than a dozen of them just within my line of sight. "This tree is absolutely gorgeous, Lily."

"I don't disagree," she says, stepping next to me, "I would love to say I had a hand in it, but I can't take any of the credit."

"Well, no matter who decorated it, it's a dream. I saw some of these ornaments when Lucian and I shopped at Harrods a few days ago."

"Oh?" she says, "I haven't been there in years. My decorator typically makes the trip for me." She glances over at Byron and William. "If you'll excuse me again, I must check on dinner."

"No worries, I'll figure out a way to keep the boys busy," I jest. Crickets chirp at my attempt at a joke while Lily quickly darts her eyes toward her husband.

"I'll be right back," she assures as Byron stalks up, cutting my view of Lily's eye exchange with William by extending my freshly poured drink to me. His deep ocean eyes and dark hair match his mother's. Lily takes her leave as I thank Byron and take a large sip.

"Are you the older brother?" I ask.

Byron dips his chin and opens his mouth to speak but is abruptly cut off.

"If you've been shopping together," William inquires from his seat next to the fire. "Am I to assume you and Lucian have more than a working relationship?"

"Actually, no," I say, walking toward where William sits as Byron rounds the couch and rejoins him. Their posture is so ramrod straight that it looks painful.

"We're friends. We have a lot of downtime before the surgery, so Lucian's been kind enough to show me around."

"What surgery?" Byron asks, his eyes drilling mine unforgivingly. Jesus.

Sending up a quick prayer for Lucian's fast return, I'm thankful when it's answered, and he walks in, balancing a ridiculous number of presents stacked to the high heavens in his arms. Sweat dots his brow as he eagerly searches my person for any sign of harm, and I give him a wink in response. Meeting him at the tree, I unload them as quickly as I can, unable to help my light laugh as I catch the drop of sweat gliding down his temple.

"Couldn't make more than one trip?"

"I wouldn't dare do that to you," he utters low, a small smile simmering on his lips.

"I'm fine, Doc," I whisper.

"Report back," he utters warily before elevating his voice. "Byron, I told Ben and Jasper they could open a gift before tomorrow with your permission, of course. Jane and I found one in particular we feel they'll enjoy."

"Fine by me," Byron says without any emotion as Lucian's eyes light slightly, and I grin, our thoughts the same.

Images of last night flit in and are in stark contrast with the feel of the room now. All I want to do is sweep him away from here and back into our happy place. A place where he feels somewhat comfortable to act like himself or to seek in finding out who he is more easily. Which is a far cry from the reserved man he is now, who's taking great care to contemplate every single word he utters and seems terrified to leave me alone too long with his own flesh and blood.

Ben and Jasper come stumbling in, both of them close to losing their grip on the strategically stacked presents in their arms as Lucian and I break an eye lock I didn't realize we were engaged in.

"Father Christmas!" Jasper shouts, using the term as more of a swear word. I laugh, and Lucian chuckles as we relieve him of the packages. Ben stumbles blindly toward Lucian as he quickly unburdens him as well. Once unloaded, both boys stand back and gawk at the pile of presents.

"Christ, Lucian," Byron speaks first. "Don't you think this is a bit over the top?"

"You bought all of this *for us,* Uncle?" Jasper asks.

"I owe you three Christmases, do I not?" Lucian replies, ignoring his brother's comment.

"Pathetic," William snaps, and none of us are spared as I dart my gaze to Lucian, who again ignores him and bends, gripping a box in question. "Is this the one then, Jane?"

"Yes," I nod, confirming it's one of the two that holds the costume before grabbing the other and looking over to Byron. "It was me. I'm to blame for putting a dent in his credit card limit," I joke.

"Well, that's no real surprise, is it?" William sounds up, tilting his rocks glass and pretending to inspect the contents.

"Groundless, Father," Lucian counters in my defense, as if this is a typical, natural exchange between them.

*What. In. The. Fuck?*

The bastard Lucian introduced as his father just insinuated—no, flat out accused me of being after Lucian's money, and the lingering look he gives me just after lets me know as much.

*Easy, Jane.*

Ignoring William for a second time, I grab my drink and drain it as Jasper and Ben start to animate with excitement.

"Right, Byron, where's your childminder?" William snaps, and instantly, I know his intent. He's going to try and cut this reunion short.

Lucian snaps his attention to his father before staring back at his nephews. It's in his gaze that I see his want to connect along with his observation of how they've grown. It strikes me then that I can read him so much better now. His subtle tells, the intent behind each of his lingering looks.

From the look and feel of this house—along with his recollection to me that night in Oxford—it seems like Lucian's been deprived his whole life of giving and receiving affection. It's becoming even more apparent with the way he leaned into my touch last night—like he'd been starving for it. Especially now, as he hesitates and rattles with indecision on how to interact with his nephews.

"What is it?" Jasper asks, pulling off the last of the wrapping paper and eyeing the box.

Ben's smile grows as his eyes light. "It's a costume."

Jasper's expression shifts to match his brothers. "Can we try these on, Father?"

"I see no need to change so close to dinner," Byron says in quick refusal.

"Actually," I chime in, thankful for the whiskey starting to warm me, "these were designed to wear over clothes and are a cinch to get on." Partial lie, at least for adults. "If you'll let me, I can help them."

Byron stares over at me as Lucian speaks up in inquiry, answering a budding question of my own about their mother's whereabouts.

"Where is Hannah, Byron? Is she coming along?"

The air thickens as William scoffs, as though he's been waiting for this, as Byron replies. "I'm assuming she's spending tonight with her boyfriend, seeing as how we divorced *four months* ago."

I mutter a low "shit," which is evident in Lucian's expression as he looks over to his brother. "I'm sorry, I didn't realize—"

"And how would you?" Byron bites out bitterly. "Seeing as how we haven't spoken in nearly a year, *brother*."

The use of brother might as well be a bullet, and I see it penetrate as it slams into Lucian.

"Criminal," William taunts. "I suppose your brother has been busy . . . *shopping*," he chastises, eyes cutting toward me, and Lucian visibly stiffens as I imagine clawing them out to spare us all.

Inhaling a breath of patience, I rip my eyes from William's affronting ones and dart them to Byron, who notices my gaze and holds it with just as much resentment. It's safe to assume at this point that both collectively believe I'm part of the reason Lucian remains in Boston. They have no reason to think otherwise yet, which has just made me Aston enemy number one. It's also clear William doesn't like having any one of his family members an inch on either side of his thumb—just firmly under it.

Though I know their presumptions will eventually be cleared up, I recognize it won't change anything about how horrible this dynamic is.

Nothing at all about this situation feels right or in any way fixable. Even with the giggling boys feet away, there's not an ounce of warmth to be found in this house despite the roaring fire—which currently blazes—highlighting the man whose horns are becoming more visible by the second.

And from the way we're being regarded, it's as if Lucian's only been invited to be ambushed. Absolutely no one is acting otherwise, aside from Lily, whose absence is becoming painful.

"What's this surgery?" William prompts, all too eager to dig into Lucian again, though I'm unsure of his motive for shifting the conversation in this direction.

"I'm sure you've read it in the Oxford updates," Lucian replies without a hint of emotion in his tone.

"I'm not aware of it," Byron says.

"Father, may we try our costumes?" Jasper sounds up, nudging his brother and eyeing me with a smile. That's all it takes for me to become smitten. "Jane said we can—"

Byron cuts his hand through the air, stopping them short with a curt, "Fine."

I press my lips together, now aware of why Lucian hates it, but I can't help but think it might be an inherited movement from the head of the household.

Lucian, distracted by his brother's news, rounds the couch and takes the seat closest to Byron before speaking. "I am sorry, truly, to hear about Hannah. I liked her so much for you."

"Yes, well, she rather preferred her free time with her trainer," Byron says before sipping his drink.

"I see," Lucian says, his tone somber. "I wish you would have rung me."

"I don't see how that would have made any difference," Byron sighs as Lucian gives a faint dip of his chin as if he deserves to be dismissed.

"May I?" I ask, holding up my empty drink to William, who all but rolls his eyes at me with a nod.

As an adult, I've never felt so uncomfortable or unwanted in a room in my life, and I give enemas.

"Had it been going on long?" Lucian asks, his eyes still on his brother.

"Not a topic that should be discussed in front of young minds," William snaps, his scolding appearing to be for us all.

I sink in my skin as Ben and Jasper chat me up, their spirits seemingly high as I unpack their costumes and attach their battery packs. Once they're off and running, squealing in delight, I'm relieved when they exit the room, if only to escape the horrific surroundings. Making a beeline for the drink cart—knowing I shouldn't drink much but convinced it's the only way I'm making it through however long we're stuck in this purgatory—I watch on. As I do, it's like watching a tennis match, the ball itself battering as it flies back and forth, mostly served from William to each of his sons. In observing the grueling exchange, I feel like an unwanted fly on the wall in a den full of vipers—or rather, one viper, as it toys with its victims, with Lily still nowhere to be seen. And good on her for it.

It's when she finally summons us to the table for dinner that I feel any sort of relief—at least in the sense that this night is progressing and there will be an eventual end to it. My face is flushed, and sweat slides down my back due to the liquor I'm numbing with—combined with the heat coming from the roaring bonfire, which seems to be hosted by the devil himself.

As we file into the dining room—Lucian's and my posture matching someone walking death row—I glance over to give him a reassuring 'hang in there' and 'we've still got this' look, to which he acknowledges with a faint dip of his chin. Though, I'm pretty sure by the way William Aston is studying the two of us right now, whatever *we've got*, he's going to do his damndest to make sure we don't leave with it.

# TWENTY-THREE

## LUCIAN

I was right to leave.

Within minutes of crossing the threshold of my childhood home, I was made aware of exactly why I practically fled London. It cements in further as the minutes pass that it wasn't just my inability to freely grieve over Alexander's passing—I just couldn't see it clearly through the pain.

Fully sober to that truth now, I realize that in my absence, I haven't missed William Aston.

Not in the least.

No fond memories of him ever stirred during my hiatus, causing not one second of discomfort or longing to regain or be in his presence. A truth I've known for far longer than I've admitted to myself.

I lost absolutely *nothing* when I cut him out of my life, and in return, I gained a freedom that threatened to evade me the minute I stepped back into the place I've only ever identified as my own personal hell.

Jasper and Ben's collective giggles interrupt my thoughts as Jane entertains them once again, mimicking father's absurd mannerisms whilst his attention is safely elsewhere. This time, she over-exaggeratedly dabs her mouth with her napkin before wobbling her head and mock speaks while plucking at a nonexistent piece of lint from her sweater, nose melodramatically lifted. She's executing her impersonation so effortlessly that I've caught Byron's lips quirking a time or two.

By my count, she's nearly four drinks in and, by my guess, feeling little pain at this point. I would be more concerned if she hadn't eaten, but she's cleared her plate. No doubt, she was doing so in an attempt to keep her mouth occupied to withhold her temper. I harbor no grudge for her numbing herself to this horrific fucking nightmare disguised as a family dinner, and I wish I had the ability to do so myself.

"Jasper, Ben," Father snaps, faintly catching onto Jane's game. Both boys' eyes widen as Ben speaks up. "Yes, Grandfather?"

"You're both excused," he says, not so much as looking their way, his stare carving into Jane.

"Bid farewell to your uncle and Jane before you go," Byron adds, eyeing me.

Both scramble from the table, but Ben stops short just in front of Jane, his compliment heard by everyone dining. "I hope you come back tomorrow, Jane. Happy Christmas!"

"Happy Christmas, buddy. I don't think we'll make it back tomorrow, but I hope to see you again sometime."

"Happy Christmas," Jasper calls to her as he rushes and throws his arms around me, causing me to push back in my chair slightly.

"Etiquette, Jasper," Father snaps as I embrace Jasper, who pulls away smiling, ignoring Father's scolding whilst reminding me of a younger Alexander.

"I hope to see you again, Uncle. Happy Christmas!"

"Happy Christmas, Jasper," I reply, "I'll be ringing you soon."

"Okay," he says as Ben collides with me next, their easily given parting affections taking me slightly aback. In return, I embrace Ben while connecting gazes with Jane, whose eyes are alight with sentiment.

After their collective goodbyes, they quickly clamber out of the room. I catch sight of them just outside the door of Father's study as they scramble to put their T-rex costumes back on.

Lifting my chin to Jane, she follows my prompt, catching sight of them. The most perfect of smiles graces her lips before staff blocks our view, removing some of our plates. The fact that I'm unfamiliar with my father's current staff is no surprise because he goes through them like water due to his temperament, or rather, his daily antics.

Tense silence fills the air in the boy's absence as Jane picks up her drink and drains more from it before speaking. "Dinner was delicious. Thank you, Lily."

"You are most welcome," Mum replies, her eyes soft on Jane.

She likes her, and Byron seems to be coming around somewhat as well, engaging in conversation with her more.

My stare fixes on the man at the end of the table opposite of me as his gaze darts between Byron and Jane—no doubt plotting—and my anger once again begins to build. I'm confident that while I'm trying to come up with appropriate words to explain my actions—and offer an apology—he's trying to decipher just how far he'll go to ruin the rest of the evening for everyone remaining at this table.

This only brings me to the same conclusion. William Aston is still the same insufferable bastard he's always been, and he's been just as acerbic toward Jane as I suspected he would be, which fuels my mounting fury.

My hatred for him only grows as I ultimately decide an apology to him would be worthless.

Any apology I could muster for him specifically would be an utter waste of breath and effort he doesn't deserve. As would any attempt at resuming a relationship I now know was always one-sided in the familial sense, as well as a relationship I have no desire to resume.

Coming here tonight was a mistake, and from how it's been tearing Jane apart to see this play out, it hasn't been worth a single minute of her discomfort.

Twice in the last hour, I watched her eyes water due to his scathing remarks for me, though she did her best to shield it. More than once, her eyes have beseeched mine to defend myself from the monster who fathered me.

In fact, during dinner, when William struck hardest, she searched every face at the table—Byron's especially—only to be disappointed when no one came to my defense. It was of no surprise to me.

It's how we survive in this godforsaken fucking house. How we've survived him for all these years. We simply let him have his say until he's satisfied, believes he's done lasting damage, and finally leaves us be.

But I stopped allowing him to inflict any significant damage when I left England—again, something I realize in hindsight. This realization transitions into a firm decision—I will not invite him back into my life to pick up where he left off. To guilt me, manipulate me, to make me feel inferior only to make himself feel superior.

His treatment tonight is typical, as are our reactions to it.

For Byron, Mum, and me, this is our normal.

A bully and his victims, because that's all William Aston is and all he has ever been—a fucking bully.

The time away has clarified that, and in leaving, I got the space I needed to see the wood for the trees—to finally be able to call a spade a spade.

A bully a bully.

Who's never wrong.

Who's never sorry.

Never remorseful.

And God forbid he ever admits he made a mistake.

But he did, his most significant—having children.

Looking over to Jane now, I can't help but want to take her hand and fucking run, if only to spare her any more of this unnecessary torment.

Because of his treatment of her, my brother, and my mother, the anger brimming inside me starts to paralyze me once again. I haven't been able to defend her much due to the rage that continues to bind me to my chair—and now mutes my tongue.

*"Of course you don't. You never fight for anything, do you? Never*

*fight at all or raise your voice an octave higher than appropriate because you've never bothered."*

Gwen's words haunt me as I realize she's right.

Alexander might have brought some peace and harmony to this house, but my war with my father has always been silent on my end—resentment unspoken through no one's fault but my own.

Just like everyone else at this table, I've muzzled myself for too many fucking years and eventually allowed my own father to mute me to the point that I now voluntarily mute myself.

What a fucking coward Jane must think of me.

But if she only knew how futile fighting him is.

Rage sweeps into me as Jane's sweet voice filters in as she speaks to my mother. "He's been giving me a lot of history lessons. He's so knowledgeable. I'm lucky to have him as a tour guide."

Another plea on my behalf for my character, a wasted plea for my father to see that I'm a worthy man. All I want right now is to sweep her away and well out of the reach of William Aston.

Staring over at her, I inhale the look of her once more. I feel as if I may go blind with my need to kiss her, touch her, taste her, claim her body, and whatever else she'll allow me to access.

To confess to her that I haven't had a single thought that didn't include her since I opened my eyes this morning. More so when I wrapped my hand around my cock and groaned her name upon release. An act I repeated in the shower this afternoon after she emerged from her room looking like a living fantasy. Her attire was simple, but the mere sight of her brought me to my knees. Not only that, but it was also her efforts in spending her day to make me look a better man and much less selfish to my family and nephews.

Ironically, my thoughts are selfish now. I want to forget my reasoning for being here and take her somewhere remote and private. Somewhere I can admit all these things, preferably while thrusting every confession into her until she stops refusing our chemistry.

But what could she possibly want from a man who allows himself and his family to be degraded in such a way?

She's refused my advances for the best of reasons—namely,

because she's aware of what a fucking mess I currently am. A mess I allowed myself to become. How is that in any way desirable?

Unbearable tension continues to build beneath the surface of the light conversation as I square off with my father at the other end of the table.

My nephew's roars fuel my hatred as they filter in from the great room, and my fear sets in for their future if they continue to be subjected to this monster. Fear for the imminent loss of innocence sure to come in keeping company with the man sitting opposite me at this dinner table.

Unable to stop myself, I have the darkest thought of my life— wishing my father more swiftly to his grave, to *an early* grave.

Anything to spare Ben and Jasper from succumbing to his cruel behavior and adopting the like. To keep my mother from enduring more life with him than she's already withstood and to free Byron of the same invisible shackles he himself has been blind to all these years. Shackles I can only see clearly now—long after having freed myself from them.

Though I didn't have to leave England to liberate myself, I don't regret my path just the same.

For the whole of my life, my father has disguised his abuse under familial obligation, claiming some false sense of family in that our heritage deserves the utmost respect and boundless devotion. But ultimately, it was used as an excuse to keep us close and accountable to him, all the while remaining under his scrutiny.

Christ, how could I have been so blind?

Fury becoming rage, I tune into Mum and Jane's conversation to aid myself in the vain hope that Jane's sweet voice may coax me into a calmer state.

Jane, who has done nothing but to remind me in our time together that there are good people in this world—selfless people who will care about you without the expectation of binding devotion or submission. Who don't consider emotion a weakness but rather a strength and embrace it, showering those worthy of it freely and without reservation. Trustworthy people, and it's evident that in a mere week, I've trusted her with more than I have most close to me in the entirety of my life.

And fuck, how I want her, and it burns that I'm nowhere near a man worthy of her in my current state.

Determined to change that, to sort myself out, I mentally set a cleansing fire to all remnants of the coward who believed the liar sitting across from him for so many years. Who made me believe family is an obligation that allows authority over you to the point you lose all sense of self.

"Did Lucian clue you in on any of the *Aston* history?" Father rudely interjects *again*. "Because Aston men have a fair amount of history."

"Some," Jane replies, her tone indicative that she'd rather not engage with him.

"Allow me to give you a befitting lesson," Father drones on. "Lucian comes from a long line of influential Aston men. He has royalty in his blood."

"He told me this house belonged to a former duke," she glances over at me, holding my eyes in silent support. Intent on taking her and leaving as soon as possible, I look over briefly to my mother and brother, knowing that though my fight with my father is over, my fight for the family I *choose* has just begun.

"Yes, well, had I known Lucian had no plans to further contribute to our lineage, I might not have wasted time and money investing in his education. As of late, I find myself thankful Oxford tuition was so easily paid."

Jane's eyes flare as she tosses her napkin on her plate. My father continues, his expression sparking with unguarded satisfaction in the knowledge that he's finally gotten the best of Jane.

*Big mistake, William,* I muse, unable to help my growing smirk as I read her posture and know she's done holding her tongue and accompanying wrath.

"In case you weren't aware," Father continues, "Oxford tuition is cheap—"

"I've enjoyed my time in England," Jane interrupts him, using a tone I'm becoming familiar with—*fed up.*

I press my lips into a line to suppress my smile, having zero intention of stopping her.

"Of course, I had a lot of grandiose ideas about what London would be like through media—mostly movies—which is kind of silly, I know," she continues. Though she's hiding it well on the surface, I can feel the anger emanating from her from feet away.

"Jane," I softly call her name to relay—without words—that she doesn't have to defend me. Her eyes flit to mine, and I see the apology in them before she breaks our stare and sets her sights on my father.

It's much too late.

Indignation starts to filter into her expression as she continues to speak in an even tone. "In fact, Lucian and I had a discussion just the other day about the fabrication of what's on screen for the sake of drama versus historical facts," she continues as the paradigm starts to shift. It's felt throughout the dining room as Byron and Mum exchange looks, and I settle in.

"I admire a lot about the British and British culture," she continues, "but what seems to be portrayed quite well and so often on screen is people of your pedigree's inability to acknowledge emotions while in turmoil. This seems to be a common denominator in a lot of the stories because, as we all know, wounds have a way of festering, of making a mess of people who can't recognize them."

She shifts her narrowed eyes on Byron. "Because of that, relationships can become paralyzed in time. Opportunities are missed, and words are left unspoken. When that happens, sometimes people have no choice but to walk away . . . and when people," she divides her glare between father and Byron, "particularly the family you're supposed to be able to rely on during the worst of times, have their heads shoved so far up their asses they can't see the forest for the trees. Who could ever blame someone for hightailing it out of their company to search for better company—company having a pulse being a huge step up."

Jane looks over to me then, her expression apologetic. "I know

I couldn't and should never judge them for it because I would be wrong for that."

I gently shake my head as she holds my expression a beat longer before zeroing in on my father. Byron looks over to me, briefly stealing my attention from Jane, his brow lifted in question. In response, I stick my tongue into the corner of my cheek and quirk a brow right back at him.

*Brace yourself, brother.*

"I'm sure you probably look down on us Americans for being more vocal, more emotional, but as unhinged as we may seem at times, I'm starting to think we're a lot wiser in that respect. We try to sort ourselves out as things happen, but you," she snaps at my father, "you've taught your sons differently, haven't you? Hell, if I didn't know better, I might think you're trying to *regress* them. I realize you're probably getting up there in age, but please tell me you do realize this is the year of our lord twenty seventeen, correct? Not seventeen twenty?"

Jane digs into my father, who is now openly glaring at her, displaying his contempt. Sitting back, I cross my arms, loving that she's managed to get under his skin. Byron starts to pale, eyes darting around in fear as Jane continues her diatribe.

"I mean, I'm sure you have some woman ironing your knickers, but, outside of your manor, *sire*, times, they are a changing," she finishes as I bark a laugh.

The whole table turns to look at me as I cough into my hand. "Apologies, you were saying, Jane?"

"I'm not sure what point you're attempting to make," Father says, his glare darting between us now as freedom zings through my chest and my anger starts to dissipate. He's not worth fighting with or for. Never was.

"Sure you do," Jane hisses, "and I wouldn't worry too much about passing on traits of an Aston man, William. When I met Lucian, he imitated your stiff upper lip and mimicked your inhumane behavior. Then again, he came to his senses enough to realize his error in judgment in making sure he's nothing like you."

"How dare—"

Jane cuts her hand through the air, and it's a miraculous sight to see him get a good dose of his own medicine.

"Save it, *Billy boy*. Not one person at this table has listened to a damned word you've said all night, and as an outsider, I can see why clear as day. No one here likes or respects you enough to give a damn because, frankly, you're a horrible person, and Lily," she addresses Mum, and I stiffen in slight fear. "You are gorgeous, polite, beautiful, and an intelligent woman, so please pardon my candor in telling you no swinging dick is worth putting up with this bullshit."

It's then I know drink four was the one that did her in as Jane turns to my brother, "though I will say I got a generous peek of the family jewels. From the jaded expression you're sporting—along with your shitty disposition—it seems that, sadly, you *didn't get the shaft* in that department and want nothing more than to share in that resentment by luring your brother here."

Byron gapes at her, and I softly say her name as she refutes my interruption.

"Seriously, Byron, why? Because of some misguided familial obligation you've been brainwashed to believe outweighs decency? Or just to allow him to be berated? To hurt him? Because misery loves company? My sister would never allow anyone to speak to me that way. You're the older brother, are you not? Is it not your job to protect him? Have you *ever* protected him? And if you're going to speak up and give the excuse that you're both grown men, that's fair, but why in the hell aren't you two protecting each other? You have to know this isn't right," she shakes her head in disgust as Byron remains wordless.

Father cuts in, his face reddening. "That's quite enough."

"Well, then, I guess I won't get started," Jane says, standing and stalking toward me. "Come on, Lucian, there's no use in apologizing to people who won't accept." She looks pointedly at everyone at the table. "And until they can, maybe they shouldn't extend another dinner invitation."

"You have no right to come in here and sling accusations," Father says. "Your opinion is of absolutely no importance to this family."

"It is t-to me," I snap as Jane looks down at me, but she's too far gone to be reasoned with as she glares back over to him.

"If you call *this* a family, you've got a lot more problems than worrying about me, *Billy boy*."

Byron's eyes bulge as Mum's jaw drops.

Jane gazes down at me with tears in her eyes. "I'm so sorry I encouraged you to come. Please . . . can we please leave?"

Standing, I swallow repeatedly as my nephew's shrieks filter in from a room over. The sound tugs at my chest as panic sets in. I turn to Byron, doing my best to appeal to him.

"I want to be a part of their lives, d-desperately, and yours—but not as a part of *his* family. Please let me know if that's ever going to be a possibility. If you don't, please spare them, Byron. She's right on every count, and you know she is."

Byron drops his gaze to his plate in lieu of a reply, and my heart sinks with the knowledge that we may never bridge our gap as I address my mother. "My apologies, Mum. Please excuse us."

"Walk away, nothing unusual," Father snarks at my back, and it bounces off. Even so, I take advantage of the freedom running through my veins.

*Maybe he's not worth the fight, Lucian, but you deserve the last fucking word.*

I turn so suddenly that I have to steady Jane next to me. I see my father eyeing his tumbler as if what just transpired means absolutely nothing to him. Knowing him, it most likely doesn't.

"Look at me, you b-bastard," I snap as all heads turn my way, including my father's, and Jane squeezes my hand. "I'll cut you a cheque for the total sum of my tuition and any other fees you feel you incurred from your pathetic excuse of attempting to be a parent. Because that's all being your child has ever felt like—a fucking debt." I swallow. "Take a good look, William, because this is the last time you'll ever see me. From this moment forward, I will have nothing more to do with you."

My father glares back at me, and I take him in, knowing this will most likely be the last time I lay eyes on him and make peace with it. "That leaves you *down* two sons, so I'd advise you to be good to the one you have left."

A sob erupts from my mother, and the sound of it lands squarely in my chest as Jane keeps our hands firmly grasped until I'm at the front door.

"Go to the car. I'll collect our coats," I tell her as she carefully eyes me for cracks that aren't coming, and I nod.

Jane walks out the front door without protest as I collect what I need before following her out. Stalking toward her, she stands idly at the passenger door, rubbing her hands briskly up and down the arms of her sweater.

Opening the car's back door, I lay my jacket on the seat. I keep hold of hers, wordlessly wrapping her snugly inside it as her tear-filled eyes trail my every movement. Sliding my hands along the back of her neck, I free her hair of the jacket's confines before cradling her beautiful face.

Searching her tear-filled eyes, I seek and find the permission I need. Bending, a breath away from crushing her mouth with mine, I hear my name called at my back.

*Fuck!*

# TWENTY-FOUR

## LUCIAN

Jane's latched eyes break from mine, roaming over my shoulder as I turn to see my mother standing at the foot of the porch waiting for me. Quickly tucking Jane into the passenger seat, I feel her eyes following my every move as I reach over the console and press the ignition button to start the car and crank up the heat to warm her. Pulling back enough so we're face to face, I pull another tear away from her cheek and gently shake my head just as she goes to speak.

"Don't, Jane. I'll be right back," I murmur as I catch another tear with my thumb before indulging myself and softly pressing my lips to hers. The kiss is far too brief as I reluctantly pull away without gauging her reaction. I snap the door closed to leave her bundled inside the car.

Quickly stalking over to where my mother stands, her eyes remain focused on Jane as I reach her as she speaks. "She's nothing I would expect but absolutely suited for you, Lucian."

She flits her focus to me then, her lips lifting as she grants me a cheeky grin. "And I must admit, I'm quite fond of her frivolous tongue."

"You believe she's suited for me?"

"I do, and admittedly, I never really saw Gwen as your rightful match."

"Honestly?"

She nods. "You were already engaged when I reached that conclusion, and things were in motion by then. I didn't dislike Gwen. I knew she would make a fine wife—but for someone else. You've always possessed a more passionate side, even if you've made every attempt to hide it. Gwen doesn't possess it, so she could never recognize it. However, our dinner guest seems very attuned to it, and from what I've seen tonight, naturally draws it from you."

"Jane and I, well, we're ... not exactly ... involved in that capacity for the moment," though I don't mention I have every intention of changing that, as I glance back toward the car, "I don't dare define what we are at this point."

"Happy, it seems," she muses, a sparkle in her eyes. "Whatever relationship you have, whether it be work colleagues or friends or more, the friendship is admirable. You seem to care about one another and get on well, so try not to worry yourself over it."

Her eyes glaze over as she tightens her sweater around her. "But she was right in so many respects and was easy on me in many of them. I, too, have failed you. All three of you, and for that, I'll forever be sorry."

"You haven't, Mother. We've all been sorting ourselves since Alexander passed, but what happened in that house tonight was inevitable."

"I have failed you," her voice breaks as she shakes her head in disgust, "and you'll never convince me otherwise. I'm so sorry, Lucian."

"We haven't been boys in years," I admit. "We allowed it as men, and maybe all of us have failed each other in accepting it for so long, but it's not too late. Not for any of us."

"Fifty years," she croaks, referencing the length of her marriage. "I can't even picture another way to exist at this point."

"If you ever decide to create that picture, I'll be there for you.

Byron will, too. You have to know you are the reason we endured him, Mum."

"That's how I failed you," she whispers, eyes averted.

"I can't allow him to be a part of my life anymore. Please understand I can't and won't in any capacity, and I hope you and Byron make the same decision."

She nods solemnly, the implication of my words clear. "Alexander's loss took what remained of the man I once so fiercely loved. If he's eventually left alone to fend for himself, he'll truly have no one else to blame but himself." Her eyes catch mine. "I beg you, son, don't concern yourself with this. I will sort it."

"Is he so cruel to you?"

"Nothing I can't handle, but it's not your place to worry yourself for me," she sniffs again. "Just promise me you won't return to the States until we see each other again. I'll meet you wherever you choose. Please don't leave without saying goodbye. I couldn't bear it a second time."

"I won't, Mum, and I am sorry for my absence. I hope you do believe me and realize that your happiness matters . . . very much. I won't leave without seeing you. You have my word."

"Your word is good enough for me. Now go," she nods toward the car, "and try to enjoy your holiday." Hesitantly, she lifts her hand before palming my jaw in a rare show of affection. "I love you, Lucian. I'm incredibly proud of you and the man you've become."

"You too, Mum."

"Merry Christmas," she says, tugging her sweater around her as heavy snow begins to fall, and she makes her way back inside. Byron stands at the door, staring at me intently as she passes, and I turn and head back toward Jane without deciphering what his lingering presence means.

It's his decision now, and whatever he decides will affect me significantly. I feel that truth along with the pang in my chest as I make my way back to the car.

Once inside, I turn to Jane just as she launches herself at me, or rather, into my arms. Her body shakes in my hold, her selfless tears for me. "I'm so sorry, Lucian."

She cries quietly into my neck as I grip her just as tightly, enjoying her warmth, her scent, and the fact she's shedding tears for my sake—while hating them for the same reason.

"Is this my Christmas hug?" I jest in an attempt to lighten the emotional toll on both of us.

Her laugh tickles my throat, sending a surge of need through me. Mere minutes ago, I was so close to taking her lips and claiming her mouth. Though the urge fills me again, the moment has passed. Her emotional state takes precedence as she pulls away and searches my expression. "So, how mad are you at me?

Cupping her face, I begin to wipe the black streaks lining her cheeks. "Not in the least."

"I couldn't handle it. I thought I could, God. I thought I understood what you were trying to tell me, but that was," she shakes her head in my hands, "unbearable."

"So, you don't want to return for New Year's?" I joke as her face crumbles and her eyes again mist.

"They d-don't deserve you, Lucian. They don't, and I can't help but be a little pissed at your mother for allowing that shit, and I'm sorry if that upsets or offends you, but it's not right."

"She's aware and just sincerely apologized to me for it."

"It's a start, but she deserves it if you can't forgive her."

"All three of us fell victim to him, and not one of us has ever handled it properly. It's all three of our crosses to bear."

"I'm sorry I made things worse. I went too far."

"All your actions told me back there is how lucky I am to have befriended you. You are, by far, the best new best mate I've ever had. No one in my life has ever stood up for me the way you just did. Christ, I didn't stop you because it's as if you were speaking *everything* I was thinking and have been for years. God knows I've been maimed in that respect when I'm overly emotional and irrationally angry and did no better tonight. So, mad? No. If anything, I'm thankful you put a voice to it in a way I never could or have. But," I say, sliding my thumb down her wet cheek, "please, no more tears for me. Especially because of him. He doesn't deserve them, and I assure you, I'm fine."

"But your brother," she sniffs, "and Ben and Jasper."

I nod. "I can't lie. I worry, especially for my nephews. But I have to trust that Byron will come around, and honestly, I hope he does. I'm glad you told him what's what. I admire your ability so much to say exactly how you feel and refuse to give a fuck what anyone thinks about it."

"Yeah, well, no one gets to openly belittle me—but *me* and you just made the same decision," she grins. "Can I be proud of you for that?"

"Fine, but pathetically, I should have ended this so much sooner," I sigh. "Some Christmas I've given you. I apologize."

"I'm so glad I was there, really, and it's still salvageable," she says, pulling down the visor mirror, "and as soon as I can get myself together, we're going to turn this night around." She turns to me, a resilient smile blooming on her face. "You believe me?"

"I do," I say because it's already turning around as her tears dry and her smile emerges. Her heart has just broken *for me*, something I'm still reeling from. She cared so much that my hurt and anger became hers, and I can't, at all, ignore the meaningful stretch in my chest because of it.

"You know, as shit as that dinner was, and trust me, it's in my top three of shit dinners," she sniffs, clearing her face of any lingering black streaks, "I'm only disappointed we didn't get to wear those crown hats I've seen in the movies."

"Ah, you were hoping for a cracker."

"A *cracker*, are you kidding?" She pushes the mirror up and turns to me, eyes wide. "That spread was magnificent, even if the company sucked. I'm *stuffed*."

I throw my head back and laugh.

"What?" She narrows her eyes, "what am I missing?"

"Nothing I can't remedy," I say, pulling my jacket from the back seat and placing it on her lap.

"This again?" she says, regarding me suspiciously. "Lucian, I'm not cold."

I laugh again and shake my head, "Unroll it, Nurse Cartwright."

She unrolls the top of the jacket and gasps, lifting the gold bauble eye level, her expression matching the one she wore when she first saw it. "You got me the love ball?"

"Not exactly, more so *stole* you a love ball," I admit.

"You totally just stole from your family for me," she boasts.

"Well worth it because by them, it will go unnoticed. For you, it will be treasured."

"Damn right it will," she says, looking over at me and whispering a soft, heartfelt "thank you, Doc."

I nod, and it's all I can do to keep from taking her mouth, but my fear now is that I won't be able to stop. I want as much distance between Jane and the ghost I've just placed forever in my Christmas past as possible—never to allow her anywhere near him again.

Priority shifted momentarily, I take one last look at the house and put the car into gear set to drive away from it for the last time.

Jane puts her hand over mine on the gear shift, knowing exactly what my thoughts are and what this means as she leans forward in her seat, tracking the rapidly accumulating snowfall.

"I'm taking this as a good sign. Tomorrow everything will be covered white and new. So," she says, fastening herself in. "Any ideas on how we turn the rest of this night around?"

"A few. Firstly, I'm going to find you a proper cracker, and then I'm going to catch up with you in seeking and consuming a proper fucking drink."

"Ohhhh," her ice-blue eyes light. "Are we getting drunk tonight, Doc?"

"I should think we deserve it after all we've endured."

"Hell, yes!" She pumps a fist into the air. "Though I should warn you, I think your dad pissed me off so much I burned the alcohol off as I drank it, and my tolerance might have shifted from lightweight to Godspeed."

"I'll take that under account," I say, "just please don't make me regret this."

I turn on the headlights as she flashes me her cheekiest grin. "No promises."

Just after finding Jane a proper cracker—which was hard to locate as most of the shops were closed—I presented her with the shiny, plaid, treat-shaped package. She takes it, slightly confused, as I instruct her on how to open it to get the proper sound, hence its namesake.

"Ahh, a cracker. Got it, duh," she says sheepishly as I dump the contents into my hand and hold it over the console for her to examine them. She lifts the tiny rolled scroll of paper first.

"It's a joke and totally up our alley," she exclaims before clearing her throat. "Question: What do you get if you eat Christmas decorations?"

"No idea," I reply, appreciating every bit of animation in her expression.

"Tinselitis!" she delivers with a giggle before plucking the small box from my palm. "A dice ring," she says, immediately sliding the plastic ring onto her ring finger.

"So that's what a cracker is, huh?"

"Yes, but you're forgetting the most important part," I say, urging her to examine the open cracker further. She grabs a package and fingers it before pulling the shiny gold paper from it and unfolding it.

"It's my crown!" She hollers, donning herself instantly before insisting I crack my own and do the same. An order I don't protest, knowing I would probably do just about anything to see her smile tonight.

Once christened with our shiny paper hats, I'm drawn into another appreciation-filled Christmas hug. Embracing her back, this time, I take full advantage of the feel of her while inhaling her clean, citrus scent.

Our hug is cut slightly short when Jane spots some traffic outside of the windshield of the bustling Richmond town center.

"Lucian, look," she nudges me with her shoulder, forcing me back as I follow her line of sight to a group of couples rounding the corner.

"I bet you anything if we follow them, we'll probably find our proper drinks."

Exiting the car, we trace their steps to find a marquee sign just around the corner that reads INCOGNITO.

"Well, if this isn't a sign for you, Dr. McProper, I don't know what is," she jests as I scrutinize the sign and surroundings. Seeing no other indication of what the establishment is, we open the thick wooden door behind it.

Much to our surprise and delight, the pub just inside is the perfect place for us to congregate and indulge.

After tipping a hostess handsomely to garner a table—which she insisted at first didn't exist due to the pub being fully booked—she led us to a corner booth inside the main bar.

"You totally just gave her your "come fuck me" smolder eyes to get this table," Jane says as I peel off her coat and she takes her seat.

"I so did not," I deny, shouldering off my own.

"Oh please, you just totally abused your smolder," she accuses.

"And you would know what my 'come fuck me' eyes look like because?"

She knows damn well what the look is because I gave it to her last night—right before she turned me down—but I don't allude to it as her lips part and then close. Jacket in hand, I bend, catching her lowering eyes. She's recalling one of a hundred scenarios I've dreamt up, which easily elicits such a look as I slowly take my seat, and she gapes at me. "You shit, you are *totally aware* of your *smolder.*"

"Which you're clearly immune to," I grumble, going unheard as I soak in the bar's atmosphere just as she does.

"This place is insanely cool," Jane says as we look around. "Our luck is changing by the minute."

"I couldn't agree more," I say, tamping my fist to her offered one in a bump before glancing around and soaking in the atmosphere.

The pub itself seems a novelty, with a speak-easy vibe. The furniture is both plush and posh, with dark leather and brass. The walls are lined with framed photographs of tuxedo-clad animals wearing top hats and adorned with other various laugh-inducing knickknacks.

The tavern being one of a kind in that it has an old-world feel and charm. The main bar where we sit has a carnival-type atmosphere. A large, antique Ferris Wheel sits to the side of the bar, spinning continually to add to the ambiance.

Even more impressive is the drink selection, in which each cocktail isn't simply delivered but is *themed* and *presented* theatrically by the staff. Staff, who are dressed to the nines, most of whom wear masquerade masks that only add to the mischievous atmosphere.

We're even more taken when, minutes later, Jane grows giddy as her drink is presented. Titled "Royal Charlie Foxtrot," the tumbler is housed in a hot pink, outdated iron scuba mask. The interior of the mask is lit in light ocean blue and highly decorated in a heavily detailed sea life theme.

"This is too cool!" Jane exclaims, opening the mask's door to grab the heavily garnished rocks glass from the perch on which it sits, coconut-scented smoke billowing out of the scuba mask and filtering around our table.

Just after the masked waitress explains the contents of the drink, Jane holds it out to me for taste. We exchange smiles before I take a healthy sip, refuting the 'stick in the mud' title she branded me when I initially tried to order a scotch. Since then, I've ordered several specialty cocktails out of curiosity just to see the presentation. The last having been delivered in a century-past Parisian-looking hot air balloon, in which the basket dispensed the cocktail into my tumbler.

The pub is impressive and immersive on every level, so clearly thought out in detail. A true hidden gem amongst the everyday shopping center and delight to all those surrounding us, lifting the spirits of all who enter, Jane's and my own included with each specialty drink delivered.

It's when I sit alone for an extended time—after Jane excuses herself for the restroom—that I start to worry we might have over-indulged as suspicions rise that she might be getting sick.

Buzz thrumming through me, and knowing I'm half pissed al-ready, I shoot out an apologetic text to Mike—due to it being a hol-iday—and request he meets us here at the pub to see us safely back to our hotel.

As another minute ticks past without a trace of Jane, I'm just about to push back in my seat to seek her out when her voice filters out through the pub's speakers as the entirety of the bar's light dim close to a full blackout. "Paging Doctor Aston . . . Dr. Aston, if you're in need of a nurse, now would be the time to raise your hand, you sexy prick."

Shouts and whistles ring out around me as I palm my face briefly in one hand before slowly raising the other.

"Right here," a bloke a table over says as the cheers grow louder, and Jane's giggle is cut off as another voice rings through the speak-ers, one I recognize as the introduction of a song I'm familiar with.

"*'Teen drinking is very bad . . . Yo, I got a fake ID, though.'*"

"Christ," I mutter as the beat drops and the opening of J-Kwon's "Tipsy" fills the bar, the patrons cheering at the music's arrival as the bass kicks in, rattling the walls and filling the air.

Lowering my hands, I tap my fingers on the table to the beat just as a dozen or more sparklers ignite behind the bar and start to fizzle.

"What have you done now, Cheeky?" I mutter in slight dread and anticipation as the faces behind the bar start to come into view with the sparkling light. I manage to catch the devilish smile of one mischievous nurse whose crown is now fitted around her newly-ac-quired top hat.

Just as they round the bar, the sparklers split as the staff parts, half of them moving throughout the tables to deliver shots while several head in my direction. Jane comes into view as she makes a beeline for the table—for me. With her sweater now tied around her waist, she wears nothing but a black camisole shirt that fits her snuggly, showcasing the ample curves of her breasts, which I trail down to her swaying hips as she points her sparkler at me.

Pushing off with one foot, I slide my chair back, pointing both my fingers toward my lap in time with the beat—an invitation to let her know exactly where her destination is as she sashays toward me, looking like the perfect mix of heaven and sin.

This woman, this fucking woman.

Images of the ways I want to devour her perfect pussy, of stretching her mouth, of making her moan begin to take shape as she taunts me from feet away. Her curves are highlighted with every purposeful and skilled movement of her hips, which she works in flawless synchronization with the music.

Fisting a sparkler in one hand, she holds the neck of a liquor bottle in the other and stops briefly, pointing it toward me as if leading a charge.

Giving her my best come fuck me eyes, she reads my expression easily, her lips curving up as I impatiently wait for her to take her designated seat. All the while knowing that I'm going to take full advantage of the permission she's wordlessly giving me as soon as we have some privacy.

I've never lusted so much for a woman in my fucking life, and I vow in this chair, in this pub, I'll make sure she's just as needy for me. That I'll have her lips begging, her pussy weeping and aching, I'll have tears and pleas and both punish and pleasure her for stirring this lust within me to the point I'm going insane. Only then will I give into my need for her.

Smile growing with plans of punishing her for extending my wait, I take in every detail, every purposeful and seductive move of her hips until she's within reach. As she takes the step to close the last of the distance, I snatch her onto my ready lap, situating her sideways to accommodate her laden hands. Grinding her arse onto my rapidly swelling cock, she laughs when I practically snarl before burying her head into my neck.

"You're playing a very dangerous game," I inform her as her eyes lift to mine."

"I like dangerous games."

"You are so in for it, Nurse Cartwright," I growl into her ear.

"Promise?" She whispers as one of the waitresses tables two empty shot glasses before giving us a parting grin. But not before relieving Jane of her sparkler while leaving the bottle of booze secured tightly in her other hand.

Eyes hungrily roaming, I sweep the curve and contour of her chest and slowly peruse her milky, flawless skin. I then trail my way up to lock my thirsty gaze to hers as I wet my lower lip, and her eyes follow. "I should have known I was in for *something* when you disappeared."

"I figured you deserved a special kind of bottle service tonight," she rasps heatedly. "Because even though technically it's not your birthday, it is kind of your *re-birth* day, isn't it?" Her voice is pure sex as it reaches me. "That calls for celebration. You're free now, Lucian. Your life is completely your own, and you did that. Whatever life you truly want is yours for the taking without anyone else's expectations weighing you down."

She palms the bottle, holding the spouted tip with her finger and pressing it to the side of the shot glass.

"So, here's to you, my friend," she says before she unleashes the alcohol, raising the bottle in a long pour, filling the glass to the brim before quickly moving it to the other, skillfully twisting her wrist to cut off her pour before tabling the bottle. She flits her focus solely on me as I eye the bottle and quirk a brow at her. "Absinthe?"

"Hmmm, well, it's on the list of things at this table I want to taste," she states, her implication clear.

"Is that so?"

"Tis so . . . which brings me to my proposal. Tonight, I say we go *all in*." Her fingers curl around my neck before she starts to stroke the hair at the nape in a seductive sweep.

Fuck. Me.

Fisting my hands in order to restrain myself, my cock rouses further to life at the suggestion of her posture. Fuck, how I want her, and her next words sound like music in my ears.

"I'm proposing a temporary amendment to our deal. One night only, for the sake of the continuation of our awesome new friendship and to keep things from getting messy."

She palms my chest, my heart thundering beneath it as she continuously strokes the back of my neck with the other—it's all I can do to keep from touching her. But before I do, we have to get some things straight, and like every other fucking time tonight when it comes to getting intimate with her, the timing is off. I can't have the conversation I need with her in a noisy bar surrounded by so many watchful eyes.

*Patience Lucian.*

"I'm listening," I say, cock straining against my fly. Her ample chest heaves, and the temptation to capture her plump skin—which is just within reach, along with my need to mark it—increases tenfold.

"Just for tonight, we live in the moment. Without adulting, without a worry about anything other than the here and now, no consequences." Her insane blue eyes bore into mine, "we just go wherever it leads and do what we want." She pulls back, weighing my reaction. Seeming satisfied with whatever she sees, she leans in again, the fucking picture of temptation as she purposefully rocks herself against my cock. "And *anything goes*, Doc."

My pulsing dick eagerly agrees as the rest of me disagrees, knowing one night won't come close to satiating either of us.

That I can convince her thoroughly of later as I temporarily give in to the lust overtaking me. Lifting my hips slightly, I roll the evidence of my answer beneath her before I voice it, and her lips part.

"I think you know my answer, Cheeky, but we have some terms and conditions to work out."

"I'm all ears."

"Not here," I tell her.

"So," she bites her lip and scrapes it with her teeth before releasing it. "Tonight?" She prompts, lifting my shot in offering.

Not answering, I take the offered glass as she lifts her own, and we clink them together.

"Merry Christmas, Doc," she murmurs, a lush smile lifting her lips.

"Merry Christmas indeed, Cheeky," I whisper roughly, plans solidifying in my head as we collectively toss our shots back, sealing the deal.

# TWENTY-FIVE

## LUCIAN

Incessant ringing attacks my pounding head as I crack my eyes open and groan due to the strength and amount of light filtering into the room—which temporarily blinds me. Completely unaware of where I am or how I got here, a painful drum pounds steadily behind my temples. The hammering brings me further into consciousness, as well as the awareness of the soft, warm flesh encased in my palm.

The ringing continues, agitating me to the point I fully rouse to realize I'm palming Jane's hip, her knicker-clad arse firmly tucked against my thinly covered cock. Barely able to glimpse a sight of her due to the overwhelming need to locate and stop the noise, I manage to get to my feet. I stumble through and *over* several barriers I can't identify as my vision goes in and out while stalking the source of my annoyance.

Cocking my head to pinpoint where it's stemming from, I finally locate the hotel phone buried beneath an upturned couch cushion resting just near my foot. The phone blares in my hand as I pinch my forehead between my fingers to relieve some of the pressure—I press the button to stop it.

"This is Dr. Aston," I growl.

". . . Good afternoon, Mr. . . . er, Dr. Aston. I'm sorry if we woke you. This is the front desk."

*Afternoon?* "And?"

"We . . . just wanted to check in with you both to ensure you were feeling well?"

"Why wouldn't we be?"

"Sir, . . . you and Mrs.—"

"Ms. Cartwright."

"My apologies, it seems you and Ms. Carwright were in a bit . . . of a state last night when you arrived back at the hotel, and it was reported by staff that one of you got sick in the elevator."

"Please allow me to apologize for that. I'll be happy to pay for the cleanup."

"That's not necessary, Mr. Aston. We've handled it. Your driver . . ."

"Mike," I fill in gruffly, hoping the urgency in my tone will help to expedite this increasingly painful conversation.

"Yes, he ensured that you both arrived safely to your room, but we just wanted to inquire on whether or not you were feeling better?"

"Fine. Your concern is appreciated," I say, glancing back to where Jane sleeps on the floor, running my gaze from her painted toes, along her bared legs, up to her lacy knickers, and further. Her bra is askew, exposing the side of her breast, which has me tightening my grip on the phone.

Though seemingly unharmed, much of what is exposed is covered in dark brown smudges, some of them resembling . . . fingerprints?

An empty champagne bottle rests on the floor next to her head, and I tilt mine to see that it's been decorated with what looks like plastic . . . googly eyes?

Christ. What in the fuck happened last night?

Thrusting a hand through my hair, it's stopped short by a rat's nest filled with goo, and I quickly untangle my fingers to examine them to see they're newly coated in . . . chocolate?

Praying to God that's both the case and the substance in question, I note my thighs and calves are coated as well. Pulling on the waistband of my briefs, I glance down to see my cock wasn't spared either.

It's all over me, and seemingly . . . everywhere.

Coming to enough to finally take in my surroundings, my jaw drops as I scan the room. Not a single furniture cushion is in place, most of them covered in similar chocolate smudges and handprints.

No doubt I'll owe the hotel thousands to replace them due to the number of stains on both the couch and floor and—tilting my head to gauge the state of the wall between the ruined lounger and sofa—I mentally add a painter's fee to the growing tally.

Glancing back at Jane as the front desk drones on about our state while indirectly reminding me they're not the type of establishment that tolerates this kind of behavior from guests, I narrow my eyes on her sleeping form. "I assure you it won't be happening again."

"We truly are just calling out of concern, not to make a complaint."

"Good thing," I snap, "because we have yet to make a rightful complaint against you," I counter, though completely mortified at what they might have witnessed.

"Understood, Dr. Aston."

"Glad that's settled. I'll see to it that this remains an isolated incident and ask if you could get the cleaners up here as soon as possible."

Silence and then. "I'll send them up directly. Anything else?"

"Yes, coffee please, and paracetamol. I'll order breakfast shortly."

"Right away, Dr. Aston and Merry—"

Hanging up, I toss the phone on the dining table and make my way back toward Jane as I survey the destroyed penthouse living room.

Anger lighting my veins, I stalk back over to where Jane lays comatose as she comes into clear view.

Sleeping on her side, dark hair splayed out on the carpet, lips parted, her chest heaves, drawing my attention as a good amount of breast and nipple peek out beneath the cup of her dark red bra. The contrast of the color against her white skin seems as sinful as the abundant curve of her hip, which is only magnified by how she's positioned. One of her long legs is propped on a pillow that she has clutched to her while surrounded by several others.

It's then I spot a tray not far from the fireplace housing several pints of ice cream, some empty, some melted, some unopened. Just next to them are bowls of toppings, limp whipping cream, nuts, and cherries, including several sauces—two bowls of them empty. Another piece to add to the growing puzzle, the biggest one being why I can't recall a second of it.

Scanning the room in search of more clues, I spot another champagne bottle teetering on the edge of the cushion-less couch, uncorked and seemingly empty.

How much did we drink?

The answer rings clear thanks to the ceaseless throb in my head just as a bout of nausea threatens.

After recovering from a nasty dry heave, I walk back to hover over Jane and pause, noting her lips are swollen, and she's covered in an array of light and dark red marks. Marks I'm intimately familiar with. And there are many, from her ankle to her calves and hip, her midsection, one on the side of her breast, and trailing further from the collar bone to her shoulders and neck.

*Fucking hell!*

Cock threatening to stir at the sight of them, my anger and utter confusion win out as I snap her name while frantically trying to piece the night together, and yet not one remnant comes freely to me.

"J-Jane," I call again and get no reply.

"Jane," I snap a third time, already at my wits' end due to the fact that we'd been intimate, and I can't remember a single fucking moment of it. Furious that I lost total control of my faculties, I can't help my bark.

"Jane! Wake up this instant!"

She jerks awake, wincing before her eyes slowly open and focus on me. A smile, which convinces me we were extremely intimate, breaks on her bee-stung lips.

"What's wrong?" she croaks in confusion, slowly releasing the pillow she was straddling and lifts to sit. She blinks and then blinks again, looking down at her exposed flesh, and makes no effort to cover herself as she lifts a finger.

"It's coming to me." Her lips slowly lift in a full-blown smile. "Yeah, that was *fun*."

"Was it now?" I query sarcastically, doing my best not to linger on her dark, rose-colored nipples or fixate on the marks covering her body.

"I think it was, you don't?"

"W-was it fun when one of us got sick in the lift? The front desk just rang."

"Yeah," she grimaces, "that was you." A grin quickly replaces her grimace, "but you rallied like a champ and came back swinging."

"Well, I guess fucking cheers to me. Was it fun when someone bit your breasts?"

"Also you," she says, her expression drawing in confusion. "Remember?"

"So, am I to assume I also put handprints all over the couch?"

"That was *us*, a collective effort," she laughs lightly.

"Did we fuck?" I bite out as she gapes at me, or rather my delivery. "Jane, answer me this instant. Did we fuck?!" I practically shout, to which she flinches.

"We came close," she says, searching her memories to recall what I can't as another infuriating smirk graces her face. "But you told me not to be a tosser, kissed my tits goodnight, and passed out instead."

Ripping at my hair, I glare down at her. "I'm glad you find this amusing, but just so you're aware, I'll be acting *age-appropriate* for the rest of the trip."

"I'm thinking I'll join you," she says through a pained sigh. "My head is killing me."

"Well, you should dress. The cleaners are on their way up."

"I don't think these stains are coming out," she frowns, finally realizing the expense of our little chocolate champagne party.

"Really?" I snap. "Do you think?"

"Is that sarcasm?" She draws her brows. "Lucian, why are you so upset?"

She stands, her mouthwatering, tear-drop-shaped tits now on

full display as she squares off with me. "Hey, bud, I didn't force you to drink the absinthe with me."

"No, you didn't, but you might as well have."

"I had no idea the strength of it," she says. "But we were in a controlled environment. I made sure of it. Mike picked us up. Remember?"

Eyeing the mark next to her nipple, my anger only multiplies. "Cover your breasts," I snap.

Her palms instantly lift to cover them a second before her eyes narrow. "Why?"

"Why?" I balk. "Because you're indecent."

"*I'm* indecent?" She scoffs. "Newsflash, Doc. You have a hard-on that could hammer a box of nails into steel and googly eyes covering your nipples. You plannin' on answering the door like *that*?"

She juts her chin toward me, and I follow her prompt to see that large plastic eyes are, in fact, covering my nipples. They are staring back at the two of us as my angry cock points directly at her.

Ripping the large stickers from my chest—without inquiring as to how in the hell they got there—Jane squares off with me, ripping off her bra and planting her hands on her hips before pushing her chest out defiantly.

"What's your issue all of a sudden, huh? You loved these tits so much last night. Hell, with all your high praise, you practically wrote them a sonnet!"

"Well, obviously I was out of my fucking skull," I counter, words becoming harder to articulate as more annoyance filters in because I can't summon a single memory of kissing her, touching her body, or marking and mapping her skin.

"I was buzzed too, Lucian, but . . . I remember." Her lips tremble as she stares over at me and cocks her head before regarding me suspiciously. "Oh, God, you're not using that stupid denial tactic men use sometimes, so you don't have to cop to it, right?"

"Cop to it?"

"It means owning to what you said and did last night, Lucian."

This accusation only angers me further. "I'm not sure what type of toddlers you have been dating—"

"Men my own age," she counters, "and in venturing a *decade past that* with you last night for the first time, it seems there's not much of a difference because you *all act like toddlers* under pressure."

"Well, I'm not that man, so your accusation is unproven. I don't shy away from matters such as these," I counter indignantly.

"You seriously mean to tell me you don't remember *any* of it?"

"Not a minute past . . .," I'm stopped short with one detail that rings in clearly. "The bottle, Jane, the bottle read 179 in *bold*."

This has her pausing too, and pinching her lip.

"Jane, please tell me we didn't take three back-to-back shots of one hundred and seventy-nine proof alcohol?"

I'm granted my answer when her eyes drop, and she mutters a low "shit. That would make sense, wouldn't it?" She brings pleading eyes back to mine. "It wasn't purposeful. I just thought it was some fancy name. I asked the bartender to give us a bottle of something strong because they were closing up early. That's ridiculously high, though. I've never heard of a liquor with that high of a proof, and I'm a part-time *bartender*."

"Well, there's your reason no one ever orders absinthe, Jane."

"I swear, I didn't know it was that strong! Cuervo eighteen hundred isn't eighteen hundred proof. It's just the name. It was an honest mistake, Lucian."

"Christ, it's no wonder I was buggered up so bad. But I could've . . .," my fury threatens to boil over, "what if . . . what if I would've— fuck," I run a hand over my jaw.

"It would have been completely *consensual*, Lucian," she rasps out, hurt leaking everywhere in her voice.

My fight leaves me temporarily as she looks over at me, devastation evident as her ice-blue eyes water. "Sure, it would've been drunken sex, and clearly, *you* would have regretted it, but I wouldn't have. I'm sorry, I didn't realize . . . you seemed cognizant enough. I swear. Or maybe I just thought you were, but we said and did things . . . I guess it doesn't matter if you really don't remember."

"Not a second," I say, my anger returning for that fact alone.

"You've made your point," she snaps before shaking her head

and glancing around. "And you're right. It was a bit irresponsible, and I did initiate taking the absinthe. Let me go get dressed, and while I do, I'll cancel the cleaners for now to see what I can get out myself before we're billed for the furniture."

"That's not necessary, Jane, I've already—"

She reels on me, her eyes battering. "Your time is up," she declares, pure venom in her tone.

"My time?"

"You don't have to understand it, I do. And it's exactly why I didn't want to go there . . . you know what? Fuck it, forget it, *and you* . . . and for once, I'm going to need you to shut the hell up because as much as you like to believe it, you have no damned say in what I do or not do. You're not in charge here. If I want to clean up, I'm cleaning up, but I'm doing it alone, so leave me to it and go," she points to my room, "I'd like to do the adulting this morning if this is all *on me*."

"Jane—"

"God, just get the hell away from me," she orders, her back already to me before her shoulders slump. A tense silence follows as she shakes her head and then turns to address me over her shoulder, only granting me the side of her profile as she speaks, her tone defeated. "You know, we didn't drive or endanger anyone. We didn't get arrested, we made it safely back to the hotel, we got a little wild, a little loud, and had one hell of a make-out session, and I'm sorry you missed it."

Her last words are the true reason for my upset in that I did miss it. I scan her milky skin, which I christened good and fucking proper with my love bites. Even when sleep rumpled and covered in chocolate, she's stunning—which infuriates me all the more.

Regret starts to war with my anger at seeing how I'm hurting her.

"So, we got a little messy," she carries on, "but it's not like we committed murder. You're still a brilliant, well-respected surgeon, and I'm still a surgical nurse, and only Mike and a few of the hotel staff are the wiser. If you weren't freaking the fuck out right now, we could have laughed about this at some point, but I don't see it being funny at all, now or *ever*."

"So, your war story is lost, and that's what concerns you?"

"No, Lucian," Jane turns, and it's then I see the tiny tear trailing down her cheek. "Without plans of telling a soul aside from Charlie, last night was one of the best nights I've had in a very long time, and I'm alone in remembering it. That's what *saddens* me."

She darts her gaze away, and at the loss of it, my chest tightens with regret. In truth, I am overreacting, but I've never once lost control of my senses, not ever. Most of my anger stems from the fact that my brain has been continually failing me since I woke without any recollection of finally touching her. A night I'm furious I can't summon and that she apparently holds in such high regard—which I have no remembrance of. Not any of it, and thanks to my behavior, I most likely won't be granted a single detail.

"Please go," she whispers, "before you say anything more than you have. Get some sleep. By the time you come out, it will be as if it never happened, and I *assure you*," she mocks my delivery of the phrase, "I'll treat it as if it *never did*."

"You're not going to make me feel guilty for being upset about this," I snap, as the guilt cloaks me, and I feel every bit the bastard I'm behaving as.

"No one can *make you do or feel anything*, Lucian. That's so obvious," she says, turning her back on me. Knowing she is giving me the cold shoulder, I opt to give her space as I attempt to sort myself out. I am two steps away when I hear a whisper that I'm certain she hadn't meant to reach me. "Merry Christmas *to me*."

*Fuck.*

Hours later, I'm roused by the same annoying ring that woke me this morning, and I'm not feeling any better than I did then. Just as annoyed by the disturbance, I blindly reach for the phone and answer, biting out my greeting.

"This is Dr. Aston."

"And Merry Christmas to you, Lucian," Matthieu spouts comically, getting an instant gauge of my mood. Moving to sit, I run my hands through my sweat-soaked hair—no doubt a side effect of the alcohol we consumed last night. Though I'd showered and scrubbed before falling into a fitful sleep, I still feel like hell—primarily because of my behavior this morning and Jane's rightful reaction to it.

"Sorry, Matthieu, I assumed we didn't have discussions today, seeing as it's the holidays."

"I'm actually calling for Jane. We have dinner reservations."

Stiffening, I turn my head in the direction of her suite. "I see."

"Unless you have any objections?"

"It makes no difference to me," I lie.

"Okay, then," Matthieu replies, "please give me Jane, Merci."

If she so quickly agreed to have dinner with him, it's apparent she's completely dismissed me and any connection we might have made in the past week—or last night. She said it had meant something to her, but I can't see how if she's willing to dine with another man with my marks all over her body. I grin at the fact that they're there—and she'll have one hell of a time concealing them—but my smug smile disappears just as quickly that once those reminders fade, she'll be entirely divested of me.

Jane has been good to me, and I can't, at all, say I blame her in the least if she's decided I'm no longer worth her time or effort. She's at least been a friend, and I haven't acted like much of one or given her anything in return—aside from ruining the trip that she's repeatedly said means so much to her.

That truth amplifies my guilt. As of this morning and due to my behavior, I'm not worthy. Sadly for me, Matthieu is in the best position to give her the memories and stories she so desires. Though not much of a commitment man, he is a good man, one I trust to look out for Jane.

But am I bowing out too easily?

"Right, let me get her. Give me a moment, I'm not decent."

It's a lie. I want time to gauge her reaction to me.

Phone in hand, I put it on mute and walk over to her suite door, knocking once before it easily gives a few inches. Just inside, I hear the shower running in her ensuite bathroom. I approach the second door—also partially open—and spot her behind a steam-filled cloud. I instantly lower my eyes as I've lost the right to her body and the temporary permission she granted me, all of which helped fuel my anger this morning.

Jane sings lightly along with a country song, which blares from her phone on the counter beside the sink. The screen is within my line of sight, and I eye the title. "She Is His Only Need," by someone called Wynonna. Jane sings reverently, having memorized not only the words but also the delivery, and that's how I know it's a song close to her heart. A heart I know I've taken for granted as I listen intently for a full minute while knowing Matthieu is in wait. The song is essentially about a man who lives for and is devout to the woman he loves.

Clearing my throat, I knock loudly on the bathroom door.

"Jane?"

A pause. "Yeah?"

"Matthieu is on the phone about your dinner reservation."

"Well . . . I'm in the shower."

"Obviously, do you want me to tell him to ring you back?"

"*Obviously*," she mimics dryly, pointing out, yet again, what a prick I am. "Please, tell him to give me ten."

"Will do," I say.

"Did you see I got the chocolate out?" She calls to my retreating back. I hadn't even noticed while walking through the suite. Her cleanup job is miraculous. I eye the living room from her bedroom to see that it's exactly as it was upon our arrival at the hotel. I can't even imagine how she managed it.

"Truly impressive, Jane, and greatly appreciated."

"Yep," she says, adding a "*never happened*" for emphasis.

She's still bothered, which means she still cares. Which means I should hang up on Matthieu or tell him he can't have Jane for dinner because I had her for dessert last night. The marks on her body came from me, and therefore, she's not at all ripe for his picking.

It occurs to me then that I'm being a territorial wanker and have absolutely no right to her—unless I make things right, but I have no idea how. There's no apology worthy enough because of my abhorrent behavior—which is why I haven't yet tried to deliver one.

I've probably given her more whiplash than she can withstand by this point with how all over the place I am.

And after what she did for me last night? I'm irredeemable.

If her wish is to move forward—and with Matthieu—then I need to leave her be.

I click on the call just as Jane cuts her shower off. "Matthieu, she's showering but said to please call her back shortly."

"I will. Last chance, Lucian," he says in half question, part taunt.

"I have no objection," I say as Jane and I lock eyes in her bathroom mirror just as she wipes the steam from it. Secured in a robe, hair wet, I note a darker mark inches beneath her ear.

A possessiveness floods my veins at the sight of it as I make my way out the door. Ten minutes later, Jane enters the living room to retrieve the phone just as it rings.

Feet away in the chair with my hardback, I watch as she makes herself busy in the kitchenette as she takes his call.

"Hi Matthieu," she rings out, her tone enthusiastic and seeming genuine. "Sorry, yeah, I was in the shower . . . Absolutely . . . Sounds perfect. No, I can meet you there." She picks up a nearby pen, jotting down what I assume is an address, and nods, a smile gracing her lips as a laugh escapes her. "Sounds good. Seven. See you then. Merry Christmas to you."

Hanging up, her smile dissipates when her eyes find mine and drop.

Fuck, if it doesn't feel worse than not remembering. I've hurt her—*again*. A mere week into our trip. How is it possible? She's better off, I decide as she walks through her suite door and closes it softly. But that click might as well have been a shotgun blast to my chest.

I bristle the entire time she readies herself. And when she appears a little over a chapter later—a chapter I re-read for ages and couldn't retain for the life of me—she steals my breath.

She looks ravishing, dressed in tight, black leather pants, a form-fitting pale pink sweater, and boots. The outfit isn't too racy but is sexy as fuck with the added effect of her pink, glossy lipstick.

She looks both sophisticated and downright fuckable.

It's then my cock stirs as a whisper surfaces and not of an image but of a sound. The soft call of my name, followed by a moan, and the timing of this recall couldn't be more painfully ironic.

In seconds, I'm hard, and not a minute later, the second close of a door befalls me as dread filters in and jealousy seeps into my rapidly heating veins.

She's gone.

And currently walking directly toward and possibly into the hands of one of my oldest mates, and I can't fucking stand the thought of it.

# TWENTY-SIX

## JANE

London passes in a blur out of the window as I ride in the back seat of the sedan while battling memories of what transpired in this very spot less than twenty-four hours ago. Heavy snowdrift limits my view of the London street as Mike slows to a stop while recollections shutter in—Christmas lights blurring in the background as I drink in Lucian's dimly lit profile and the way he regarded me after our first real kiss. His fast exhales against my parted lips as he pressed his forehead to mine, along with the words he spoke. Ache fills me in knowing I'm left alone in that memory as Mike rounds the car, opening the door for me, outstretching his gloved hand to my bare one.

Heart heavy, residual hurt drives me to take his offered hand while anger fuels me to press through the hours ahead.

"This city is so damned big," I glance at our surroundings. "I don't think I've seen a single landmark twice since I got to London. I have zero doubt I'd be lost without your help in getting here, so thank you so much for the ride, Mike."

My exhales become more clouded due to the freezing temperature as Mike warms me with his return smile.

"Always a pleasure. Merry Christmas, Jane."

"Merry Christmas, and I'm sorry I bothered you. I was just worried I wouldn't be able to catch a cab on the holiday." I glance around at the traffic surrounding us and grimace. "Looks like I worried in vain."

"I told you I was doing nothing but watching the telly."

"No family to see today?" I ask, the thought of him alone on the holiday with no one to share it with tugging at my heartstrings. It's no mystery why, and entirely because of the man I'm trying my best not to think about being in a similar predicament.

"Ah, quite the contrary, family overload this morning. There were thirty of us. I'm the fourth of twelve siblings, and only four have had children so far."

"Holy shite," I laugh, and he does too.

"Enjoy your dinner. I'll be nearby if you need a lift back to the hotel."

"Oh, no, I'll find my way, no worries."

"Jane," Mike prompts, drawing my eyes to his.

"Yes?"

"I'm more than happy to drive you *anywhere*. Ring me if you need a lift back, okay?"

Extending a ready bill that I plucked from my wallet toward him, he instantly refuses my offered tip. "Oh, now don't insult me. Dr. Aston has already tipped me handsomely for the duration of your stay."

The sound of his name alone pathetically starts a pain that quickly threatens to branch out and spread before I rapidly reel it back in, determined to see my plans through.

"So what? I dragged you out of your warm house to drive in this mess," I argue. The snow furthers my point as it begins to pour down on us.

"Put it away, Jane," he scolds lightly.

"Fine," I sigh. Glancing back, I eye the restaurant, which looks every bit like a highfalutin establishment. The entrance alone is regal with a highly polished stair railing, the awning hovering above brandished with a gold lion's head.

"Ever dined here?"

"Not my kind of place," he says with a wink.

"Mine either, if I'm honest," I relay. "I got a heaving helping of high society last night," *along with a giant dash of prick this morning,* "and well, let's just say it's left a bitter aftertaste."

"We have that in common," he says, "I got a taste of that myself long ago and decided not to partake again *very purposely.*"

"Really?" I ask, intrigued. "Do tell."

A horn honks obnoxiously behind us as I glance back at Mike reluctantly. "Crap, guess you better go. But maybe a story for another time?"

"I'd be all too happy to replace your dinner date tonight, but I have a feeling the Dr. would have an objection to it," he muses distractedly, glancing back toward the restaurant.

"Why do you think that?"

"For one, I drove you back to the hotel last night," he jests.

"Oh shit, yeah, about that," my cheeks heat at the idea of just how much he witnessed. "Please know that was all alcohol-infused, but trust me, Lucian doesn't give a rat's ass about any date I may have in the present or future."

"I don't think that's entirely accurate, Jane," he counters.

"Why is that?"

"Call it an inkling," he says, lifting my hand for a polite kiss. "Text me if you need to. I must insist on that."

"You're a good guy and true gentleman, Mike. Thank you."

"Well, unfortunately for me," he flashes me a sexy grin, "I don't have a choice."

Before I can question why, he leaves me with a parting wave before hustling inside the car and pulling away from the curb. Stalling, I watch the sedan until it disappears into the rapidly accumulating snow drift.

Dreading the rest of my Christmas—but steadfast in seeing it through—I turn to face the music and slam right into a hard body instead. A yelp leaves me as fear filters in until I recognize the gloves on the hands currently working to upright me. "Apologies, Jane. I didn't mean to frighten you."

Gathering my wits, I shake free from Lucian's hold.

"Well then, maybe you shouldn't be frickin' hovering like you're my damned shadow or something," I glare up at him. "How long have you been standing there?"

"Long enough," he answers unapologetically.

"So, you're the evil who scared our good driver away. *Figures.*"

"There is very little Mike is afraid of, I assure you, and he's not at all oblivious to what's happening between us."

"Which is nothing," I harrumph, "you made certain of it this morning. Now, if you'll excuse me, I have a dinner date to get to."

"You didn't seem so anxious to get to it when you were conversing with Mike."

"He's much better company in comparison, and do you eavesdrop on all conversations or just mine?"

"I walked upon it," he counters, "didn't realize you needed privacy on a public street."

"From you, I need priv-a-cee at all times," I mock.

"Jane, I need a word."

"No," I say in an attempt to sidestep him, and he immediately blocks me.

"My behavior this morning was deplorable and unforgivable," he starts anyway, and I jerk my chin, denying him.

"All things you could have said back at the *hotel.*"

"I knew you weren't going to allow me the opportunity to apologize," he blows out a long exhale. "I knew it would be pointless."

"Oh, I'm sorry," I palm my chest, "am I *inconveniencing* you? When you're the one who just rudely dismissed our driver, and are currently interrupting my date *before* it starts? Wow, your amount of self-importance is astounding, Doc. If this morning was any indication, the upkeep of being your girl must be hell. My condolences to all of them, past, present, and future. I'll take *past* for two hundred, Alex."

His brows furrow.

"Jeopardy reference," I clue him in, "and I'm late."

When I move to sidestep him again, he gently but firmly grips my upper arm and begins walking me to the side of the restaurant and down the sidewalk.

"Just what in the hell do you think you're doing?" I grit out, attempting to free my arm, "unhand me right now, you ignorant brute."

"I'm intercepting your date," he says matter of fact, "until you hear me out." He releases me as snow begins to pummel us both.

"Again, you had all damned day to apologize. Big surprise, you took the prick route and remained mute, and like I said, your time is up."

Glancing around at the few who pass us on the street, Lucian grips me again and drags me out of the path of foot traffic, crowding me just outside one of the bright red phone booths London is notoriously known for. I curse the fact that it's the first time I've seen one up close since our trip to Oxford, and that timing was just as shit then to snap a photo as it is now.

Snow pings my face and starts to coat Lucian's hair and the shoulders of his trench coat as he laces his fingers, tightening his gloves.

A tick I've seen before when he's . . . *nervous?* Though, if I'm gauging him correctly, he seems more *agitated.*

*You don't care. His time is up.*

"What I meant to say, Jane, is that I know that no apology I make will suffice. I know that."

"Then don't bother, but tell me, what in the hell is your real damage, Doc? You keep pulling me close, only to smash me in the face before pushing me away twice as far. It's dizzying, and frankly, our little tango is exhausting, so I'm done trying to figure out what your steps are. I'm tapping out."

"I am sorry," he relays, every syllable sounding sincere.

"You're already forgiven," I tell him honestly, "I told you I would forgive you even when you pissed me off after that night, in Oxford, remember? But unlike you, I mean what I say, no matter what state I'm in."

Shit, that sounded extremely bitter, but how can I not be?

"What's that supposed to mean?"

He crowds me closer to the door of the phone booth as a few passersby eye the two of us before flashing us matching smiles as if we're in on the 'happy couple' secret. I manage to muster a small wave of my own, adding a "Merry Christmas" before turning back to Lucian.

"What it means is that I'm covered in memories of last night, things that were said and done, even if you can't remember them. And that sucks, and so does the way you acted out this morning, but you're forgiven. I know for a control-necessary guy like you, blacking out must be your worst nightmare, and I can't blame you for being freaked out. However, I can blame you for making me feel like a disease and stay mad at you for it until I can get past it. I'm allowed to be mad and stay mad at you for that, *friend*."

"I see you as anything but a disease, Jane, and to be clear, I was angry about far more than that," he clips out, "and am growing more so at the moment."

"Oh, yeah, well, grab your pitchfork and join the party, Doc. Though I have no idea what you could be so pissed about, considering I'm the one who had to endure your wrath this morning. But hey, we didn't *fuck*," I spit the word out like he did this morning, "so no real harm done, right?"

"Please stop your lecturing and listen to me," he clips impatiently, and my jaw drops.

"No man in the history of ever has kept his privates intact ordering a woman to do that, and you're lucky it's Christmas, or I'd rip your cock right off your body. And why should I listen? You don't deserve my ear. Right now, you deserve less than shit."

"You might deserve an apt apology," he says, looking so fucking gorgeous standing in his suit and trench coat while being pounded by snow. "One I'll rightfully give you until you can get past it, but I am curious as to why you accepted a date after playing hurt."

"*Playing* hurt?" I repeat incredulously. "I wasn't *playing anything,* asshole!"

Lucian glances around briefly, clearly uncomfortable with the drama playing out publicly, before crowding me further. "Tell me, Jane, those marks all over your body were made *by me*, were they not?"

"Stupid question . . . wait," I shake my head, "you aren't fool enough to think that gives you some damned claim on me?

He lifts his shoulder in a shrug, though his unforgiving eyes drill into me.

*Jealousy?*

"Maybe I'm curious as to how you intend to explain them to Matthieu."

I gape at him. "I'm having dinner with him, not sleeping with him, you presumptuous—"

"Not after being under my tongue, you're not," he snaps, eyes flaring, his latest declaration temporarily stunning me as his guard starts to slip.

Definitely jealous.

"Unless you want me to obnoxiously laugh in your face, Dr. Astonhole, you better step away because you did not just say that to me."

"I did, and allow me to elaborate and make it clear," he leans in, dropping the rest of his guard in a blink, his replacement expression—fury. "I will not have you going to him with my bites all over your body and my kiss fresh on your lips."

"Hey, there, Doc. Do you hear yourself right now?"

"Yes, and I sound ridiculous." He agrees readily, which again stuns me into momentary silence. "Christ, I know I sound ridiculous," he runs a glove through his hair, and it's then I see he's not all that well put together. In fact, it looks like he barely had a chance to clip his cufflinks before he left the hotel—and from his timing in intercepting my date—he left in one hell of a hurry.

*Ignore that flutter, Jane, he's the devil.*

"Reason being," he explains as his wind-blown hair—which isn't styled at all—falls limp across his forehead, "or as you might have gathered by now, when I get angry, or when my emotions start to get the best of me, I'm terrible at expressing myself. I'm angry now and getting more so by the second about the fact that you, that you m-made a date."

Snow quickly accumulates around us—and between us—he inches closer in silent demand that I answer him. I inch back, which backfires because now I'm plastered to the booth's door and debating on whether or not to enlighten him. Instead, I decide to hold that card close while slightly enjoying his display of jealousy.

Okay, really enjoying it, but he deserves to sweat, and the lingering sting in my chest agrees—though the sting itself is slightly soothed that he is jealous. The man is too damned good at guarding his emotions and looked nothing but disgusted and mortified this morning while I was all but naked, which can be quite a confidence blow. The memory of that jerks me back into flight mode.

"Well, sorry you get all tongue-tied when you're upset, but I'm freezing my ass off, and I have yet to start the damned date because you're holding me up, so I'll see you back at the hotel."

"NO!" He booms as an older couple passing us startles and gasps before scurrying away. He shakes his head, frustration in his expression, and my eyes bulge at his outburst.

"Lucian, you're scaring little old ladies. Just get to the point."

"You won't hear it. Christ, n-none of this will d-do. You've solidified your opinion of me, and that's obvious, but p-please allow me the time to attempt to speak the words."

"Save them, Doc, okay? And save us both some time. Matthieu is waiting on me."

"I bid you not to say his name to me again," he warns.

I gawk at him. "Did you just threaten me?"

"I'm angry," he clips out.

"Uh huh, so you keep telling me." The fact that he keeps repeating it and is taking his time in between speaking is pretty telling in the sense that he might not be bullshitting about his emotion-driven speech impediment.

A long minute passes and then another as we stand in the snowfall, and as it does, I start to believe him as the truth sets in.

Last night, at the table with his father, I could see something was brewing inside him, even if his guard was up. But he hadn't spoken up once in his defense—or anyone else's. In the car afterward, he flat-out told me that he was maimed in that respect and that I'd put words to what he never could.

I hadn't taken that to mean *literally*, but if that's the truth of it—which seems to be the case—then he's fighting right now just to be able to *speak* to me. Not to come up with words but to get them out. It's not a lack of emotion Lucian's struggling with. It's the fact that he's dealing with too much emotion at once, and it flusters him to the point of stammering or going catatonic.

Chest threatening to cave in from the vulnerability he's showing me—and the truth now so clear to see—I nearly take a step back toward him. That is until I remember that he had zero issue making me feel like shit this morning, but he hadn't yelled. Not really, and once he did clam up, he didn't utter a word after.

Had he been that upset?

Convinced that it's the truth of the matter after another long bout of silence passes, I war between gripping him to me and slapping the shit out of him for the words he did manage to speak.

"I want my hour," he finally says.

"What?" I ask, gawking at his word choice after so much loaded silence.

"Our deal was that I have an hour at any time of my choosing, and I want it."

"Oh, this is unreal," I gape at him. "You can't be serious."

In a flash, I'm ushered inside the phone booth. The snow coming down is close to white out at this point, but I can hardly register that past the fire in Lucian's eyes as they command mine.

"I was angry," he swallows. "That I couldn't remember touching you when it's all I've wanted for the entirety of the time we've been here. I'm, I-I'm fucking furious I can't remember leaving this." He palms my neck with a gloved hand. His eyes transfixed on what I'm sure is one of a dozen of the marks I have covering me. Lifting the glove to his mouth, he bites the pad of the middle finger to remove it, freeing his hand before again covering my neck and reverently brushing the skin with his thumb, which elicits an instant full-body shiver from me. "So responsive to my touch, Christ," he rasps, his eyes bolting back to mine, "and I missed it."

"Could've had a lot more where that came from if you'd not woken up and shanked me," I blurt, already breathless due to the way he has me pinned, my body once again betraying me as the last of my hurt leaks out.

"You limited it to one night," he reminds me, his thumb steadily stroking my skin.

"You really don't remember," I utter hoarsely due to his coaxing touch.

"Why would I lie about that, Jane? It's my biggest regret alongside my reaction this morning," he says as he continues to pin me in every way imaginable—with his body, eyes, and gentle touch. "Contrary to what you believe, I do give a rat's ass about who you date in the present and future. I should think it's obvious by now. And let me make myself clear, I don't have one-night stands and had zero intentions of fucking you last night or going along with your one-night rule. I just lost the fucking plot before I was able to tell you as much. I'm not the one-night stand man and haven't been for quite some time, and that's not at all what's happening between us. I won't have it. So, if you think for one second, I'll allow any man on this fucking continent or any other to have you when I can't even remember your taste, you've got another think coming."

"It's thing," I correct weakly, his words stunning me, "another *thing* coming, and yep, you've lost your damned mind."

"Whatever it is, know that I'm the only date you'll be having," he bites out. "In London or *Paris,* for that matter."

I shake my head. "Let's face it. You and I are oil and vinegar in every way. We will never mix well."

"We get on perfectly fine," he counters. "When you aren't bullshitting," he spits, mocking me, seeming to gain more of his bearings.

"You sound ridiculous saying that."

"A vast majority of your vocabulary is confusing for me, but I'm trying."

"Well, because of arrogant men just like you, I'm fluent in *jack-ass*, so you're good there."

Forced to finally take a full inhale from trying to hold my breath for so long, his masculine scent fills my nose and instantly surrounds me. I become dizzy as the heat starts to build below, my needy clit pulsing due to the look in his eyes, and his declarations. Sadly, pathetically and especially, his admission of jealousy.

All of his actions scream, claiming, but it's not enough. Not after the way he made me feel this morning. Giving Lucian the power to hurt me again would be idiotic at this point, and so my fear speaks up for me.

"I don't know why you keep pressing for us to happen," I rasp out hoarsely, "with the way things are, we won't last a week," I argue. "First of all, you're too uptight, and second, too set in your rich bitch ways to handle a girl like me. You're too much of a control freak . . . and I'm not a girl to be controlled—unless I want to be. I'm just too much for you. *Period.* Too loud, too opinionated, and too independent, something you probably find threatening."

"Oh, is that what you believe?" His eyes darken and hood as my heart starts to pound along with the steady beat between my legs.

"Yes, I do. Put simply—and since we're still in brutal honesty territory—I'm too much fucking woman for you, Lucian, whether you discover that *now or later*, which will be *your issue, not mine.*"

His mouth is on mine before I can give any more reason to stop this, us. I catch myself and my moan before it escapes, breaking the kiss and glaring up at him.

"What are you doing?"

"Giving you a kiss I can remember."

"You don't even know if you want it or me. You're just confused right now and in no place to venture into the girl-boy area. What's happening right now is just some misplaced territorial bullshit."

"Do not again presume to tell me what I want," he grits out as he grips my hand and slides it down his toned chest and torso before using it to cup his cock. I revel in the full feel of him under my palm as his eyes bore relentlessly into mine. "I've been hard and wanting for you every goddamned day, Jane. Including the day we landed, but you know that because you caught me, didn't you?"

"Lucian," I groan in protest as he surrounds me, his fast exhales hitting my lips.

"You say that you're interested in what makes a man like me tick, but allow me to flip that narrative for my own use in revealing that I'm just as interested in what makes *you tick. More* so, what makes you *come apart,* and how many of the precise licks of my tongue it will take to get you there."

"But—"

"But shit, Jane, take my fucking kiss."

# TWENTY-SEVEN

## JANE

Releasing my hand, Lucian thrusts both of his into my hair, cradling my head before crushing his mouth to mine.

Even with our mouths closed, I feel the connection down to my toes. Instantly, I go limp in his hold and become pliant as he starts to dismantle my willpower with the strength of his kiss.

My resolve is further obliterated when he uses the tip of his tongue to trace both my lips, coaxing them open. The second they part, he deepens the kiss tenfold, delving into my mouth while sweeping my cheek gently with his thumb.

Fire ignites throughout my entirety as I become enraptured in the most sensual, intimate kiss of my damned life. The kiss to beat all others as I grip the shoulders of his jacket to keep myself upright while furiously kissing him back.

Our tongues tangle in a frenzy, becoming more urgent as all the pent-up sexual tension between us starts to unfurl. He coaxes me in further with every thrust, drawing every imaginable reaction from me as he wholly claims my mouth, his gentle thumb continually gliding along my cheekbone.

When he finally ends our kiss, he pulls away, resting his forehead on mine as he lowers his ungloved hand and slowly lifts the hem of my sweater to the waistband of my pants, running the pad of his finger along the top of them.

"Jane," he whispers roughly, his voice pure sex, "can I touch you?" All I can do is nod.

Within the same breath, he flattens a palm against my bare stomach before running it up to cover my breast, and I melt into his touch. Cupping, molding, and massaging me through my bra, I gape up at him as he draws in my every reaction. It's when he sweeps a thumb over my drawn nipple that I shudder, my hands re-gripping his jacket to keep me standing on now shaky legs. My attraction to this man is debilitating, especially when he presses his erection against my stomach briefly before gliding his palm to my other breast, repeating his movements as I tremble in his hold. Mixed moans and pants rush out of me as he continues to sweep his thumb back and forth over my peaked nipple, panties flooding as my clit starts to pulse. Wanting more, needing more, I arch into his touch and press back against him in silent request.

"Christ," he whispers coarsely, his rough tone filling the space along with the roar of the snowstorm outside and the wind battering the booth. Gusts of the chaotic breeze whirr loudly outside the door, matching what I'm feeling inside as Lucian covers me in his warm, sensual touch.

Though we're on a seemingly busy street, the cover of the snow and the quiet in the booth makes it feel like we're trapped in a bubble.

A very fucking hot bubble as Lucian runs his deft finger over my nipple once more before adjusting his hand so he's able to slide his palm into the tight fit of my pants. The second he nears where I'm aching, a moan rips out of me as he doesn't stop or pause, slipping past my underwear and running his fingers through my folds before driving them straight into me.

"Oh God," I croak as he captures my mouth, muffling my moan as he starts to ruthlessly fuck me with his fingers and tongue. Skillfully and purposely, he stretches them inside me before pulling them out enough to spread my pussy lips and lightly glide a finger over my clit.

He draws my mouth in another dizzying kiss as my legs continually shake, and my return kiss turns desperate. When he cuts the kiss and pulls back, his eyes flame as he plunges his fingers into me again, and I crack at the feel, my body jerking while calling his name.

His honey eyes light with satisfaction as he drives in again and again, and my orgasm starts to build. My head falls back into the hand still cradling it as I brace myself while he ruthlessly fucks me with his fingers.

"Jane," Lucian whispers hoarsely, pausing his touch and bringing me back from the brink. "Give me one hour to replace everything you felt this morning. I won't even ask you to forgive me."

He pulls his fingers from me, and I damn near jump out of my skin at the loss as he keeps my eyes hostage. He lifts his glistening middle finger to his full lips before closing his eyes and sucking my arousal off. It's as if he's been waiting forever to taste me, and I burn his reaction into memory, ranking it easily as one of my hottest ever.

"Please," I beg. "Please don't stop."

I want more. I want him and have since I first laid eyes on him. So, when he poses his question again, I don't hesitate.

"Do you agree?" he prompts. This time, it comes out as more of a demand, and I nod in reply.

Stepping back, he lifts his jacket and shirt cuff to reveal what I'm sure is a stupid-expensive watch before pressing a button on the side of it.

"One hour," he states, quickly situating my clothes before zipping my jacket, "let's go."

Dazed and aroused and close to the point of going bat shit due to lust alone, I stand in wait as Lucian quickly hails a cab before ushering me inside.

We remain wordless on the ride as Lucian strokes the inside of my wrist with a single finger, his touch mimicking the one in the booth.

Time blurs during our ride to the hotel until we file into the elevator. Once inside the doors, my body becomes completely aware of him and his every movement. The slight twitch of the gloved fingers at his sides, the length of his inhales, the set of his jaw. Alone now, he keeps his distance from me, standing on the opposite side of the elevator, which confuses me. As if reading my mind, he speaks up. "Last night, I told you I had ground rules, remember?"

I slowly dip my chin, and my eyes fixate on the thick lips that just swept me into an epic tailspin.

"We never got to those rules, as far as I recall."

I shake my head softly in reply.

Three more floors are all I can think of as I rattle in anticipation, growing wetter by the second. What he just made me feel, and what I feel now, is indescribable, and it was from just a kiss and his fingers. While last night was epic in its own right, it seems like child's play in comparison.

"I won't force you to tell me what happened last night, but I do want to know if I touched you intimately and if you touched me."

"No," I reply, ignoring the residual sting he doesn't remember and most likely won't. "We didn't make it that far. It was just a lot of kissing and over-the-clothes heavy petting."

He nods, seeming pleased with my answer as I follow him to the penthouse door. Once he swipes the card and we're inside, he stalks straight toward my bedroom. Stupefied by the way I'm still tingling and mostly aching, I stand just inside the door as he walks toward a small bedside table and chairs bordering the wall opposite my bed. Snapping the lapels of his jacket onto his biceps—a move I find sexy as fuck—he then shrugs it off before laying it over the arm of the chair.

Anxious because his clock is ticking—and I know we burned at least twenty minutes getting back to the hotel—I resist the urge to cross my legs and squeeze due to the need thrumming through me. My body is so damned lit up, I know it won't take much.

"Permission is *very important* to me, Jane," Lucian says, slowly loosening the knot in his tie. "It was instilled in me early by my father, mainly for the protection of our familial wealth," he admits dryly. "It was self-instilled later as my sexual appetite grew, and now it's something I need and require from every partner I have in order for us *both* to feel safe." Undoing a cufflink, he begins to slowly roll up the sleeve of his starched white shirt.

It's all I can do not to speak up that time is being wasted, while at the same time loving this version of Lucian—controlled, seemingly methodic like he is in the operating room, and just as intense and demanding, if not more so. Within the next second, he unbuckles his belt and rips it out of its loops. Pulling it free, the end lashes out, snapping the air before he tosses it into the seat of the chair.

Fuck me.

*Please.*

"The major reason why I was so angry this morning is that I need that permission in order to feel good about what I want—want specifically to do to you." He pulls his tie from around his neck, his hesitance clear. "So, to answer your very first question, I haven't had sex with a woman in nearly three years, and that's by my *own* design. The long abstinence was my decision for a few reasons, but mostly because I was too numb and uninterested. During the entirety of that time, no woman has had such an effect on me as you have in a mere week. So, if you want the blunt truth—"

"Yes," I answer instantly.

"You're sure?" He asks, slipping his wingtips off.

"*Please*, Lucian." His eyes close at my plea before he re-opens them where they remain half-mast, a golden fire roaring to life in his return gaze. A mix of nerves and butterflies swarm me before he levels me with his next words.

"To tick off the start of the list, I want to fuck your perfect pussy, mouth, breasts, and arse in that exact order. If you'll trust me with your body and give me permission and time, I assure you I'll make it both pleasurable and memorable for us both. Never to be fucking forgotten."

All breath leaves me as I stare back at him, entranced. Instead of unbuttoning his shirt, he untucks it, eyeing me the entire time as if weighing just how he's going to carry out his task list. The sight of him, the way he's looking at me, the anticipation of the feel of him, it's all so incredibly hot that all I can do is stare back.

"It starts with trust and permission, Jane," he challenges.

The sound of my zipper at my hip sounds so loud that I startle myself, fumbling with the fabric before pushing the material over my hips and peeling them off. Keeping eye contact, I lift off my sweater and toss it before unclasping my bra and doing the same. Fingering the sides of my panties as his gaze roams me hungrily, I pull them off and clutch them in my fist before walking over and holding them out to him. "Permission enough?"

He sweeps my body with deep appraisal before taking and pocketing them, and sadly for me, pocketing both his hands as well, intent on having this conversation.

"You're exquisite." The words cover me in a caress, and I can't help my question.

"You said I caught you. You mean the night we got here," I start to ask because I initially dismissed what I thought I saw the night he darkened my door. "The night we got here . . . you . . . were really," I trail off.

He smirks, and I know then he's going to make me ask. "What about it, Jane?"

"So, you really were," I swallow, brazen Jane nowhere to be found at the moment due to the vibe he's putting out. It's so damned sexy and controlled, and there's nothing I want more right now than to make him lose it.

"Ask me, Jane," he clips in command.

"You were really," I bit my lip, "you were—"

"Imagining a hundred or more ways to fuck you? Yes. I wanted you that night almost as much as I do now."

He wanted me *before* he needed me, and relief washes over me at his confession. It's enough to tip me over into *all-in* and *down for whatever*.

He seems anything but vulnerable right now as he scans me like he's about to unleash three years of pent-up sexual tension, and I am so frickin' here for this release party.

"Fuck, I think the order might have to change," his whisper hits my neck, "that's if you agree."

Confused in thinking that I just gave him permission, all my thoughts fall away when he bends and runs his tongue along my lower lip. I chase his mouth with my own, remembering the kiss we shared earlier and how amazing it felt when he dominated my mouth.

Hands still in his pockets, he dips and captures my nipple between warm, wet lips. Gripping his head, I watch as his eyes flutter closed while he takes deep, long pulls as if he's feeding from me. His every move ignites me further as I grip his hair, freely running my fingers through it. Time slows as I memorize his movements, though I know it's ticking by faster than I want it to.

Eagerly, I draw out his name, begging him to hurry so I can get any sort of relief.

He releases my nipple and licks around it with the tip of his tongue, his eyes on my drawn skin as he poses his question. "Are you wet for me, Jane?"

"Soaked," I say on a moan as he darts his tongue along my collar bone before pinning me with his words.

"Fuck, the ways I'll have you if you'll let me, and once I do, you'll be mine to have—only mine."

He says this with such surety, and I don't doubt him. I'm literally putty in his hands, and they aren't even on me. Last night was the most intense make-out session of my life. Although it was consuming, it seems weak now in comparison to the heat in the booth and the fire building between us right now.

"Lie back on the bed," he commands, jutting his chin over my shoulder. I start walking backward as he stalks forward, only stopping when my thighs hit the mattress. Lying back, I put my heels on the edge of the bed and palm my thighs.

He hovers over me, eyes blazing, hands still pocketed as he delivers his next heated order. "Spread for me, Jane. Show me my feast."

His words would be laughable if they didn't sound so fucking sexy coming out of his mouth. But there's not a damned thing funny about anything happening right now as I follow his order.

"Wider," he grits out, his eyes sparking more fire between my legs as he studies me bared to him. I'm practically whimpering as he peruses my body, taking his time, his eyes and timbre the only thing giving his hunger away.

"Why aren't you naked, and why won't you touch me?"

"Patience, Cheeky."

I bite my lip to stop myself from reminding him of the ticking clock.

Drawing his hands from his pockets, he palms the mattress next to my feet and kneels.

His breath whispers over my soaked pussy before his words do. "Could I even be sated of you? I've tasted your pussy for a single second and feel I already have my answer. Can I have it again, Jane?"

"*Please*," I urge as he continues to hover so close to where the pulse pounds—I can *feel* his every word.

Instead, he lowers and sucks on one of the marks on the side of my ankle as I practically writhe beneath him at just that feeling alone. As he releases the skin, one of his rare, devilish smiles takes over his face.

"You see, I don't really need the details of last night, Jane, because even though I was inebriated, I was wise enough to map you."

"To what?"

"I mapped you," he repeats gruffly, his hot stare trailing along the marks he left. "You see, while the lighter marks bring you some pleasure," he brings his point home with a light suck on one of the love bites on my calves.

"The darker marks," he continues, his eyes fixing on one at the top of my inner thigh before he lowers and takes a heavy pull. My back arches as he "hmms" in response before releasing the skin. "I think you get my point."

"Sneaky," I say breathlessly as he spends the next few minutes retracing his map, making me feel worshipped until I'm a needy, quivering mess. He draws out more moans and pleas until he's again hovering above my pussy. Eyes locking with mine, he dips, placing a full-lipped kiss on my sensitive lips, and in response, I weave my fingers through his hair.

"Thighs, Jane," he reminds me before he lowers again, licking me smoothly with a flat tongue, and I immediately bow, losing instant grip on my thighs.

"Jane," he draws out in a mild scold as I grip my thighs before dipping again, torturing me with the same maddening, thorough sweep of his tongue.

"God, please, please," I plea as I writhe uncontrollably beneath him as he edges me to the point of insanity.

With a few more passes, he becomes impatient. Covering my palms on my thighs with his own, he pushes them wider apart before clamping his mouth over my entire pussy and sucking feverishly.

"Jesus . . . oh my God," I lose all sense of self as pleasure unfurls throughout my every limb, and my thighs shake as he continues to suck my whole pussy as if he doesn't want to divide an ounce of his attention. In seconds, I'm building, the noises he's making so damned filthy. It's only when I'm covered in a thin veil of sweat that he releases me.

Rimming my entrance with his finger, I buck again, the ache becoming unbearable before he fills it with both his fingers and tongue. His eyes continually find mine between his tortuous workings, and I see nothing but satisfaction in his expression as he continues his agonizing new routine.

Despite my begging, Lucian continues to switch between perfect, precise licks and suction. Within one or two switches, my entire lower half begins to coil. Animalistic hunger takes over as I break out in a full-on sweat, fevered and on the verge of something other worldly.

Pulse pounding in my ears, and as if he senses my orgasm, Lucian fills me with his fingers to the point of discomfort, stroking along my walls and flicking my G spot. Digging my nails into my thighs, I cry out, calling his name over and over, begging, pleading, praying as my lower half coils up so tight I feel the strength of the orgasm just before it hits.

Tongue jackhammering against my clit, he hastens his fingers as I detonate, my entire body shuddering as I come completely undone on his perfect, wicked tongue. My body convulses as I'm blinded by wave after wave of bliss.

Through it, and then some, he continues to eat me like I haven't just exploded on his tongue. Relentless, he doesn't stop, milking every second and prolonging it as I cover my mouth to muffle the insanity pouring out. Scolding me, he bats it away, still fucking me furiously with his fingers as he pulls on my clit again, lengthening my orgasm until I'm a shaking, watery mess.

As it starts to subside, my entire body sags on the mattress as I go boneless, unable to keep my hands on my thighs, as they drop lifelessly to the bed.

I'm done for, and it's obvious to both of us. There's no use in pointing out that he just delivered the strongest orgasm of my life. I'm certain from the sounds that left me that he's aware, and the entire hotel might be, too.

Pushing my thighs open even further so I'm completely exposed to him, Lucian starts to lazily lap at me, bringing me through another orgasm and then another until I'm sure his jaw is aching.

I have never been touched like this. I have never reached peaks this high through kiss, and touch alone, and I doubt I ever will in the future. Because, along with his skill, I've never been *treated* like this. Dominated so masterfully while being so sweetly tended to.

Seemingly satisfied when he lifts from his lazy worship, his expression remains heated. Unsure of how I'll survive the first round with his cock, but eager to feel all of him, he lays on the bed next to me in lieu of undressing. Confused, I lift to take the lead and lower to kiss his chest, but he stills my hands just as his watch goes off.

"That's my hour," he reports softly.

I gape at him, realizing he's still fully dressed and I'm completely bare, and more than that, I feel like I've been thoroughly and utterly fucked. Even so, I can't deny my disappointment. "You aren't seriously calling time on this. We haven't even had sex."

"I told you, I'm not the man to do a one-off. That's not for me.

I made a selfish exception tonight, but this is as far as it goes—unless you agree to more."

Frowning, I turn on my side, propping my head on my hand as his eyes sweep my naked body. "Are you talking about the ground rules?"

"Yes," he reaches out and covers my hip with his palm, slowly gliding it over the curve of it. "I don't want you to ever feel manipulated into a decision and needed you sated before we had this talk."

"Mission accomplished, Doc, and . . . kind of not because I'm dying to get you naked. So, do we really need to have a talk?" I slide my hand down his chest, which, to my dismay, is still covered by his shirt.

"Yes," he says, stilling my hand before I'm able to lower it to stroke the impressive bulge in his pants. "Trust me, I would much rather be fulfilling the command so clear in your eyes."

"I think it's obvious I want more," I say, feeding my eyes just as greedily with a thirsty sweep. "I gave you permission, and you still have too many clothes on."

"More how? I need you to take this seriously, Jane," he says, running his thumb along my jaw. God, that touch in particular, it's every damned thing, and I lean into it, letting him know as much.

"I'm listening."

"I'm not saying I've never had a one-night stand, but those days are long gone. Before I got engaged, and when I was around your age, I started doing partners only. Not all of them were serious, but a combination of dating and sex—no real exceptions. I realize our situation is different, and this could get complicated, but I'm not making an exception here. I want the same with you."

"Are you saying you want to *date* me?" I grin. "Really?"

"Why is that so surprising?"

"Because you—"

"You assumed things you shouldn't have because you were hurt, and I didn't help matters. Yes, I was angry I lost my memory, but I'll make this simple because honestly," he turns me to lay on my stomach and runs a warm palm from the top of my back smoothly down my spine and over the curve of my ass while shifting so his heated whisper lands directly in my ear. "I had zero intention of fucking you last night while we were drinking. Thank Christ that I had sense enough to follow my moral code even if I was pissed drunk. Also, I'm positive we could never be satiated of one another with just one go."

He continues to run his palm down my back, his whispers lighting fire along my skin as he molds it into his touch. "My devil has wanted to fuck yours since you gave me a glimpse of her on that plane, and I would love for our devils to meet," he pauses, his hand on my ass. "So, tonight could be just the beginning," he wedges his hand between my thighs to cup my pussy, "or the end of it. Again, the decision is yours, but know this . . ." he dips a finger just inside me and my hips buck into his touch, "if you truly want more, fair warning, I can be a sexual fucking heathen with an insatiable appetite and I will push every boundary you set for me."

He rims my entrance with a slick finger. "If this starts, my goal will be to make it to where your body craves mine—*constantly*. There will be little to nothing we won't experience together sexually as long as it lasts. The decision is yours."

He continues stroking me, stoking the fire he's relit within seconds, his touch and whispers leaving a trail of goosebumps along the entirety of my arms and neck.

"You're so beautiful, Jane," he rasps out, his voice gravel as he slows his hand before stopping it altogether, and I immediately deflate at the loss. "And I don't want to pressure you. Take your time—"

"Yes," I say breathlessly, "with the condition that you get inside me right now."

Loaded silence fills the air, and when I move to turn over to gauge his reaction, he stops me by palming my ass back to the mattress.

"You'll hear no complaint from me on your condition," he says as he lifts my lower half to prop me on all fours. In the next second, I'm being stretched and readied by his fingers, the sound of just how wet I am filling the silence as he shifts behind me.

"Lucian, I want to see and feel you."

"Well, that's too bad, Jane, because there's the matter of your punishment," he draws out, on his knees now.

"Punishment?"

"For making a fucking date," he grits out as the light sound of fabric rustles behind me. A smile he can't see buds on my lips as the need to see him wars with the ache growing inside. But it's my need to be filled by him that silences any confession or complaint I have.

His hand covers me again in a long sweep down my spine as the other continues to ready me. "Birth control?"

"Covered. Completely," I tell him.

"Do we need a condom?"

"No," I rasp as he runs a reverent palm down my back in the most soothing caress. "It's been a long time for me too."

"How long?"

"Over a year," I confess breathlessly. "Lucian, please, I'm aching."

"Christ, I'm about to explode. This is sure to be embarrassingly fast," he utters as his zipper sounds, which draws a moan from me.

"I don't care. I want to feel you."

"Then we do this, Jane?" He questions just as I feel the thick head of his cock brush against me. My heart begins to pound, his bare thighs brushing mine as he runs his full length between my pussy and ass cheeks.

"Yes, please, fuck me, Lucian," I mewl as he slowly wraps my hair around his fist.

"With pleasure," he replies in a growl as he runs his head through my lips one last time before he slowly begins feeding me his cock, inch by inch. I gasp at the full feel of him and the knowledge that I'd underestimated his size—greatly. He continues to fill me to the point of discomfort while doing his best to ease into me. Not being able to see him do it is exquisite torture.

"God, yes," I cry as he starts to gently pump to fit in more of himself.

"Shame you can't see this stretch," he both taunts and grits out, lust coating his voice, "fuck, this pussy was created to fit me."

In the next second, he thrusts in fully as all the air leaves my body, and Lucian releases an animalistic curse.

"Fucking hell," he stills, "are you okay?"

"Please, Lucian, I'm going to come. Please move."

Releasing his grip on my hair, he lowers it to clamp my neck, using his other to grip my hip before he starts rocking into me. The second he's fully covered in my arousal, he goes feral, pounding into me like a madman, and it's all I can do to keep from collapsing under the weight of the pleasure.

"Perfect, I . . . knew it . . . Christ," he grunts, thrusting relentlessly as I hold on for dear life, my orgasm building, the full feel of him hurling me straight toward release.

"No need to announce," Lucian whispers roughly, his voice so sexy it spurs me on, "I feel you bearing down . . . fuck, Jane, I'm done for." He slams into me, not a drop of mercy to be had as he buries himself again and again, and I can't get enough.

I fly off the edge he thrust me so quickly to, coming apart as my loud cry is cut off due to the sheer force of it. Lucian's powerful thrusts increase to a maddening pace, prolonging it, milking it, until his groan fills the air. He stills, gripping my hip tightly as he fills me with his release just as I start to collapse into the mattress.

Locking me to him, Lucian follows me down, gently pumping his cock into me as if he doesn't want to stop. He continues to grind into me, his chest covering my back until he's fully spent. Seconds or minutes pass as we gather our breath before he gently pulls out of me and disappears into the bathroom.

Roused by the feel of the washcloth and sweep of his hand minutes later, I turn to see him studying me, and I stare right back. For minutes, we simply gaze at each other in comfortable silence, both dazed about what just transpired until our lips both gradually and simultaneously lift.

"That was so damned—" I start.

"Incredible," he finishes as we again smile at one another until his starts to fade. He sweeps his fingers along my skin, dragging me into a lull as I give him the time he needs to give me the words.

"I don't know what comes after," he finally says, a tinge of vulnerability in his voice. "You know I'm in the midst of sorting myself, so I don't know exactly what I can offer. This might be ... or get messy, but I'll do my absolute best to be good to you."

"Your best will do, Lucian," I whisper back. The fact that he's currently sorting through thirty-plus years of repressed emotions and family trauma has me forgiving him for the heartache he's sure to deliver at some point. I reach out and palm his jaw. "We'll take each day as it comes. No pressure, no expectations, and make the most of it."

"I'm completely agreeable to that," he murmurs, running a lock of my hair through his fingers.

"Good," I smile over at him, eyes hooded from exhaustion as he smiles back, keeping me captive with his coaxing touch.

"Merry Christmas, Lucian."

"Indeed it is, Cheeky," he whispers before pulling my upper half to rest on his chest. Taking my cue, I wrap myself around him completely, running my fingers through his hair and strumming his skin in return.

And for the rest of the night, between bouts of deep, restful sleep, he continually unwraps me.

Best. Christmas. Ever.

# TWENTY-EIGHT

## JANE

*Jane sent a SPOTIFY link to Ludwig van Beethoven's Ode to Joy*
*Jane sent a GIPHY of CAT HEAD being drenched by water.*

**KITTY OBLITERATED. KITTY PUUUUURRRRRED ALL NIGHT LONG. TONGUE EMOJI, CAT EMOJI, SWEAT EMOJI, CAT HEART EYES EMOJI**

The shower continues to run in my ensuite bathroom, where one gloriously naked, freshly sated doctor still stands beneath the spray where I just left him. Fastening the tie on the plush terrycloth robe, I plop down onto my bed—which desperately needs a sheet change—just as the response bubbles start to pop up.

**Barrett: Jesus fuck, little sis, did you forget I'm a visual person? SCREAM CRY EMOJI. PUKING EMOJI.**

Barrett sent a GIPHY of a Woman screaming WHY, GOD WHY?

**Oh, shit, I keep forgetting you rejoined the chat, bro. Sorry!**

**Charlie: OMG, tell me everything!**

**Barrett: DO NOT DO THAT!**

I can't anyway, we're leaving for the pub and pitch soon.

Charlie: Pub and pitch?

Yep. Lucian's brother extended an olive branch this morning with an invitation to play in a flag game of football. Apparently, Pub and Pitch is a Boxing Day tradition that Lucian's missed the last three years while he's been in the States.

Charlie: So, what in the hell happened? When you FaceTimed yesterday, you were done with him.

To spare Barrett therapy, let's just say he manned up in a big, BIG way. EGGPLANT EMOJI. WATER SQUIRT EMOJI

Barrett: How is that message better?

Stop being such a prude . . . But get this . . . we're kind of dating now.

Charlie: What?! What is kind of dating?

I can't help my smile as I type.

Dating, as in it's a no-pressure situation while we're on the trip. He told me he doesn't do one-night stands, that he's not that guy. He said it's gotta be something or nothing. We both chose something for now.

Charlie: I'm really starting to like him.

Barrett: Me too.

Me three, but don't get too excited, he can be a bit of a shit. But yeah, we're like . . . dating at his insistence.

Charlie: I'm so happy!

Barrett: Cool. What is Boxing Day?

The way Lucian explained it, it's a holiday over here, kind of like our Labor Day.

Charlie: BORING! Tell me about all the hot sex.

Charlie sent a GIPHY of CAT MEOWING

Charlie: So, so, happy for you. PARTY HAT EMOJI.

Barrett: Do I need to leave this chat again?

Barrett: And at least one Cartwright sister is getting some.

Charlie: Don't be jealous you aren't petting the kitty.

Are you being stingy with the kitty, sis?

Charlie: ABSOLUTELY. Especially since he decided to throw away my birth control. Apparently, maybe means right now to this jackass.

Knock her up proper, brother! I want that new niece or nephew. FIST BUMP EMOJI

Barrett: Bet on it! FIST BUMP EMOJI

Charlie: MIDDLE FINGER EMOJI

I have to go. Kiss my boy for me. I love y'all. BABY RATTLE EMOJI

Barrett: Love you, little sister. But please, spare me the future kitty statuses.

No promises.

Barrett: Oh, Big Bird is going to be in Paris when you are. Just talked to him today.

Oh? Send him my number and tell him he had better text me! It's been too long!

Barrett: Will do.

Charlie: More details please.

Charlie sent a GIPHY of TAPPING FOOT.

Charlie sent a GIPHY of CAT PURRRING

Charlie sent a GIPHY of CAT RIDING MOTORCYCLE.

Charlie sent a GIPHY of MAN BREAKDANCING WITH CAT HEAD.

Barrett: Okay, I think we get it, babe.

Charlie: But you ain't getting it! BURN EMOJI

Charlie sent a GIPHY of NOPE NOPE NOPE CAT head shake.

Barrett: All right, that's it. Please excuse us, little sis. Someone needs a reminder . . . and should probably run.

Charlie: Run? PALEASE in your drea

I can't help my laugh knowing that Charlie's been tackled by Barrett wherever she is in the house, which left her incapable of finishing her text. When they first started their dueling, Barrett had surprised us both with the ferocity and tenacity with which he refused Charlie's excuses and batted away any attempt she made to keep him at bay. A Southern boy to his core—and though mostly soft-spoken—once Barrett Jennings had his sights on someone, namely Charlie, it was all she wrote.

Which left me happy for Charlie—if not a bit envious. Lucian's voice rings out feet away, interrupting my thoughts just as I toss my phone on the mattress.

"Good report to Charlie this round, I hope?"

Glancing over, I see Lucian wrapped in a towel, filling the door of my bathroom, water dripping from his gorgeous frame.

"*Very good review*, too bad there isn't a YELP category for what you got swinging beneath that towel—and how you work it—you'd be the best on-call doctor that ever lived."

He shakes his head, and I notice his ears turning a little red, which I find endearing as hell.

"Are you blushing, Doc?"

"You are incorrigible," he grumbles.

"Damn right," I give him a wink. "But everyone else can fend for themselves and find their own dirty Doctor Prick because I'm sure as hell not sharing mine."

He quirks a brow. "That so?"

"'Tis so. Besides, you came out of the gate trying to be stingy with the penis."

"Correct me if I'm wrong, Nurse Cartwright, was it not you yelling at me on the street less than twenty-four hours ago to keep my penis away from you?"

"No, it was just you, I have no beef at all with your penis," I grin. "He's my greatest ally and newly acquired necessity, where you're still optional."

"You're shameless," he grins back.

"You love it," I say, glancing down at my phone to see Charlie still hasn't managed to text back. "But yeah, that was Charlie and

Barrett, who, upon reading my latest report, have decided they might like you, so don't screw it up."

"I'll do my best," he says, sauntering toward me.

"Your best will do," I inwardly sigh, thinking about how good his best has been so far.

"Anyway, they're going to start trying for another baby, and I'm glad because they're still as crazy about each other as they were the day they met. Well, not the actual day they met. That day was, whoa," I say, "but now, well, I guess you could say they're relationship goals for me," I look up to see Lucian staring intently at me.

"What? . . . I'm babbling, I know."

"You're beautiful," he says so sincerely that it stuns me.

"And you're mad," I mock in my shitty accent as I run my hand through my wet hair. "I probably look freshly fucked."

"That too," he says, a grin on his lips, "because you have been. But you need to get dressed and bundle up tight. And you need to hurry up, or you'll make me late."

"Aye, Aye, cap-i-ton. Would you like fries and a shake with that order?"

His eyes darken as he gives me a telling stare.

"Well, if you want me dressed, get out of here," I wave him away, "before you impregnate me with that there smolder," I drawl.

He shakes his head, grinning, before turning and making his way to his room to dress.

Clawing the air at his retreating back, I release my running commentary on the down low.

"So. Frickin'. Hot . . . come back baby and make this kitty PURRRRRRR . . . I gon' take that dick. Gon' take that dicka . . . Gon' take that dicka . . . gon' get that dicka all up in my vag—"

In seconds, it becomes very, very obvious that I *did not* keep my running commentary *low*, and I clamp my mouth closed when Lucian stops dead in his tracks a few feet outside my door.

As he slowly turns to me, a clear 'what the fuck' in his expression, I lift my phone and pretend to text. When he doesn't move for a solid fifteen seconds, I have no choice but to give him facts, cheeks blazing as I refuse to look up from my phone.

"If you're feeling any sort of buyer's remorse right now, I think it's important you know it's much too late, Doc. You already took the kitty home and petted it. No refunds."

You know those scenes in movies and on TV where British blokes huddle together in long-sleeved collared polos, and drunkenly shout-sing songs of their favorite team or alma mater?

Well, thanks to Byron's invitation to Lucian, I've just witnessed the real deal.

After Mike swept us from the curb of our hotel, we were swiftly delivered to a charming little pub in Richmond—a pub where a dozen or so of Byron and Lucian's oldest and best mates met and congregated. Just after their enthusiastic greeting, they proceeded to chug a dizzying number of pints brimming with a dark, stout lager, seemingly without taking a breath in between.

Lucian had surprised me by partaking, downing his fair share of foamy dark beer with a mischievous twinkle in his eyes.

In a sudden turn of events, Mike had turned in his keys for the day and emerged from the pub restroom in matching attire—tiny sports shorts, a multicolored, striped polo shirt similar to Lucian's, and cleats. Or, as Lucian called them—'studs.' Studs that Mike brought for Lucian and himself to wear for today's match—which only confirmed my suspicions about our driver.

Thinking them all a little crazy for wearing short shorts in *teen* degrees, or rather freezing Celsius weather, I have to admit I'm not too upset about Lucian's tiny shorts. Or at all opposed to the fact that they showcase every inch of bulging muscle in his thick thighs.

When we arrived—and through a cloudy haze of testosterone—I was briefly introduced to the whole group. Their names evade me now as we all set out to the field or, as I've been corrected—the pitch. A pitch which is conveniently located across the street from the pub, where the friendly, no-contact match is set to be played.

As we made our way over, I saw some of the girlfriends and wives—who I was also briefly introduced to—setting up field-side tables, including hot drink dispensers and snacks. While others fill coolers to the brim with more beer, no ice needed due to nature's refrigerator.

It seems sobriety isn't required for the game—the opposite greatly encouraged.

Within minutes of hitting the field, I'm thankful I took Lucian's advice and dressed more for comfort rather than style. Wearing bright white joggers and a plain sweatshirt, I topped it with my white marshmallow jacket and matching pom-pom beanie. The only pop of color in my outfit is the icy blue snowflakes on the tip of my boots.

With all the white I'm wearing, I could easily blend with our winter wonderland surroundings, a good amount of the snow banked around the entirety of the field, correction—'pitch,' which someone has miraculously plowed in preparation for a drunken game of soccer, that they keep referring to as football. A joke I told in the car that neither Lucian nor Mike found funny but I deemed hilarious.

*Men . . .* and their damned football. And as it seems, these folks don't mess around even when it comes to a simple rookie game.

Though the wives and girlfriends seem nice enough, I stand solo at the end of some plastic bleachers during pre-game so I can keep a sharp eye on Lucian and Byron for any sign of progress, good or bad.

When Lucian showed me the text this morning in bed, the threat of a smile was definitely there, as was the hope filtering in his eyes. Hope that yanked firmly on every damn string in my heart. It's obvious to me how deeply Lucian still cares for his older brother, and I can't help but hope there's some potential there for reconciliation.

Byron had been cordial enough in the way of a greeting when we got here—if not a little more friendly—which I took as a good sign. Especially since I made a comment about his junk being inadequate the last time I saw him.

*Whiskey. Oops.*

As it seems now, they're barely speaking, but speaking they are, which I also see as a glass half full because it's steps above not at all.

Ears stinging red as I stalk the Aston brothers, I tug my beanie down close in preparation for freezing my ass off while watching grown men guzzle booze and fight for control of a ball.

Not that I'm not a sports fan, but in extreme temperatures, it's a bit much to subject yourself to this cold while not playing for real points.

The nurse in me is already gauging which players I should worry about injuring themselves by who's currently stretching and who's guzzling more beer. But it's the dirty blond God in the center of one of the stretch huddles that captures and keeps my attention.

Though smaller in stature than some of them, his build is still incredible. I know from our own private match last night, in which he literally fucked me until I passed smooth out, that when it comes to stamina, there isn't a bloke here that can match his.

That thought alone has me smiling like a dick-matised idiot on the side of the field.

*Dear God, it's me, Jane. He's so pretty . . . can I please keep this one? I'll be good. I'll do better. I'll recycle more and swear less. Please?*

As if he senses my prayer, Lucian's eyes lift to mine as his words from last night come back to me.

*I'm a sexual fucking heathen.*

"Yes indeedy, that you are."

*With an insatiable appetite, and I will push every boundary you set for me.*

"I'll take *that shit* for five hundred, Alex."

*If this starts, my goal will be to make it to where your body craves mine*—constantly.

"Mission already accomplished, Doc, but I'm still going to make you work for it," I muse as Lucian eyes me curiously, no doubt wondering what I'm mouthing while standing alone. Though his resting bastard is firmly in place because no leopard changes his spots overnight, I can see he's more at ease in his posture and, no doubt, amongst his friends.

He's come a long way already in the week we've been here, and frankly, I'm proud of him. It was his behavior last night that shocked me most in the fact that he wanted us to date and didn't want this thing between us to be limited to physical.

Something I still can't quite manage to get my head around as he stares back at me, gifting me a slight lift of his lips when I give him a little wave.

*Get ahold of yourself, Nurse Cartwright!*

But I can't, so instead, I bask in my happiness and rake my eyes down Lucian as his stare suddenly grows heavy, and he begins stalking toward me.

Confused as to why he's suddenly moving toward me like a man on a mission, the mystery is quickly solved when my view of Lucian is blocked by a Frenchman. One I stood up last night.

*Oh shite.*

"Good afternoon, Jane. How are we feeling today?"

Matthieu asks, standing before me in his own tiny sports shorts and polo. He peers back at me, his curious gaze searching my person as Lucian quickly approaches from behind.

*Well, this is most inconvenient.*

"Hey, M-Matthieu. Didn't know you were coming today," I squeak out as a dark blond blur starts to torpedo in our direction. Lucian's eyes glide down Matthieu, and as he draws closer, I catch the visible tick of his jaw. With every step Lucian takes, I scramble to figure out how to make a quick escape, just as Matthieu inevitably speaks up. Which so happens to be the exact second Lucian comes within earshot.

"I see you're feeling better today. I was sorry you canceled our dinner last night."

Lucian stops dead in his tracks a few feet away from Matthieu, who's completely unaware of the honey-brown twin daggers that just shifted from his back to pin me.

Dread fills me because I know Lucian's wheels are spinning, and it's just a matter of seconds.

"So then, you are feeling better?" Matthieu prompts because I hadn't answered him.

"Much better now, thank you," I say just as Lucian's eyes narrow on mine.

*Yep. Busted.*

Raking my lower lip with my teeth in an attempt to conceal a threatening smile, I fail miserably, and Lucian's nostrils flare in response. I tilt my head. Is that smoke coming out of them?

Scrambling for a way to make a quick exit, what comes up comes out.

"Lucian, look!" I shout, jarring Matthieu, who turns back and spots Lucian standing feet away. "Matthieu is here," I say, all but presenting him with jazz hands.

"I can see that, Jane," Lucian says, taking a few feet to reach us before politely turning to Matthieu. "Good afternoon."

"Good to have you here, Lucian," Matthieu says, palming Lucian's shoulder. "We have missed you on this day these last few years."

"Happy to be here," Lucian says, sounding anything but as he levels me with a dead stare.

I. Am. So. Fucked.

"You know what?" I squeak. "I'm suddenly dying for a cup of coffee. I'll let you two catch up." I turn to Matthieu. "Lucian was just stretching. You should stretch with him. As medical professionals," I verbally vomit, "we all know how important it is to stretch! In fact, I could use a good stretch now, have a great game, guys!"

I wave furiously between them like an idiot before turning and high-tailing it out of there. True to my word, I stretch my legs as much as possible to get myself to safety while catching the tail end of their interaction.

"Go see Byron for your position and team assignment," Lucian tells Matthieu, "I'll be right back. Oh, *Jane*," Lucian calls as I practically flee.

"Jane, a quick word," Lucian bites out as I speed up while huffing and nervously laughing as he practically chases me down the side of the field. Searching for refuge, I spot two of the girlfriends crowding the coffee table and make a beeline for them.

Much to my dismay, the minute I get there, they both walk off, leaving me defenseless. Defeated and knowing my boots are nowhere near tall enough for the amount of shit I'm now in, I wave my white flag by grabbing a coffee cup and staying put.

I've just started dispensing it when I feel fire licking along my profile.

"You sneaky, cheeky fucking woman," Lucian hisses standing just to the side of me, his exhales hitting me so he's literally breathing down my neck. "It was all for show yesterday, wasn't it? You lured me in, entrapped me."

"Hey, hey, let's not sling those types of accusations. I did no such thing," I defend weakly before pressing my lips together to hide my guilty smile again.

"You're so damned guilty, you can't even *look* at me."

"I can. I just choose not to," I squeak, stirring my sugar into my coffee before capping it.

"Look at me this instant, Jane Cartwright."

Crossing one arm over me, I lift my cup with the other and turn my head to meet his accusing return stare. "Does this really constitute first and last name seriousness? And are you really complaining?"

"You plotted the whole thing, didn't you? Left the address for me to easily find. Dressed up, looking so fucking fit, no doubt to drive me mad. All for show."

"Well, looking 'fit' is a matter of opinion, and yours is mighty flattering," I lift my coffee in cheers. "So, thanks for the confidence boost."

"You had already canceled your date before you left, hadn't you?"

"Semantics, Doc, and who needs details when all's well that ends well? We ended *really well*, don't you think?"

"I thought you were angry with me," he bites out. "And oh, how the tables have turned."

"Nah, you're not so mad," I squirm under his stare. "The cat doesn't have your tongue, so I'm thinking we're good."

"You're assuming wrong. And Oh, Cheeky, how your pussy will pay for this—*dearly*," he offers in clear threat. "Especially when it's obvious you're feeling absolutely no shame."

"What can I say? A dozen or so orgasms will do that to a girl."

I wink at him, and he practically growls in response, crossing his arms as he does.

"Oh, come on, Doc, it wasn't *all* me. I had no idea if you would show." I glance past his shoulder to avoid his debilitating smolder, which, as it turns out, is even sexier when he's angry.

"I'm going to bide my time, and I suggest you do the same. But, Jane, know this—at the time of my choosing, you will be *severely* and *thoroughly punished*."

"Promises, promises," I snark, sweeping my tongue across my lower lip, all of my current confidence completely false because of the vibe he's sending off.

Closing the space between us, he leans in, his lips so close that I can practically taste them. Heat gathers below as I dip my eyes to study the mouth that recently pleasured me to the point of comatose.

"The possibilities are endless. By the time I'm done with the thorough retribution I'm plotting, you'll be well aware I'm not at all keen on being toyed with."

"Don't threaten me with a good time," I shimmy, slightly quaking in my boots due to the vibe rolling from him.

"It will be torture, I assure you."

"If your mouth is involved, that's doubtful," I jibe.

"You're so fucking cheeky," he scorns.

"And don't you forget it," I quip.

"Oh, I won't. Trust me. You're now suspect for everything." He shakes his head, his expression incredulous. "Christ, that was bold."

"Go big or go home, right?" I dip my eyes. "I opted for *big*."

He leans in further. "Flattery won't save your arse. Jesus . . . how have you bewitched me *this much* in just a week?"

"Talent," I say, shimmying due to the cold but mostly the anticipation. "Now, you have a different match to concentrate on and eleven drunk men to contend with. I suggest you get your head in the *right game*, Doc."

"I suppose I should," he glances back at the other players starting to crowd the pitch, "but Jane," his eyes darken as his guard dips and his devil peeks out.

"Yes?" I swallow.

"Plans are set."

"Looking forward to it," I snark, thankful Christmas isn't quite over for me yet.

"I see we've decided on 'walking on water' Jane today?" He deadpans.

"No, more like floating on cloud nine," I admit honestly.

"Again, flattery won't save your arse."

"No, I saved my arse just for *you*."

His eyes light fire at my admission, and I drop my imaginary mic and make my way toward the stands, admittedly with a little more pep in my step.

Just after taking a seat, I watch as Matthieu approaches Lucian. Shortly after, both men's focus shifts to me. Instantly on alert, I get an inkling and it's not a good one.

Matthieu leans in and whispers to Lucian seconds later, his lips rapidly moving as all animation leaves Lucian's expression before he slowly turns his head, setting his sights on Matthieu—Matthieu, who's still looking at me. It's then I see the shift in Lucian's posture. It's subtle at first, until it isn't, ultimately reeking of wrath.

Shortly after the match begins, all hell breaks loose.

# TWENTY-NINE

## JANE

"You really need to start focusing on trying to use your words, Doc," I say before pressing my lips together as Lucian stews, facing me where we sit perched on the edge of my bed—a position I practically had to wrestle him into when we got back to the penthouse. I forced him to nurse a Gatorade as I cracked open the first aid kit that I asked the front desk to send up. The moody man in front of me looking much worse for wear than he did when we left this morning.

Grass and mud stains now cover a majority of his clothes and skin, his legs littered with debris where his shin guards ended, and a little blood splatter now staining his solid white collar.

From minute one, their annual *friendly* match progressively turned into a massacre—at least from my vantage point. Maybe it was the alcohol, or that all of them had some pent-up aggression they needed working out or the nature of the sport itself. But as it played out, not one footballer left that pitch without some blood splatter or fresh bruising.

Lucian had more than held his own but had highly instigated a lot of the brutality that transpired. The 'no touch' concept had gone right out of the window in a matter of minutes.

"Have to admit," I say, soaking the cotton ball with antiseptic before dotting the cut on Lucian's lip, "it's pretty entertaining watching men engage in a cock fight for a woman's attention."

"That's not what—" Lucian starts to protest as I lower the cotton ball and quirk a brow. In return, I'm granted a sheepish grin.

"Did it work?" He finally asks, his beautiful lower lip swollen as I gently dab the small cut with antiseptic.

"Oh yeah, I witnessed every painful second of the crash course therapy session with your brother and best mates. It was highly entertaining, really. And in case you didn't notice, my eyes were on you the entire time. There was no need to toss your flag and go all Godzilla."

"Pointless it seems, as I lost," he grimaces a little as I dab at a deep scratch on the underside of his jaw.

"Your team lost, not just you, and you're displaying bad sportsmanship by sulking." Which, honestly, I find adorable. "Jesus," I say studying the aftermath up close, "the whole side of your face is swollen."

He gently grips my wrist. "I'm fine, Jane. Leave it."

"Tell that to your priceless vision and billion-dollar hands. Considering what we're here for, that was pretty reckless, Lucian."

"Perhaps . . . but it was fun," his smile costs him a discomforting wince due to the cut on his lip but lights up his gorgeous face just the same. He looks so boyishly handsome, staring back at me with his hair a wreck, a lot of it dried in a sweaty heap across his forehead. His makeshift uniform is now hanging by tattered threads, and his ruined new cleats are discarded nearby on the floor.

"Fun, huh?" I ask.

"Yes," Lucian nods emphatically as I replay the whole thing.

From what I've gathered, the second Tremblay told Lucian of his game plan involving *me*, Lucian decided to dismantle Matthieu's plans by *not* using his words and instead spent the entirety of the game trying to rip his head off his body.

"You know, I can still hear Matthieu begging for mercy at the bottom of the dog pile that you *tripped him into* before you pounced. Your name was all muddled as he begged for mercy. "Lu-sheeannn-an, palease, mon dieu, merde, Christ Jesus," I recite in my most pathetic, French-infused impression.

Lucian tips his head back in a maniacal laugh, and the sound fills me up as I resume tending to his superficial wounds. "Yep, terrible sportsmanship, Aston, but if it helps the sting of the loss, and you can sink this into your currently Neanderthal-drenched brain," I say, gently pressing the antiseptic to his skin, "my attraction for you doesn't depend on whether or not you win a soccer game."

"Football," he counters.

"Always correcting me," I scold playfully.

His face sobers instantly. "My apologies, I'll try to stop."

I pause the cotton ball. "No, you won't, and *don't*," I shrug. "It's kind of our thing now."

"Is it?" His eyes follow my every move.

"Hmm," I dab at a few more light scratches. "Geesh, handsome," I say, patting another cut on his neck, "did you wrestle a rose bush? I must have missed that part."

Lucian grips my wrist, pressing his lips against the inside, his eyes holding mine hostage before he lowers it and sweeps his thumb over the same skin as he speaks. "I fancy you, Jane."

His admission is so sincere that it immediately sends my heartbeat skyrocketing and, pathetically, seduces me on the spot. It makes it clear that I've got it bad already, and we've only been dating a day— less than a day.

*Careful, Jane.*

"So I've been told," I say, clearing my throat, "by everyone *but you* . . . until now." I grip his hair playfully. "Gotta say, it's nice to finally hear it from the source. Although," I sigh, "it is another alcohol-infused admission."

"Jane, I haven't had a drink in hours, and I'm nowhere near as inebriated as I was two nights ago. Tell me you believe that."

He presses in with an earnest expression, and I nod. "Okay, Doc. You fancy me."

"I do." His smile has me reeling as my heart gallops, threatening to grow wings and fly right out of my chest. Lucian, with his guard down, is utterly charming, disarming, and endearing.

Said heart straps itself up as it prepares for battle, or at least some defense. I can't give in to these feelings for him so easily, but he's making it so damned hard. Even so, I remind myself of the situation—that our dating status is most likely temporary. *Five weeks* temporary, to be specific.

"And I've been in love with your pussy since the second I saw it," Lucian says, a wicked grin lifting his lips.

"And you call *me* incorrigible?"

"The second I laid eyes on it, I wanted to fucking feast."

"Doctor Aston," I tug the hair my fingers are entangled in, "you're quite the pig."

"Title me what you will. I'm not ashamed to admit that the night I examined you, I wanked off thinking about it."

"I'm absolutely shocked," I feign surprise. "And to think I considered you a true gentleman.

"To be fair, it had been years since I've seen a woman's bare flesh in any respect."

"Well then," I say, capping the bottle and closing the kit, "I guess you get a pass."

"Ah, but this pussy," he says, quickly pulling me to sit on his lap, my back to him as he slides his palm down to cup it, his heated whisper tickling my ear. "Fuck, I was mesmerized."

"I can honestly say," I rasp out, "she's pretty fond of you, too, and," I add, turning to look at him as his fingers trace my sex outside my joggers, "I fancy you a little too."

"So I *heard*," he says, shifting us to pin me on the mattress, eyes playfully glittering down on me.

"Will you please *stop* reminding me you heard everything."

"What did you say to Charlie that first night?" He tilts his head playfully, completely ignoring my request. "Ah," he grins, and I brace myself for embarrassment. "'If he wasn't such a dick, I would let him full-on *crack my back.*'"

"Jesus," I say, cheeks heating, "do you have to embarrass me?"

"Titt for tatt, Cartwright, and don't think I've forgotten you played me last night."

"I just gave you a little push," I shrug, "men need those from time to time."

"I see, and what would you have done had I not shown?"

"Dined alone," I state simply. "I wasn't wasting good makeup and a kick-ass outfit. But," I relay on a shaky breath, "whether this lessens my future punishment or not, you need to know dinner is all I agreed to, and it was *before* our walk that night in Oxford. Before you ever touched me or kissed me. And after you did," I swallow, "I didn't want dinner with *that* doctor anymore. I was too busy fancying another. So, I didn't make a date, Lucian."

His eyes soften at my confession. "Why didn't you simply tell me that?"

I bite my lip briefly. "Because you stung me pretty good—"

"And so, you decided to sting me back," he finishes.

"I'm sorry," I say.

"No, you're not," he grins, stealing my breath.

"I am a little bit," I admit, as he grips the hem of my shirt before slowly pulling it over my head and I lift my arms to help him. Eyes scanning my upper half, he unclasps my bra as my pulse speeds up, anticipation soaking my panties. As crazy as it is, aside from the butterflies, I'm already completely comfortable bearing myself to him.

So, when he pulls on my joggers and drags my panties down with them, I lift my hips to help him do it. Fully naked beneath him, I stare up at him as he fists off his polo, exposing his sculpted upper body and making my mouth water. When he loses his shorts and boxers and positions himself between my legs, he hovers above me.

"As you well know, you succeeded," he whispers in admission. "Good thing I had a nurse nearby to tend to such a wound."

All talk ceases as we just stare at one another, though our eye exchange feels every bit like we're carrying on a conversation. That is until he bends and takes my lips in a sweeping kiss.

As it lengthens and overpowers me, I decide Lucian's kiss is my kryptonite, and it's brought home further as he brands me with it.

Lost in another deep kiss, he pulls my thigh to hitch it on his hip before driving straight into me, capturing my gasp in his mouth.

Pulling back, our eyes bolted, he begins steadily thrusting into me, the feel of it, the connection surreal and so next level. With every single push of his hips, he grinds slightly past bottoming out, a mix of groans and rumbles sounding from him as he draws on my reaction.

The threat of an orgasm has me clawing his shoulders and tightening my legs around him. I lift my hips to meet his thrusts, which sets him off as he starts frantically pumping into me.

"Christ, Christ," he grunts as I widen my thighs and angle my hips to take him deeper. It's then he truly snaps, fucking me like a man possessed. His unsuppressed groans of pleasure fill me as he ravages me, and I eagerly run my hands over his flexing biceps, his heaving chest, and everything else within reach. His movements become less controlled as we both spiral and time lapses without measure.

Harsh breaths continue to leave as he hovers above me, refusing to look away or break our gaze. Our sounds mingle, our bodies moving effortlessly together, the connection intensifying tenfold.

"Oh . . . God," I cry as he shifts his hips again, and that's all it takes. I explode, feeling every inch of him as my body clamps around him while the rest of me shatters. Topping last night, it's the most powerful orgasm I've ever had, and he palms my stomach, pressing it down while dragging his cock perfectly along my walls, making it last a blissful eternity.

Tears of ecstasy slip down my temples as he moves his palm from my stomach to frame my face while still staring intensely into my eyes.

"Jane," he whispers as he lifts me easily from my back to sit astride him, and we both moan at the feel of him sinking in impossibly deeper and the inevitable click that follows. Too overcome with the need for more, I immediately start to move, and as I do, the world begins tilting on its axis as we both get lost in sensation, in each other.

My mouth parts just as his goes slack as our bodies work in sync, so much so another orgasm seizes me. I bear down on him as it sweeps me, and he crashes his mouth into mine, kissing me so ferociously I think we might not survive it.

For long minutes, we kiss, that connection just as intense as our joined bodies.

Jesus . . . Can he feel this, too?

God, I pray I'm not alone.

"Feels so right," he murmurs against my lips, mimicking exactly what I'm thinking and feeling as he considers me, too, our bodies only gently rocking at this point. Though I'm eager for more with the light friction, in a way, it feels like enough just by the way we're linked.

"So good," I murmur back, wishing for it to last as long as he can hold out. My wish is granted as we exhaust ourselves, and he continually breaks me against him—my soft curves to his rock-hard *everything*.

It's sensual and deliberate and delicious and so perfect. Before, I could never imagine a life where sex was ever this good. But here I am, living in it with my fantasy man, who's staring back at me like I matter.

Like this sex matters, and we're only a day in.

In one sudden movement, he grips my hips. His lips part against mine as he pours into me, the sound leaving him too fucking perfect to be real.

"Lucian," I chant as he stills my hips and bucks, lifting us from the bed as he groans out his release, and I furiously grind against him. Once he's spent, we collapse in a heap, his back on the mattress, me on his chest, him still buried inside me.

When I pull away to peer down at him, his hairline soaked, skin glistening, I lose a little more of the self-preservation I'm still trying to hold onto.

It's too much too soon, and what we did felt a lot like making love. Even so, I owe him the admission budding on my tongue as he stares up at me, his expression becoming more curious as he continually strokes my face.

"Can I be honest?" I ask, running my palm over his chest.

"I want nothing less. I don't wish for that aspect to change in the slightest."

"That's the best I've ever felt with any man, ever, Lucian."

"I have to agree on my end," he offers, running his pointer along my profile.

"Well, that *sucks*," I joke, "guess it's all downhill from here."

He gives me a dead stare. "And you believe I'm emotionally stunted? Are you aware you make jokes when you suffer emotional overload? Seemingly at the worst times?"

"Ouch and touché."

"Just an observation," he whispers, trailing the pads of his fingers down my back.

"Well, I don't want you to think you have to say things like that just because I—"

"Stop, immediately," he whispers harshly. "I'm being honest, Jane. I'm positive there won't be a better comparison for either of us after having one another."

"Me too," I whisper, though it scares me. I collapse back on his chest and exhale. "All right, the real truth is . . . my pussy just fell in love with your cock."

The bounce of his chest has me grinning. Several strokes of his fingers later, he pauses them. "Can you sleep?"

"Yeah," I say, my voice full of the lull his touch put me in. "I was just about to doze off. You?"

"No, I'm rather wound up, actually."

"Really?" I ask, utterly depleted.

"*Really*, so I'm going to leave you to sleep, but I'll be back."

"Lucian, don't feel like you have to—"

"Enough, Jane," he scolds as I scowl at him, and he makes it a point to hold my eyes. "I'm fine with intimacy and don't at all stray or veer away from it. I crave intimacy as much as anything else when it comes to sex. Believe me when I tell you that sex is meaningless, pointless, and empty to me without it."

"Well . . . that's," I bite my lip briefly, "refreshing."

"Well, that's also dating an older man," he counters. "At least *this* older man."

"I crave touch, too. A lot, if I'm honest, so that works for me."

"Good." He takes my mouth in a kiss meant for an ex-rated fairy-tale before he ends it with a long press of his lips, easing from beneath me and off the mattress.

Inwardly sighing, I turn on my side in time to catch him click off the light where he now darkens my door like he did a week ago. One week and our dynamic has drastically changed. I can't wait to see what the next one brings.

"Sleep well, Cheeky."

"Oh, I'm positive I will, Doctor."

Sometime later, I wake and cover the billion-dollar hand that palms my stomach, pulling me into him. His warm lips glide along my neck before his breathing starts to match mine. Tucked inside his warmth, I drift away.

# THIRTY

## JANE

*JAN 2018*

*S*wipe.

A snap Lucian reluctantly took of me while I lightly heckled a queen's guard outside Buckingham Palace.

*Swipe.*

A picture of Lucian and me on our penthouse balcony, matching New Year's Top Hats on, both of us smiling, faintly captured fireworks littering the night sky in the background. It was a damned good night, and our midnight kiss lasted well past the strike of the hour.

*Swipe.*

A candid of Lucian in Hyde Park in his suit and trench coat, gloved hands at his sides. His profile was lit perfectly by the sun rays peeking out of the cluster of trees he stood next to while lost in his thoughts.

I heart that photo and add them all to my favorites as I re-live the last two incredible weeks while we ride passenger in the sedan. This trip to Oxford has a different vibe than our last as Lucian and Mike chat. Closing my phone, I glance between the two of them as they talk candidly and roll my eyes before finally letting them know their jig is up.

"So, Mike," I prompt, just as Lucian starts to thumb through his email.

"Yes, Jane?"

"How long have you been Lucian's *personal driver*?"

Lucian's thumb stills, hovering over his phone screen, and I glance in the rearview to see Mike's eyes bulge before he answers, his expression sheepish. "Before he left London, it was nearing 'round seven years. We've been mates much longer," Mike confesses. "And I didn't tell her," he adds for Lucian.

"That's because *she* is intelligent enough to have figured it out in week one," I mutter dryly. "Did you jackasses really think I wouldn't catch on? Seriously, it's insulting. I've been patiently waiting for one or both of you to come clean," I scold between them. "So why haven't you?"

"I'll let you take this one," Mike says, chuckling as I turn expectantly toward Lucian.

Lucian pockets his phone and turns to me, running his finger over the top of my hand resting on the seat between us.

"Don't be upset with me, Jane. If I'm honest, you terrified me with your squirrel-like attention span and by blindly walking into the streets." He bites his full lower lip, smolder in full effect, while looking delicious in an all-black suit adorned by the dark purple tie that I picked out this morning.

"I simply wanted to keep you safe," he admits. My chest flutters at his confession as Mike chimes in.

"I believe his exact words were," Mike clears his throat as Lucian murders him visually in the rearview, "I'm traveling with a very mad, very cheeky American woman who is a danger to herself and others. It would be the miracle of all miracles to keep her in one piece until France. So, when you come around, don't tell her you work specifically for me, as she currently detests me."

"Thank you for clearing that up, *mate*," Lucian mutters derisively, "and you're fired."

Mike and I laugh, and I shake my head, knowing Lucian probably recruited him right after our fish and chips fight in the street because Mike chauffeured us to Oxford the following day.

"Okay, I get that, but why continue to hide it all the way up to *now*?"

"Frankly, you're unpredictable, and if you got or get 'pissed,'" he mocks me, in a surprisingly spot-on impression, "you might stop allowing him to drive you."

"Which means you would lose your *personal spy*. Don't feign innocence."

"It was never about invasion of privacy," he defends.

"Well, we both know priv-a-cee is a hard commodity to come by with you around."

He quirks a brow. "Are we complaining, Nurse Cartwright?"

"Not today," I wink. "But for your information, I wouldn't have ditched Mike. I happen to like him more than you," I jibe as Lucian's jaw goes slack. "And he's not even the one giving me a daily helping of the *Aston shaft*."

Mike bursts into laughter as Lucian's eyes light fire and narrow.

"Ahh honey, don't take it so personally," I coo. "I'm touched, really, that you fancied me so much that you hired me my very own stalker," I palm his jaw. "It's like we're a legit couple."

"Stow it, Cheeky. I just wanted to keep you safe, as well as the people of London, for that matter."

"And kudos on succeeding, handsome," I say, nudging his shoulder.

"Not quite. You and the whole of Europe are still at risk, seeing as how we still have three weeks to go."

"Hilarious, but I am sad we're temporarily losing our driver," I push out my lower lip as I meet Mike's smiling eyes. "I'm going to miss you while we're gone, buddy."

"You as well, but you'll be back."

"Or maybe I'll just disappear in Paris, never to be found again," I chirp excitedly. "*Le sigh*. I can practically hear the uplifting accordion music already. Birds sing along as the sun shines on my postcard view of the Eiffel Tower while I sip my morning coffee at one of those street-side cafes and nibble on a fresh *croissant*," I drawl. "I *cannot wait*. Oh, and I reserved the most adorable place to stay, too."

Lucian turns to me, brow quirked. I lean over to address him, though Mike is the only person we're open around with our relationship. To everyone else, once we're outside the penthouse—and aside from our exchanged heated and lingering looks—no one would ever be the wiser.

On the days we do spend together publicly, I get a kick out of watching him interact with others—resting bastard face firmly in place. All the while knowing what it's like to have him pumping furiously inside me while whispering filthy as hell things into my ear.

Leaning over, I keep my voice low, the topic private enough to call for it. "I was going to talk to you tonight and see if you would stay with me. It's not like the penthouse or anything super fancy, but it is a hideaway meant for *lovers*," I drawl in my best Pepe Le Pew.

"Flattering, but what you're omitting is that you initially booked it for you and your *French* lover. That was on the itinerary, was it not?"

"Shit," I sink into my seat. "Heard *that part* of the convo with Charlie, did you?"

He gives me the hairy eyeball in return.

"Well, in my defense—"

"You have none," he clips dryly. "At all."

"The hell I don't. We didn't exist yet, Aston. You can't really hold that against me."

"Can't I?"

He sips from his to-go espresso cup as I roll my eyes and scold him with a whisper. "Such a jealous man."

Possessive is more like it, and not in an unhealthy way, but just enough to make me giddy when it happens. After two weeks of dating, I've memorized some of his behaviors and quirks.

For one, he prefers to read hardbacks. My love for that quirk stems from the sound of them snapping closed, which often means I've pulled his reading focus away and probably have an orgasm coming.

His work ethic is impeccable. Though we have spent a good amount of time distracting each other—when Dr. Aston is in the house—he's all about his profession.

He's spent several days in the lab with Matthieu in the last few weeks—who had a good laugh at Lucian's expense when Lucian had to tuck his tail between his legs and apologize. Matthieu had accepted instantly and admitted that he had purposefully baited him, laying it on thick, knowing it would get under Lucian's skin. In the end, according to my hot-headed Englishman, their friendship 'hasn't suffered in the least' along with Matthieu giving us his full blessing.

Though I missed him during his long days at the lab, I spent my free time exploring London, checking things off my itinerary, and sharing the details of my days once Lucian got back to the penthouse—often while he ate a late dinner, or we shared a midnight dessert.

Just after, he would wordlessly let me know just how often he thought of me during his long hours away.

Just like everyone else, Lucian has his good and bad days.

On the days he's more subdued, I'm becoming more certain it's due to his grief over Alexander. Sometimes, on those days, he'll talk about him, and I'll just listen. There have been a few times that talking hurt him to the point that he went silent, and instead of trying to cheer him up or compensate for the quiet, I allowed him to just feel it.

During those times, it seems as though his pain is fresh, the loss of Alexander seeming days old as opposed to years ago. But in Lucian's mind, it probably is, and he more or less explained the reason for it during our walk in Oxford. Which is, when Alexander died, Lucian became frozen in time. Now, thawing years later, Lucian's finally allowing himself to feel it fully, and though it hurts something awful to be the one to witness it, I consider him acknowledging his grief progress.

I've gathered a few more notes, too—pop culture references are almost always lost on him, though he has surprised me a time or two. He also takes immaculate care of his health and works out religiously and vigorously.

In the same respect, he had not been exaggerating at all about his sexual appetite. If anything, he downplayed it, and in turn, I've been subject to regular workouts, as has my kitty, who purrs daily with *zero* complaint.

We haven't gotten as vocal about our feelings for one another or our connection as we did on Boxing Day—which, in a way, is odd because we're more intimate and closer now than we were then. But it's a huge relief because it was startlingly premature and kind of scared me due to the overwhelming intensity. I'm thankful it was isolated to that day because it takes any and all pressure from us both as far as expectations.

No matter the case, it's been a fucking dream to be the object of his affection. Instigating on my end for the sole purpose of watching him come apart is my absolute favorite new hobby—and one I take very seriously. More than once, we've damn near spontaneously combusted trying to make it to the penthouse. Our new game for the moment is to see who can make the other come first, and so far, I'm losing.

Big time. And losing has never felt so damned good.

My goal before our trip ends is to weaken him to the point that he gives in and we get busy somewhere publicly. Breaking a man who seems to always enforce sexual discretion at all times would be one hell of a feat, but I'm up for the challenge.

"I've only ever been jealous over you," Lucian whispers, breaking up my reverie. I turn to see him staring at me. And God, that look and the way it makes me feel. I take a mental snapshot, my psychological hard drive filling up rapidly with dozens of ingrained images of him already.

"You're *flattering me*, Doc," I whisper.

"Well, you're *unraveling me*, Cheeky," he whispers back.

God, we're becoming so damned gooey already, and all I can think is *good*. There are enough couples out there making each other's lives miserable on a daily basis and doing nothing to remedy it. I should know. I was in a few of those relationships before they turned into relation*shits*. So, I'm okay with owning being content, happy, and giddy for a while, no matter how this turns out.

But this content? This happy? This giddy? It scares me, as has our connection since before we started. In a way, it feels dangerous to me, which is why I resisted it so hard, but the payoff of giving in has been the sweetest damned reward.

Two hours later, Lucian's gloved hand lightly brushes mine as we walk toward the building. True to his professional nature, once the elevator doors open, Dr. Aston takes over.

This is fine by me, as my nerves are a bit frayed from having to face off with Gwen today as opposed to the last time we were here. Last time, I could plead my innocence in my involvement with Lucian. This time, I have to woman up and deal with the fact that I have partaken in the most glorious sex with her ex-fiancé but have absolutely no plans of making it obvious to Gwen or anyone else on staff.

In fact, I plan on taking great pains not to look at Lucian the whole day. At least not longer than what would be professionally acceptable. But as luck would have it, the second Lucian and I walked into the classroom—and Gwen scrutinized us—I knew our jig was up, and like an idiot, I let my guilty eyes drop, confirming it for her.

Fuck.

Entering the bathroom during break later that day, I apply my lipstick as the door opens, and Gwen walks in, sidling up next to me. Inhaling deeply, I face off with her reflection as I pull out my mascara to keep my hands busy.

Just as Gwen opens her perfect mouth to charge me, I hold my hand up to cut her off, wondering if she hates the gesture as much as Lucian. To be fair, it really is rude, but right now, it is entirely necessary.

Turning to her, I face her head-on because it's warranted.

"Gwen, before you say a word, please know I have a great deal of respect for you *professionally* and the fact that you were with Lucian personally. I watched you in there, and I admire the way you handle yourself amongst them. I know how tough it is to navigate a male-dominated field, and the way you conduct yourself and command attention is something to aspire to."

My words have her pausing as I continue.

"But what I truly despise and will take away all personal respect I have for you is if you continue to throw shade my way or insult me to somehow make yourself feel better. Because we both know it won't feel good for you in the long run. I'm sorry he hurt you, but again I didn't, and I don't deserve any of your wrath, so fair warning, if you bark and bite me this time, I'm going to fucking bite back."

"Wow," she says, bracing her hands behind her on the counter. "And to think I actually followed you in to apologize."

Seeing the shock register on my face, a small smile appears on her lips. "Yes, Jane, I'm not all that bad, despite what Lucian may have told you."

"He's been completely respectful of you in the way I know very little, if that helps."

Her eyes lower. "I wish it did, and I do apologize. To be honest, I've been a little sick about it."

"Accepted, and I get it, you know. I've been there—one too many times. Not exactly the same way, but I have been there, and it feels awful. I'm sorry you're hurting."

"That's," she gives me a thorough once over, "remarkably kind, Jane."

"Lucian aside, I really love the balls you show when you get revved up. You don't put up with shit from the swinging dicks."

Her lips part at my candor before she bursts into a short bout of laughter and shakes her head. "This is rather odd. I never expected to laugh with the woman I hoped to despise."

"Well, that's the boring thing about adulting, right? If we act like them, it doesn't equal too much drama."

She nods, looking gorgeous in a form-fitting pencil skirt, puff-sleeved blouse, and high ponytail, which compliments her thin, toned figure. I hate the few seconds I spend comparing our bodies and am thankful for the distraction when she speaks up.

"I looked into you as well," she confesses, and I can tell the admission pains her. "You have dedicated a great deal of time to get here. Don't let anyone allow you to think it's undeserved, even if you're at the bottom of the board."

"Thank you, I'm really trying," I admit, wishing things were different so I could pick her brain. But they aren't, so I don't dare. It's enough we're being cordial now, bordering friendly, and frankly, as I think of Lucian, it's a lot to ask.

While I would never, ever fight any woman over any man, for Lucian, I would definitely go an easy thousand mental rounds, and I've only had him for weeks.

"I may not be lead," I say, "but I'll be there for *all of you* as much as I am him. You can count on it. In any way you find me useful."

"I'll be honest, I believe Brian has been chosen for the lead," she says, and I swallow that down, along with my pride. "It's simply—"

"I know. I told Lucian I'll be a team player. The success of the surgery and patient is what's more important."

"Agreed," she says, her eyes trailing down my frame, but a lot less harshly than the first time, this time more out of curiosity. For those few seconds, I do the same and glimpse what Lucian saw in her. As I do, I feel a sort of jealous sting.

"Well, I'll see you outside," she says, her voice a little wobbly as she turns and walks into the first stall, closing the door. I hightail it out of there because I don't want to hear her so much as sniffle. Even though we both took the high road today—her especially—it doesn't really make it any less uncomfortable.

Guilt riddles me for the rest of the day, and I don't look Lucian's way at all, even when I feel his golden stare burning into me.

# THIRTY-ONE

## JANE

Our medical team breaks for the final time in Oxford, and our next scheduled meeting is in Paris for the patient consult and surgery, so Lucian takes me on a short tour past a few more notable landmarks. One of them being The Bridge of Sighs—which I recognized from a Harry Potter movie—before he whisked me to The Eagle and Child.

According to Lucian, the pub itself is a historic watering hole that was another stomping ground for Oxford-based writers like CS Lewis, who wrote one of my childhood favorites—The Lion, The Witch, and The Wardrobe. Amongst other legends like J.R.R. Tolkien, whom Lucian relayed along with Lewis, were members of the famous Inklings Writers' Group, which convened here back in the thirties and forties. Though the pub doesn't look like much streetside, the true character residing within makes itself known mere steps inside its door.

The tavern itself isn't a lone room but is divided into several rooms, big and small. I note that one is titled The Rabbit Room as Lucian and I briefly tour the historic landmark. I take a few snaps of the walls covered in novelty pictures and memorabilia before glimpsing the snow-covered skylight above one of the main bars, which enhances the intimate feel for those gathered in this unique time bubble.

Many of the white walls are yellowing and accented in dated shiplap. Some of the seating areas are made up of high-back booths that look just as weathered, making it more special to me.

To be in a place where legendary novelists and great minds convened is fascinating and slightly surreal, and I tell Lucian as much as I scan the space. My eyes land on a chalkboard that stands perched at the foot of the bar.

Walking over with Lucian on my heels, I take a picture of the stand, which is chalked up with a quote by Lewis that reads, "My happiest hours are spent with three or four old friends in old clothes, tramping together and putting up in small pubs."—CS Lewis.

"He was down to earth," I glance over at Lucian, who nods.

"It would seem so."

"God, just to have a cup of coffee with someone like that, to pick their brain, it would be so cool," I nudge him. "Should we have a beer to honor them?"

Lucian nods. "Feels appropriate."

"Thank you for bringing me here," I tell him, gripping his hand subtly and squeezing before releasing it. I want to kiss him in thanks, and it strikes me then that it's the first and only time the no PDA thing has bothered me. Voicing that I want to kiss him would probably only make him feel guilty, so I don't.

"I thought you might appreciate it," he says, studying me as carefully as he has since we left the campus.

"I do, immensely," I relay sincerely before averting my eyes. Today has really done a number on me head-wise, and I'm failing to hide it.

I know Lucian's picked up on it too, especially as he scrutinizes me while we're led back to the front of the pub and sat at one of two tables that crowd a smaller, more private room.

Ever the gentleman, Lucian ushers me into the only seat with a view. Outside the centuries-old, four-paned window is a glimpse of the bustling Oxford street. A bright red phone booth sits at the edge of the curb, and a light snowdrift is lit and visible because of a nearby street lamp.

Normally, I would crack a joke or make a waggling brows comment to Lucian about the booth, but I can't seem to stop the gnawing that's been in my chest all day after seeing Gwen upset.

How in the hell do you get over a guy like Lucian Aston?

Am I currently lining myself up to find out? Am I keeping this casual enough?

Stop it, Jane. Beautiful man, perfect setting including snowfall, kick-ass ambiance, and food. Your wish list has been granted—just fucking enjoy it.

"Do you mind if I order for us?" he asks, and I nod. Once he's politely tasked our waitress with two shepherd's pies and dark pints, I feel his steady, probing gaze on me as I shed my coat, my eyes following the snow's progress behind him.

"All right, Jane, I've been patient enough, let's have it."

"Have what?" I ask, knowing damn well what. Unfortunately, so does he, and he puts a voice to it.

"Why have you been avoiding my eyes, me, all day, and why can't you look at me now?"

"Pass," I answer.

"No," he refutes, "not when it's bothering you this much."

"It's not."

"I see. So, we're lying today?"

Shit.

Lifting my eyes to his, I try to choose my words carefully before remembering our deal and the fact that I don't have to.

"Did you really love her?"

His brows draw as I stare over at him, so undeniably gorgeous—the dim light above us catching the halo blond of the natural highlights in his dirty blond hair. The man is surreal-looking and could probably have any woman he wanted. It's the truth, and for some reason, it really irks me at the moment.

"You understand the question," I tell him as he hesitates with a reply. "Be honest."

"You're bothered by Gwen?"

"I'm not bothered by her, and I'm not jealous," I say, toying with a coaster. "I mean, I'm a little jealous, but I suppose that goes with the territory. This thing between us is new and undefined. You have a real history with her. You were going to marry her. That's serious. She's so heartbroken, still—years later. It's sad to witness, Lucian, and here you are, sleeping with me."

"That sounds . . . accusatory. Am I to believe you're upset for my ex-fiancée right now, Jane?"

"Why not? I guess you could say I'm not bothered by her, but for her," I say as our beers are set before us, and I take a sip, as does he.

"I don't owe you any explanation," he says, his voice carrying clear warning.

"Maybe you don't, but how about you put the fact that we're fucking to the side." His eyes flare in annoyance at my word choice. Though I know I'm not crossing any line that should make him uncomfortable in the public sense, as the tiny room we're occupying only houses one other table—and it's empty.

"Or if you can't, remember I'm a new lover, and this is no longer off-topic."

"I'm not sure I like this," he says, considering me, "at all."

"Humor me, Doc."

Knowing I sound like and am resembling an asshole, I soften my tone.

"I'm just trying to understand you and, I guess, men in general. How can they walk away from women they have a history with and make it seem so damned easy? I mean . . . I know men and women are built differently," I explain, "and react differently to things, especially matters of the heart. But I really don't get it, though."

"Get what, exactly?"

Oof. He's not happy with my line of questioning, but I carry on anyway, my need to know getting the best of me.

"Why we're made so different and how we're supposed to work

long-term at the same time. That's why marriage isn't something I think about much anymore because it just seems like we're set up for failure. Having different personalities is one thing, but why are women predisposed to be so much more emotional and men the opposite? It's kind of a flawed science, isn't it? It's like we're chemically designed not to be compatible long-term. To me, the science is fucked. Women, we have our hormones working overtime against us, and you all are filled with testosterone, which often drives you and some of your decisions. All I'm saying is it seems like a shit bet to gamble on chemistry."

"Once again, Jane, I'm not speaking for all men," he replies dryly.

"Then speak for yourself. Why was she crying in a bathroom stall today? Meanwhile, you're all hunky dory and seemingly indifferent, and now having a beer with your new fuck buddy?"

"Stop," he snaps. "Stop being so crass about us. Your barbs are obvious, as are your passive-aggressive comments. Why are you so intent on having this conversation?"

"Hey, I tried to pass, but you asked for it," I sip my beer again and shrug. "I'm taking the opportunity to question a man because I have free reign to do so and to get honest answers. I've wondered for a long time how men seem to get out of emotional entanglements so easily. Seemingly without a scratch. Completely unscathed, while a woman often loses a piece of herself. So, I guess what I want to know is, does it even bother you that she cried today?"

"Of course it does."

I rake my lip. "Sorry, but I don't believe you. I don't see it in you—at all. Not a tenth of her heartache is anywhere on you, and I feel like you just answered that way to appease me, which nullifies our agreement."

"Some nerve," he scoffs, "but you still can't read me full-on, now, can you?"

"No, but I bet she can read you and your indifference, and I guess it saddens me that you can be so cold-hearted about it because you're not that way with me. So, just answer me, Lucian, and be honest. You said you didn't want things to change, so don't change them by lying to me right now."

Our food arrives, and neither of us takes a bite as he stares back at me—considering me.

"Fine, fine," I say, tucking my hair behind my ears. "I'll drop it," I add, taking a drink of my beer.

"Gwen denied me a conversation the last time we were here. Well, actually, she accused me of not wanting to speak to her for reasons I can't fathom, but it was true. I didn't want to speak with her or rehash the decimation of our relationship, and I'm still trying to pinpoint why. Once I do, I will have the proper conversation with her, which she deserves because I did love her—years ago. But I grieved our relationship long before I left her, and it's been years. It doesn't affect me much anymore because I wanted to leave her by the time I left. My reasoning for doing so is for her to hear when the time comes for that conversation. I'm over her—entirely at this point—and I'm sorry if you feel that makes me heartless. I did feel remorse when you told me she cried in the bathroom. It doesn't please me she's upset."

His golden eyes pin me as he lifts his spoon, running his thumb over the back of it.

"I can only deduce that your musings and diatribe are intended to further probe into what we're doing—and my thinking as far as you and I are concerned. And while I again can't speak to or for the entire male fucking population on why men feel less deeply than women on certain matters of the heart. I speak for myself when I say," he leans in, his intent stare unwavering. "I rather enjoy fucking you, and I should think the honesty part of our situation will make things easier as we go and much less complicated. If such a thing is possible for men and women—as you have so little faith and low regard for chemistry—which I also can't explain and have no place in doing so. So, Jane. If you're indirectly asking how I feel about you at this point . . . I've yet to sort a single one where you're concerned at the moment—other than the possessiveness I initially felt, the want of keeping your constant company, and the desire to continue to fuck you as hard and as often as possible—including the moment we're currently in."

"Wow," I mouth, more than say.

He digs his spoon into his pie. "Yes, I loved her very much. But I fell out of love with her before I left. So, there's your honesty. Now, I feel I should warn you that I'm famished, and I'm going to eat my pie whether you decide to dine with me or not."

I press my lips together as he digs into the savory dish and scoops up a heaping forkful, taking a hearty bite and chewing defiantly. I can't help the lift of my lips as I table my beer and grab my own fork. "You know you're kind of hot when you get all pissy."

He stares back at me with dead eyes as he takes another bite and chews his food—very purposefully. Unable to help myself, I grin over at him.

"Is there something you want to add, Doctor?" I taunt, knowing I'm now playing with fire, but he's so damn sexy when he's irritated.

"As you can well tell, Jane. Yes. But I'd rather not speak it for the moment. So, I'll pass."

"Okay then. Let's eat."

Not long after, Lucian tables his American Express, glaring at me in response when I offer to cover my own dinner. Exiting the pub, we take a tense, loaded, but silent walk back to our hotel.

With our silence currently uncomfortable—where it typically isn't—I continually press my lips together to try and hide how his irritation tickles me. It's not that I want him angry with me. It's just . . . he's so fucking hot as he stalks toward the hotel, eyes purposely averted, looking so edible—a lot like my old school Dr. Prick.

I don't like that I'm the bad guy right now or that I totally ruined the good vibes we've successfully maintained in the last few weeks—or rather, the atmosphere we organically created in our time together with our chemistry. But I don't voice that yet as I struggle to keep up with his fast strides.

Frustration rolls off him as he leads me toward our hotel. I know it's not the line of questioning so much as the way that I fronted him out. The truth is, I let my fear speak for me tonight, and I know better.

I learned a long time ago that nothing ever goes right or well when you let fear speak for you. He deserves an apology, and I decide to give him one as I follow him through our hotel and to the door. When he pulls out the keycard, he gives me a nasty side eye before pushing through the door.

Damn . . . well, okay then.

Sighing, I decide to hasten my apology to quash this and palm his back. "Lucian, I—"

He turns on me instantly before backing me against the kitchenette counter. "I'm no longer interested in conversing with you tonight, Jane."

"Whoa, Doc. Take it easy, I was just going to say—"

"Again, I'm uninterested in anything you currently have to say," he grits out.

The vibe coming off him now reeks of warning. Even the little devil on my shoulder appears, firmly shaking their head no. But it's my very curious, very thirsty kitty that pops up next, using her furry paw to slowly push his anger like it's a breakable keepsake toward the edge of the table. "You know, Doc, not using your words is very unhealthy."

His eyes start to flame, his expression riddled with warning even as he voices it. "Jane, I'm warning you right now. You don't want to provoke me further."

"All I'm simply saying," push, inch. "Is that it would be good for us to discuss," push, inch, push, inch, swat, "why you're so upset."

Push. Push.

He snaps off his jacket and tosses it before pulling out his belt—which lashes the air and only spurs me on. "Hear me, Jane. Not another word."

"Word," I blurt, my kitty swatting his temper right off the edge of the table and seeing his restraint shatter the instant of impact.

"Right," he snaps, hellfire and retribution in his expression as he leers at me while my kitty both celebrates and salivates in anticipation. "Since you seem hellbent on ruining every part of tonight—including our dinner and ultimately deciding to waste yours—let me solve both our problems."

He tilts his head menacingly, his voice dripping in a mix of lust and condemnation. "Aside from that, what kind of gentleman would I be if I let you go to bed hungry? On your knees," he orders—zero room for argument in his tone.

My mouth pops open in surprise as his eyes darken, his intention clear.

"What was it you said the other day, 'closed mouths don't get fed?' Well, by all means, Jane. *On your fucking knees.*"

He scowls down at me in challenge as wetness immediately starts to seep out of me. I glare right back, but more for show than anything because, damn. I'll take this for any amount, Alex.

Using his waistband and hips as leverage, I slowly sink to my knees.

Within the sound of his zipper, he unsheathes his mouthwatering, inches above average, very thick, very angry dick while winding my hair in his fist.

"Grip it," he orders gruffly as my panties start to flood. He's been this dominating before, but never while he was angry, and I can't help how much it's turning me on—while knowing it's wrong. But he seems fine with taking his frustration out on me, and I have no regrets in giving him permission—or instigating it.

Doing what I'm told, I grip him firmly in my hand and leisurely lick the head of his fat crown.

His eyes flare as his lips simper, but not in a good way. Whoa, am I in for it while at the same time—yes, please. Lucian's dominated me a lot in our time together, but never quite this way. I'm about to be punished. Bow chica wow—

"I believe you've done enough playing tonight." Pushing past my parted lips, he thrusts his length in, to the point I gag and my eyes water. Nothing but satisfaction flares in his angry return gaze as I choke on him and try to relax my throat. Giving me no recovery time, he draws back and thrusts in again, eliciting the same reaction. "You are to swallow every time I push in, understood?"

I "hmm" in reply around his ridiculous, thick length as he pulls back and drives in again—purposely gagging me, my jaw already screaming from the stretch.

Determined to top him from the bottom, I relax my throat fully and begin to take him with every thrust. Swallowing each time as ordered, his eyes blaze, and he starts to fuck my mouth more forcefully.

The room is otherwise quiet. The sounds of my gags and slurping fill the air—which is obscene, filthy, and so damn hot that I can't help the moans that start to leave me. It's with their arrival that Lucian starts to show small signs of cracking as he pumps his hips.

He tightens his grip on my hair and thrusts in hard. His cock jerks when, with the next thrust, he's able to fit himself fully inside my mouth. In response, his jaw goes a little slack. When I light up victoriously at the state of him—which he easily reads—it seems to fuel him to thrust harder.

He punishes my mouth, my jaw aching as I inch my hand down beneath my skirt. He immediately denies me by jerking my elbow up and thrusting in faster and deeper as my eyes widen.

"So fucking beautiful with your mouth full of my cock. A true shame about your insolent tongue. Should I coat it?" he threatens as he stills his hips when our eyes finally hold.

Cursing, he pauses his thrusts and lifts me to stand before turning me and placing my hands on the small counter. Ripping the hem of my dress in haste to get it over my ass, he scoffs when he sees what's underneath.

"I see we decided knickers were optional today and opted out, will you ever fucking learn?"

"Probably not," I quip, pushing my ass back in taunt.

"Let's see about that," He grits out, hooking my waist and pulling my lower half back before bottoming out inside me.

My legs nearly give due to the feel of him just as he covers my palms with his own on the counter. Pinning me with his hips, he begins furiously fucking me. I take his thrusts and back into them, egging him on. My body is taut with the memory of the mix of heated and angry looks exchanged back at the pub. It's the sound of his palm connecting with my ass that startles me out of my lust-infused haze and has me tensing as I clench around him on the verge.

"Again, please, again," I moan at the sound of the connection. The feel of the heat blooming on my ass brings my orgasm to the forefront, and my legs begin to shake uncontrollably.

Unforgiving in his retribution, Lucian pushes me to rest my upper half atop the counter so my feet are dangling off the floor. I'm pinned by his hips and thrusts alone.

Uncovering one of my hands, he fists my hair, leaning over me so his chest covers my back. His next thrust is so penetrating that I damn near pass out. My clit pounds, begging for attention, and is ignored as he brings me to the brink over and over and continually denies me, knowing my every tell.

"Please let me come," I mewl, pushing my ass back in a request for more, and he stills, granting a few more stinging slaps instead while taking the friction away.

Pushing back in to taunt me, he gives me exactly what I need, and just as I'm about to fly over, he pulls out of me. Throwing a tantrum, I pound my hands on the counter at the loss as sweat starts to cover me.

Lucian's dark chuckle fills the air as he bends, lifting my leg and propping my knee on the counter before slowly impaling me.

"Christ, your pussy is perfection," he groans as he unleashes, his hips working overtime as he pounds into me furiously before finally allowing me to topple over. The orgasm rips through me as I cry out hoarsely.

His curse reaches my ears as my body surges at the weight of my release, my dangling toes curling as I call out his name. The sound of our bodies greedily joining has me climbing again in seconds.

Pulse pounding in my ears, I clamp around him a second time and explode, coming so hard I go completely lax on the counter.

Cursing, Lucian hoists me up the rest of the way, turning me to face him—wrath in his expression. He hooks my knees onto his shoulders while simultaneously pulling my ass to the edge of the counter and onto his cock.

Moans and cries pour out of me as he ruthlessly fucks me. He rips at the buttons at the top of my dress, releasing a breast from my bra and suckling a nipple painfully into his mouth.

"God, Lucian. Oh God," I cry as the sharp pain brings me right back to the brink as he drills into me. With another hard pull and the slight shift in his hips, I detonate a third time, disbelieving how fast my orgasms are coming but knowing why.

I foolishly thought I'd met Lucian's heathen before tonight, but he's made it perfectly clear we're being introduced now—and in the best imaginable way.

The sounds of our bodies slapping only increase my arousal as I soak his perfect dick with my orgasms. His thirsty, heavily-hooded, angry eyes sweep me as he continues to fuck me holding a clear grudge.

Knowing he's purposefully denying our connection, I palm his jaw and finally speak up. "I'm sorry."

I see it the second he realizes I mean it.

"Goddamn it, Cheeky," he snaps before crashing his mouth into mine. Pausing his hips, he kisses me and kisses me. Dizzying me and lighting a fire inside me as he slowly starts thrusting in again, his strokes matching the intoxicating licks of his tongue. Within those seconds, our connection overtakes us both.

Lucian pulls me flusher to him while leaving just enough space to grind into me. Though my thighs burn with the way I'm being sandwiched by him, the discomfort takes a backseat to the pleasure as he buries himself again and again, grinding into me. With one incredible thrust, he buries himself so deep that we gape at the other, his eyes softening as we start to collide in an entirely different way.

In the same instant, our hands and lips begin to roam in worship between murmurs and heated whispers, and it's . . . every fucking thing.

Pumping into me slowly, Lucian turns his head, suckling the skin of my leg at his shoulder while sliding down his palms to massage my burning thighs—soothing my aches as emotion threatens in my chest.

What's happening inside me must show in my expression because he immediately releases my legs. He hooks an arm around my back and anchors me to him as he starts to roll his hips. He grips me so tightly, it's as if he never wants to let go—and I don't want him to.

"Watch us," Lucian prompts, his eyes already on where we connect. I do the same, watching my stretch around him, and it's the most intimate thing I've ever experienced.

"Lucian," I whisper hoarsely as I continue to watch him thrust in and out of me. The sight of us is so filthy but perfect in the way we fit.

With the sight of it and the feelings swarming me, I unravel one last time as his own groan fills the space. He follows me, coming long and hard, before crushing me with another kiss.

When he pulls away, we pant against the other's mouths as he lifts me from the counter. Still wrapped around him, and with him still inside me, he gently lowers us to sit on the floor.

Both of us are half naked from the waist down, my dress destroyed, our hair a wreck, skin splotched, lips swollen, and sated. We stare at each other in the aftermath of our first fight—and make up sex.

For long, silent, but meaningful seconds, we simply . . . stare.

My first thought is that I can't wait to fight with him again and he must think the same because our lips gradually lift in a shared smile. Not long after, another silent conversation commences as his soft brown eyes bore into mine before gently—so gently—he takes my mouth in a worshipful kiss. This one is far more explorative and tender than the last before he closes it and pulls away, a hopeful glint in his eyes.

I can only hope he can see the same in my own because I feel it, too—the hope. I was hard on him tonight, and I'll apologize to him again tomorrow because neither of us knows where this is going. But we both know we want to be right here, doing what we're doing and in it together. It's more than enough.

I let the conversation end without another word and kick my fear into the back seat—where it belongs—knowing it should never have been the driver.

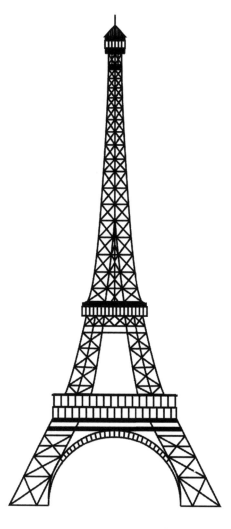

PARIS

# THIRTY-TWO

## JANE

Admiring my new passport stamp, I catch sight of a better view as Lucian carries a tray full of coffee and pastry toward our table—the two of us already checked in at the Eurostar station. We decided to take an earlier train due to the weather report and the impending snowstorm heading our way—which Lucian said was going to be a zinger. After rebooking our original tickets—and an hour-long lecture on packing during which Lucian decided to teach me the roll method—he rid me of one of my tattered suitcases, lessoning the count. A suitcase he denied me any mourning period for due to his need to be punctual. Because of his insistence, we made it to the station with a little time to spare. Lucian's lips lift in a smirk as he watches me watch him set the tray on our table.

"As a Brit, would you be offended if I say this stamp is the one I most looked forward to getting?"

"Without question," he deadpans. I start to unload the tray, including two coffees and a large, sharable pastry strategically covered in glazed peaches, kiwi, and strawberries, along with what looks to be Bavarian cream.

"This is almost too pretty to eat, and why do I get the feeling you're not a fan of Paris?"

"Oh, but we are eating it. And I'm respectably fond of Paris. London is more comfortable for me, of course—more my speed. Paris has always felt . . . a thousand miles an hour for me for some reason—though certain areas in the city can be quite relaxing. Hard to explain, but you can judge for yourself soon enough."

I can't help my excited outburst at his words, a mix of an expelled squeal and simultaneous giggle. Thankfully, his reception to it is warm as he mixes sugar packets into my coffee. Notably, Sugar in the Raw, which is my preference and lets me know he's taking notes.

"So, you're not like lingering on to any centuries-old grudge involving the two-finger salute?"

"I like to think of myself as more open-minded. I don't have issues with entire cultures due to historic beefs. I find I have more issues with people in the present by their actions."

"I like that answer *a lot.*"

"Glad I passed," he muses.

His lips curve up when I, in turn, add a splash of cream to his coffee and stir it. It's then I realize we're at the annoyingly gooey point, no doubt irritating to outsiders by how *together* we look, and I can't find a shit to give.

Last night, there was another shift between us. This morning—as soon as we woke up—I wholeheartedly apologized. First with my mouth and words, and after wordlessly with my mouth and tongue. From Lucian's reaction, it was gloriously accepted as was the rest of our morning . . . until I got the packing lecture.

Lucian hands me my coffee and lifts his.

"Fair warning, Doc. You should probably stop catering to me."

He frowns and pauses his cup. "Why in the hell not?"

"Because I'll get used to it, and if it stops, I will totally resent you for it." Movement outside the large window of the small café grabs my attention as two women step onto the escalator leading up to the platform.

"I promise to always fix your coffee, Jane."

Lucian steals my attention with his decree. "A promise?" I tilt my head, grinning. "Really?"

"A solemn vow," he widens his eyes. "Because only a twat wouldn't be able to carry out such a simple task to please a woman—especially one so simple."

"You know, you really aren't that big of a prick, Doc," I say, inwardly swooning. In the moment with him, I'm jerked back out when it dawns on me why the two women on the escalator stole my attention.

"Lucian, how long until our train?" I ask, grabbing my phone from the table.

He checks his watch before following my line of sight. "Ten minutes to board," he replies. "Did you recognize someone?"

"I saw someone that I swear . . . I know, but I don't know. No," I say quickly, logging into social media.

"That makes total sense," he says dryly.

"Sorry," I say, flustered. "I could have sworn I just saw one of my favorite indie authors."

"Does this author's work include the one you tortured me with on the plane?" He gives me a sarcastic flash of perfect white teeth.

"Watch that gorgeous mouth of yours, buddy," I scorn as I check her group for any mention of overseas travel, certain my eyes are playing tricks on me.

"She's truly one of the best indie writers out there, and yes, along with her divine writing—which includes some explicit sex scenes—she writes completely outside of the box. No two books of hers are the same. They're original, but yes, she delivers the goods," I give him a warning look. "And before you get judgy, Mr. Scholar Pants, I prefer books with those scenes to feel that intimacy rather than just an indication it happened."

"That was obvious."

I look up, eyes already narrowed. "You're judging."

"I'm listening to your explanation."

"I shouldn't have to explain it. Frankly, I don't know why books with explicit scenes get a bad rep by prudes like you who dismiss their literary merit on some principle that if it contains the use of cock and pussy, it's not art."

"Jane," Lucian glances around, "could we have this discussion in a more private setting?"

"Sorry," I grimace, briefly stopping my scrolling. "But it irks me that you'll dismiss a book that mimics our very bedroom behavior. It's a little hypocritical, don't you think?"

"It's a fair argument," he considers my words. "I guess I'm just not a fan of reading the act and more of a hands-on man."

"That you are," I grin. "I'm a fan of your hands-on, but sex is such a natural and beautiful part of living. It's one of the best perks of living—as I've been made well aware as of late."

"No arguing there," he says, raking his gorgeous lip with his teeth before taking a bite of the pastry.

"Hell, I've learned a trick or two from those books, one of which I have yet to use on you."

"We should remedy that immediately," he says without an ounce of humor, which has me giggling.

"So agreeable now, huh?" I say, lazily scrolling while not really paying attention—a little too distracted by the way Lucian is devouring his pastry. He's not purposefully being sexy. He just fucking is.

"Bite?" he asks, quirking a brow.

"Please," I say as he extends it toward me. I take a bite, not at all sexy in my execution as my tit shelves a half-bitten peach.

"Damn, and this is why I can't have nice things," I say, picking off the peach and soaking a napkin with my water bottle to attempt to get the sugary glaze stain off my sweater.

"Shit," I give up. "Another one bites the dust. Anyway, one more point to my argument, and I'll leave it be. Plenty of artists have used sex as an artistic medium. So many of them, in paintings, statues, and music—it's frickin' everywhere in every form of entertainment. So, what qualifies as art in one form is porn or smut for others? I call bullshit." I toss my napkin. "I propose another amendment."

"How about we skip those and just have a simple verbal agreement."

"Okay," I agree easily, resuming my search and tapping into Instagram.

"I'm listening," Lucian says, none too happy with my split attention.

"I propose you read and listen simultaneously to one of my favorite indie novels—explicit sex included—and I'll read one of your snore fests. By the way, I do read a little of everything. I just prefer romance."

"I'll agree to it."

"Including the sex scenes, with audio," I taunt.

"I agree," he says simply.

"You're easy to please today."

"The day is young," he teases, full resting bastard sliding back into place.

"Your ability to do that is unreal."

Glancing back down at my phone, I start to ask him not to punish me with War and Peace or Moby Dick and freeze when I confirm my eyes aren't playing tricks on me.

"It's her. That was her," I say, eyes bulging. "And I'm willing to bet she's on our train."

He takes another bite of the pastry as I give him my best pup-py-eye expression. "I need a favor."

"Okay," he says, dabbing his mouth.

"I love the way you eat that," I tell him.

"Jane," he scolds playfully as I stand and shoulder my purse.

He sighs. "Does this favor mean I don't get to eat my pastry?"

"I'll buy you a dozen in Paris, please, Lucian? I just want to meet her and maybe ask her to sign my Kindle case."

"All right, if it means so much to you."

"I'm mentally sucking your penis," I say just as an older man walks past us, and Lucian's stare hardens.

"Any guesses as to what I'm mentally doing?" He clips.

"Pretty sure it includes your hand and my arse?"

"You would be correct."

"Hurry up," I say, gripping my suitcase and hightailing it out of the café and onto the escalator. Lucian follows with his suitcase and my other bags in tow.

The second we step off and make it to the platform, I'm going full speed as Lucian struggles to keep up with me, herding my bags with his carry-on.

"Crap, I think we're too late."

"It's not even boarding call, Jane, look, just there," Lucian says. "To your right."

"Oh, that's her. You rock, Doc!" I exclaim, navigating us through the small crowd just as she nears the train.

"Jewel," I call, taking a few steps forward as she turns to me and pauses, confusion on her face. Mine reddens a little from fan-girling, but I press on.

Stopping right in front of her, I note how gorgeous she is. She is a granola girl to her core, with long blonde hair and what can only be described as wise blue eyes. A long pause fills the air as I smile at her and the woman standing next to her, unsure of what's happening, as they stand frozen before me.

It's when I notice their collective gazes fixated on the wet dream behind me that it hits me. I almost forgot I'm with the hottest man in London, and their deer-in-headlights behavior is due to the Lucian Aston pause.

"I did pretty good, huh," I utter low as both their eyes snap to mine, and I bust them. They both have the sense to look sheepish.

"Anyway, I know you probably get this a lot, but I'm a huge fan of your work, and I was hoping to get you to sign something for me?"

"Thanks so much," she says, snapping out of her Lucian stupor, "and of course I will."

"I'm excited about your new book," I tell her, "I'm in your reader group." All this is being relayed as I dig into my purse, searching for my obnoxiously large Kindle while doing my best to keep the conversation flowing. "Are you going to Paris for a signing?"

"No, just to visit. I signed in London a few days ago. There were over a hundred of us."

"Oh? That's awesome," I say, pulling stuff from my purse and stuffing it in Lucian's hands to search for my *ten-inch* Kindle.

*Where in the fuck is it?*

The answer comes to me when I find it jammed inside the back of my purse, wedged in perfectly. Gripping the side, I immediately start to tug it free.

Lucian frees a chuckle behind me as I struggle with the damn thing for a few seconds before finally ripping it out of my purse. Shit flies everywhere when I finally free the fucker. I hear a distant ping on the tracks beside us, knowing I probably just sacrificed my thirty-dollar lipstick for her signature, which was my only splurge this month.

Worth it.

Embarrassed in front of both Lucian and my favorite writer as they all gather my shit from the station floor and hand it back to me, I thank them profusely as my cheeks go a ripe shade of tomato.

*Great, now you have to ghost her group!*

Knowing my time and her grace are probably running out, I verbally vomit as I search for a Sharpie. "We're headed to Paris, too," I say, praying God will help me Jedi mind trick a Sharpie as I dig and dig.

"Do you have a Sharpie?" Her friend asks.

"Somewhere in here," I say as her kind dark brown eyes soften, reading my desperation.

"I have one for you," she winks at me.

*Thank you, merciful God.*

"Great, thank you so much."

"So," Jewel asks, "are you two here for vacation?"

"We're here for work, too. Surgeon," I jut a thumb toward Lucian, who idles behind me, and then point to myself. "Surgical nurse, but we're doing it together. I mean, we're together, but not romantically, well, er we . . ."

Lucian's chuckle sounds behind me again, and oddly, it settles my nerves rather than elevates them.

"Sorry, I'm a little nervous," I admit as Jewel smiles and takes my Kindle, her friend offering her a Sharpie.

"I believe what she means to say is, I'm Lucian, and this is Jane. We are, in fact, here to work and are *doing it,* too. Romantically or not, depending on the time and day. It's my pleasure, ladies," he says, "both to meet you and even more so that this interaction is making Jane nervous. It's a rarity, I assure you," he jests as both women openly gape at him and his accent.

An accent he just used to freely admit we're romantically involved and doing the dirty and that even in my awkward-as-hell-ass state, I'm doable to him. He's winning today, and I'm going to reward the shit out of him the first chance I get.

Jewel palms her friend's shoulder as she hands me back my Kindle. "This is my friend, Cleida."

"Nice to meet you, Cleida. Thank you so much for the loan." I back up so I'm shoulder to shoulder with Lucian, "We don't want to keep you any longer. Have fun in Paris," I say before I start to usher Lucian away.

"Hey," Jewel stops us, "you said you're in my online group?"

"Yeah. That's how I figured out it was you. I thought I recognized you when you got on the escalator. A lot was going on in the group, but I saw a screenshot on Insta that you were overseas and put two and two together."

"I'd love to post a picture with you in there if that's okay?"

"Oh, I'd love it," I say, thankful I don't have to leave the group just yet.

"How about a group shot?" Cleida asks, producing her phone instantly as all four of us crowd into the frame.

Once it's snapped, Cleida asks for my last name to tag me in the photo.

"Cartwright," Lucian offers as I stand a little shocked by the moment.

"Thanks so much. Jewel," I say. "This made my day."

"Best believe it's the same for me, and hey, thanks so much for reading. Message me sometime if you're up for it."

"Really? I'd love to, and I guess," I flash all my teeth. "Let's go to Paris."

"Right, you two have fun," she grins as they board their car, and I turn back to Lucian.

"Too damned cool," I say as we start walking toward our own car. "Did I make a *total* ass of myself?"

"Not in the least. She was nervous, too."

"That part was all you, hot shit. Hell, I wouldn't be surprised if her next main character is British and looks a lot like you."

"That was a big deal for you," he muses at my expression.

"It really was. Thank you for being so awesome about it. I'm seriously going to find a way to let you know how appreciated you are—and soon."

I nudge the saint, balancing both my excitement and over-abundance of luggage. "You are so getting some devotional loving when we get to the city of *lovers*."

"My pleasure, Jane," he rasps out.

"Oh, it will be," I say with a wink.

"Always so cheeky, Cheeky."

Once we locate our car with our seat numbers, we climb on board. Lucian loads our luggage onto a waiting rack before ushering me forward to find our seats.

"Wait, so. We just leave it back there?" I ask, seeing other luggage stacked up next to ours.

"Yes," he says simply.

"Wow, it's like an honor system, huh? Lot of trust going on here."

"Well, they can't exactly get away with it," he relays before biting his bottom lip.

"Oh, I forgot, this train travels *under* the ocean for like twenty minutes of the two and half hours, right?"

My nerves threaten about that tidbit I conveniently forgot. Lucian must see it because he squeezes my hand as we take our seats—I glance around nervously.

"You'll be fine," he whispers. "I assure you."

"Keep assuring me, just for a bit, okay?" I ask him. "I'm just . . . a bit claustrophobic, and this feels weird. This is weird, right? We're on a train that travels through a tunnel in the ocean. It's weird."

"It's all right, love," he says, taking my hand in his. I glance down at our hands, and my eyes damn near water at the sight of it. He's purposely breaking his own PDA protocol to console me.

"I'm fancying the hell out of you today, Doc," I say. "I wanted to kiss you last night at the pub to thank you then, too. But it's okay that you don't do public affection. I'm totally okay with it. I want you to be *you* at all times, okay?"

My blurted sentiment seems to take him a little by surprise.

"Was that too much? I'm sorry, ignore me. I'm just nervous."

"It's fine, Jane. I want you to be you at all times as well."

"Okay," I say, releasing his hand and letting him off the hook before pulling out my phone and ticking off my checklist. Seconds later, I realized I ticked all but one of my tasks and snapped my fingers.

"Crap, I didn't do the money exchange thing before we left. I was going to get it out of the way." Reaching into my purse, I start to dig for my wallet to see how much cabbage I have left—which I know is close to a hundred pounds—if not more. I haven't spent much recently because of Lucian's insistence on paying for dinners, but I have only allowed it a few times.

"No need, today," he speaks up, "I have a few Euros in my wallet from my last trip."

"You're a saint, *moneybags*, but I have my own money, and that's not up for discussion." I dig deeper in search of my wallet just as London begins to blur past us and frown. "Hey, Lucian," I ask. "Did I hand you my wallet?"

"No, you handed me a Ziplock bag of crackers that have probably seen better weeks, two lipsticks, and a very, very long strip of condoms," he mutters the last part dryly. "But nothing resembling a wallet."

"Those condoms were from a bachelorette party nearly two years ago," I report. "Oh, how you fancy me with your little green-eyed tint," I draw out.

"Sure I didn't hand you my wallet? It really doesn't look like a wallet. It's square," I lean in, "it's a scan-safe wallet that keeps thieves from getting your card info."

I can see the laugh forming in his eyes. "I see."

"Don't knock it, buddy. Thieves are hella smart these days and can just walk past you and get all your card info with a scanning thingamajig."

"Sounds entirely complex."

"Smartass," I drawl. "When you get taken by some old lady with a thingamajig, you'll wish you had one. Hey, I could get you one for your birthday," I snark. My panic rises, as does bile, while I frantically search my purse.

"Splendid."

"When is your birthday, anyway?" I ask, not hearing his reply as my pulse starts whooshing in my ears, and full-on panic sets in because my wallet is not in my purse.

My wallet is *not* in my purse!

A faint reminder of a ping sounds in my subconscious as I ignore it and dig harder until I'm forced to stop.

Because it's still not in my purse.

Panic soaring, I feign a smile as Lucian opens his hardback, and I stand, grab my purse and tell him I'm going to the bathroom. Racing back to our luggage, I sit next to the luggage rack and frantically search my purse, only to confirm it's not in there. Foolishly convincing myself that I had moved my wallet, I open my bags and search them as well.

Nada.

I lost my wallet. I lost my fucking wallet on an overseas trip!

Or did my favorite author just pickpocket me?

"Of course, she didn't, you idiot," I say to no one, "she's got cash. You're the poor one!"

Panic fully takes over as I rack my brain, and the truth sets in.

The ping.

The ping I heard on the tracks was my fucking travel wallet.

My travel wallet is currently on the track of the Eurostar station in London, and I'm about to go beneath the ocean to get to France. Once I get on the other side, I will be broke. So very broke.

While I was just broke in London, I will be *piss-poor* in France.

That wallet had every single one of my credit cards in it and over a hundred pounds—as well as my license and the social security card I signed when I was seventeen. Which, to me, was sentimental because the number finally belonged to me again.

"Fuck!" I croak out, but low enough so Lucian can't hear.

And I don't want him to. He's rich and has a lot of green, which hasn't been an issue at all between us—so far. I've allowed him to buy those few dinners but little else. And I refuse to let money be an issue now, that is, if I can somehow conceal my epic fuckup. I can't borrow money from him—even temporarily. The idea repulses me.

Though we have a daily stipend allowance for food, lodging, and other expenses, we must produce receipts for reimbursement. Every single one of my receipts was in that magical wallet.

I am so fucked.

"Think, Jane, think!" I say as sweat coats my upper lip.

*Okay, your electronic bank statement will get you reimbursed.*

But without those cards and the last of the cash I had in pounds, I'm fucked for the moment.

"God, no." I panic, racking my brain for anything I can do. A second later, it dawns on me. My emergency credit card! I read a travel tip to put a card with a decent balance in an entirely different area than you keep other cash. Such amazing advice!!

"Thank God," I sigh. In seconds, I'm sitting back next to Lucian with a plan. I still have my passport, and my Uber is attached to my PayPal. I'll just pull up the online app, cancel the credit cards that are floating somewhere at the bottom of the train station in England, and use the card I have tucked in my Ta-Ta for incidentals and meals for the rest of the trip.

It's not an optimal situation, but it will work. I can't help my smile that I did good in following travel tips.

"What's that smile?" Lucian asks.

"Pride, I'm proud I met her," I say, hating that I'm lying, but he's already given me a good spanking on packing. I don't want him to think I'm totally irresponsible.

Lucian resumes his reading, and I take that time to be sneaky, positioning my phone slightly away from his line of sight to cancel my cards, still miffed I'll have to get a new license and social when I get back to Boston. And that I lost a hundred pounds, which isn't chump change to me. But all is not lost.

Pulling up the app, I click on the cards I lost and hit the *lost or stolen* button.

A confirmation button pops up to cancel them, and I hit confirm.

It's when I see *all three* of my cards light up red, including the card that held my salvation, that I lose my shit.

"No!" I shout as Lucian startles next to me.

"What? Jane, what?"

"Sorry," I say, concocting a lie on the spot. "I screwed up and didn't ship Elijah's Christmas present on time. He just now got it." I shrug. "Frickin' UPS."

"You're overseas. I'm sure he'll understand."

"Oh, yeah." Overseas without a single penny.

Not a single dollar. Who in the fuck loses their wallet, finds a savior card, and accidentally cancels it?

This idiot right here.

"This view," I say, faking the fact that we're facing one direction and the train is moving in another. "I'm going to go take a minute without it."

Lucian frowns. "Feeling sick?"

*Well, my asshole just hit the back of my throat, Dr. Bubble Butt. How are you?*

"Yeah, I'll be right back."

"Jane?"

"Hmm."

"Are you being honest?"

"About the fact that I can't wait to get to France? Absolutely."

He gives me the bullshit eyes but allows me a pass as I haul ass back to our luggage and frantically dial my card company. Fifteen minutes later, I'm on the phone with them, and the good news is, they can send me a card in five business days.

"I have no money," I say.

"Is there another card?"

"I canceled it by accident, remember," I grit out, "which is the reason for my call."

"I often tell those traveling overseas to put an extra away from where you keep the bulk of your money for emergencies."

"Great advice. I'll follow that next time," I grit out knowing they haven't listened to a damn word I said. "Five days. Okay, I'll look for Fed Ex. Thank you."

Ending the call, I slap at my face, more so the annoying tear escaping me. I could ask Charlie to wire some money, but she currently has zero. Winter is a tough spot for Barrett as a farmer, and they use every bit of Charlie's salary to get them through. And I know Christmas wiped them out.

I have nothing and no idea how I'm going to do this.

Thinking on my toes, I quickly shoot off a text to my work wife. We're not close, close, but she may be able to help me with enough to get me through until the one replacement card I ordered arrives.

*Please don't be as poor as me, Tammy.*

I'm resigned to the fact that I might have to tell my new English lover I'll be forced to fornicate for money, and he needs to make room in our bed. When I stand to face whatever the future brings me, I'm stopped short to see him hitched against the doorway. His arms are crossed, watching me from a few feet away, his brow quirked in a call of utter bullshit.

"You aren't sick, so let's have it, Jane."

"How do you feel about menage?"

"I don't," he says, his eyes flaming.

"I'm joking, Doc."

"You better fucking have been. Out with it."

"Just got shitty news. Please let me pass for now until I'm in a better mood."

He nods. "Fine. We're set to arrive soon. I was getting concerned."

"K."

He smiles at me. "You're in France, Jane."

"Yeah," I say, adoring him for trying to lift my spirits as my brain murders any happiness it might have brought.

*France-1 Jane-perpetually in the negative.*

# THIRTY-THREE

## JANE

Utterly discombobulated as we arrive in Paris, Lucian spares me another concerned glance as he pulls my luggage to the platform. This time, I take the bulk of it, stacking one of my smaller cases on top of my roller as he protests.

"Deal with it, *mate*," I say, drawing another hairy eyeball from him.

"I can only help you if you voice the issue," he urges.

"Yep, yep, closed mouths don't get fed orgasms, sensei. Let's just get to our place and get settled, okay?"

Lucian, knowing the way, begins to lead us out of the massive, bustling station, and I find myself thankful to have him as a travel partner as remorse courses through me.

"I'm sorry," I softly call over to him. "I don't mean to be a dick. You definitely don't deserve it. You've been nothing short of amazing today."

"It's fine, Jane," he replies without a hint of grudge. "Let's just get to wherever home is and get some food."

"Maybe some wine, too?"

"I wouldn't mind it," he says as we exit the station.

It's while taking my first steps in Paris that I realize the sun is completely absent, and the birds are most definitely not singing. The Eiffel Tower is nowhere to be seen, and the accordion music that's been playing in my head for the last twenty-four hours is cut off like a record scratch as we're swept into a nightmare.

Several women and men rush us, rapidly speaking French as my eyes bulge and a man shouts at me. "American, yes?"

"Non," I lie, using one of the only French words I know, though it's obvious.

"Jane," Lucian calls as we're separated by the dozen or so people swarming us—all seemingly with different agendas. Some hold up what looks to be brochures, others asking questions I can't understand.

"Lucian," I call back as the crowd surrounds him, practically drowning him as I stand by helplessly in wait. Glancing at the curb as Lucian inches his way toward me, fighting them off, I spot a man waving frantically to me. He's standing in front of a sleek sedan behind him, a driver's uniform on, the trunk of the car propped and ready as he gestures me toward him. I wave back, thankful our reprieve is close.

"Lucian, our ride is here," I holler, walking toward the man and handing him my bags as he gives me a warm smile and immediately starts packing them into the trunk.

"Merci," I use my second French word, "thank you so much. I'll just go grab Lucian," I say, and he nods in reply as I stalk toward Lucian. He successfully navigates his way out of the crowd and finally reaches me.

"Bloody hell," he snaps as he shakes his head in exasperation. I rake my eyes over him in relief to see he's unharmed as he regrips our bags.

"What did they want?"

"A few asked for money or cigarettes. Others wanted me to attend shows, offering tickets, things of that nature."

"Well, our car is here," I tell him.

"What car?" he asks, features twisting in confusion.

I gesture over my shoulder.

"The car," I say, glancing over. "That car that has . . . my . . . bags in it."

I swallow as I stare at the empty curb for long seconds as Lucian replies to me as if he's underwater, his words coming out in Kung Fu Panda slow motion.

"Jannnnneeeeee IIIII ddddiiiiddddnnnn't orrrrrddddeeerrr aaaa carrrrrrrr."

In an instant, I'm brought back as chaos surrounds us with the exit of more new arrivals while sweat breaks out, covering every inch of my body.

"Oh, God, please no!" I scream, running toward the street frantically while searching for a car that's long gone—with ninety percent of my luggage in its trunk. "Nooooooo!"

Lucian's call sounds faintly behind me as my pulse whooshes in my ears, and I grip my head in my palms, shaking it furiously back and forth. "Jane, stop this instant! Stay where you are!"

At that exact moment, snow begins to dump out of the sky, like someone had been waiting idly by to pour a bucket of it over Paris.

Hyperventilating, I palm my knees as Lucian catches up with me.

"He looked at me," I wheeze, "both of us like he recognized us. I was so sure he knew who we were—that he was our driver. How stupid am I?"

My watery eyes find Lucians through the pouring snow, which only adds to the utter commotion while ramping up my anxiety.

"It's okay, Jane," Lucian soothes, "I'm sure it's a common tourist trap. It happens."

"Yeah?" I whisper as my eyes spill. "Happen to you recently?"

"Well, no—"

"That was rhetorical," I say, freeing a tear and swatting it away. "Because, pathetically, we've had this conversation before, remember?"

He swallows at a loss for words, no doubt due to my utter idiocy as I attempt to pull my shit together.

"Okay, so that happened. I glance down at the bag Lucian still has of mine and nod, deciding I'll make do with whatever the contents are. "I'll figure it out. Let's just get to the BNB."

"I'm sorry," Lucian coaxes.

"You have nothing to be sorry for. I do. I'm sorry I'm such a gullible jackass." I blow out a stressed breath. "It's been a fucking day," I say, my voice laced with defeat. "Wine is so happening."

"Agreed," he murmurs softly, taking my hand. "I should have told you I hadn't arranged a driver for us here."

"I shouldn't have assumed. It's not your fault I'm an idiot, but in my pitiful defense, he was ridiculously convincing."

"You're not an idiot—don't do that," he gently scolds.

It takes us the better part of twenty minutes to get through the clusterfuck of cars at the station and finally locate our Uber driver, who had to send five different pins for us to find him. An Uber driver who I insistently verified a paranoia-induced number of times, matching the license plate and profile pic before we got within a foot of his vehicle. Lucian was patient during this time, though I know it wore on him.

Our driver didn't make matters any better by being rude as hell by the time we got in the car. I can feel Lucian's irritation building now as he reads off the address on my screen to make sure the driver has it correctly. I'm not taking any more chances today.

Within a few minutes, we're off, and when I say off, I mean a hundred fucking miles an hour in six seconds flat.

"Lucian," I call in a panic as Parisian streets blur past me, as well as the insane amount of snow drift. "Is this what you meant by Paris being a thousand miles per hour?"

"More or less, but he's pretty fucking erratic. "Ralentissez," Lucian snaps at the driver.

"Meh," the driver says, which needs no translation. When we take a curb and bite it, I scream out, and Lucian snaps at him again as I white knuckle the door handle.

Lucian makes another attempt. "Ralentissez tout de suite. Vous faites peur à ma petite amie!" *Slow down right now. You're scaring my girlfriend!*

"Thank you," I say, "for whatever you said."

With another terrifying and dicey turn—in which I piss a little in my pants—I turn to Lucian. "Please, baby, I know we're working on your people skills, but I need you to go full-on prick. I'm so scared I'm about to piss myself."

Lucian's eyes flare with anger as he snaps at our driver again to no avail, and in a sudden fun, circus twist from hell, our driver begins to inch dangerously close to the car speeding beside us. The situation only escalates as our driver curses and gestures at the driver a lane over, who's maneuvering through the residential streets just as recklessly.

"Luciannnnn," I draw out in fear, vomit rising in my throat as we speed down a Paris street at breakneck speed. "I'm going to be sick."

It's when Lucian goes eerily quiet that I know he's at Defcon 1 because I can feel the rage emanating from him.

Not ten seconds later our car comes to a screeching halt, and I'm thrust forward with backbreaking momentum due to a thoughtless lack of seatbelt. I am reminded of just what a mistake it was not to strap in as my face smashes full force into the computer screen strapped to the headrest of the front passenger seat.

Screaming out in fear and pain, Lucian quickly and gently grips me in his palms, his frantic eyes searching my face as he examines me. "I'm so sorry. I reached for you too late, Jane. Are you okay?"

Tears pour from me as I nod, pain radiating from my neck to my face as he peers back at me, his complexion paling.

"I'm okay," I whisper, unsure if I'm lying, as his expression goes from terrified and concerned to livid just as a commotion breaks out at the hood of our car.

To both our horror, we turn to see our Uber driver in a fistfight with the driver of the car he was just racing. Scrutinizing the car in front of us, I realize it's a taxi. A real-life Uber versus Taxi fight plays out before us, the two men beating the utter shit out of each other in the middle of zooming traffic. Horrified as we watch on, I can feel the budding explosion inside the man sitting beside me before it happens.

"NO!" Lucian booms, making me jump back a second before he gets out of the car and stalks to the hood. Cupping my mouth in terror, I watch as Lucian boldly steps between the fighting men before easily ripping them apart. In the next second, he's screaming at them *in fluent but stuttered French* before focusing on the taxi driver—to the point that the driver is bending back toward the hood with each word.

Palms up in surrender, the taxi driver manages to slip from beneath Lucian's back-bending wrath before hightailing it to the open door of his car and speeding off. Not a second later, Lucian clamps the back of the neck of our driver and practically drags him back to the driver's door before shoving him in. Gripping our driver's hair at the passenger side door, he keeps it in his fist as he maneuvers himself into the back seat to ensure the driver doesn't take off without him—with me still in the car. Once beside me, he releases him while spitting orders in venom-filled French in a way that even intimidates *me*.

"Conduisez-nous à notre putain d'adresse sans incident ou je vous tue de mes propres mains." *You get us to our fucking address without incident or I will kill you with my bare hands.*

A second of tense silence ticks past before Lucian hisses at him in French again, and the driver has the good sense to hold up his hands in surrender before slowly pulling back into traffic.

I'm utterly catatonic when Lucian pulls me firmly to his chest, speaking soothing words at my temple. His scent fills my nose as I close my eyes, and he instructs me to concentrate on his voice.

"I w-won't let a-anything h-happen to you, ag-again, C-Cheeky. I p-promise. I'm s-so sorry."

I have no idea how much time passes when Lucian gently nudges me to open my eyes. The sun has fully set now, and behind his shoulder is a beautiful, historic building with a wrought iron gate, soft yellow light peaking through it in welcoming. Feeling a little relief, I shift my focus to the even more beautiful man whose eyes are gently prodding mine.

"We're really here?" I croak.

He nods and brushes my cheek with a feather-light touch.

"Okay, good," I nod.

"L-let me d-deal with t-this, and I'll g-gather you."

He's still furious, still emotional, his stammer seemingly worse, and my heart lurches toward him just as he leaves me in the back of the car. At the trunk of the car, I hear Lucian speak more stuttered-hissed French. I know he's berating our driver, and right now, I couldn't care less if he goes Hulk on his ass—it's deserved.

Once we're at the curb, the Uber from hell speeding away, I turn to Lucian.

"What you did for me warrants a hell of a lot more than thank you, and it was extremely fucking hot," I say in a lifeless tone. "I'm just going to say thank you for now and spend the next three weeks showing you how grateful I am."

His eyes close briefly. "No need to thank me, I'm just so—"

"Please don't apologize to me again," I say, wanting to simply hand him my fucking heart on the Paris street. "You're my new hero, Lucian."

Without letting him shy away from the compliment, I pull out my phone and press in the code on the instructions. Once through, I open the mailbox as written and retrieve the key. From there, we climb up some very narrow, very creaky stairs, and I'm finally able to free my tongue enough to crack my first joke.

"On the bright side, at least we don't have a lot of luggage," I snark breathlessly as we hit floor three, my thighs burning at the steepness of the steps. When we finally hit the landing of the fourth floor, it houses just two doors.

Putting the key in the first as instructed, I breathe a sigh of relief when the lock easily gives and turn to Lucian with a grin. "This is where things get much, much better."

He grins back at me just before we take our first collective step into *hell*.

Lifting my phone to compare the pictures to reality again, I glance over to Lucian. "This can't be happening."

His expression matches mine as we survey our surroundings.

The Airbnb I booked, in short, is a fucking dump. The walls, which look freshly painted in the picture, are heavily stained with various substances. The fluffy, inviting loveseat couch displayed online is now limp, lifeless, and heavily stained with little to no cushion. The wood-burning fireplace is covered in soot, and handprints surround it as if someone crawled out of it—or maybe into it to escape this place. As promised, there is a stack of wood piled neatly beside it.

"Should we even brave seeing the rest of it?" I ask.

"Might as well, the storm is . . ." the wind furiously howls outside as he trails off, not wanting to deliver the news that we're more or less trapped here—at least for the night.

I nod solemnly as we venture into the kitchen, which surprisingly seems to match the online picture and has all the promised appliances. Knowing the door adjacent leads to the bathroom, Lucian follows me back through the living room into the bedroom, and . . . "Yep, not as advertised, either," I sigh.

The bed is dilapidated, as in tilted at a ridiculously unfixable angle due to having a broken frame. The TV on the dresser opposite the bed is a foot tall if that. The robes hanging in the inch-wide closet are paper-thin and crispy-looking.

"Soooo," I say, turning to Lucian, who looks like he might burst into tears at any second, and I can't blame him in the least. "Do you think we single-handedly had the worst first day in France in the history of ever?"

"Loads behind those brave souls who endured the battle of Normandy, but I believe we're close to topping the tourist list."

"I'm so sorry," I whisper. "I feel like the biggest fool alive, and please don't say it happens. I have the worst luck in the history of ever. It's part of the Jane Cartwright luxury package, and unfortunately, those who pet my kitty subject themselves to it."

My tone is somewhere between laughter and tears as he stalks over to stand before me.

"This is all temporary, Cheeky," he assures me. "We'll make our own fucking luck. Let's bear with it until the worst of the storm passes and find more suitable accommodation. I may still be able to resume my reservation."

I don't bother to tell him that I have to stay here—or be here—when my replacement card comes. I was told that once the order was placed, I couldn't change the address for any reason. All things I decide I can sort when I have more brain power as Lucian's stomach audibly growls, and my guilt sinks in further. Due to the empty cupboards in the kitchen—which we checked for the complementary wine bottle promised, which *surprise*, doesn't exist—I know I can't remedy his hunger.

I can't help the short burst of laughter that leaves me. "There's the fairy tale idea of what your first Paris experience will be, and then there's reality," I all but whimper. "I would say they aren't matching up."

"It's all temporary," he whispers again. "I assure you."

"I love your assurances," I say. "Thank you for not hating me."

"Not possible," he murmurs.

"We'll turn this around. I mean, it can't get much worse than—"

And that's when the power goes off, leaving us in the pitch dark.

FUCK. THIS. TRIP.

# THIRTY-FOUR

## LUCIAN

Jane's teeth chatter along with mine as she watches me prepare a fire. We spent the night on the mattress in front of it and let it be because we weren't sure if it was fit for burning—hoping the power would resume. We came to heavily regret it every hour we left it unlit.

When the sun rose and light finally filtered into the apartment, we decided enough was enough.

We made it through the night, gripping each other tightly for warmth. In the early morning light, I decided that the dim yellow lighting did our surroundings a favor by softening the small apartment last night. In the bleak light of day, the Airbnb is fucking terrifying and looks very close to a crime scene.

At sunrise, we also discovered that our batteries were low on every device we had. We decided to save what life they have left in anticipation that the power would remain out for the duration of the storm. Which sadly seems a rightful prediction.

Jane had lectured that we were too spoiled in first-world living, thinking everything would be 'hunky dory' once the power resumed.

I now agree because we're in dire straits. The storm has only worsened since we arrived as expected, leaving us helpless and trapped without food, running water, and barely suitable shelter.

"After we get you warmed up, I'll see if I can find an open store," I tell her.

"No, Lucian," Jane protests fearfully. "We'll be okay."

"Jane," I glance over to reason with her. "It's a literal matter of survival. We have to have water at the very least, and I'm not quite ready to melt snow yet."

"I'm sorry," she whispers, eyes watering. "Me and my stupid romantic notions."

"Not at all stupid. Neither of us could have anticipated this. We will turn this around," I swear to her, and I will, even if it means I have to become a fucking survivalist within a day. I was honest when I told her that I hadn't compartmentalized a feeling for her the other night at the pub—I hadn't examined any one of them closely thus far.

That's drastically changed. From our collision after the pub to the utter terror I felt yesterday in not being able to see her through the crowd that surrounded me at the station—witnessing her fear in that cab and being helpless to stop it, and just after getting hurt. I'm pretty confident I know exactly what my feelings for Jane consist of.

Not only that, I've discovered recently that there's nothing I hate the sight of more than her tears. Though she's as tough as they come, I can't at all blame her for her reaction so far. Both of us are exhausted from freezing our arses off most of the night. We are in dire need of warmth, food, and baths. Simply being able to relax our contracted muscles due to the freezing cold would be a fucking luxury at this point.

"In a way, I feel like we're in the goodbye Jack scene of the Titanic," Jane jokes. "Except I won't rip your frozen fingers off a door you could totally fit on and watch you sink into the ocean. If we go down, we go together, Doc."

"Good to know," I say, examining the fireplace.

"I won't take a bite out of your ass, either. You know . . . resort to cannibalism."

I can't help but grin. "That's reassuring, but let's hope it doesn't come to that."

"It's like we've been tossed into an episode of Survivor—*Antarctica*. Except it's Paris, and everyone has disappeared, so it's like God's rapture and a survivor combo."

"Interesting take," I say, tilting my head to look up the chimney as she continues with her theories. I listen as attentively as possible, knowing she just needs to talk—to work it out in her head. It's what I've learned about her in my time with her and one of her most endearing qualities.

Just short of standing inside the fireplace, I catch a hint of an icy breeze but can't see any light, which means something might be blocking the flue. Deciding to take my chances, I step out, stacking two logs in place to test it. With the strike of a match from the square box I found next to the pile, the wood sparks and fires to life without issue.

*Please, God, make it that simple.*

Jane shouts with glee as I look over and grin at her. She is sitting on the pathetic excuse for a loveseat, bundled in the heavily worn comforter—a comforter I would prefer *not* to be touching her skin.

"My hero, *again*," she proclaims proudly.

"My pleasure," I palm my chest playfully and bow my head just to evoke her smile. "Always."

"Hmmm, get over here and get some well-deserved lovin'," she says, opening her blanket like she's wearing a cape to usher me next to her.

"Happy to, but I'm in desperate need of a—"

My words are cut off as Jane's eyes widen at what she sees over my shoulder, and I turn to see smoke start to cloud the apartment and snap to immediate attention. "Christ!"

Jane springs from the couch and jumps into action, rushing toward the kitchen and turning on the faucet.

"No water!" I call out in reminder, brain racing as I try and decipher the best way to put out the fire. "Look for an extinguisher."

"I believe you're betting one in a million with that request!" She shouts back.

"Fuck!" I roar before an idea strikes. I race into the kitchen and open the cabinets, grab a small water pitcher, and haul arse into the bathroom. I pause when I see the size of it before lifting the toilet lid and sigh in relief when I see that it's full. Doing my best to get a good amount of water into it, Jane shouts at my back.

"Big surprise, no extinguisher! I'll go get some snow!"

"I think I've got it," I call back, rushing toward the fire and pouring the water I was able to gather onto the flames as Jane tosses a laughable spoonful of snow in contribution to top it off. Fearfully, we watch for any inclination of residual flames and sigh in relief when there are none. Staring back at Jane—who stands newly traumatized beside me—our new motto circles my head, but I don't dare say it.

Fuck. This. Trip.

An hour later, the apartment door is still open to dispel the residual smoke. Having knocked on every door surrounding us in the vain hope of receiving a helping hand—which we get none—Jane and I sit in front of a nonexistent fire. Both of us frantically texting our medical team for any help they could possibly give.

"Any signal?" Jane asks.

"Very little. Only two have successfully received my texts, and they're all stuck because of the storm. Does no one live here?"

"Sorry, Lucian. I know as much about this place as you do," she relays, to which I nod.

"Looks like we're alone in this," I glance over at her, knowing I may have a fight coming. "Jane, I have to try to find an open store."

"It's too dangerous," she refutes.

"I'll be all right," I assure her, eyeing the heavy snowfall out of the kitchen window behind her. It's pelting down and hasn't stopped since we arrived.

"I'll be terrified worrying about you." She stands and lifts her chin. "I'll go, too."

I bite my lip to stifle my smile and then give her my answer. "Absolutely not."

"Why? If you can, I can," she says, hands on her hips—my cheeky girl.

"Jane, let's not debate this. Please just let me go alone. I assure you I'll be back."

She pinches her lower lip, something I've deduced is a nervous habit. "I have no signal, like at all. You won't even be able to text me for updates."

"I'll be back, Cheeky. Thousands of people surround us even though it might not feel like it. If I can't find a store, I'll knock on some doors."

I quickly dress in my warmest clothes and empty my messenger bag before walking to where she rattles apprehensively from the bedroom door, watching my every move. "I'll tell you what, if I'm not back in three hours, then send an SOS."

"Three hours," she repeats. "That long?"

"I'm hoping not."

"I'm hoping we wake up from this nightmare," she whispers hoarsely. "Please be so, so careful, Lucian. You *are not* replaceable."

"Glad you believe so."

"It's the truth," she says, palming my jaw.

Her sentiment warms my chest. "And as soon as I get back, I assure you, I'll fix this fucking flue, and we will have a fire."

"Such a badass," she murmurs. "If my breath wasn't kickin', I'd kiss the shit out of you."

I grin down at her, knowing my teeth need a good brushing, too. "Want to brave it?"

She smiles, which is answer enough as I crush her mouth.

# JANE

I spend the first hour doing inventory on what supplies we do have in the apartment. I also examine the contents of my remaining suitcase, which sadly only houses my beauty products—including stolen shampoo bottles from the London penthouse—and hairdryer, which are useless to me without water and electricity. The kick in the teeth is the only clothing packed in this suitcase is my godforsaken purple dress, tutu and dino costume. No panties and not a stitch of clean clothing to change into. Though, if the power comes back, there's a washer in the kitchen. Until then, we're living the essence of off-grid.

Peering out of the kitchen window—which is covered by bars, something I would probably find charming if this place didn't feel like a prison—I stand in utter shock at how drastically our circumstances have changed. Just days ago, we were living in the lap of luxury in a penthouse and wanting for nothing.

I got us into this mess, and right now, Lucian's battling a life-threatening storm just to get us fed, watered, or both.

Determined to be proactive and do my part, I zip myself up in my fluffy coat and boots—thanking God I had sense enough to wear them yesterday—and exit the apartment, walking against the debilitating gusts of breath-stealing air in hopes of getting some signal to send a secret SOS.

I'm about three thousand steps from the apartment door I left unlocked for Lucian when I get some signal.

Charlie thankfully answers within a few rings.

"Oh, shit, it's nostrils Jane again," she says with a laugh. "What's wrong now, baby sis?"

"Charlie," I croak, staring at her on the screen underneath the lip of the building, which is doing little to shield me from the numbing wind. "I don't know how long I'll have a signal, but I need you to listen to me and take me very seriously."

She instantly sobers, "Barrett, get in here!"

"What, babe?"

"Now," Charlie barks.

"I'm listening, I'm here."

"I'm in Paris with Lucian, and to make a horrible twenty-four-hour story short, I lost my wallet, my luggage was stolen, and thanks to an Uber driver who needs therapy for anger issues, I almost died on the drive from the train station to the Airbnb. Which I might add is a fucking dump of epic proportions, and right now I'm standing in a twenty-year storm that blew in from fucking . . ." I falter briefly. "I can't believe these words are coming out of my mouth."

Barrett slowly appears next to Charlie on screen, jaw unhinged.

"From *Siberia*, a storm from fucking Siberia, y'all, and it's freezing, and our power is out. We have no heat, food, or water, and I have no clothes or money."

"Holy fuck," Barrett whispers.

"I need you to call Big Bird and tell him where I am and see if he can help in any way. I would ask for someone to wire money, but money is useless right now because the part of Paris I'm in is a fucking ghost town because of the s-storm. It's so eerie and quiet, and we have no neighbors to help us. So, if you can call him and just see if he can get to me with help, I'll give you the address."

"I'm ready," Barrett says.

"Thank you," I croak as I pull up the address and sound it off. "Please tell him if he can get here that I need a little loan, just a little until I get my replacement card, not that it will do any good right now. If he can bring some food or water, we—" I break against the mounting emotion because the more I speak, the scarier it becomes. "Lucian's somewhere in this storm trying to get us some food and water so we can make it until the worst passes."

I crumble briefly under that truth. "I'm terrified he won't make it back. I've only been out here for fifteen minutes, and I can't feel my fucking arms. Not a single person in the building we're staying in opened their doors. It feels like ice Armageddon out here. I might be overexaggerating and tired and just emotional, but I'm scared, you guys."

"You need to get out of that weather, little sis," Barrett all but orders.

"I know, I'm going. Please tell him to meet me here in the morning, outside around eight am if he can. Oh, and tell him not to knock. I don't want Lucian to know I lost my wallet."

"Because that's what's important," Barrett scoffs. "Are you fucking serious right now?"

"It's important to me," I tell him. "And right now, he's being all valiant and all 'me man, me build fire,' and I don't want to hurt his pride, but we're in deep shit here for the moment. Or, again, maybe I'm overreacting. But this feels really, really desperate and scary and just please see if he'll come."

"Okay, babe," Charlie says. "We've got you."

"Look at me," Barrett commands, and I do.

"If anyone can get to you, he can. He'll be there."

"I know," I sniff, "but don't make him feel guilty if he can't. It's insane out here," I say, looking around at a frozen Paris. "I can't even describe this, and I live in *Boston,* where winters can be brutal."

"Jesus Christ," Charlie says in the background, "you're not exaggerating, Sis, it's a fucking anticyclone. England and Ireland are getting pummeled. To be honest, you're safer in Paris."

"That's why Lucian had us take an earlier train, but when he tried to tell me the magnitude of the storm, I wasn't paying enough attention. I didn't take it seriously enough, but I am now," I whisper tearfully. "Charlie, please check on Poochie. I can't text Agatha. I have no signal at all."

"K, babe. Don't worry about your dog right now, and get the hell out of that snow. You better damn well text me the second you can. I'll be scared shitless until you do."

"I will, I'm sorry to bug y'all." I let out a tear or two. "This is . . . I feel so out of it."

"We've got you, Sis. We'll do everything we can," Charlie assures.

"Thank you," I say. "Love y'all."

Ending the call, I make my way back to wait for Lucian. Each minute feels like an hour as I continually pop my head out of the apartment door every time I hear a creak in the building. Eventually, I catch him on the right one. The second it sounds, I open the door, tears in my eyes when Lucian appears. The messenger bag he took with him is filled to the brim—along with his arms.

"Hey, Cheeky," he says with a grin.

Unable to help it, I burst into tears. In response, he quickly walks in, ridding himself of his bounty, just before I fly into his arms.

"I hardly went to war, Jane," he chuckles. "I haven't been gone that long."

"I didn't listen when you told me how bad this storm is. I didn't listen. I'm just so glad you're okay," I say. "I went out in it to get a signal and feel like I nearly froze to death." I'm being so dramatic, but I don't give a damn. I can't let go of him.

"Why would you do such a thing?" He scolds.

"To be a responsible dog owner," I lie, gripping him tightly and inhaling him deeply.

"It's okay, Cheeky," he whispers as I start kissing his neck, desperate to feel him—for more of him. "The world hasn't ended."

But it's then I know exactly what it would feel like if I lost Lucian Aston in any capacity, and what has me grappling to get closer.

"Jane, I brought you—"

"I don't care," I say, ripping at his jacket to get it off him. "I don't care what you have. Not yet, please, Lucian," I say, meeting his stare. Reading my need, he instantly starts to help me undress him before claiming my mouth hungrily. And for minutes or hours, in the middle of the worst episode of biblical rapture survivor—Antarctica-Paris, AKA hell on earth, on a very, very lumpy mattress, my Englishman makes hell feel a lot like heaven.

# THIRTY-FIVE

## JANE

Fire crackles next to us as Lucian, and I lay tangled on the mattress. A few traces of the soot we spent a good hour trying to get off him are still smeared on his neck and the edges of his ears. He manned up in a big way and seemed to have endured a *great battle* on the rooftop. The noise above the apartment was deafening, including pounding footsteps and crashes, along with a mix of ladylike screams met with shrieks from very angry birds. Not long after, a cloud of smoke came barreling out of the fireplace, and seconds later, I was rushing to the apartment door when it slowly opened. Lucian was standing on the other side, covered in black ash, only the whites of his eyes visible. He opted to 'pass' on the details of how he managed it as I did my best to de-soot him. He stared blankly at me, clearly shaken by what had transpired.

After cleaning him up as much as I could, we stuffed our bellies full of the sandwiches he'd gotten from a bakery he found open. After Lucian explained what we'd endured to the baker, she loaded him up with days' worth of food, pastries, and bottled water. She had even given him a pint of whiskey to help take some of the sting out.

Unfortunately, he couldn't find a single store open for any other supplies, but we have at least another day or two worth of wood if we
burn it conservatively. So, for the most part, we're as safe as we can be.

Warm enough, stomachs full, with a light whiskey buzz—feeling like the world is no longer ending—we've spent the day on the
mattress next to the fire, mostly naked.

Naked now, our legs tangled, Lucian lazily traces my nipple with
his finger as I run my nails along his scalp, my body cradling his. "How
are you still single, Jane?" He asks, pulling back to look up at me as
if it's some great mystery.

"How are *you*?"

"You know why I am currently, but you're different."

"True, I am a goddess," I say with a smile and cat-like yawn.

"You are," he says with zero trace of humor.

"Meh, you only like me because I'm shiny new booty. It will wear
off. It always does. You're ignoring my flaws right now."

"As you are mine," he claps back. "So tell me, why aren't you
taken? How am I so lucky?"

"Like I said, you only like me now because it's new. You haven't
had to try too hard to wrestle me into the version of me you would
want yet. And you have the luxury of a short-term fling to hide behind in that respect."

"I'm going to ignore the timer you just set on the situation,"
stopping his fingers, he looks at me pointedly, "and concentrate on
getting the answer I want. Is that what happened with the last man?
He tried to change you?"

"You've been in a few long-term gigs before Gwen, I'm sure."
He nods.

"Well, for starters. Post high school, I had a string of bad luck.
My first serious boyfriend, Brandon, slept with my roommate. He
wrecked my car the same night, the day after I made my last frickin'
payment. I've been hoofing it around Boston ever since. So, I had to
wade through those types of assholes for a bit. Then I found a few
decent men, but it never lasted. I guess the long and the short of it
is that I was too much for the few men I chose to spend some years

with." I pause, gathering my thoughts. "I gave them all I had, loved them the best I knew how, and while I think a few might have loved me, they left me without looking back. Toward the end, they wanted a *modified* Jane, a more muted, watered-down version. Less mouthy, kind of like you did when we met."

"Don't do that," he counters testily, "That's not fair."

"You're right, I'm sorry. I won't," I run my fingers through his hair in apology.

"I can handle you just fine, Jane Cartwright."

"Yeah, you can, now. But only after running in the other direction for the first six solid months."

"Guilty . . . and what a fucking fool I was," he sighs, running his own fingers over my skin.

I take in his expression and pause. "You meant that."

He draws his brows. "Of course I meant it. We're going to continue to be honest. I don't wish for that to change. Not ever."

"Well, if you're going to say things like that. I'm up for it."

He lashes his tongue against my nipple before nipping it—*hard.*

"Lucian, Lucian, geesh. Leave some for the others."

"Others?" His eyes narrow.

"I meant my future children, caveman."

"I feel possessive of you," he declares, tracing my skin. *"Very."*

"Couldn't tell when you shoved me in a phone booth and fingered me to within an inch of my life."

He grins. "I'm glad you're single."

"I'm glad you're glad."

He frowns. "I can't seem to win a compliment from you today."

"You have a God's oral skills and should give a master class, along with the most perfect cock on the planet. I'll give you another one when you really deserve it. Tell me about your ex-fiancée, about Gwen. What was that like?"

He bites his perfect upper lip and rakes it before answering. "Easy. We had similar backgrounds and were raised much the same. We were attracted to each other and had common goals."

"See? It's less of a pain in the ass to find a woman who doesn't need modifications. That's probably why you put a ring on it."

"Or maybe that's why it was easier for me to leave her." He winces. "I know I'm horrible for saying it, but there was hardly any emotion at all in the relationship—even when I proposed. Which, looking back, wasn't a good decision. Though I truly did love her, and we got along perfectly fine, I didn't feel one-tenth of what I feel when I'm with you, and we've just started."

I gape at him and the easy admission that he feels more for me than the woman he was going to marry. He shifts, so he's looking right at me.

"Come on, Jane. I see no sense in denying it. I've grown very, very fond of you in our short time together, and I'm sure that's evident."

"I mean, yeah, but men don't often *come right out and say it.* Some women never get to hear things like that. Like ever."

"And you are one of them?"

"In a way, yes."

He nods. "Glad I changed that because it's nothing less than you deserve. Like I said, I don't want things to change. I like our arrangement. I'm mad about you and want you to know it."

I can't help my smile. "Mad, huh?"

"Bonkers." Mirth-filled eyes on mine, he peppers my chest with kisses. "Criminally and extremely mad for you."

Unable to deny myself this moment—this man—I give him honesty without a trace of humor. "I feel for you too, Lucian."

His answering smile seals the deal of what I already knew. When my chest starts to burn, and the fear sets in, I close my eyes to hide the threatening tears of the unknown and the fact that I'm utterly, madly, stupid in love with him.

Sneaking out of the apartment the next morning, I walk the thousands of steps necessary to see if I have any messages. Powering up my phone, and as I wait for a signal, I can't help but feel like a total jackass for sending my stress-induced SOS yesterday and worrying my family half to death.

But hunger, fear, and sleep deprivation can do the worst to people. Sadly, I was the opposite of stoic when the shit hit the fan and pathetically cracked in less than a day. Though we're still without power, we have water and food, we're warm enough, and we're entertaining each other perfectly well—often and thoroughly.

But as I watched the fire flicker while in Lucian's arms last night, I decided that I will make it a priority to learn more about survival techniques. As the saying goes, you don't think situations like this can happen until they happen to you, and I'm living proof.

When my phone comes to life, I note I have twenty percent battery left, and I mercifully manage to grab two bars of signal before seeing several texts waiting. A few from Charlie asking for updates when I can, also letting me know Poochie is okay—the last from a number I don't have programmed, sent two minutes ago.

**ETA Ten minutes, Tweety.**

Smiling, I shoot off a quick text.

**10/4 Big Bird. Can't wait!!**

After shooting an update to Charlie, I hustle back to the entrance of the apartment, knowing I'm being a shit for keeping this from Lucian. I don't have much time to mull it over because, not long after, a fully equipped powder white Range Rover with snow chains rolls up in front of the building. A crack of a driver's door later, black snow boots crunch the ice-covered street.

Within a blink, Tyler appears, rounding the hood, wearing insulated black pants, a matching thick long-sleeve shirt, a puffer vest, and a beanie that covers his ear-length brown hair. His matching warm brown eyes glitter on me as he comes into view. "Hey there, little sister. Aren't you a sight for sore eyes."

"I mean, that was so damn rockstar of an entrance. You deserved background music," I laugh as he scoops me up easily in his hold and I hug the shit out of him on the snow-covered Paris street. "God bless you for coming, Big Bird," I whisper, gripping him tightly. "Sadly, it seems like you're saving my ass every time I see you."

"You're completely worth saving, Tweety," he says, squeezing me just as tightly, using the nickname he gave me when we were just kids.

As we pull back—me still wrapped in his hold, my feet dangling—we smile at each other and notice the differences.

"Not so little anymore, though, huh?" He drawls. "Such a beauty you turned into."

"You look amazing yourself, so handsome," I palm his jaw briefly as he lets me to my feet. "It's been too long. What, three years?"

"Too damned many," he agrees.

"What in the hell, buddy?" I nod toward his white horse. "Only you could get a weather-equipped vehicle like this in Paris in the middle of a blizzard and come save the day."

"Not that hard when you know the right people," he winks. "So, Barrett called and scared the shit out of me." He scans the apartment building behind me. "What the hell is going on?"

"Oh, Jesus. Better question is, what isn't? I'm assuming he gave you the low down."

He nods as I scour his appearance and can't help but linger a bit on how handsome he is. Tyler Jennings was a beautiful boy but turned into a gorgeous man, and it's not bias—it's facts.

"An adult I may be, but apparently, I can't stop finding new and creative ways to get myself into the same type of predicament. I didn't mean to scare you. Things have just been so fucking scary the last two days. Thank you so much for coming."

"Stop. You're family, and I'm just glad I was already here." He again glances at the building. "So, no electricity?"

"No. It's out."

"It's spotty all over Paris. No city is really equipped for these types of storms, but I can still get you the hell out of here if this place doesn't suit you. Hell, I'll take you back to my spot."

"I'm with someone," I say. "A surgeon and I kind of didn't tell him how much of a mess I'm in—or that I lost my wallet." I grimace while showing him all of my teeth.

"Why?" he frowns. "Is he an asshole?" He asks, his jaw ticking.

"Don't get all protective. It's just that he's wealthy, and I don't want to borrow money from him. It gives me the ick. But when things got as shit as they did, I panicked and asked Barrett to call you. Things aren't as dire now. He did the hunter-gatherer thing, got us food and water, and managed to get us a fire going, but I still feel weird telling him I'm broke. He's . . . really rich, Tyler. I don't want him thinking the worst of me."

"Ah, I got you, but if he's worth a shit, he won't care."

"He is, but I don't want to test that just yet."

"You're prideful, and I respect that. But maybe a bit too prideful considering the circumstances?"

"Yeah, probably. Sorry, I hope it wasn't too much trouble for you to get here."

"I'll always get to you, always. I've got your back."

"I've missed you a lot since I left Triple."

"Same, but I'm rarely there anymore."

"Yeah, I know. You're never home when I visit, and man, we need to catch up."

"Sweetheart, I would love to, but," he gestures toward the Range Rover, "want to step into my office to get out of the cold?"

"I can't. I want to get back in there before Lucian notices I'm gone. Anyway, if the power is out in a lot of the city, I guess we're in as good of a situation as any, right?"

"More or less, but I have a few things that will help make it easier." He opens the back door of the Range Rover and unzips a duffle. "There are instructions on a lot of this shit. The rest is pretty self-explanatory." He pulls out two small bean-looking bags and begins to rough them up with his hands before handing each of them to me. Grabbing them, I instantly feel the heat from them as they start to rapidly warm my freezing hands. "Oh wow, these are awesome."

"Pocket warmers, and where in the hell are your gloves?"

"I didn't properly pack," I admit. "Doesn't matter now. My clothes are somewhere in Paris without me."

"I'm sorry. It sounds like you had one hell of a rough introduction to France, and I hate that it happened."

"I'm an idiot. I've fallen for two tourist traps so far. This shithole we're staying in being one of them. I've been so freaked out, but if I'm honest, seeing you helps," I say tearfully. "Damnit, sorry," I slap at my tears. "I've been this emotional for days, but it's just good to see a face from home. I'm so sorry I needed help, and we couldn't have a cup of coffee to catch up like normal folk."

"Stop apologizing. Shit happens every day, and *shit happening* just so happens to be my *specialty*," he grins.

"I know, and I'm so thankful for you. Lucian has done everything he possibly can to make things bearable."

"You like him," he winks.

"Lot more than that," I admit. "He's so good to me, Tyler."

"Good to hear."

"How about you?" I ask softly. "Anyone new?"

It's been a horrible couple of years for one of my oldest and dearest friends, and I see the traces of sadness in his eyes as he answers.

"No, and there won't be anytime soon. A lot has changed, and we do need to catch up. But maybe not in a snowstorm in the middle of a street in Paris?"

"K," I look down at the loaded duffle as he unloads and drops another beside it. "Damn, how am I going to explain this?"

"Can't help you with that, but honesty would probably go a long way."

"This is awesome," I say, surveying the bags. "Thank you so much."

"There's a couple thousand Euros in this one," he kicks one of the bags. "If you need more, I'll—"

"It's too much, way too much, Tyler. I just needed a little loan here," I say, bending to retrieve the money. He grips my arm, stopping me.

"Nothing's too much," he says firmly.

"I'll pay you back," I tell him just as firmly.

"The fuck you will," he counters, and I know arguing with him is a lost cause. I see it then, the years between us from kids to adults. The thing about us is that we were family before Charlie and Barrett got together, and our past stretches long before their coupling. A group of us who found one another and formed a sort of trauma bond for our collective struggle just to survive. Tyler's suffering was due to the volatile state of his household. His father, an ex-Marine, endured and continues to endure the worst PTSD imaginable and is far more of a terror to deal with than Lucian's dad.

Somehow, we all managed to find each other like magnets. The disadvantaged, poor kids, all coming from broken homes in some form—a group of misfits with a common bond of struggling. There was many a night when we were in junior high, where we would meet up and have pathetic potlucks consisting of Hot Pockets and Doritos. No other kids we knew were in a similar boat. So, when one of us got lucky, we would share that wealth. I see the recollection of those days in Tyler's eyes.

"I know just how well you've done for yourself, Tyler, and I'm proud of you."

"Jane, I know this might seem out of left field, but seeing you now, it's . . . that time is coming back, and I just want you to know if you ever need anything—"

"With the exception of this current shitshow, I'm doing so well, Tyler. I promise I'm not hurting for anything. You're not the only one hustling. I'm on my way to doing bigger things."

"Just know, the offer stands, always."

Reaching into his vest, he retrieves a necklace from the pocket, and I eye it as he drops the raven wings into it. Heart rattling, I close my palm around it, knowing its significance.

"I've been meaning to get this to you for a long time now," he says. "Charlie has hers already."

Overcome with emotion at how far we've come, I pull him tightly to me and whisper to him. "You know I went to visit him last time I was in Triple," I sniff. "I miss him all the time, Tyler. I loved him so much."

"He loved you too, sweetheart."

"So, how is Tobias?"

"Who's this then?" Sounds behind us.

"Shit," I whisper to Tyler as we both turn to see Lucian standing just outside the gate, his resting bastard on fire.

"Tyler, this is Lucian, my—"

"Significant other," Lucian supplies in a clipped tone.

I bulge my eyes at Tyler, who smiles over at him.

"This is my *significant other*, Lucian," I say, whispering back to Tyler, who still has me clutched in a bear hug. "You better put me down, buddy. My new man is getting jealous."

"Is he aware that you're under my wing?" Tyler whispers back.

"I'm pretty sure you've made it obvious, and I don't think he gives a damn at the moment," I jest as he sets me back on my feet. We walk over to where Lucian stands—or rather bristles—his eyes volleying back and forth between us.

"Lucian, this is Tyler Jennings, AKA my Big Bird and one of my oldest and dearest friends. We're kind of a family too. Barrett is his first cousin, you know," I prod, "Charlie's boyfriend?"

Lucian nods as I continue.

"Well, Charlie happens to be Tyler's version of your Paxley Buxton. They dated for two days in middle school."

"'Til your evil sister tore my heart out," Tyler quips. "Two days, and then she went and fell for my cousin. Unreal."

"Slight exaggeration, that was *nine* years later, Big Bird."

Lucian's eyes lighten slightly, a little less lethal. "So, Charlie dated you?"

"Yes, well. It's only because her little sister was too young," Tyler teases, stoking the fire.

"You know damn well you weren't my first crush, and you didn't tell me, how is Tobias?"

"He's an asshole. He's here with me. He would have come, but he's handling some things. What are you two doing in Paris?"

"Work thing. You know I'm a surgical nurse now. Lucian here is a cardiothoracic surgeon. He's doing a groundbreaking surgery here in a few weeks."

"Ah," Tyler offers his hand to Lucian, "Well, Lucian, nice to meet you. Any friend of my favorite little sister is a friend of mine."

Lucian takes his hand, and they firmly shake as I smile between them.

"And what is it that you do?" Lucian asks, eyeing the Range Rover, his curiosity getting the best of him.

"I'm a former Marine, and now I guess you could say I'm kind of a wingman," he winks at me, and I shake my head.

"And before that," I chime in, "he was breaking the hearts of every teenage girl in Triple Falls."

I turn to Lucian. "Tyler and Barrett are two of four cousins who share a six-generation farm their grandfather left them.

Lucian nods, mulling us both over as I turn back to Tyler. "You ever planning on doing anything with your acres?"

Tyler palms the back of his head. "I did actually, years back, and then kind of let it go."

"Barrett didn't mention that."

"It didn't last long. We'll talk about that some other time."

"K," I say, dropping it instantly before turning to Lucian. "Tyler was in Paris, and Barrett sent out the bird signal after I called yesterday. So, he stopped by this morning to check on us and drop off a few things."

"It's appreciated," Lucian says with a slight grudge, as I hold in my eye roll.

"Get inside and get warm," Tyler says, hoisting the bags toward Lucian in offering. Lucian takes them with an audible enough "thank you."

Tyler scans the building with concern, which I must admit looks a lot less inviting in the bright light of day. "You sure this place is safe? If you want, I can give you both a ride, or you're welcome to stay with me at my spot. It's not much, but it's got running water."

"I think we're okay to ride it out here," I say, turning to Lucian, who nods, his eyes fixed on Tyler.

Tyler meets Lucian's stare, his words coming out far more of an order than a request. "Treat her well."

"I have every intention to," Lucian claps back as I give Tyler 'behave' eyes.

"It's a good thing," Tyler prods, "because I have a way of knowing if that's not the case."

"Big Bird," I scold in exhale as Lucian starts in.

"I'm not sure what you're trying to—"

I palm Lucian's chest, walking him back a few feet as he keeps his grip on the bag and his fiery gaze on Tyler.

"Lucian," I say, grabbing his attention. "Remember when I told you that someone saved me and Charlie from the streets?"

Lucian nods.

"This is him. He's just really protective of me, okay? Give me a minute more with him, please?"

Lucian looks between us, and I can see his jealousy dimming substantially as he dips his chin toward Tyler. "Pleasure to meet you."

"If only I believed you," Tyler grins, giving no shits he's pissing him off. "Take care, Lucian," he tilts his head, "and what was your last name again?"

"I didn't say," Lucian snaps before turning and heading toward the gate. I turn back to Tyler when it slaps closed behind him.

I step up to Tyler. "You always were a shit-stirrer."

"Only with outsiders, and he's clearly under your spell, but he needs to know not to fuck with little sister."

"I'm pretty sure you just got me in trouble," I say, shaking my head.

"I'm positive you can find your way out. You really turned into one beautiful woman, Jane. I always knew you would go far. Charlie, too." I hug him one last time.

"I love you, buddy. Thank you so much for saving my ass *again*."

"Love you too. You call me anytime, and don't lose my number again."

"Yes, sir," I say, giving him a salute. "Please take care of yourself and say hi to my Frenchman for me."

"Will do."

Tyler makes his way back to the Range Rover as years of

memories—good and bad—filter in. He stops just at the driver's door and hollers back at me. "I'm here for the next week or so, so I better damn well get daily texts and updates until you're through the worst of it, or I'll be back."

"Promise, thanks again."

"Always a call away, Tweety."

I give him a wink and join Lucian, where he idles just inside the gate. Knowing he won't let me carry a duffle, he starts to trail me up the stairs, waiting all of ten seconds to start firing questions.

"So, let me guess. Your first crush, this Tobias, is the reason you wanted to have an affair with a Frenchman, isn't it? . . . and should we expect some paratroopers to arrive around noon?"

All I can do is laugh.

# THIRTY-SIX

## JANE

You know those montage scenes in movies where some cute, uplifting song is playing in the background while a couple zooms around a room in a time-lapse, doing multiple activities as the sun rises and sets?

That was the rest of day two and three in Francartica for me and Lucian.

Picture Lucian jump-roping next to the mattress at Olympian level while I watched on in fascination. The two of us constantly stoking the fire and hauling ass back to the mattress to keep warm after using the bathroom. Eating, talking, laughing, and listening to one of my audiobooks as he painted my toenails with us on opposite sides of the mattress, my feet propped on his chest.

Lots of sex, but maybe don't picture that part in fast-forward because it wouldn't at all do justice to real-time.

Thanks to Tyler's bags full of little miracles, we were able to take the equivalent of old-school whore baths with sanitation wipes, sprinkle the toilet water with a treatment that both cloaked and masked what was festering in the bowl so we weren't constantly gagging, or holding our breath. Tyler even provided us with a gadget with enough battery power to charge our devices.

On the morning of day four, the power finally resumed, and I swear the angels sang as the clouds parted and the snow began to melt. Life—as we once knew it—commenced as traffic noise sounded and residents slowly started to emerge. The streets outside of the apartment now showing signs of life. It also meant that somehow, I would have to talk Lucian into at least one, possibly two more nights in the cesspool we managed to convert into a love nest despite the odds against us.

Being the asshole I am, I hadn't come completely clean about losing my wallet, but it hadn't mattered until this morning. If I could somehow manage to convince him to stay—when I got my new card, which was already in transit according to Fed Ex tracking—we could get the hell out of Satan's lair.

With power, running water, and slightly better reception, I didn't think it would be a huge feat to get him to stay. Especially considering how close we've become during our time here, shivering by the fire, telling one another about our lives and all the details—big and small—of our trials and triumphs. At this point, I feel closer to him than any other man I've ever dated, and that's saying a lot.

Lucian had woken me up this morning just after the power had sparked back on and told me he was going on a mission to see just *how open* Paris is. I was so excited to be able to shower that I enthusiastically left him to do it solo, not having realized what a feat it would be. Why?

The three-foot-wide fucking shower stall—and that estimation is generous. Not only that but it's got a bolted, immovable glass partition in the middle that cuts its width in half.

My self-esteem diminished with every second of the ten minutes I spent trying to get into the damned thing, smashing my boobs and sucking my stomach in to try and make it into the stall one titty at a time. On my fourth attempt, I got wedged in between the glass and almost lost a nipple, trying to get back out.

Not an ideal situation when you're trying to remain groomed

and smelling decent for your dream man. Giving up, I decided to take a one-legged shower, drenching the floor in the process. After barely managing to get my body somewhat clean—and damn near crying because it would have been my first real shower in four days—I suck it up and wrap myself in a cardboard towel before putting on one of the paper-thin robes.

Determined to look my best for Lucian, I exit the bathroom closet and find the correct adapter plug in my suitcase for my hairdryer—excited for the hot air alone.

Glancing out of the kitchen window while searching for a suitable plug, I take in the sight of the rapidly melting snow currently pouring from the rooftop, my spirits lifting at the sight of it. Just after, I find a suitable enough plug space just above the washer—which was entirely lacking in the bathroom—as I continue to mentally draft the most damning of Airbnb reviews.

With the sight of a bird landing on the ledge of the window just outside of the bars, I release a joyful smile as it begins to sing before I click the button on my dryer and lift it . . . and flames shoot out of the blower before it practically explodes in my hands. Screaming bloody murder, I drop the smoking flamethrower a second before the scent of burnt hair reaches me.

Wretching due to fear and the stench—wondering how in the hell I managed to burn my soaked hair—I unplug the dryer to make sure I don't burn the apartment down in the process. I rush to the bathroom to weigh the damage with the disconnected death trap clutched in my hand. I wipe the moisture from the mirror to see one of my eyebrows is, well, it's . . . I tilt my head—yeah, it's singed to the roots. Using the smoking gun in my hand as a mouthpiece, I lift it to my reflection, adding my pointer for emphasis. "Fuck *you*, fuck *you*, fuck *you*, fuck *you*. You're cool, and fuck *you*, I'm out!"

A deep chuckle fills the bathroom before Lucian's voice does. "Another pop culture reference, I presume?"

Jumping due to his undetected Houdini appearance, I turn, only allowing him the view of the left side of my face. I see him grinning at me from the bathroom door, quickly covering my new lack of eyebrow. "It's from the movie *Half-Baked*, which I currently am, so don't look at me!"

It's then Lucian starts to sniff the air. "Jane, what's that smell... what's happened now?"

"What hasn't? Just go on without me, Lucian. Leave me here to wither in ruin," I groan.

"Come now, Cheeky. It can't be all that bad."

"Can't it?" I say, screwing my face up at my reflection, refusing tears. "Maybe it won't be if you could . . .close your right eye *indefinitely*?"

"Jane," he groans, "don't be ridiculous."

"Fine, but I warned you," I say, turning to him to see his perfect lips part.

"How in the hell did you manage that?"

"Are we even asking questions now? Like, it's pointless, isn't it?"

"Right," he says, holding out his hand while pressing his lips together to stifle his laugh. "Come. I've got just the thing to cheer you up."

"Unless it's a lobotomy, nothing else will do."

He laughs, full-on laughs, as I take his offered hand and trash my hairdryer on the way out.

"I got the right adapter. I made sure of it," I grumble, glancing back at my latest assassination attempt, now lightly smoking up the waste bin.

"It's this building," he states as fact. "It's cursed. The electrical wiring on the roof was an absolute disaster to work around while I was sorting the chimney." He guides me into the living room and sits me on the love/limp seat, where feet away, the only clothes I have left are currently strung up haphazardly and drying by the fire.

It's there I take note of several high-end clothing bags just as he twirls a large suitcase toward me. "Your new luggage," he presents proudly.

Taking in the mammoth pewter, bordering purple travel case, I twirl it on its shiny new wheels.

"It's so awesome, thank you," I beam over at him, smoking brow and all.

"And," he begins to unload the bags and presents me with some new pants, shirts, underwear, and a bra.

"You bought me clothes? How did you know my sizes?" I gawk at him.

"I checked them when we started our wash this morning."

Tears I can't help fill my eyes as I gape at him. "Just so you know. Your best is fucking awesome, Lucian," I say, pulling him to me.

"It's going to get better, Jane," he runs a palm down my back.

"Yeah? Wouldn't happen to have any eyebrows in those bags, would you?"

"It's almost over," he assures me.

"Two weeks left," I remind him, though now it's more of a warning.

Paris—in a word—is closed. Though a large part of the city might have reopened for some business, the more tourist-prone areas and attractions haven't or are closing on a whim, earlier than what's stated on the web. This means that as of today, and four days in, I haven't so much as made a dent in the Parisian part of my itinerary. After thanking Lucian in a way he felt thoroughly appreciated, I put on some of my new threads, and we both set out optimistically to get started. So far, every place we've managed to freeze our asses off in line for—the latest being the catacombs—closed right in our faces and without apology by its employees. After letting in a small group before us, Lucian and I got to the front of the line and were turned away. We hit the doors for The Louvre just after, which were slammed shut the instant we made it to the entrance. All I managed to get at the world-famous gallery was a picture of the pyramid just as it lit up in the courtyard.

I sulk now just across the street in one of Paris's infamous cafes, where we share a bottle of wine and a gorgeous pear tart beneath some provided heaters. Thumbing through my list of unchecked destinations and weighing the free time I have left, I start deflating with each passing second. We meet our patient in three days, and from then on, we'll be here to work for pre-op, surgery, and post-op. With the clock ticking, I've selfishly dragged Lucian around the freezing, seemingly closed city for most of the day, and he's been nothing short of a saint about it.

"I'm sorry . . . about today," I tell Lucian as he cuts into the tart.

He looks over to me, reading my sincerity, and per new Lucian fashion, says exactly the right thing. "Jane, it's fine. I assure you."

"You and your assurances are appreciated, as are you. None of this is your fault, okay? I just need to give it up. There'll be other trips," I lie. "I'm going to run to the restroom, and we can call it a day. Okay?"

Sensing my white flag is at half mast, he nods as I leave him the rest of the tart—he deserves it. Sadly, as of late, he's become an optimist as I continue to terrorize him with my grand notions and plans—refusing to give up my idea of Paris rather than my reality. Though the city itself is gorgeous—the architecture alone is breathtaking. The buildings themselves culminated in such an imaginative way to create an entire city crafted with the finest details. It's truly everything I thought Paris would be—the experience, not so much.

Determined to narrow my list and lower my expectations to spare Lucian, I take the four staircases down to the bathroom. I've recently learned that every bathroom at every café or restaurant always seems to reside at the lowest imaginable level. Once buried underground, I enter a dark corridor looking for Madame or Mesdames. After opening the door, passing through feels every bit like entering The Twilight Zone—the thought only punctuated when the light flickers above me. To my right sit rows of tall, solid black doors that look more like scary portholes to middle earth or worse—the contrast between this ambiance and the upstairs eatery is surreal.

Choosing the first stall, I do my business and reach into the toilet paper receptacle to find it empty. Sighing, I start to shake it off when I sense a presence in the room. Quickly pulling up my phone for a 'please give me some paper' audio translation, I call out a quick hello. In reply, I swear I hear the faint sound . . . of a cat's meow?

Thinking I'm losing it, I sound off my phone to ask anyone who might be in the bathroom for some toilet paper and jerk back on the toilet when a huge black cat enters my stall.

"Erm, shoo," I say, hitting the sound button again to see if anyone else is in the bathroom and can help me out.

No dice.

The cat sits on its haunches expectantly . . . simply staring back at me as I question how in the hell a cat has taken residence in a bathroom four floors underground in a restaurant. Is this the norm here?

Putting it on my list of what the fuck questions to file and ask later, I stare back at the callous eyes peering back at me as though it knows of every one of my bad life choices.

"All right, you've had your fun. Go, go on," I wave the mammoth black cat away and get a hiss in response as all the hairs rise on its coat and back.

"Listen here, you do not want to mess with me today," I warn. The hairs on my own arms rise on end as the cat seemingly prepares for battle with me.

God, no, this can't be happening!

"Get the hell away from me!" I shout just as the biggest cat I've ever fucking seen swats at me. I swipe back with a lot less claw and vigor—my swat the puniest swat in all of swat land—all the while vigorously shaking my ass to continue my drip dry.

Intimidated but resigned not to give into this gigantic pussy's egocentric bullying, I begin to threaten the cat just as it starts to prowl, walking back and forth in the stall, *stalking* me. As I watch, I swear it starts to devise a combat plan while real fear starts to set in.

Is this how I go? Death by pussy, while drip-drying in a bathroom stall deep within the Parisian underground?

Seems . . . fitting.

Terrified as the cat begins to paw at me aggressively, I go Hollywood gangster in an effort to scare it out of my stall, but to no avail.

"I'm not going out like this!" I shriek at the crazy bathroom stalker as it continues to hiss and paw at the air, getting closer and closer. Thinking on my toes, I rip the empty dispenser roll out and launch it toward the stall assassin, and it ducks, expertly avoiding it.

Mustering the last of my day's courage, I yank my pants up and spring for the door, catching a swat to the leg before I shoot past the deranged cat and out of the bathroom, running up all four flights of stairs to get back to Lucian. The minute I'm back at the table, I keel over. Sweat is raining down my face along with my newly drawn on eyebrow, hands on my knees as he takes in the state of me.

"Christ, Jane, what could have possibly—"

"Don't. Please just don't ask anymore, Lucian."

Lucian pays the check, fittingly wary of me and my current state. Just after, he surprises me with both an idea, and a Tony.

Tony being an Uber driver whom Lucian decided to hire for the night by continually changing destinations to cross a few sights off my list. An idea I immediately deemed brilliant because it meant forgoing freezing our asses off—and considering my recent run-in with the animals of the city—leaves me feeling much safer.

Our first stop was the Eiffel Tower, where we quickly got mobbed by those selling mini towers and soliciting souvenir pictures—which had the PTSD from days ago kicking in overdrive. This quickly led to me taking a picture of just the top of our heads and the tower. Only after we got back in the cab did I realize it was my one shot of the globally known landmark, and I laughed so maniacally that I scared Tony and Lucian.

After that awkward little moment of lost sanity for me, Tony—who speaks better English than I do—chatted us up happily as Lucian strategically matched my itinerary with the stops. Our last for the night is the Arc de Triomphe, which stands in a crazy roundabout Lucian relayed as Place Charles de Gaulle—historically known as Place de l'Étoile. Once Tony pulled up curbside off of Champs-Élysées—one of Paris's most famous strips—and got us as close as possible, Lucian gripped my hand like a vise and navigated us safely through speeding cars and beneath the grand arch-shaped monument. Former prick, now turned savior, Lucian gives me insight as I snap some pictures.

"Napoleon had this built to celebrate the victories of the French army."

"The short twerp everyone jokes about who coined a whole complex, huh?" I jest.

"Short by today's standards, but around your height of five-foot-seven."

"I'm five-eight, buster," I snark as I snap a few photos. "I give you credit for all your inches, don't short me mine."

He shakes his head and all but gives me an eye roll.

"Sorry," I clear my throat comically, "I'm listening."

He studies the grand structure as he speaks, his voice captivating.

"Well, the thing about Napolean—while he is the butt of so many jokes, he was an unbelievable battle strategist, which eventually earned him his title of King and Emperor. The problem was that his ego far outweighed his humanity, and in all his many victories, his ruthless ambition cost his countrymen hundreds of thousands of lives. He's notoriously known for having left France with six-hundred-thousand soldiers in his crusade for domination and only returned with forty-thousand—which eventually got him banished."

"Jesus," I say, "that's . . . *wow*."

"He ordered this built after one of his most brutal battles, and it took thirty years to erect."

"Unreal," I say, snapping a few more pictures.

"His history is quite fascinating, and his personal life is as well."

"Oh? Do tell."

"The letters he wrote to his long-time love and first wife, Josephine, were stolen when she died and have been published. Their love story is quite the tale and had its fair share of hardships. Of course, it didn't help she used him for his station when they first met, and her initial, non-discreet affairs made him a laughingstock."

"She used him for his money and position?" I ask, carefully studying his reaction.

"Yes, she saw him as an opportunity, whereas he was smitten with her from the start," he relays.

"Yeah, that's shitty," I swallow as he spends a long minute appreciating the architecture as I appreciate him. He senses my eyes on him before catching my thoughtful gaze and tilting his head.

"What, Jane? What's that look?"

Fear, because I never want him to view me in that light. The same way his brother and father so easily did in seconds—categorizing me as some gold digger with an agenda.

"It's gratitude," I finally say. "Thank you for telling me about this and for once again turning another shitty day around."

"My pleasure," he says, gripping my hand. "Shall we?"

I grip it back and muster a smile. "Lets."

# THIRTY-SEVEN

## JANE

W e're almost done with our latest expedition the following afternoon when the dreaded announcement comes.

"I've booked us into a new hotel tonight," Lucian relays, slowing his strides to a more leisurely pace. "I don't know what in the hell I was thinking yesterday, not getting us out of that god-forsaken apartment the minute we were in the clear."

He slows his strides even further in keeping with the other foot traffic of the sacred cathedral as my wheels spin on how I can keep us in the apartment another two nights. According to Fed Ex tracking, the storm inevitably delayed the arrival of my replacement card by another day.

"We should have one more night," I say in an attempt to buy the first one. "You know, just to give the place a memorable goodbye."

"Or perhaps light a match and toss it on our way out, in good riddance," he mutters humorlessly.

"Hey, have some respect. We did have some good times. I think we should buy a bottle of wine and give it the proper send-off."

He glances down at me warily. "You can't be serious."

I ceremoniously lift my nose to mock his pomposity. "Oh, but I am, sir."

"I can't even begin to imagine you are. We're packing when we go back, as I'm certain we've suffered enough," he says with finality before coming to a stop. I follow his line of sight as he stares up at the large window, his voice bewildered as he speaks. "I studied this glass for a quarter of a term at Uni."

"Really?" I ask, staring up along with him at the colorful and artfully crafted glass.

"You see, the south rose, otherwise referred to as the 'midday rose,'" he whispers, "was gifted to Notre Dame by King Saint Louis IX and was crafted in the mid-twelve hundreds."

"That's," I look at Lucian to see him mystified for once. "That's my learn something new today. You're really good at giving me those," I tell him as we appreciate the intricacies of the window until Lucian prompts us back toward the entrance of the church.

On our way out, I spot a small section to our left littered with several people lighting red votives while others load pocket change in collection urns. I nudge Lucian, and he sees my intent and, seemingly hesitant, decides to follow me.

"You don't believe?" I finally ask, seeing as it's the only subject we haven't addressed in our time together. A subject I purposely haven't broached, knowing it might be touchy for him due to his brother's loss.

"So much realism resides in me," he says thoughtfully, "but then I see significant miracles within the design of our bodies—which seems far too intricately crafted not to have a grand architect at play. If I'm completely honest, so does our world, but I'm neither here nor there regarding a firm position."

"I get that. So, how about we light a candle for others instead? One for Alexander and one for a friend I lost back home, whose roots were here in France." Lifting one of the long-offered matchsticks, I light one votive and look over to Lucian just as he pockets his hands and nods. "I don't have to, you know, if you don't feel comfortable."

"I'm fine with it," he says, and I feel him tracing my movements so carefully—I know he's having a moment. I give it to him, and when I look back into his light brown eyes, I see a flicker of hope in them that has my heart aching. It's the need to believe. After putting the stick out, I turn to see Lucian stuffing the urn with large bills.

"Your heart has grown three sizes, Doc!" I compliment, maybe a little too loudly. Seconds later, the cathedral is filled with the voice of a monk—an obvious recording that descends upon us all—rumbling through the whole of the church. "SHHHHHH. Silence and Peace."

I jerk back, knowing the recording is probably played often when the church noise spikes to an unacceptable level. The crowd respectfully settles into more muted tones just before we slip out the doors.

I can't help laughing as we exit the cathedral, and Lucian turns to me, unmistakable mirth in his eyes as well.

"Lord be," I grin over at him. "Once again, the loud-mouthed Southerner has been shushed, this time on holy ground, by a Monk," I say sheepishly.

"Ahh Jane, to hell with them," Lucian says, stopping me at the foot of the steps and brushing my hair behind my shoulders.

"Nice of you to say, but not to hell with the monks, right?" I chuckle.

"Certainly not. No," he murmurs, his gaze glittering on me.

"Well, once again, you've given me the absolute best tour imaginable. If you hadn't told me, I would never have known half that info. See, that's the stuff I find fascinating about—" I cut myself off as my cheeks threaten to heat.

He frowns, and I shake my head. "Never mind," I dismiss. "I'm just talking gibberish."

"I might pull that gibberish from you later. Let's go," he checks a watch I know would pay a year's worth of my rent. "We should be able to check into the hotel now."

Blowing out a long breath, I deflate, knowing I'm screwed. "You go on ahead, okay? I'll stick to my Airbnb."

He stops our walk abruptly just outside Notre Dame in the courtyard as other tourists take pictures of the landmark while the pigeons circle a few feet away, soaking up the midday sun.

"Why in the hell would you opt to stay there?" He asks in evident confusion.

"Maybe we should take some space. I mean, we have been stuck together like glue since we got here. Couldn't hurt to put this thing in perspective."

So *not* the right thing to say, which is driven home when his eyes turn that golden fire and his jaw pulses in irritation before he speaks. "Right. Don't you think it's time you come clean, Jane?"

"Fine, I like the place," I lower my eyes. "It's grown on me."

"Try again," he counters, "and what in the hell are you insinuating by saying 'put *this thing* in perspective?'"

"Lucian," I sigh. "Let's not get into this."

"Oh, we're sorting this," he demands. "Right now."

I tighten my purse on my shoulder. "I mean, you are a surgeon with a familial estate, and I'm a nurse who's just a credit card swipe away from eternal debtnation. God, you can't be this thick-headed and brilliant."

I move to sidestep him, and he blocks me instantly, not giving an inch.

"Let's have it."

I glance around. "You really want to do this here?"

"Damnit, Jane—"

"Fine, I lost my wallet," I confess, "before we left for Paris."

"Finally, I was wondering when you would 'cop' to it, but what a horrible way to do it, using space as an excuse."

"Well, sorry, but you don't think about this, obviously," I gesture between us.

"What of it?" He snaps.

"Oh, I don't know . . . maybe about the glaring tax bracket difference between us. In case I haven't made it clear, I'm nowhere near your pay grade."

"I'm perfectly aware."

"Are you now?" I counter sarcastically. "Well, are you aware that I had to take out a personal frickin' loan to afford to pay my portion of the *downsized* room you chose in London just to cover the initial cost before reimbursement? Thank God they comped the damned Penthouse, or I wouldn't have eaten for a year."

He stands stunned at my admission. "Jane, my apologies, I had no idea—"

"Which only goes to show you don't think about this. Do you really believe this thing we've got going on is lasting past getting back to reality? I mean, kudos for roughing it for four whole days, Lucian, but some of us have extremely low limits on our American Express."

"Where is this coming from?"

"To put it bluntly, you're a wealthy man, and I'm a poor woman, and we don't mesh in real life."

"Well, I'm not faking breath right now, Jane. Are you?"

"You know damn well what I mean. You wouldn't proudly introduce me to your circle of friends back in Boston."

"As you well know, I don't have friends in Boston, and I believe I introduced you to every mate I fucking have mere weeks ago. You're being an arsehole."

I gape at him. "What?"

"You told me that assuming makes me an arsehole. I would say it fits the scenario for your current behavior. I'm sorry for not taking your salary into account when I initially booked the room, but this, what you're doing, is utterly uncalled for."

"You can't see it," I swallow again. "God, I didn't want to have this conversation. Fact is, you don't get it, and you won't."

"Try me," he grits out.

"You and me, we're a storybook tale. The rich guy that comes from some noble line and gets with the poor girl. But let's be real and just admit that shit doesn't exactly pan out in reality."

"I'm not believing a word coming out of your mouth right now."

"Fine," I swallow. "How's this? You go to your new penthouse, and I'll stay at the poor man's Airbnb. How's that for *sorting* it?"

"Jane, stop talking *at me* and talk to me this instant," he snaps.

"I lost my credit cards—actually, all my money at the train station in London. So I ordered an emergency card, and it won't be here until the day after tomorrow. In the meantime, I got a temporary loan from Tyler, and I haven't used a dime of it because I didn't know how to explain to you how I got the cash because I didn't want to borrow it. But now you've been paying for *everything*, and I hate it," I swallow. "I hate the whole fucking money thing, and I didn't want it to be an issue between us, and I don't ever want you to think I want anything to do with your money."

He stares back at me, utterly affronted. "Why would I think that?"

"Your father insinuated I had an agenda the night I met him, talking about noble blood—"

"My father is a *twat*, whom I loathe and have recently disowned in case you've had a lapse of memory. A father who I would never take a word spoken by as sound under any circumstance. A father who's been hiding behind his *wife's wealth* from lack of his own fortune since he married her."

It's my turn to look shocked.

"Yes, Jane. It's my mother's blood that has noble ties and her familial wealth that spans generations. My father simply boasts as if it's his own, and she allows it."

I stand there feeling like a fool but still wanting to make my point clear. "I just don't want you ever thinking that I—"

"You could have and should have told me, Jane. I'm not an idiot. Minutes before you started to sweat and panic, you asked me if I saw your wallet. Not to regress too much back to the station of *prick*— along with your additional current accusations—but I am considered highly intelligent in some circles, and it wasn't rocket science to figure out. Eventually, I knew you would come clean. I just wasn't sure why the truth was so hard to gather from you. And for the record, I would never, and could never, think so little of you after hearing your history."

His relentless eyes bore into mine as I rake my lip.

"Well, shit, I'm sorry," I say, humiliation stinging my chest. "I just . . . this isn't something . . . a conversation I ever wanted to have with you. But now that the cat's out of the bag, dinner is on me. I'm hungry. You?" I verbal vomit, feeling like an idiot.

"Talk to me and tell me why your expression is pained right now."

"Because I'm fucking embarrassed," I rasp out, eyes misting. "Which is my state a little too often with you. You're this brilliant, stupid rich, stupid handsome, well-traveled, well-mannered man who has so much to offer, and I'm—"

"What, Jane, say it?"

"You're playing ignorant, but it's the whole reason why you dismissed me, knowing me, in the first place. And you're only insulting me by acting like you don't know."

"We've remedied that in the nearly four weeks we've been traveling together. So no, I don't *see it* now—at all. Yours is the perception affected by this, not mine. So you get to explain it to me. I deserve that truth before you take your needed space," he delivers icily.

"That," I say, pointing to the church, "in there, what you told me about the window is the kind of stuff I want to learn, the stuff I'm dying to know. That and all the things you've been teaching me— back in London and now here. People of your stature and educated background, the elites, often seem to know things like that." When he goes to speak, I jerk my chin to keep from lifting my hand. "And before you say I can Google anything these days to get the same education, you're right. Sure, I can Good Will Hunting my way to a Harvard degree if I want, but tell me where to start."

"Meaning?"

"Meaning, like so many others I was raised by pop culture— and that education is limited. Someone who doesn't know there's a damned *history* behind a church window can't research something they aren't aware has a history. So, I need a good grasp of history itself to start. But how would I ever know to research a window in a church or that it has any significance at all without a prompt? Unless it was instigated by a teacher or someone patient enough like you to tell me."

"And you can't have that history lesson?"

"Of course I can. Eventually, but when you hustle your whole damned life like Charlie and I had to—live and function in *survival mode*, working day and night just to make it to the next day—you don't exactly have time to catch up on all the education and culture you missed out on growing up. The way we've been living the last four days, Lucian—with the exception of cleaner walls, running water, and electricity—is the way I live back in Boston."

I smash the tear from beneath my eye. "With just enough food in the fridge to make it to tomorrow, hanging on day by day on a wing and a prayer to keep the lights on and the water running while working twice as hard just to keep fucking doing it over and over again on a loop. There is no safety net, no one to fall back on but myself. Come Friday, I turn twenty-seven, and I still don't have a true pot to piss in or anything real to call my own. That's my world," I admit, "and I'm fine with it. I'm fine with the hustle. I don't know anything else. And working this hard is going to make the other side of this so much sweeter and rewarding, but I'm not there yet. So, if you want to understand, then know that we've been living close to *my side* of the coin for the last four days, and I can't upgrade my life with a simple *reservation*. I know nothing about art. I haven't read the greats or classics by people like Hemingway and Lord Byron. I have no idea how to pair wine to what, nor the names of any. I know the names of maybe ten classic songs, and I've never been to the opera. I haven't even *heard of* half the shit you've ordered in both the countries we've been to, and there's no quick *sort* for that." I slap the last tear I'll shed away and lift my chin defiantly. "That's the girl you're *dating*."

His eyes soften, and I shake my head.

"Don't look at me like that. I'm happy for you. I'm happy you had the privilege of not having to hustle for necessities and learn these amazing things. And please don't think for one second that I don't know you busted your own ass to get to where you are despite having that type of privilege. You don't have to tell me, Lucian. I see it in the OR when I assist you. The way you are is as controlled as you are disciplined. It's such an art form. It's fucking awe-inspiring, and that's one of the major reasons why I had such a crush on you. Sure, you're good-looking, but you're so artistic in there. God, and here, the way you've handled yourself and our situation—and just, you amaze me . . . and having said that," I sigh, my heart starts to hammer as my head tells me to shut the hell up. "Can we just? I just need to be there in two days when FedEx ships my card. Can we just stay at the apartment until then? I don't want you paying for anything else. I don't want your sympathy. I'm sure as hell not the girl to take handouts. And I'm most definitely not used to having someone—" I stop and reel my emotions in as much as I can as I swallow one last time and exhale. "So, I lost my wallet, but I have a card coming. I need to be there to get it. I have some cash, and if you'll let me buy it, dinner is on me tonight. That's all I meant to say."

*That's all you should have said, Ms. How-to-Lose-a-Guy-in-Ten-Paragraphs, dumb ass!*

He stares at me long and hard as I blow out a breath, his expression unreadable as my fingers itch at my sides. I said way too much and basically showed my ass while bearing frickin' everything else.

"Jane?"

"Hmm?"

"Stand still this instant and stop fidgeting."

"Why?"

"Because I'm about to kiss the fucking breath out of you."

Gripping my face, he pauses a hairsbreadth from my lips, his eyes boring into mine, and steals my breath with the amount of warmth shining in them before he ever takes my lips. My attempt to brace myself is shot to hell as he deepens it, exploring my mouth leisurely with his tongue. His kiss is so powerful, so consuming that I lose myself completely—clutching him to me with everything I'm feeling, and pour myself right back into him. Just when I think it can't get any better, he thrusts his hands into my hair, cupping my head and angling us to go in deeper, making it last. When he pulls away, we're both panting. He keeps his lips so close to mine as both our eyes slowly open. It's in his that I see he's just as affected by it. Our lips slowly lift in soft smiles before I speak.

"You just obliterated your no PDA thing, Doc," I say breathlessly.

"Do I have your attention now, Jane?" he whispers just as winded.

"Mmm."

"You're equally as thick-headed as me—probably more so," he both scoffs and scorns. "And you're the most engaging sparring partner I've ever had, so you'll allow me my rebuttal now," he commands roughly. "In the ways that matter *to me*, you're highly intelligent as well as street-smart, mischievous, exceedingly entertaining, and are an absolutely stunning woman. I'm offended *for you* that you fell for the lie *I'm walking away from*—thinking that knowing the history of a window or reading a dead poet could make you any less significant company to me. As you well know, I don't listen to classical, and the opera means fuck all to me. Hear me, Jane. In the ways that matter *to me* you're my equal in every way and exceed me in so many others—even if you need a few history lessons. Lessons I'll happily give, but only after I spread you out on that lumpy fucking mattress."

This man and his damned . . . everything. He circles my waist and pulls me flush to him. "Let's have it your way and go back to the apartment right now."

"For?"

"I would think it should be obvious."

"I'm all for that, really. But I'm hungry, Lucian."

"Jane," he whispers heatedly. "I'm fucking *ravenous*."

My entire body spikes with need at the look in his eyes. "You win. Let's go."

Gripping my icy hand in his, he rubs them between his warm palms. "You need gloves, Nurse Cartwright."

"I'm opting out if you're going to continue to warm them up."

His lips quirk, bringing all the warmth back. "You're mad. Let's go, Cheeky."

He threads our fingers together and walks alongside me, never letting go of my hand. I try in vain to steady myself, my heart threatening to grow wings and fly right out of my chest. Despite his mission to bed me, he leads me to a nearby bakery where we order baguette sandwiches and other mouthwatering sweets to go along with two steaming cups of coffee. *I pay.*

Sitting across the lumpy mattress not long after, I gorge on Croque Monsieur—which is just a fancy name for a hot ham and cheese sandwich. As simplistic as it is, I moan due to the taste, which draws Lucian's eyes to mine as he finishes his own sandwich. Swallowing due to the look in his eyes alone, I can't help but grin as an instant fire sparks and my desire starts to run rampant. Anticipation amplifies it as we wordlessly continue to stare at each other. My mind races with possibilities as he knuckles the mattress to pivot to where I sit. I take another bite as he approaches and dips before he starts to kiss my neck.

"Lucian," I sigh as he peppers hot, wet kisses along my throat, moving the material of my sweater to bite down on my skin.

"Okay. Well, I'm full," I rasp out, clear heat in my voice. He pulls away and eyes my hand. "I'm not carrying on until you finish that."

"Seriously? You were okay with starving me twenty minutes ago."

"Eat, Jane," he orders roughly. "So I can, too."

My breath accelerates as he continues to kiss what skin he can reach while I force myself to take another bite. When he lifts my hair to lick and nip the nape of my neck, I stop breathing altogether. A second later, his absence is felt.

"You stop, I stop," he taunts.

"You're making out with me while I eat a ham and c-c-cheese," I stammer as he runs his thumb along my nape.

"And you're complaining?"

"No, I'd just prefer to participate."

He eyes my sandwich. "You're almost finished."

Drawing my sweater back, he bites down on my shoulder, and I shudder beneath it.

"Lucian," I whisper. "I'm full."

"Two more bites," he says around a mouthful of my skin, "I'll entertain myself."

"Jesus, you're killing me."

"My sentiments exactly. You could be done by now if you'd stop whining."

"You're acting kind of caveman at the moment. You know that, right?"

"You don't eat enough."

"It's a mystery why I'm so big, huh?" I mumble before going statue still.

He stills as well and pulls back as I keep my eyes down. I can't believe I just fucking said that out loud. There's been no issue, no mention of my weight whatsoever. I haven't shied away from his touch, and he hasn't at all been reserved about touching me.

"Forget I just said that," I order, taking another hearty bite of my sandwich for emphasis.

*What in the actual fuck, Jane? Is it show-and-tell-insecurities day?*

"Lucian, stop staring at me. Just forget I said that."

"Why did you?" he asks, his tone demanding.

"I instantly regretted it, so that has to count for something. I like my body, and I know you do too. This is a non-issue."

Humiliation threatening again between the Church, and now, I just want a do-over for the whole damned day.

Lucian pulls the packaging from my grasp as I swallow the last of the baguette, and he hands me my water. I take a sip, and he waits for me to finish eating before clearing the trash from the mattress and lifting my arms to strip me of my sweater. His silence feels damning, his eyes intent, as I fumble through the silent seconds at a loss for how to come back from what I just said. Of all the times I've been embarrassed in his company, this is highest on the list.

"You're not the only one, you know," he says, tossing my sweater as he unfastens my pants. "I've had a reflective moment here and there on if you were simply with me due to your attraction for me—especially considering your decision after we got to England to no longer pursue me and comments about my lack of personality."

I gawk at him. "You have to know that was before—"

"Of course I do, but it's natural then, right? To question what your partner thinks of you, isn't it? Especially in a new relationship."

My cheeks redden. "Okay, this is so not a conversation I expected to have with you for a second time today."

He tilts his head, mulling over something as he discards my jeans on the floor. "That's because a lot of the back and forth between couples is often masked with bullshit, isn't it?"

"You should really stop saying that word. It doesn't suit you."

"It's the best word for it," he argues. "Typically, relationships consist of pleasantries exchanged—constantly bordering lies to keep the peace. I've mused over that, too, since we got together. I was never so honest with Gwen or any other partner. The reward in exchanges such as these is true intimacy, which makes everything so much better. Looking at you, touching you, kissing you, fucking you, making love with you."

"Geesh, this is . . ." My blush coats my body as he continues undressing me.

"Simple. It's simple, Jane. You're acting like it's some task to discuss, but it was a decision to hand myself over to you in the same way you trusted me when this started. So, if you truly want to know what I think and feel about your body, I'll be brutally honest." Discarding my bra, he thumbs the sides of my panties and slides them slowly off my legs, eyes challenging.

"Shit . . ." I whisper as I prepare myself. "Okay, *hit me.*"

He moves to hover above me before taking my lips in a hungry kiss. I kiss him back just as feverishly while tangling my fingers through his gorgeous, mixed-blond tresses. He rains kisses from my forehead to my neck before circling back to pressing a long, slow kiss to my lips. When he pulls away, his eyes are lit by fire, and it's not the one burning next to us.

"As a scientist and surgeon, I find the human body fascinating," he whispers against my parted lips, eyes penetrating before he lowers them to trail his kiss, adding in his explorative tongue. Licking around one nipple, he takes my other breast into his hand and grazes the peaking flesh with his thumb. A groan leaves him as he closes his thick lips around my nipple with his hot, wet mouth.

My lower half bucks for friction until he releases it, studying it briefly, his breath hitting the taut peak as he continues.

"As a man," he exhales harshly, purposely, drawing the peak tighter to obey his silent command, "I find the female form utterly intoxicating." His eyes slowly drift along the skin he's branding up to mine, pinning me. Satisfied he has my full attention, he slowly lowers, his tongue darting out with a preview of the precise flicks of his tongue. His honey-colored light eyes reflect raw hunger as he lowers further to hover above my slick, aching slit.

"But when feasting on *your body*, I find myself utterly fucking consumed. Now spread your legs for me, Jane, so that I can soak you in my conviction."

Breaths choppy, I do as he asks as he keeps me hostage with the heat in his eyes, the command in his voice, and the way he demands my attention just before he lowers and flattens his tongue from my entrance to my clit. It's all I can do to keep from squirming as he voices his next order.

"Wider, Jane. Bare yourself fully to me," he demands—and I do. Fire burning uncontrollably at my core, I watch, utterly rapt, as he darts his tongue along my clit, before lapping at my core. My hips buck of their own accord as he grips my wrists between my legs and braces them on my thighs to keep me pinned. He continues these mind-bending repetitions over and over again until I'm a shaking mess. Desire and need course through my veins as my heart ramps up, and pressure builds as he brings me close and keeps me lingering.

"I'm going to make this perfect pussy weep and your body sing. And then I'm going to do it again, and again, and again until you beg me to stop. Even then, I'll be hard-pressed to until I'm certain you know your body's value *to me*, never to fucking be disparaged *by you*, ever again."

"Lucian," I go to object that I just had a moment, and he adamantly shakes his head.

"I've never been so attracted to a woman in the entirety of my fucking life, Jane—on every imaginable level. Watch me appreciate that, appreciate you, because it's a gift I don't intend to waste a second abusing."

With that, he jackhammers his tongue along my clit, as I buck and am brought right back to the mattress by his hold. Releasing his hold on one wrist, he lowers my fingers to my core. "Fingers in, Jane. Feel how wet and warm you are as I undo you."

Lowering my fingers beneath where he works his mouth, I press them as far as I can inside of me and find myself soaked. He briefly pulls back, watching my fingers glide in and out before dipping in and sucking my clit again, this time so hard it's almost painful. Just as I mewl at the bite of pain, a tidal wave overcomes me, and I erupt, the orgasm unfurling throughout my limbs, leaving me a shaking mess. True to his word, Lucian continues to lave, lick, and suck as I writhe beneath him. By the time I come down from the last orgasm, he's already working toward another.

"Lucian, I need you," it's not a plea. It's a full-on cry as he keeps me bound and at his mercy.

"And I'm still hungry, Jane," he scolds, and there's nothing disingenuous about it. He's offended by me, for me, and I'm being punished.

"Please," I say, shuddering as he suckles my clit, before pressing his fingers in along with mine.

"Oh . . . God!" I croak, voice hoarse as he runs his fingers along my G-spot while I keep my own shallow and moving.

Staring down at him, seeing the flames in his eyes as he focuses on my most intimate parts, is one of the hottest things I've ever witnessed—and I can't help but ask for more. More of him, all of him, my core aching now that I know the fit of him.

"Please, Lucian, I need you," I murmur. His eyes remain fixed on my core, and just when I think he'll ignore me, he stops the workings of his fingers. His flames scorch a trail to mine as he presses his mouth into my center and begins kissing my pussy as he kisses me, setting a whole new bar—and far higher than his last.

After thoroughly exploring me with his tongue, he sips my clit one last time and closes the kiss. In the next second, the sound of his zipper has my anticipation spiking to euphoric levels. Gazing up at him as he makes quick work of ripping his shirt off while kicking off his boots, I regret and resent the fact that I ever doubted if I was Lucian's type. Especially as he aligns his beautiful body with mine before threading our fingers and pressing into me until he can't go any further, and I feel our inevitable *click*.

# THIRTY-EIGHT

## JANE

You know those days where you feel bitchy, and you can't at all pinpoint why? There's nothing wrong per se, but you just have a shit attitude and can't really stand yourself and want to do better—but don't. Today is that day for me, and the man trailing behind me in the bodega near our apartment is starting to get fed up. I'm off kilter mentally and emotionally, and I reek of asshole right now. Which makes this day two of crazy, erratic questionable behavior for Jane Cartwright, and I can't, for the life of me, seem to get myself or my shit together.

As requested, Lucian has allowed us to spend one last night at the Airbnb, and per my latest FedEx tracking update, my card is scheduled to be delivered tomorrow morning.

With that timeline in mind, we decided to peruse local shops and get an array of eats to feast on tonight in the spirit of celebrating surviving nearly a week at the hellhole. Even with a promising night ahead, the bitchiness won't stop. It's been a somewhat good day—besides sighting my bully cat, well, its tail as it rounded the corner of our apartment building when we left this morning. Last night, when we got home, I swear I heard it taunting me with a hiss mixed meow.

Maybe I'm delusional, but with the way the Parisian leg of this trip has gone, I wouldn't be at all surprised if it wasn't the very same deranged pussy that assaulted me in the bathroom. Living the dream with Lucian aside, there have only been a handful of moments and some partial days of the France portion of my trip that have gone right.

Pushing the cart around the start of the store, I try to tick off the *why* of my pissy attitude.

Don't I deserve one good trip in my lifetime? Who was I in a former life that fate decided to pay me back by setting fire to my eyebrows and sending attack cats at me? Was I Napoleon? Because I am technically more toward five-foot-seven, but Lucian is every bit the eight, moving toward nine inches, I give him credit for. I didn't measure, but I'm excellent in that respect after years of dick disappointment.

And what about that? Why did I have to go over a decade of having sex to finally get some really good Vitamin D? I ran up some kitty mileage for one too many years on all the wrong penises. Is that why I'm feeling bitter?

Or maybe I'm still a little weirded out that I outed all my insecurities and confidence issues to my dream man yesterday—and I'm still recovering—despite the way he assured me last night into a submissive coma.

And what's with him anyway? He went from total prick to 'happy as shit' guy. Was it his lack of alley cat that had his face twisted so bitterly for the six months prior to our involvement? All these things are suspect, and I give Lucian a good side eye to let him in on it as we set off to peruse the street-side grocery store.

"You've been rather obtuse today," Lucian declares while out of earshot of anyone else.

Yep, I'm totally reeking of asshole.

"Well, if you would climb out of my *arse*, I'd be a little less bitchy."

"That is not at all what I said."

"It's what you implied, Doc."

"I'm only concerned for your wellbeing. You've been sniffling since The Panthéon, and you're looking clammy."

And then there's the fact that I'm in denial that I'm feeling a bit under the weather.

He reaches out to palm my cheek, and I shake my head, dodging his touch. Because I am being bitchy, and I'm feeling sick. I can't shake it, or the fatigue taking over while refusing the idea I might have a nasty cold coming.

"I'm fine," I lie. "Nothing I can't get over."

"With *rest*, you should be, which is all I suggested."

I look over to see him smirking as I visibly shudder with the next chill.

"Don't do that. Don't give me that damned smolder," I point to him as if he's the one causing the aches in my body and the sniffles.

"The what?" he asks, grinning.

"You know exactly what," I counter.

"'Tis your imagination, I'm afraid," he rakes his lip, not at all hiding the smile behind it.

"'Tis not," I say, snatching a bag off an endcap and opening it up. "You know precisely what you're doing when you give me that look. Maybe I'm just hungry, bordering hangry."

He eyes the bag briefly and shakes his head. "Jane, do not eat that."

I stand there—defiant against the cold I'm fighting more than him—while tossing some of the chips in my mouth and exaggeratedly crunching the snack in rebellion.

"Jane, *stop eating that*," Lucian snaps, reaching for the bag.

"Hey, bud. I know processed food is bad for you, but it's what I'm biting on, so get over it," I say, shoving another handful of the snack into my mouth and chewing defiantly.

Lucian winces as I swallow and cup another handful.

"What? Like you've never eaten a bag of *crisps*," I snark at the British name for chips—my something new everyday fact I learned a couple of days ago—which is weird because they call fries chips.

"I eat plenty of crap," Lucian defends, continually trying to snatch the bag, "just not that," he says on exasperated exhale.

"Why is that? Afraid you'll be able to pinch an inch on that perfect flat board belly if you partake?"

"You know, Cheeky, it's quite the talent you have complimenting me and insulting me within the same sentence," he snaps, stalking toward me. "Ever heard the saying 'only a dog takes bones to bed?' I prefer your perfect curves and arse as is—and fully support whatever sustenance keeps them—and could have sworn I made that abundantly clear last night with both my tongue and cock," he says, closing in. "But, if you keep this up, I might just gag you quiet again." Pinning me with his man strength, he snatches the bag from my hand and lifts it in his fist.

"And I don't eat these," he shakes the bag in front of me, "because they aren't meant for *me to eat.*"

He turns and begins to stride toward the front of the store as I call after him, my mouth loaded.

"Hey, asshat, that's fine with me, but those are mine, and we're not done, shop—" I stop dead in my tracks as Lucian retrieves one of the snacks from the bag and approaches a woman, or rather her large dog, and extends his hand out to it. Lucian glances back at me, brows lifted as the dog devours his offering while I spontaneously blow everything out of my mouth without covering it. I slap my tongue repeatedly just after to get the rest of the remains out . . . because I was eating fucking dog treats.

That ought to learn ya, *asshole!*

Lucian's laugh engulfs me as my face catches fire, and I glance around to see if anyone else witnessed me eating them. Because the hottest man alive—who licks my mouth daily—just watched me inhale half a bag of them.

My eyes scan the store for anyone else who might have caught it, and I see a woman nearby, cupping her mouth to try to control her laughter. Narrowing my eyes, I give her the two-finger salute. Hearing her intake of offended breath, I turn the cart and flee in search of a drink to chug as Lucian's laughter follows me to the other side of the store.

Evading Lucian successfully for some isolated minutes, I pull the sticker tab from my purse to decorate a can of Pringles. I'm on my third one when I feel his warmth inches from my back.

"Mystery solved," a deep chuckle rumbles from behind me. "Though I really should have investigated why there were googly eyes on my nipples Christmas morning—but there was a lot to be interpreted that day. Though I admit I'm rather alarmed I didn't examine it after the fact," he muses. "But when it comes to you, I should know better than to think I'll ever find a simple explanation."

"I'm taking that as a compliment."

"As it is meant to be," he says fondly, and I turn back to see him giving me the perfect organic smolder. God, he's been so good to me lately, and I've been such a jerk today. "Do tell me, Cheeky. What are we up to now?"

I can't help my smile as I turn back to playfully flick one of the eyes.

"I guess what I'm up to now is thinking about other bitchy people," I admit admiring that the Pringles man looks much more chipper with a large pair of googly eyes. "I think about other bitchy girls or boys. Maybe they're having a shit day, and on the way home, they go to the store and scan the aisles, thinking about everything wrong in their life. And then they look up and see this," I say, pointing to the mustached fella. "It's a reason to smile or laugh, and maybe it gives someone who really needs it in that moment one or both."

Braving a glance back, I see him admiring my handy work, expression full of mirth.

"If you think this is mad behavior, wait until you meet Goldie Honkers and Kurt Russelfeathers," I shrug.

He chuckles. "And they would be?"

"My Geese."

His eyes bulge. "You have geese?"

"Not breathing ones. They're two-foot-tall ceramic geese I have outside my front door that I dress up for the holidays."

"And why do we have non-breathing geese we dress up for the holidays?"

"Why not?" I glance back at him. "To make the delivery drivers laugh for one, and honestly, because it makes me happy."

I googly eye a few more cans before looking back at him and grinning. "So, are you ready to run for the hills?"

"Not in the least," he utters, pulling me back into him and nuzzling me affectionately. "You are such a rare bird, Jane Cartwright."

He's been a little more affectionate today in every shop, and I can't get enough of it and decide the bitchiness ends here. Palming his hands where they are around my waist while loving where we are right now—in the sweetest spot imaginable—I give in to my affection for him and run my nose along his.

"Sorry I've been acting like an asshole, babe," I whisper. "You're right. I feel like shit, and I'm trying to make you miserable company."

I don't bother to acknowledge the 'babe' slip, and it seems to go unnoticed. My nose threatens to drip, which prompts me.

"My nose has been leaking something awful the last hour. Let's try to find some Kleenex mini packs if they have some because there's apparently a shortage of toilet paper in French eateries around here, and I'm sick of finding out the hard way. But before we do, will you forgive me for being a jerk today? And do you think you'll ever kiss me again after watching me eat kibble?"

Chuckling, he turns me in his arms and presses me into my googly Pringles display. He lays a convincing kiss on me, coming close to deepening it before I stop him. "Lucian, you can't. I could be sick."

"I don't give a fuck."

"You have to, *Dr. Aston*. You have a patient to see." He stiffens at the thought and backs away, uttering a low curse.

"It could be just allergies. I have days like this," I report. "Feels like one of them. My throat is a little sore, and I'm kinda just feeling run down, but don't panic. Just tell me you forgive me for being a dick. You didn't deserve it."

"We all have our moments," Lucian assures before grabbing

the cart. "Let's get you home to rest. You said you wanted to browse the shop over?"

I nod. "Souvenirs."

"Let me help expedite this. I'll find us the right buffet for tonight, check out and meet you over there, okay?"

"K, let me give you some money."

"Jane," he eyes me evenly, his tone a request to be reasonable. "We're seeing one another. Please allow me to get some things, like Kleenex, and pick up the occasional dinner. A gift here and there. It would please me immensely."

"All right," I agree readily, hating that he's wary of the money talk and it's my fault.

"Thank you, I'll meet you next door," I say, walking toward the exit while watching him walk away only to catch another woman on the same aisle, also currently in the midst of a Lucian Aston pause. In those seconds, I feel like the luckiest girl alive.

Le Sigh.

Not long after, Lucian finds me a store over at a table scouring souvenirs.

"Found anything good?"

"Cheap is the key word here," I lift my hand to guard my whisper, "cheaper souvenirs for the people that I like least," I joke, snatching a few Eiffel Tower keychains off the hook for some of the staff on our floor before glancing back at him. "Hey, you sure you forgive me? I've been feeling off the last two days, but you poor man, I've been all over the place since we got to France."

"Forgiven, *babe*," he utters, Dr. Prick expression on display for additional comical effect as I cover my face in mortification.

"What?" He chuckles, pulling my hands away.

"I didn't mean to like . . ." I bulge my eyes at him.

"Make me feel like your babe? How incredibly rude," he taunts.

"You know," I lift and roll my hand, "make it like we're Home Depot couple bound."

"I happen to like Home Depot," he digs in.

"Lucian," I draw out, knowing he knows what I mean.

He plays ignorant and looks good doing it.

"Like domesticate us, Doc."

"I'm simply offended you don't find me Home Depot material. That's unforgivable. It's my second home."

"Can you do home repairs?" I ask.

"Perhaps," he hedges.

"Fine, when we return to Boston, you can audition for the role of *babe*. We'll get you in a tool belt, and you can change my broken bedroom lock in nothing but . . . oh wait," I say with a giddy clap. "I have a better idea. If you can complete a few things on my honey-do list in nothing but a Home Depot smock like Ben First from The Dead Sergeants, I'll consider you Home Depot babe material."

"Ben . . . he's the lead singer, right?"

"Yeah, and I know he's a little older, but just so you know, he's my hall pass."

"Way to ruin a day, Cheeky," he says dryly.

"Oh come on, you have to have a hall pass girl," I narrow my eyes.

Lifting the grocery bags in his hands to rest on the table, he crowds me and bends to whisper directly in my ear. "If we're talking fantasy here, Cheeky, what could be hotter than fucking the hell out of your surgical nurse on your consult desk, watching her perfect teardrop breasts bounce as she tightens around your cock?"

Instantly, I go lax and lean against him as he moves to my other ear for his next loaded whisper. "Or lowering her scrubs and rimming her sweet arse with my thumb as I drive into her pussy from behind."

"That's," I wheeze, "rather specific," my chest bounces. "You must have put some thought into that, and you better damn well put that imagination to work the second we get home," I finish in order.

"Oh, it's a promise, Cheeky," he utters, his voice pure sex. "These fantasies are multiplying daily. In fact, I've already sorted how I'm going to eventually take your tight arse."

"Okay," I whisper on the verge of explosion, "you can be my babe."

"No more audition?" He teases, running his hard cock perfectly along my backside.

"We'll see where the day leads us," I blow out harshly as his warmth leaves me.

"Maybe you'll be the one forced to audition," he jests. "Because I'm certain you'll have another mood or two before the trip ends."

"Challenge accepted," I smirk. "But I veto my audition because I dealt with six months of moods in advance."

"Point taken and given, Cheeky. But it's probably getting a bit hard being away from home," he says, to which I frown.

"No. You think that's it?" I ask, the notion surprising me.

"I think it's been a few days short of a month since we left Boston, and we've endured a hell of a lot so far at the hands of luck, weather, and Christ knows what else. So it's very plausible you're homesick, Jane."

I look down at the table full of, well, crap, but affordable crap, and continue to pick up keepsakes. "I mean, I guess I miss Poochie. Okay, I do miss him a lot and my bed. I like my bed—it's like a cloud and the best reason I've ever maxed my card. But," I catch his gaze, "don't take that personally, okay? I'm having a really good time with you. Like the time of my life, and I hope you believe me."

"Me too, babe."

"Assure me? Please?" I ask, lifting and kissing the side of his jaw.

"I'll assure you as soon as you're feeling better," he whispers as we start to walk to the register. Once we've checked out, we start making our way out of the store, passing racks and racks of I Love Paris T-shirts in an array of colors. Feeling a little lighter, I glance back at Lucian, heart alight, as I exit the store. "You know, you can add today to another day you made better. Things are—"

# THIRTY-NINE

## JANE

"Ohhhh God Nooo!" I hear myself screech as I trip over the foot of the last T-shirt rack just next to the open store exit—stumbling headfirst into a full rack of calendars, which only prolongs my fall. I once again land squarely on my back, this time with the added luxury of it being a *cobblestone* street.

Frantic bursts of French break out around me as Lucian's horrified face pops into view, and the entirety of my back lights fire, my body seizing with the horrific onslaught of pain.

Eyes watering, I stare up at Lucian as defeat fills me from head to foot, and my white flag appears before I mentally raise it in surrender.

Various other men pop into view as Lucian speaks fluent French and relays what I can only assume is that he's my doctor—and God help and save him for it.

"Jane, love. Please talk to me," Lucian speaks rapidly. "How is your pain?"

How is my pain?

How. Is. My. Pain?

Anger outweighing the pain, I let the eruption happen.

"FUCK. THIS. TRIP!" I roar in a half laugh, half sob. "I mean it. Fuck it, Lucian. It ends today. It has to end today. I'm done. I give up. J-just leave me here, or better yet, bury me in the catacombs if they ever reopen the fucking place," I cry. "But do yourself a solid and run for your life! I can't do this another day. Do you hear me? I can't do this anymore," I release another anguished wail as Lucian's eyes scan me, as he again attempts to scrape me off the cobbles, this time in a different country, as I full-on meltdown.

"I want to eat food in places where I can read the bag and ingredients!" I air to him as he lifts me to sit.

"I want to be warm for more than five minutes!" I relay next as I tick off my list of grievances.

"I want to take a two-legged fucking shower!" I sob into his chest as he gets me to my feet.

"I want mediocre coffee! I'm fine with mediocre coffee!" I sob as he palms my back carefully, and I grip his shirt in my fist and cry into his neck.

"I want to find toilet paper when I reach for it, and for one damn day, just one, I want to feel fucking safe!" I finish as Lucian retrieves our bags before slowly and gently ushering me back to our apartshack.

An hour or more later, I lay on the box springs in the bedroom, having asked Lucian for some time alone so I can cry myself out. I spend most of whatever time passes sobbing into a pillow, the pain in my back radiating as I just let my disappointment flow. My tears have slowed for the most part when Lucian opens the bedroom door. I crack my swollen eyes to see him approaching me with fizzing water. Expression earnest, he bends down to me where I lay and offers me the cup.

"I'm so sorry," I croak, "Really and truly, Lucian. I know you didn't sign up for this shit either, and I—"

"Shhh, Cheeky. This is where you let me be a friend. I want that so much, so please let me."

"Okay," I nod, wiping my face for the umpteenth time before an ironic breath of exasperation leaves me. "What happened to *me helping you*?"

"For the moment, or a week of it, the tables have turned, but don't deny me my one chance to shine," he says with a grin, "drink it."

"What is it?"

"It's codeine. I went to the pharmacy and got it. I have a feeling paracetamol won't do the trick tonight."

"You're an angel," I say on a hitched breath before downing it all and handing him back the cup. "And you know I love your smolder, right? So, so much."

His lips lift, and he nods.

"I didn't mean all of what I said. I was just upset."

"Who could blame you if you did? I certainly will not. We've been through hell and back since we arrived in France."

"It's not France's fault either, but God, this trip isn't a damn thing that I thought or hoped for at all—in good and bad ways. You're the good," I say. "Please believe that."

"I'm with you, Jane. For all of it until I can tuck you into your cloudy bed in Boston. Believe that. Can you stand?"

"I think so." I move to sit and wince in pain. "Yeah, this time I used the calendars to break my fall, but it didn't." I shake my head, cheeks heating. "God, I hope somebody got a laugh out of it."

"Wasn't funny to me," he says softly. "I couldn't reach you in time," his eyes drop.

"Lucian, seriously, please don't you dare. Charlie says I'm a lazy walker. I believe her. Lesson learned. *Twice*. And hopefully for the last time."

"It could have happened to anyone," he offers.

"I think we should use a running bet on how many times you'll be forced to use that one."

His lips twitch at the irony.

"It's okay to smile. Hell, to laugh, and I will. One day, but not today."

"Then I'll laugh with you, one day, but not today," he says as he discards the cup on the dilapidated night table while lifting me to stand.

"Where are we going?"

He cups my face and runs a thumb along my cheek. "Not far, love."

The term of endearment warms me as the codeine begins to kick in, spreading even more warmth throughout me. "Good, because I'm okay with resting—now," I tell him as we share a sad smile.

"I hoped you would be," he whispers before pressing a kiss to my temple.

Lucian slowly ushers me into the small living room, and I gasp when I see what's waiting. A roaring fire burns in the fireplace, but surrounding it are dozens of lit candles, some of them the old school clustered fat waxy kind, dripping freely on the sides. On the lumpy mattress lay half a dozen thick quilted blankets and two new pillows. A space heater runs on high just outside the kitchen, making the room toasty as a clean laundry scent fills my stuffy nose.

Turning to Lucian, tears threatening, I see his eyes light at my expression.

"You did good. You did so damned good." I pull him into a hug. "Thank you, you incredible man. I promise I won't cry on you anymore."

"You do what you will. I'm not going anywhere, Jane."

"The pain is lessening already, thanks to the meds. Thank you so much."

"Well then, let's wash this fucked day off and get you fed and comfortable."

"Lucian," I shake my head, realizing I admitted my one-legged showers in my tirade.

"Trust me?" He asks.

I nod. He walks me to the bathroom, and I see he's removed the nightmare glass partition.

"You aren't the only one who's had an issue, Jane. I nearly lost a fucking testicle."

We both burst into laughter, and I turn to him. "I really want to kiss you right now, but instead, I think I'll just tell you that my jet-setting days are over for the moment. I don't think I'll be getting my passport stamped anytime in the near future, buddy. I can't take much more working vacation. You'll be stuck with a different nurse."

"I wouldn't travel with anyone else," he murmurs before he carefully undresses me and then himself. Though it's a bit of a struggle for him, he bathes me from head to toe in the tiny shower stall, keeping half his body outside so I can stay warm in the spray. After we rinse off, he towels us both off hastily and brings me into the living room. It's there that I see the soup and bread he got from the bakery.

"I'm just going to warm it up, he says, gently sitting me on the couch as tears form in my eyes while I take in our surroundings— crying again. I hate this Jane, who can't seem to stop needing her white knight.

When the soup's piping hot, I inhale it while thanking him as the codeine fully kicks in, taking all of the pain away. It's as I sop up the rest of my bread that I feel the run of my nose.

As Lucian finishes his soup, I run my hand along the back of his neck and glance around.

"This is like a dream. You made this dump totally romantic and bearable, and honestly, have since we got here. Thank you, Lucian. You're the best. I wish I wasn't sick. I would totally thank you with my own imagination."

"No need, Jane, truly. I'm being a good friend, right?" He asks, his earnest expression snatching the rest of my beating heart.

"I couldn't ask for better. Your best is the best of friends there is. I'm lucky to call you mine."

"You can, Jane," he whispers, placing a chaste kiss on my lips.

"Don't do that. You'll get sick," I whisper.

"I can handle a cold, but I'm not sure it will sit well if I'm unable to kiss you. Be right back."

When he returns, he's wearing the paper-thin robe and lifts mine to slip into. Propping himself against the loveseat with the new pillows, he eases me down to sit between his legs before grabbing what looks like a new hardback, having already taken off the jacket the way he prefers them.

"What's this one?" I ask.

"It's a book of love letters between the short twerp and his true love. I thought we could read them to pass some time tonight. What do you think?"

"Really?" I say, my interest sparking. "Yes. I would love it."

We sit for hours reading the intimate thoughts of a relentless Napoleon and the tumultuous love story between him and his first wife, Josephine. I listen, fully rapt, completely captivated both by the story unfolding as well as Lucian's voice.

When he turns the page, I shake my head in his chest.

"And yet another king who divorced, and wronged his wife for an heir. A wife he *did* love."

"Sadly, that was the world and still is."

I turn back to him. "But you rebuked that world, Lucian. You said it yourself. That's probably the reason you left. You didn't want to live a disingenuous life. And you won't. I know you won't."

He stares back at me, seemingly stunned by my words. "I guess we'll see."

"You're already doing it, Lucian Aston, I *assure you.*"

"Then I'll believe you, Jane," he utters, pressing a kiss to my temple.

"Hey," I say, commanding his eyes from the page. "There's one part of what I said earlier—when I was throwing my tantrum—that I really didn't mean. I feel safe with you, Lucian. I promise I do."

"I'm glad because you need to know I won't let anything happen to you, Cheeky. As soon as surgery has concluded and we've completed post-op, I'll get you safely back to Boston. That's my promise."

He bends and kisses me soundly before resuming his reading. "'I often say that men have no power over him who dies without regrets; but, to-day, to die without your love, to die in uncertainty of that, is the torment of hell—'"

He pauses and sips his water as I turn in his arms to stare up at him again, and he stares right back at me, brows furrowed. "What are you thinking?"

"That it's pretty wrecked that a man so brutal has more game and is more romantic than most modern men who use a dick pic in place of words to woo."

Lucian grins. "Too right."

"Seriously, how did we go from *that* to fast hookups and an entire lifetime of women not hearing things like this from any man—especially one who loves them as much?"

"A true tragedy," he says, running his finger along my jaw. "What are you thinking now?"

That I'm lucky as hell that I have a man who can at least appreciate the lost art of romance. A man who, in his own right, is very, very romantic. Who makes me feel beautiful and sexy, intelligent and desired, and most importantly, heard. A man who genuinely listens to me and gives a damn about my opinion. Who warms my insides and takes my breath away constantly.

"Pass, just for now. Will you read more?"

"Happy to," he says as I turn back into his arms and revel in the sound of his voice while comfort and unimaginable warmth spreads through me. Every so often, I slink back in his hold to watch him read the intimate, private words of a former ruthless, ambitious king to his beloved but heavily flawed queen. More so of a man to a woman because, at the end of the day, though people are heavily complex, hearts are much less so. Being loved for who you are is easily the best reason to open your own heart and return that love, even if it's not the only reason. My scared heart chose other reasons to love in the past, but this reason, *this man*, is by far the best one. It's in his arms—while listening to his voice—my heart's decision solidifies with every beat, locking Lucian inside.

# FORTY

## LUCIAN

I rouse to a kiss, and yet, not quite a kiss, as Jane runs her tongue along my lower lip before gently sucking it into her mouth. Instantly hard, I grip her head in my hands and attempt to chase her fleeting lips and erratic kiss as I open my eyes.

"Jame," I mumble when, in turn, she pulls my top lip into her mouth and suckles it.

"Mmm," she whispers around it, which comes out more like a moan as I tilt back slightly, digging my head into my pillow for a better view. She again feeds eagerly on my lower lip before licking along my upper, rinse, and repeat.

"I see wee feewing betwer tobay?" I muse as she assaults me with unguarded affection.

"Hmm," is her reply as I chuckle, palming my head behind me and resting back into my pillow. Her sparkling blue eyes finally meet mine, and she smiles, the sight of it so breathtaking that I forget myself briefly as she repeats her odd kiss again. When I lift to meet it, she backs away.

"What in the world are you doing?" I ask, chasing her evasive lips.

She captures my lower lip again, which she holds captive as she speaks. "Subing on bor face piwows."

She again begins to kiss me—if it can be called that. After a few more seconds of it, I grip her head firmly, so she's forced to take my kiss—this time, she jerks out of reach.

"What are you doing?" She asks, none too happy with my interruption.

"Attempting to give you a proper kiss, you mad woman."

"I am *properly* worshiping your face pillows, sir. So just lie back and let me do it."

I draw my brows. "Please tell me you realize you speak your own language and often talk to yourself even when addressing someone else."

"Yep," she says, seemingly distracted by her ministrations—not that I'm not immensely enjoying each one.

"So long as you're aware," I say. She again tugs my lower lip into her mouth and sucks in a way that I can no longer ignore as heat licks up my spine, my cock jumping to eager attention.

Is there anything this woman does that can't turn me on? My cock thinks not. Oddly enough, it's as she covers my chest with her kiss, sinking lower and lower while covering me with her lips and tongue, that everything surges to the forefront... until there's a pause. One in which my cock is released and pumped into Jane's hand as I tip my head to stare down at her... just as she speaks... directly to it.

"Hey there," she whispers intimately, "I just want to let you know I'm a *huge fan* of your work."

Laughter bursts out of me as I reach for her again, and she bats me away. "Mad, woman. You're mad, and you're driving me mad in the process. What is the meaning of this?"

"I'm in love with your lips and cock and having private conversations with them. What's it to you?"

My cheeky girl.

"I suppose there's no harm in that, but is it possible that *all parts* of our bodies could simultaneously converse?"

"Don't be crude," she scolds, pumping my raging dick, "this relationship is still pure."

"Well, my . . ." I draw my brows, "what did you call them?"

"Face pillows," she says, as if it's now a fact.

"My *face pillows and cock* have a keen memory and are quite sure they've devoured rather *sinful* parts of your body."

"Shhh, I'm almost done." Kiss, lick, suck. Suck, lick, kiss, kiss, kiss.

She tortures me as if she's tasting a lolly rather than engaging in a sexual act as I groan and try to patiently wait for her to finish. With each teasing lick, I become harder and more impatient. I prove as much when I finally tackle her and pin her arms behind her head as she giggles up at me. It's when my cock nudges her entrance, and my tip becomes immediately wet from the brief contact that all humor leaves her face, and she moans.

"My face pillows turn you on that much, Jane?"

"So much," she murmurs, all traces of mirth long gone, replaced by heat and affection she's no longer guarding as she speaks. "I'm crazy attracted to *all* of you, Lucian, but your eyes and lips ruin me." She bucks her hips toward me, and I keep her at bay for my own admissions.

"It was your eyes as well that captivated me first," I admit. "They are what caught my attention on the plane," I murmur, bending and pressing slow kisses beside them.

"Next, it was your beautiful hair, so dark and silky. I wanted to run my fingers through it in the cab on the way to the hospital on day one, and then this," I bend and press kisses along the slant of her skin and lift. "It was the slope of your breast in that purple dress, and finally," I run the head of my cock against her entrance, and her eyes fire.

"Fuck I couldn't think straight . . . and believe it or not, your voice. It's the opposite of nails on a chalkboard for me. I was baited for every word you spoke once our deal began."

"Now I know you're lying," she whispers.

"I'm not. It gets raspy when you're tired or turned on. It's so fucking sexy."

"It was all of you at first glance," she confesses. "But then it was in your eyes and the way they soften just a little when you connected briefly with a patient. You masked it well, but I saw it, Lucian. Then it was your hands," she whispers. "The dusting of blond hair on your knuckles." She runs her fingers over them.

"When you wrinkle your nose, the three freckles there, this one here," I nudge my nose along hers.

"Your shoulders, the muscle here," she says as I release her, running her hands along them. "I wanted so much to rub them after a long surgery. To let you know I was there, that I cared."

Her admission stuns me as I unveil all I'm feeling, hoping my expression matches as I drift further under her spell.

"And further down, she says, running her hands slowly along my chest and abs. "And this," she says, rounding them around my waist to claw my arse.

"The day I busted you jump roping, I became an ass woman," she declares with a wink.

"That so?"

"Tis so, but I can't leave out one of the best bits," she lifts as she attempts to pull me into her and surprisingly manages to get me an inch inside. We both react to the feeling of the connection.

"The way you say proper," she whispers as I lower to get closer, always closer.

"The way your eyes widen in surprise," I counter.

"The way you say my name," she whispers hoarsely.

"The way you look at me," I admit, just as taken. "You, Jane Cartwright. Simply you, as well as *complicated you*, but *all of you*, nonetheless.

"All of you, too. Every part, inside and out," she whispers back, emotion shining in her beautiful blue eyes as I slowly thrust forward and press into her.

"Lucian," she calls out as another confession easily rolls off my tongue.

"I'm crazy for you, Jane, absolutely smitten," I utter as I roll my hips, and our appreciation and adoration become a moving thing between us—an indescribable sublime energy more addictive than anything I've ever felt in my life. Her perfect pussy resists me before enveloping me as I get lost in the sensation of her, in every stroke of skin, in every kiss, in her. With every movement made and every word we whisper, the you that we just spoke of aloud becomes more and more of an *us*—and nothing at all about it scares me.

Jane emerges from the shower not long after I recover from the most intense lovemaking session of my life.

"Well, damn, Doc. Mystery solved. I just got my period. You suffered through my first bout of PMS. Congrats," she announces as she exits the bathroom. "I should have freaking known why my moods were swinging like a dick in joggers."

I can't help laughing at that. "Jesus, Jane. You're so vulgar."

She grins at my reaction without apology, and I swear I adore her more for it.

"Well, sadly, sex is off the table for the next four to seven days, so we best get out there and get cultured. Anyway, we have surgery coming up next week, and I know you'll be busy with Matt and Gwen until then. So our time is almost up."

She stares at me where I stand at the kitchen counter, readying our coffees, with a mix of emotions flitting in her eyes as he watches me. But what lies within them is, most prominently, hope. Hope, which I share and intend to discuss with her before we leave for Boston. I have absolutely no intention of thinking this relationship will be cut short by a plane ride.

"Bring it, the itinerary," I sigh in false exaggeration.

"There's not much left," she assures, her expression lighting exponentially.

"I'm fine with it, but I'm adding a stop today. I noticed one very important address missing from your list."

"Oh?" She sparks up. "I'm intrigued. Let's do your idea first."

"Then go get dressed," I tell her. "But I have something specific in mind for you to wear."

"Okay, now I'm dying to know." Smile growing, she stalks toward the bedroom, and I catch her midstride.

"Lucian," she groans, "my lady bits are unavailable at the moment."

"But your lips aren't," I whisper. "Take my kiss, Jane."

And she does, melting against me until we're both breathless. I'm so mad for her at this point that I would dress as a fucking dino and dance along the River Thames every day if it meant spending time with her.

When we both pull away—her lips swollen from my kiss—she beams at me. "I'll never get tired of that, Lucian."

"Neither will I."

"You're so much more than a set of billion-dollar hands. I hope you know that."

"You're so much more than the circumstances you were raised in, Jane. I hope you allow yourself to see that as well."

She plays with the hair at the back of my neck. "I do."

"Good," I playfully spank her toweled arse. "Go get dressed. We have some *touristy shit to do*."

She gawks at my spot-on impression of her, including her accent.

"That was . . . incredible."

"Too bad you can't match it," I mimic the bulge of her eyes, "at all."

She narrows her gaze, and I muffle her snarky reply with another kiss.

Because I can.

Because I want to.

Because I'll never tire of her.
I'm besotted.

I've seen many sights in my life. As a man born of privilege, I've seen most of the wonders of the world—traveled to places far and wide. But nothing has quite taken my breath as much as Jane walking a few steps ahead of me in Versailles' Hall of Mirrors. She is dressed in the soft white coat and matching gloves I insisted she wear over her purple dress. I can't stop watching her expression as she slowly glides down the hall in her new heels, seemingly speechless, eyes misting.

I'm thoroughly captivated by her and just as taken with her as she is by the hanging chandeliers, the glass, and the exquisite intricacies of the palace. I follow her—entranced by her reaction. It's when we step out into the courtyard and are met by the sound of a violin and guitar running along chords in preparation to play that Jane scans the grounds and turns to me, her eyes glowing with the very same light they held on the plane just four short weeks ago.

"Lucian," she whispers hoarsely, "this is exactly what I pictured when I imagined Paris. She palms my jaw with her soft white glove. "This is the fairytale, and you just exceeded every damned expectation," she whispers. Her eyes alight with sentiment as the music begins to take shape, and the violin and guitar start to serenade us with Elvis's *Love Me Tender*.

"Well, then. If that's the case, we'd better get to it," I extend my hand to her and give her the dip of my chin in a bow before securing her into my arms and starting to move. She giggles, her cheeks pinking slightly as she stares up at me in a way that solidifies it all for me.

I'll never tire of her because I love her.

# FORTY-ONE

## JANE

iam Temple is nineteen years old and has a defective heart, which breaks mine as I check his vitals and air tank supply. Dressed in flannel pajamas, with dark curly hair askew and brown eyes wide and alert, our patient sits in his hospital bed, studying the doctor at the foot of it. Scanning his chart thoroughly, in full Dr. Aston mode, Lucian barely spares his patient a glance.

A born Parisian, though Liam's parents are American transplants, his vast medical treatments—which span most of his life—have all taken place here in Paris, where his heart grows weaker by the day. Dangerously weaker, which is why he couldn't make the short trip to Oxford for the procedure and the reason why he was removed from the transplant list eight weeks ago—having been deemed unfit to survive such an invasive and lengthy surgery.

Though disheartening, all these things combined made Liam a prime candidate for *this treatment*. The brilliant specialist currently standing like a sentry at the edge of his bed is his only hope for survival. The Razor procedure runs a little under half the time of a transplant operation and is far less invasive—which increases

Liam's chances significantly. In a somewhat bleak situation such as this, Lucian's hands could be the way through.

The rest of our medical team stands idly by the bed, including Margarete, Gwen, and her surgical nurse Brian, who is on lead—and I'm set to assist tomorrow. Matthieu also crowds the bed with the rest of us as the room starts to fall into a slightly uncomfortable silence while we wait on Lucian.

We've all done our preliminaries, and the clock's now starting to tick down toward the hour of the operation. Though everyone has been on point in each and every pre-op task, all acting professionally, there is an underlying amount of tension in the air. A mix of the collective nerves we all can't hide . . . aside from *one,* who stands stoically at his patient's bedside, leaving me in utter awe of him.

This last week with Lucian has been a dream. After finally receiving my replacement card just before we left on our day trip to Versailles, we packed and checked into our new hotel. Which, I begrudgingly admit, has been a little piece of heaven on earth in comparison—made more so by our lengthy hours in the cloud-like bed.

I was able to get a little more of Paris in during the few sporadic hours of downtime and enjoy the local fare, along with checking off a few more sights—satisfying my itinerary enough to where I feel I haven't missed anything significant. In no way could I have felt that anyway with Lucian as my travel companion. We've become even more connected than we were while suffering the worst, which is what I mentally but silently urge Lucian to do now as I feel the disconnect between my prickly doctor and his currently terrified patient.

For the entirety of the day, I chose not to try to jar him into a better bedside manner because he's under enough pressure. Still, I can't help but pray he unthaws now just enough to give Liam something of himself to ease some of the rattling teenager's anxiety.

As Lucian closes the chart, he gives Brian a few additional pre-op orders before Brian leaves the room with Margarete. Gwen and Matthieu say their goodbyes shortly after, both their eyes meeting mine, the same flicker of hope inside them as I nod back to them in solidarity.

We're ready.

Hesitantly, I stay in the room, sensing I'm still needed with one foot mentally outside the door in case I'm not.

When Lucian looks up at me just as I open my mouth to let him know I'm taking my leave, I realize my instinct to stay is spot on. With his guard absent for a millisecond as he holds my gaze—that's all it takes to have me resume some work to remain nearby.

It's then that Lucian surprises me by taking the chair next to Liam's bed to face him head-on.

"Do you have any questions, Liam?" Lucian asks, looking every bit like the pillar of strength he's resembled for the whole day.

"Not really, no," Liam says, eyes raking over Lucian in appreciation, *my kind* of appreciation.

Ah, it's the Lucian Aston pause.

Seems like I might have misread the reason for some of Liam's nervousness and that Lucian's patient might be currently developing a bit of a crush—which doesn't surprise me one damned bit. Liam's eyes flick to mine to see if he's been caught in his pause as Lucian thumbs through his tablet. I give Liam an assuring 'oh yeah, he's that hot' wink to let him know his secret is safe with me.

It's the slight, nearly imperceptible lift of Lucian's lips that lets me know he's onto both of us as he taps a few more buttons and lifts his screen for Liam.

"Okay, one more time for clarity. I'm going to guide you through this," Lucian says before hitting play on the screen to show him a less-in-depth, virtual demonstration of the procedure Gwen put together. Just after, Lucian goes to stand but seems to think better of it, scanning Liam's face and remains seated as he speaks. "Let's speak more candidly, shall we?"

Liam nods in response as he rattles in his bed, his thoughts no longer on Lucian's debilitating looks as my heart starts to pound while an all too familiar knot threatens to lodge in my throat. While I believe in being transparent about how much I care about my patients, their well-being, and their treatment—I know that confidence is vital. Confidence that needs to be seen by the patients, especially in times exactly like this. So I maintain, and right now, not just for Liam.

"Ask me what you're afraid to," Lucian prompts, "and I will only give you honesty."

"Will this work?" he asks immediately.

"You know your chances and percentages, but I will make every effort to see that it does."

"But I'll die on the table if it doesn't?"

"Yes," Lucian relays with care. "At this point, Liam, your heart can't afford anything further."

Liam nods and nods as the damned lump forms, stinging me anyway. "Yeah, I guess . . . I know I shouldn't have made it this far," he says with an exhausted sigh.

"No," Lucian weighs in. "There is no shouldn't. That's what we will be fighting tomorrow—the forgone conclusion and *shouldn't* that goes with your condition, and your heart is battling it as well. The fact that you're still here tells us both how badly your heart wants to do its job for you. To hold its beat and to give you the length of the life you deserve. It's my job to ensure you get every beat out of it past the limits your condition set. So it's done its job, as have you, and tomorrow you and I will be the first to battle the *shouldn't.*"

Staving back the sting in my eyes, I mentally palm Lucian's shoulders. *Keep going, baby.*

Liam's eyes water as he stoically clears his throat. "Do you personally think it will work?"

"I think it could, or I wouldn't be here. I think the odds are extremely fair but not as favorable as I would like."

"Okay."

"Your parents?" Lucian asks. "Should I speak with them again?"

"They're . . . uh," Liam hesitates, and I know it's Lucian's intimidation factor. It's then Lucian drops his guard, his eyes flitting over Liam with that rare softness that gets Liam speaking. "Well, they're kind of begging a different guy right now to save their kid."

"Faith is good for them and you, so let's all try and have some," Lucian encourages.

"Okay," Liam says, "I will." His voice rattles with his words, and neither Lucian nor I miss it.

Lucian's eyes drop briefly when he speaks again. "I'll tell you something and only you—something that most of the medical staff knows—and that I probably shouldn't share with you."

"Okay," Liam lifts the end of the word, glancing over at me. I give him a reassuring smile and nod before Liam again searches the seemingly impenetrable doctor's face.

"I had a brother by the name of Alexander who, in a way, you remind me of, and he had congenital heart disease. If this procedure had been available, it maybe could have saved his life. I'm personally invested a great deal in seeing that I do absolutely everything I humanly can to see you through this—if that helps you at all."

Liam nods, his eyes full-on watering as they light with a much-needed spark of hope. "It does, a lot. Thank you for telling me."

"You know," Lucian says, a flicker igniting in his own eyes. "If this works, you and I will make medical history together. Might I suggest a shave for the closeup photos? It would certainly suit you."

"You think so?" Liam grins, palming his scruffy cheeks.

"I think I can help him out there," I offer and wink at Liam.

"I'll take you up on that," Liam says. "Thanks."

I nod with an "of course" as Lucian stands and turns to me.

"Before you freshen him up, Nurse Cartwright," Lucian says, in his very best Dr. Aston, "I need a quick word."

"Sure," I nod to Liam. "Be right back."

"Meet you at the table, Liam," Lucian says, and Liam nods. "See you tomorrow."

"Let's beat the shouldn't," Liam says, the air far lighter than it was minutes ago.

Lucian nods and exits the room. I follow him to his temporary office on the surgical floor, and close the door behind me, palming the knob.

"You did good, doctor," I whisper across the space, my need to pull him to me debilitating. "So damned good."

Lucian nods, his hands in his pockets, the long lapels of his white coat caught in his sleeve cuffs. Turning to me, I see his guard start to slip. "Jane, I know we had p-plans tonight, but I'm going to have to cancel and m-meet you back at the hotel."

My heart cracks due to the amount of emotion in his voice as he stalks over to where I stand at the door—not for me, but for the freedom that lies behind me.

"Lucian," I start, and he jerks his chin, eyes silently pleading as he lowers them.

"Get back to L-Liam, okay? He needs your nursing much more than he needs a . . . his doctor for the m-moment."

"Okay, but—"

"Jane, p-please," he whispers roughly, and I immediately move from blocking his escape a second before he opens it and stalks away without looking back. Helplessly, all I can do is watch him go.

"Lucian," I rasp, palming his shoulders as he thrusts into me like a madman, keeping his eyes averted. I can feel the anxiety rolling off him. He came in a little after midnight, leaving every one of my texts unanswered, only to wordlessly climb into bed and start ravaging me. The intensity in his expression now is one for the books as he drives desperately into me. As good as it feels, and as much as his body is fueling mine, I can't help but stop him because nothing about this feels right. More so, it seems like he's coming apart beneath my palms. Sweat lines his temples, covering his chest, and his heart pounds beneath my hand. Fear is driving him into me again and again, but he's nowhere in this room, this bed, this moment with me—not at all.

"Lucian," I say more insistently, feeling my orgasm within reach but hating the fact that I feel such a disconnect between us that's never existed. I try again.

"Lucian, please," I croak, hating that I'm doing this but hating the space so much more. Finally lifting his eyes to mine, he reads my expression and slows his hips before he stops. "What's wrong?"

"That's what I want to ask you," I say.

"Am I hurting you?"

"No, but . . . where are you?"

Knowing he doesn't want to deal, I get the answer I expect.

"I'm here," he utters.

"That's your first lie to me," I whisper before he buries his head in my neck and gently pulls out. Rolling over, he stares at the ceiling for long minutes as I wait patiently for him to talk to me.

When he finally lifts to sit at the edge of the bed, I feel his words forming, and instead, he shakes his head.

"Talk to me. I know you're nervous about tomor—"

"I don't want to fucking talk, Jane."

The venom is surprising, and like a fool, I lash right back. "Well, I'm sorry, you don't get to fuck me to distract yourself."

Bending next to the bed, he grabs his boxers and jerks them on. "My apologies."

"Which I would accept immediately if it were *sincere*. The hell, Lucian?"

He pulls on his jeans and starts picking through his luggage before plucking out a sweater.

"You're leaving?"

"I'm simply going to take a walk."

"I'm pretty sure you were walking for most of the night. It didn't help the first time. Or do you mean run? Because that's more or less what you're doing. Don't run, talk to me."

Pausing with his head through the hole of his sweater, he stares down at me with a look I've never been on the receiving end of and immediately decide I hate. His words come out clipped and bruising. "I don't want to talk to you."

"Fine, but tell me first how walking helps."

"It will exhaust me to the point I don't think anymore."

"I'm right here."

"I don't want to talk," he snaps.

"Okay," I relent, doing my best to ignore the sting. This isn't about me at all.

He shoves into his shoes and turns to me. "Despite your speech to my father, I would prefer to keep my stiff upper lip for the moment if it's all the same to you."

"Oh, I see. We're itching for a fight. Well, give me your best shot, Doc. You haven't left a bruise just yet."

His jaw ticks in irritation. "You know, not everyone needs to talk everything out all the fucking time, Jane."

"Yeah," I lift to sit with the sheet palmed to my chest, "clearly, you've got whatever going inside of you under control."

He turns to stalk out, and I can't help but bite. "By the way, you just fucked me like I'm a sex worker, so make sure to leave a tip on your way out."

He pauses at my words and turns, his gaze so full of venom that I have to look away. He stands there for lengthy seconds, and I drop my eyes, unwilling to be battered by the mix of fear and anger he's simmering in. Seconds or minutes tick by before he finally charges out of the bedroom and slams the door of our suite.

Sometime later, I wake to a slow kiss pressed directly on my lips, his apology hitting me before I can open my eyes. "I'm sorry, Cheeky."

He hovers at the edge of my side of the bed, his palm cradling my face as he gently sweeps it with his thumb.

"Come on, get in bed," I whisper.

He undresses and takes the spot next to me, and I turn and grip him in my hold, running my fingers through his hair. "You don't have to be perfect, Lucian. You can be stressed out and bitchy too."

He grips my hand and kisses the back of it, and it takes him several seconds to speak.

"I'm," he lowers his head, "Christ, Jane, I'm terrified. As many patients as I've seen since he passed, Liam has to be the one that reminds me most of Alexander? That's the cruelest irony I've ever endured. I can't understand it, and I'm fucking furious about it because it's got me all at sixes and sevens, and I can't operate that way."

"You're ready, Lucian, and please believe your best is better than good enough. You'll do everything you can, and that's all anyone can ask—especially Liam."

"I've been considering having Matth—"

I shake my head, already knowing where he's going with this, and cut it to the quick, delivering my words as soothingly as I can.

"I'm sorry, Lucian. This is where it sucks to be the one most skilled in your field. I can't imagine the pressure you're under or what you're feeling, but I'll be there, and I have utter faith in you—and I'm not alone. Everyone is behind you. Please believe me. And if you can't because of our relationship, then believe them. Your team, the board, all of us, because everyone else has decided you are the only surgeon for this."

He nods into my chest as more silent moments pass, and I do my best to stroke his worries away. Just as I think he's drifted off, he speaks up. "I'm sorry if I made you feel used. I loathe that I hurt you that way."

"I'm fine, and you can use me anytime," I jest. "I rather enjoy it. I just couldn't handle how much was going on inside you. Just don't hide from me. But if you do, I know exactly where to look for you because you made sure of it."

Lifting his head, he stares down at me before pressing kisses to my lips and cheeks, drifting down to my bare chest, circling my nipple before sucking it into his mouth. Within seconds, he's on his side at my back, lifting my thigh to rest over his hips, cradling my head on his bicep, and turning my chin with his hand so our eyes are connected as he slowly pushes into me.

"There you are," I whisper as he thrusts in and out of me, our eyes bolted until we both succumb, and after. Wordlessly, he keeps me in his hold, kissing me thoroughly before resting his head on my pillow, our eyes glued to each other until we're both pulled into sleep.

I wake up alone and deflate at the sight of the space next to me until I see a waiting text.

**Meet me at the table. Preferably on time, Nurse Cartwright.**

I can't help but smile as I text back.

**Let's kick some ass, Doc!**

# FORTY-TWO

## JANE

Lucian's gloved and steady hands hover over Liam as he meets the eyes of every one of the surgical staff in the room to see their respect-filled nods before ordering us into post-op. A second later, cheers sound from both sides of the glass in the theater-style operating room. Those cheers are matched by those applauding on the multiple screens in the corner of the room, which house medical personnel tuning in from all over the globe.

Dr. Lucian Aston is now a bona fide medical rock star, but all my heart can recognize at this moment is the man inside the stoic veneer.

My eyes water as Lucian quickly exits the operating room, nodding toward those recently ungloved and clapping in support of him as he passes. It's atypical in a surgical room, but if Liam holds, Lucian just made history and has potentially saved many lives—lives like Liam's and his late brother's.

The weight of that truth strikes me as Lucian trashes his surgical gown before exiting the scrub room in record time. Margarete, Brian, and I take great care to stabilize Liam before allowing him to be rolled out for post-care. After completing the rest of our checklist, we, too, exit the operating room.

Some of the staff linger in awe of what they've just witnessed. Some are stunned silent, while others are vocal, chatting with obvious excitement in their voices. And me? I can think of nothing but the surgeon who just fled, and I turn and follow suit, stalking the floor for any sign of him. Knowing he's not going to be in his office, I start to search every nearby room and find him in a supply closet. Stepping in, I quickly shut the door behind me.

Lucian stands feet away, his back to me, posture ramrod straight, despite the few merciless hours he spent with steady eyes and steadier hands at that table, taking one hell of a mental beating.

My heart breaks at the sight of him, knowing his fears and the inner struggle he must have gone through during every second of that surgery. It didn't stop him—he was fearless the entire time. But his stoicism—which was evident up until this moment—is starting to crumble, and I approach him swiftly in the chance he needs a soft place to land. Calling his name, I lock the door and stalk over to him, resting a hand on his back.

"Lucian," I softly repeat, "Baby, I can give you your space if you need—"

He turns to me on a dime, and all I can see are his swimming eyes before he plasters me to him, burying his face in my neck. I cling to him, my own tears spilling over as his body starts to shake in my hold, and he sets his emotions free. I run my hands soothingly down his back, along his shoulders, through his hair.

"You did so good, Doctor Aston," I relay in a soft whisper, murmuring my encouragement as he continues to shake in my embrace. Years of pent-up grief escape him as I try to ease his worries without stretching an inch of the truth.

"It's out of your hands now, Lucian. No matter what happens from here on, please know you did everything right. The rest isn't up to you."

We've got a solid week of post-op and worry ahead of us in

which any number of things could go wrong, but in this moment, I claim his victory.

"You were so brave, so strong. I'm so fucking proud of you. I knew you could do it. I knew you would. It was never a question. I'm so, so proud, Lucian. You are the best there is, and if he has any chance, it's because of you. Please tell me you know that."

He nods into my shoulder, his frame shaking, and I grip him tightly until it subsides. When he pulls away, he gazes down at me with red-rimmed eyes.

"How do you feel?" I ask.

"I don't know . . . not just one thing at the moment if that makes sense."

"Perfect sense, but it's my turn to let you know your work is done. I'm going to be on him like white on rice. It's time to let me take over, okay? Please tell me you trust me to take it from here."

He palms my cheek. "Implicitly."

My eyes water again as he opens his mouth to speak, "Jane—"

A loud knock sounds on the door, and we both turn toward it.

"Lucian," Gwen's voice rattles from the other side of the door as I gaze up at him, and he squeezes my hands in reassurance. "Allow me a minute with her?"

"Of course," I say, walking over to the door.

Behind it, Gwen's eyes are equally red-rimmed before she rushes past me and walks straight into Lucian, gripping him into her hold.

Feeling a slight sting of jealousy, I bat that shit down, knowing that while I might have had a little to do in helping him today, Gwen was the one who was at his side for most of his medical training, there for the loss of Alexander and no doubt much more. It's a history I have no right diminishing—especially at the moment—and I won't. Though my heart rages to get back to its owner, I shut the door behind me and go to check on Liam.

# LUCIAN

"Congratulations," Gwen whispers as I grip her tightly while years of memories surface. The first time our eyes met on campus. The smile she gave me that lit up my chest. The knowing. Falling for her. It wasn't at all in vain, and I hold her a little tighter while finding myself thankful for what we meant to each other. Grateful for having loved her and receiving her love in return. Gwendolyn Cavendish was my first love—and though it turned out temporary rather than lasting—she will always have a place in my heart. Maybe in the future—if she can forgive how reckless I was with our history—she can have a place in my life, and I in hers.

When I pull away, she lifts and kisses my lips, and I allow it, pulling away to keep it chaste, knowing it's our last.

Her eyes dim at the rejection, and I shake my head gently as her expression crumbles.

"Why, why couldn't it have been me?"

"It was," I tell her honestly. "It was you, Gwendolyn. I chose you as you had me, but after some years together, we had far more going on internally than just my inability to cope with Alexander's loss."

Taking a step back from her, I finally allow myself to speak the unspoken truth that aided in the dissolution of our relationship and take responsibility for my part. But in reflecting and pinpointing the actual reason why I left my fiancée and my family, I realized the blame wasn't mine alone.

"You were jealous of him," I state.

"Of your fourteen-year-old brother? That's absurd, Lucian," she dismisses, though I see the guilt in her expression.

"Is it? Hear me, Gwen," I ask, and in return, she slowly nods.

"Before Alexander died, you were jealous of my affection for him and the closeness of our bond. Mostly because of the time and attention I spent on him, obsessing over curing him—time which you rightfully deserved a good part of and didn't receive."

"I understood," she offers.

I nod. "To a degree, until you grew tired of it. Even then, you loved me enough not to speak up. Then again, you knew that eventually it wouldn't be an issue and that he would die."

"That's not true," she gasps. "Lucian—"

"It is. You're a true scientist and always have been. So, as upset as you rightfully were with me, you knew he wouldn't factor in the long term and that, eventually, my attention wouldn't be so divided. When he died, while you did genuinely mourn him, you were also relieved you wouldn't have to compete for my attention and affection for you."

"That's so cruel and callous. Please don't think that way of me," she says, a tear rolling down her cheek.

"I don't think that way of you, but only because you had never lost anyone so close to you and couldn't understand how hard it truly was for me."

"Until I lost you," she rasps out.

"I didn't leave to punish you, Gwen. My heart wasn't in us in the months leading to his death, and I think you knew that. But while losing my brother, somewhere along the way, I fell out of love with you. My true crime is not ending us sooner and sparing you."

Her tears multiply, as does my guilt.

"Regardless of when and how, I loved you, truly. I know you felt it when it was present in the relationship, but I lost myself completely in my grief and have just found my way back to a better semblance of living."

"Because of her?"

"Not entirely, no. I've known her much longer than we've been together. I just didn't and couldn't see her until recently. Another side effect of my grief, and it's not done with me yet—maybe it never will be. But I'm living again for the first time since he passed, which is a far cry from merely existing."

Tears continue to line her face as she swallows, her voice distant when she speaks. "So, you'll never return to London?"

"I'm not sure. But your question is, will I ever return to us," I say as her attention snaps to mine, "and you already know that answer."

A sob escapes her as she swallows and begins to clear her tears furiously, and I step forward and palm her cheek.

"Please try to understand. I left a life I didn't want any more that had much more to do with my father than anything. You know that. I've always been resistant to his way of life, and I was stupidly following suit. I don't know what my future is, but for the first time in a long time, I'm looking forward to what it might be—Jane has much to do with that, and I'm so sorry that hurts you. I know it does, and I'm a bastard for it, but it's a truth you deserve."

I exhale as I take in the hurt in her eyes and allow the guilt in.

"What I hope for is that you can eventually forgive me for being so selfish in my pain and one day be a friend to me as I wholeheartedly and truly want that. You're a beautiful woman with much to offer, and I didn't deserve the time you gave me after I checked out. You definitely didn't deserve desertion, but rather honesty. That's what I'm giving you much too late. I want happiness for you. True happiness, Gwen. I think the reason I never wanted to have this conversation was because I knew you still loved me. You still rang my number and texted me, and I knew if I replied, it would only leave me giving you hope for reconciliation and hurting you further. But please never mistake the fact that I did love you, was truly and deeply in love with you at one time, and you'll always hold a place as such in my heart. The bastard who gets you is beyond lucky."

## JANE

After seeing the nurses in place to monitor Liam, I couldn't help stalking back to where I knew Lucian and Gwendolyn were finally having their reckoning. Pacing just outside the door, I also couldn't help tuning in to the end of their conversation. They'd been holed up in the closet for the better part of half an hour, and the woman in me—who is undeniably insanely in love with the man on the other side of that door, currently talking to his ex-fiancée—could not, at all, help the direction of her steps in getting back here. Heart pounding out of control, breath holding on its own to hear every muffled word, I finally stop my footing inches on the other side.

"Don't marry a man you don't love, Gwen. You'll be doing yourself a great disservice."

"Well, I can't marry the man I do love, so you haven't left me much choice in the matter."

"I'm sorry for that, and again, I hope you'll forgive me one day, but you shouldn't settle, no matter the reasoning. Especially if you don't love him."

"And do you love her, Lucian? Do you love Jane?"

"Sabalabob-who-ha-doodaly-do!" I shout in my best Adam Sandler voice, not giving a damn what I sound like. The door opens a heartbeat later, and I wince and look over to see both Lucian and Gwen staring at me like I'm in the midst of growing a third ta-ta.

Flushing a shade of red that I'm sure mimics a tomato—I allow my verbal vomit to flow. "I-I," *didn't want to find out if Lucian loves me through eavesdropping on a closure convo with his ex,* "felt a chill out here," I rub my arms aggressively, "and it gave me the creeps." I toss my hands in to help convince us all of it. "You know, they say it happens when you w-walk over someone's grave or through a ghost . . . this place has a lot of history." I spread my arms wide with my declaration. "Bet it's haunted!"

As Lucian's lips slowly lift into a knowing smirk, I shrug for added effect.

He's onto me.

Of course, he is. He's always onto me.

Gwendolyn, however, is still a bit clueless and looks none too happy about my Happy Gilmore impersonation—or my timing.

I toss a thumb over my shoulder as my words tumble out in a rush. "I'm just going to go . . . find a priest real quick."

"No need, Nurse Cartwright," Gwen utters dryly, shaking her head in humored annoyance before stepping up to Lucian and kissing his jaw. She begrudgingly grins at me over his shoulder as she leaves him with parting words that surprise me. "Be good to her, Lucian."

He nods, his eyes following her briefly before meeting mine

as she brushes past me and then stops, turning back. Face to face, I study the gorgeous woman who might have been Lucian's wife by now if circumstances were different—if he hadn't lost Alexander, if he hadn't left London—and brace myself. I can't imagine being so close to having him permanently, to being his wife and losing him. That alone will keep me silent no matter what she decides to leave me with. I didn't heed her warning and am now foolishly in love with him, and so I wait on bated breath until she finally speaks.

"I do see it, Jane," she says, her eyes watering as mine follow suit. She lowers her voice to a whisper for only me. "You're an exceptional match for him."

Shit. I hadn't expected that. It's the nicest thing she could say to me aside from her following parting words. "Congratulations on today, and I wish you both every success and happiness."

In absolute awe, as she takes the highest of roads, my empathy kicks in. Eyes misting over, I nod, choking out a "you too" as she leaves us both.

Lucian's eyes follow her as she walks away before they slowly lift to mine.

"You okay?" I ask, having a hard time with hand placement, and awkwardly decide to twist my fingers in front of me.

He dips his chin in reply. "I feel incredibly guilty for the moment, but yes."

"It will pass, and I hope it's okay to say I'm proud of you."

"It's okay to say," he exhales, "and it's for the best."

"You sure?"

"I'm sure. Come here."

I point to the ground at his feet. "To where you are? Right now?"

"As if you can somehow find other meaning in that," he muses, eyes twinkling. "Come, Jane."

I take a step in as he takes several toward me with his next order. "Close the door."

Sighing, I close the door and take the extra step to get to him as he circles my waist and brings me close to his chest, tipping my chin up with a long finger, eyes prodding.

"I wasn't eavesdropping," I lie.

"You most certainly were, Cheeky."

"Okay, I was, but I didn't hear much."

"I wouldn't care if you heard it all."

"Really?"

"Really," he says, eyes glittering with affection as he leans in and presses a slow kiss to my lips, making me forget myself as I wrap around him, running my fingers through the soft hair at his nape. The kiss deepens on its own, and when he pulls away, I see the same haze in his eyes as I'm sure reflects in mine.

"A week of post-op and we go home, Doc. Whatever should we do until then?"

"You don't have anything more on your dreadful itinerary?"

I slowly shake my head as he steps forward, keeping me firmly in his grip as he closes the door to the supply closet and locks us in.

"Oh my, Doctor Aston."

*Sex outside of the penthouse, check!*

# FORTY-THREE

## JANE

"Fuccckkkkkkk thiiiiiiiissss triiiiiiiip," I bellow to Lucian in slow motion, Kung Fu Panda style, as we slide around the ice rink known to others as King's Cross Station. A stop I just *had* to make to get a frickin' picture on platform 9 ¾. A picture every true Potterhead requires and that I demanded for myself. A demand I also tasked my faithful travel companion and love with, who's currently flailing uncontrollably feet away from me on his wingtips. A desire I made clear to him couldn't go unfulfilled the second we arrived back in London—turned Londartica.

Despite the weeks that have passed, the city is still cloaked heavily in the aftermath, blanketed excessively in a dangerous mix of ice and snow thanks to the anticyclone, which has now been coined The Beast from the East.

Terrified of falling a third time, I grapple for Lucian as our bags do dizzying pirouettes around us while one of the classical songs I *can name*, The Blue Danube Waltz, plays as background music in my head. A song I find utterly fitting as my Englishman and I make a circus-worthy spectacle of ourselves outside the station in a mere attempt to get to both Mike and the safety of the sedan.

Neither of us has a grip on shit, both of us cursing colorfully as we collectively inch toward the other before going full-on treadmill, arms windmilling. At the same time, our feet run on the ice, never making any progress until finally, we slam against one another. Our dance ends when Lucian hooks his arm around me and braces us against the wall of the station. From there, we somehow miraculously gather our luggage before inch-worming our way to Mike.

After successfully managing to get to my favorite driver and giving him the little souvenirs I took great care in picking out for him—including a bright orange I love Paris T-shirt—he thanked us by safely chauffeuring us curbside to a pub called Duke's, for our English last supper. At the pub, we dined at a small table in front of the fireplace and sipped dark beer, ordering one last round of fish and chips.

Just after, I requested a drive by 221B Baker Street, the address of one Sherlock Holmes, for a quick phone-out-of-the-window snap before successfully dodging traffic on Abbey Road for a full body, arms in-the-air shot, which had me gleefully crossing the last item off my itinerary.

All thanks to the English saint I'm crazy in love with and plan on relaying that information to very soon. We haven't discussed a single minute of any future plans we have for when we get home, but it seems unnecessary at this point because Lucian made it so.

Feeling more solidified with him than I thought possible in a mere six weeks of traveling together—five of which we've been dating—I can't imagine either of us calling it a day on something that seems too good to be true.

Both of us ready to tuck in after a day of travel, Mike safely drops us curbside to check in one last time to a hotel called The Park Grand in preparation for our flight home tomorrow morning.

It's in the middle of the smaller, more quaint room I insisted we get that I mimic the news playing on the screen behind me as Lucian eats preservative-free chocolates—which, as an additive-addicted

American, I sadly find lack in taste—while laughing at me as I imitate the news anchor.

Standing between two full-sized beds—one of which we have already christened—he shakes his head at me as I use my hairbrush as my mic. I relay the news the Jane way, which is basically far more theatrical. Oddly enough, I only have to play up the exasperated news anchor by a mere fraction as he animatedly reports, seeming as though he's at his wit's end.

"Crikey mates! The substance that fell from the sky weeks ago has continued reigning hell on all our land and halted all activity, ceasing life as we once knew it! The twenty-year storm has brought catastrophic and record-breaking snowfall and icy temperatures that will not cease, which has us all buggering so hard—"

"Wrong phrase, love," Lucian cuts in, laughing harder.

"Okay, bugging out. Shhhh, Dr. Hottie-God's-Favorite-and-mine-too, I'm trying to give you the news," I playfully scold, pointing my mic at him briefly before tuning in to report more in my horrible mock accent. "Due to worsening conditions, Heathrow is scheduled to close sometime tomorrow afternoon, as all inbound and outbound flights are set to be canceled!"

I finish that bit with jazz hands as Lucian's smile disappears.

You know that up-close moment in movies or shows where the camera pans in on the clueless idiot?

Well, this is where it happens for me in three . . . two . . . one . . .

"Noooooo!" I boom, turning around and shaking my head incredulously at the screen in disbelief. "Noooooo! Lucian, say it ain't so. Tell me I heard that wrong!" I shout at the TV and him as he stands and folds me into his arms.

"Please, God no," I croak as he begins to murmur his assurances, his arms wrapped around my waist.

"It's okay, Cheeky, we're on a very early morning flight, love. We may make it out, don't panic yet. Don't give up hope. Picture yourself flying to Boston tomorrow."

"Oh, I'm panicking," I go limp in his arms as he pulls me toward the bed, my heels dragging as I marvel at his incredible upper body strength while I offer him no help—a ragdoll in his arms. Laughing, he pulls me to sit between his legs—which has kind of become our thing—as he props himself at the headboard, bracketing me in his hold.

"I can't handle another day away from home, Lucian," I say, shaking my head. "Do you hear me?" I crane my neck to look back at him. "I can't do it," I croak. "Just . . . grab your black doctor bag and sedate me right now because I'm telling you if I'm not on a Boston-bound plane tomorrow, I'll be buggering so fucking hard."

"Jane," he laughs, "you've got to stop using that turn of phrase."
"Why?"

"Because you're saying taking it up the arse so hard."

"Oh?" I stop my wriggling in his arms. "That's what that means?"

"Yes, Cheeky," he says through a light laugh.

"Oh, okay. Well then, bloody hell and bollocks!?" I glance back to see if that checks out.

"Better," he chuckles as I sink back into his arms on the bed.

"I mean, it's not that I haven't enjoyed my time here—especially with you—but yeah, I want to go home now. Like, so bad. I miss Poochie. He's probably forgotten his mother by now, and if he hasn't, he's going to piss on my bed for a week out of pure spite." Turning in his hold so I can see him, he grins at me as I air my grievances.

"I just want to be back where I don't have to decipher odd words like buggering or pronunciations like the River Thames—pronounced tems, seriously? What the hell? You guys are just setting people up with that one . . . and I want to eat outlawed neon cheese and chocolate with all the additives and dangerous food coloring yellow one through a hundred. I want to die prematurely because of it. I want to be back in the land where toilet paper is abundant, coveted, and a major priority. I want to be an *American* again. I've had about all the culture I can stand."

"Noted," he whispers, "and I made a promise to get you home, and I will," Lucian assures as his phone rings on the nightstand, and he palms it.

"I love your assurances," I tell him, nuzzling his neck and wrapping around him as he eyes the screen on his phone and stiffens in my hold.

His expression sobers considerably as he looks over at me. "It's Byron."

"Well, hurry up and answer it," I urge him, running my hands down his back. Lucian spent a little over an hour in the hotel lobby earlier with his mother as I showered and packed. I said a quick goodbye to her before I did but didn't stay long because I wanted to give them some time together. He's been a bit melancholy ever since and voiced his worry for her and his wish to get her out of the house—more so from beneath his father's paralyzing thumb.

A few seconds after answering, I leave his lap to sit bedside and give him some room for conversation. I hear the desperation in Byron's voice on the other end of the line as Lucian eyes me, seeming stunned. The conversation remains mostly one-sided as Byron speaks rapidly and Lucian starts to dress. "I'll be right there. Hear me, Byron, I'll be right there."

Ending the call, he looks over to me with a panicked expression.

"He," Lucian shakes his head. "He snapped at Jasper earlier today, and he's beside himself. He sounds destroyed, Jane. He said he needs to talk."

"Lucian, you have to go. He's at his breaking point. Go. Go talk to him. I'll be here."

"You're sure?"

"Are you kidding? Of course I'm sure," I grab my phone and start typing. "I'm texting Mike right now to come get you. Finish getting dressed."

After shooting off the text, I grab his wallet and hand it to him as he starts bundling into his jacket and scarf before pulling on his gloves.

"I've never heard him so distraught," Lucian whispers, looking haunted as he searches the room for anything else he might need. When he's dressed and ready, I palm his jaw as he stands idle at the door.

"This is the perfect time," I encourage him. "Not that I'm glad it happened. I'm just glad you were still here when it did. That was the moment he needed. He's ready for a change, and he needs you. Go talk to him, and Lucian—*really talk.*"

"We don't speak frankly about emotions, Cheeky, ever. You know that."

"Tonight, you will," I tell him. "Because you know exactly how to. If my radar is on point, he just hit bottom. I don't think he knew how to ask you for help at the game, but I could see his need to try to connect—and yours."

"Jane, I've never—"

"He's lost his brother and his wife, and you have the same father. You know exactly how it feels. Go be the man I've gotten to know and be fucking real. You can do this, Lucian. Push the rest of that poison your father tried to pump into you out, and finally go have a heart-to-heart with your brother."

"Right," he says, looking a little intimidated by the task.

"He's your brother, not your father, and he just proved it with that phone call. He probably scared the shit out of himself. If you truly want a relationship again—"

"More than anything," he cuts in, and I can see the desperation in his eyes, his need to believe it's possible as guilt kicks in that I selfishly didn't encourage him to do this before now. I've monopolized his time here, and he still hasn't fully dealt with them.

"Then this is your shot, baby," I murmur. "You've got this. Even if you don't, *go.*"

Lucian grips my face and kisses me soundly before I usher him out the door.

Intuition is a bitch. A bitch that's led me to the right conclusions on more than one occasion. It's everywhere today. In his posture as we boarded the tube because Mike couldn't reach our hotel due to the icy road and traffic clusterfuck surrounding it in both directions. It's in Lucian's eyes, which have frequently failed to meet mine through the last two stops. A far cry from this morning, where just before dawn, he returned—after talking all night with his older brother—and we had a mostly wordless but very intense lovemaking session.

It's in the low tone he's kept since we both wheeled our bags out of the hotel. It haunts me as I finally look over and catch his return gaze, immediately sinking into his intoxicating honey-infused depths.

In there, I find so much—adoration and affection being key players—but just past that, a melancholy of sorts laced with indecision. I should be happy. Thrilled. We're going home after six long weeks overseas, and I'm anything but because of the gnaw currently prodding me.

Though Heathrow is still threatening to close due to the conditions, we decided to try our luck today with our tickets, with no real backup plan in mind.

In the worst-case scenario, we're delayed on our return trip. Despite my protest, I don't think either of us would've minded a few more days flying back to Boston—to reality. But alas, the weather this morning was clear enough to make the effort, and if we missed a flight that does take off, I can't really afford to replace my ticket.

Lucian, now very attuned to that truth, though a bit skeptical our flight would leave, didn't put up a fight to save me the embarrassment of admitting it. We remain silent as we ride, the train speeding through the tunnels as the world bustles around us. In our world, I'm forever lost in his eyes, trying to decipher when the shoe will drop. Either here in London or once we touch down in Boston.

A decision has been made, a big one. That's all my intuition is telling me for now. She's a fickle bitch, intuition, and no matter how hard I try to prepare myself, to anticipate and decipher what the decision might be, she's got nothing else for me. As the train slows and stops at the station Mike told us to meet him at—to take us the rest of the way to Heathrow—I feel the heaviness set in. It's only after I roll my new island on wheels onto the platform and glance back to see Lucian hesitate just before he steps out next to me that I know.

It's here, in London, and the shoe is dropping now.

"You're staying," I blurt, knowing at that exact moment that's what his decision is. When his eyes drop—and my assumption is the right one—I feel and start to mimic every part of his shaky demeanor down to my core. As we both step out of the way of foot traffic, I grip his suit-clad arm. "Lucian, please look at me. Are you staying?" I ask in vain because I already know.

Shock registers when he brings watering eyes to mine, and my eyes instantly follow. He's not going to put on a front. It's the greatest compliment he can give me—some solace for the horrific rip that's started in my chest.

"I have to break my promise to you, Cheeky. To see you safely back to Boston. I'm so fucking sorry. I never once meant it to become a lie."

"It's not a lie," I croak, as a tear so powerful branches throughout my chest that it momentarily steals my breath. For him, I force my way through it. "I know exactly why you are staying, and I can't at all and won't blame you." I shake my head as my eyes spill over. "C-can you give me a minute?"

He ushers me away from the onboarding crowd, and I catch sight of a tear falling down his cheek before he tucks us behind one of the pillars of the station and stares down at me—his palm on the wall next to my head. It takes us both a long moment to absorb the sting and even longer for him to speak.

"If I go b-back to Boston with Byron in the state he is, with Mum still being victim to my father," he shakes his head. "I can't leave them again, Jane. Not when I have a chance to help Byron, to be a brother to him for the first time in a very, very long time. Or possibly get my mother away from him. I've been s-so wrapped up in you—"

I palm his jaw and shake my head. "Lucian, it's okay. I thought the very same thing last night before you went to him. That I, we, distracted you from making any more progress."

"Please don't you dare feel guilty. I can't regret it," he whispers. "I w-won't ever regret it."

He grips my hip as I bite my bottom lip, looking up at the ceiling of the station. My eyes spill over as I rasp out my blessing. "It's the right thing, Lucian. Absolutely the right thing. I don't blame you at all, I promise."

Deep down, I always knew I was on borrowed time. I hate the fact that I was right—though my time with him will forever remain sacred and untarnished—I have that. I'll keep it. I'll remain the friend he needed me to be.

Aside from that friendship, Lucian and I made so much love in the weeks we were together. It was a gift neither one of us abused or took for granted. Somehow, I always knew we would end when the trip did. I just wasn't sure how or why.

Intuition has become my biggest enemy as I think it. But I can't regret it. Being with him and spending the time I have with him has changed something fundamental inside of me. I know, without a doubt, it's further stoked my expectations for my life and the things I should and will demand for myself—and I tell him as much.

"If you thought I was bad before with my unrealistic expectations," I say, smiling through my tears, "you've created a monster now. You've set a high bar," I crack on that. "There's no way I'm going back to what I settled for before, Lucian. Not ever," I whisper vehemently.

"And I'll be hard-pressed to find another man who," my eyes flood again as I keep them up to the ceiling of the station so I have the strength to continue, "does anything the way you do. Who could ever touch me as you do? Make me feel so . . . fucking perfect." More tears tumble as I fall apart right in front of him—my heart shattering with every beat as the tear continues to rip through me. It's a hell I never knew existed. I'm so crazy in love with him, and only through hell will I get past loving him. I'm not even sure it's possible or that I can outlive it.

"Jane, l-look at m-me, please," he whispers, his voice hoarse.

"It hurts, Lucian," I sniff. "It hurts so much."

"I know, but I'm asking. Please, love."

I lower my eyes to his as he blurs before me, and I blink to clear them as he speaks. "Christ, I f-fucking hate how hard this is for m-me. Just p-please know I can hardly describe what this time with you has m-meant to me."

"Same."

Same?

Same?

Speak woman! Tell him that he's altered your perception, that he's widened your heart, that he lit your spirit—your whole fucking soul on fire. That he's more than any expectation anyone else has of him. That he's got a perfect heart, and he loved you with it better than anyone else ever has. Another long minute passes by as I give him the time he needs, knowing that mine isn't the only heart that's breaking.

"I can't tell you the future," he rasps out, "but I c-can tell you the one I thought of, dreamt up when I was returning with you. Do you want t-to know?"

I nod, my eyes blurring with more tears, and I blink to clear them, intent on burning his confession into memory.

"Long walks along the harbor," he swallows, taking his time as tears freely glide down his jaw. "Shared wine. Fucking you, tasting you, every chance I got. Making love to you on rainy mornings when the thunder rattles the ground. You know those mornings?"

I nod.

"Shared desserts at midnight. Seasons changing. For *years, Jane.* As many as you would give me," his voice cracks as I cough out a sob. "Please, Cheeky. Don't cry."

"You're crying."

"That's because I'm in love with the most beautiful force of nature I've ever met, and apparently I've become a master at breaking my own fucking heart."

"You're not doing it intentionally," I tell him. "I'm pr-proud of you, and I—" I falter, burying my face in my hands to muffle my cries. It feels like I'm dying. He wanted years with me.

*Years.*

And he loves me. He loves me, and even if he hadn't said it, I know—he made sure I knew.

"Can I be so selfish as to ask you to stay?" he chokes out hoarsely. "Will you stay, Jane?"

I shake my head, needing a little reprieve. "I mean, I could, but London would surely fall."

We both share a tearful smile, which dissolves almost immediately. "Honestly, I don't know, Lucian. I don't think I could leave the States or Charlie for good. I, I don't know."

"But you may consider it if I stay?"

"For you, I would consider *anything*."

He blows out a breath, a tear gathered at the corner of his lip, spraying out and hitting my neck. It feels like a fucking wrecking ball as I grip the lapels of his jacket to keep myself standing. We continue to openly cry as we soak up what time we have left—which isn't much—and it's the saddest, rawest, most beautiful thing I've ever experienced. He doesn't want to break my heart, but I don't want to keep him from healing his.

"Jane," he croaks, eyes continually shimmering, "you saved me in a way I'll never be able to repay you for."

"No," I shake my head. "You saved yourself. This truly is the right thing. As much as it hurts me to say it, it's the right thing."

"Are you sure? Because it feels horrible. It f-feels like fucking hell," he crushes me to him, and I grip him right back, holding on tight before he latches onto my mouth and kisses me to within an inch of my life. As a train pulls in, I can feel his body shaking with his hurt as I shake in his arms, sobbing into his jacket, feeling his pain and allowing him to absorb mine. Though neither of us wants it, this feels a hell of a lot like goodbye.

He only pulls away as the next train stops and stares down at me. "Jane, you have to go, or you're going to miss your flight. I c-can't. I don't at all want this to end. Can I ring you?"

"I don't want it either. In fact, I'm strongly in favor of *never*."

"Then let's not say g-goodbye at all," he prompts. "I can't. I fucking w-wont," he says, gliding his thumb along my cheek. I lean into that touch, having no idea how I'm going to go a day without it now. This can't be happening.

I nod as the bustling station drowns out any possible conversation.

He kisses me chastely and then bends to whisper into my ear. "I can't see you off. If I do, I won't stay."

"Go," I nod toward the train. "Go. Get your life back."

He hesitantly nods and starts to race toward the doors before calling back to me. "This isn't goodbye, Cheeky," he assures me, putting up a hand to indicate he'll call me. Between the announcement and the chatter surrounding us, I order him away. A second later, hellfire fills my chest at the fact that I didn't return his sentiment.

That I can't fucking live with. Not this time. Determined to track him down to say the words I've been denying myself as panic fills me from head to foot, I take a step toward the train and am stopped by the sight of him mere feet away, watching me. Eyes locked, he frees me of the agony as his perfect lips open, his declaration clear as he mouths, "I love you."

"I love you," I say back just before a passerby blocks my view of him. By the time he passes, Lucian is gone. Trailing him in vain, I catch sight of him just as he steps on the train a second before the doors close. The sight of it has me cupping my mouth to try to stifle my sob.

Within seconds, the train is speeding away with Lucian on it. My soul screams at the sudden loss. I remain paralyzed where I stand at the station, unable to move an inch to the left or right, unknowing of how I'm supposed to fucking function without my heart, which is currently speeding away from me.

I've been with him every day for the last six weeks, in a cloud, in a surreal bubble that just burst as realization sets in—that in this second and every one after that, I have to somehow start to exist, to resume life without him.

Nothing about it seems right or like it's real—like it's reality.

He's gone. He's gone.

It feels like I waited a lifetime for him, and just as swiftly as he was gifted to me, in a blink, he was taken away.

From this point on, he'll be just another local, and maybe our time together will leave him with a story or two to tell, and one day in the future, I'll be part of some of his fondest memories. That time he spent six weeks with the cheeky nurse he worked with when he temporarily left London.

The notion of that shatters me further as I sob openly in the train station, unable to see a single thing in front of me.

I always knew—felt—somehow that it was inevitable he would break my heart. I knew soul-deep that if I allowed myself to fall, he might very well be borrowed.

As the last of his train races out of sight, I feel a desperation to catch it, as though I'm already becoming a part of his past, and his real life has just begun.

The truth of the matter is—his life is here.

He abandoned it three years ago because he couldn't take the heartbreak of losing his brother. If Lucian were to get on the plane with me today, realistically, *I* would be the only one of the two of us returning home. Boston was just a temporary derailment of his path. For Lucian, England is home. A home where he'll remain a legendary surgeon, a doctor.

A really *good* doctor who happens to have a steady beating and very capable heart. I know because I've felt it beat true beneath my palm and have been on the receiving end of his use of it. It was the best I've ever felt in my life. A gift I'll never take for granted. Not a minute will be wasted. Even as I stand, hollowed out, soul screaming due to the abrupt way my heart was just ripped out of my chest, I know I'll never regret loving Lucian Aston. Loving one another made us both better people.

And from here on out, he'll be the doctor he was meant to be. A doctor and surgeon that patients will fly to from all over the world to get a glimmer of hope. And he'll supply them with every bit of the hope they need and then some.

Because he was that doctor all along.

Scraping myself mentally from the floor of the tube station, I meet Mike in shambles at the curb and make it to the airport in time to board.

My plane and flight are the very last to leave the airport just before it closes.

# FORTY-FOUR

## JANE

*February 13th*

> **Lucian: I've just had a groundbreaking talk with my brother today, and I have you to thank for that. Thank you, Jane.**

Smiling, I answer the knock on the door and open it to see two huge vases of circus roses—my favorite. I never told him.

I send him a picture along with my text. **No, thank you! Mind Blown EMOJI How did you know?**

> **Lucian: Charlie told me.**

Charlie told him because Lucian is now part of my support group chat, as he's been since the first week I got home.

> **But it's not Valentine's Day.**

> **Lucian: I don't need a designated day as a reason, Cheeky.**

We FaceTimed only once, and it was the first time we spoke—which was only days after we parted in that train station. That convo seemed even more painful than it was there, and since his long-term plans haven't been decided, I refuse to torture myself with the sight of him for now.

It's too hard—at least for me—and so I requested we not talk on screen until I can handle it a little better. However, it seems to be the case for him as well. I can hear it in his voice—though it's not tearful like mine. What helps is that he seems to have meant every word he spoke that day—though I'm too afraid to test the theory and don't have to right now. He texts every day, sometimes multiple times.

It's been a little less than two weeks since we parted suddenly in London, and I'm already losing my shit at the hospital. Daily. Every once in a while, I'll swear I see him gracing the halls of our floor and blame it on the absinthe.

I slide my thumb up to look at last night's text again as I situate the roses on my counter and kitchen table.

**Lucian: I miss you, Cheeky.**

Hitting reply to his last text, I don't bother to overthink it, giving him honesty, always.

**Missing you hurts so much, but I'm too proud of you to give you too much shit for it. I love you, Lucian. Always.**

**Lucian: It's fucking hell being without you now. You're everywhere in London.**

**You're everywhere in Boston, and we have no memories together here.**

Bubbles start and stop and start again, and I know it's because he's refusing to make promises he may never be able to keep. I text first to try to help him along. I don't want him to suffer over making the right decision. As I suspected, Lucian told me Byron had been inconsolable the night they met up—finally having hit his own rock bottom. He'd scolded Jasper in a way that he felt he might be better off cutting himself out of Jasper and Ben's lives and begged Lucian to give him some guidance. Hearing Lucian recall their conversation was horrible and broke my heart. From what Lucian said, once he helps get Byron on his way, he's determined to help get their mother away from their father's clutches—though Lucian isn't sure if it's possible.

**Don't, Lucian. It's fine. Maybe if we stayed together and came home, we would have fought like cats and dogs.**

Maybe our attraction would wane, and we'd go back to hating each other.

Lucian: I never hated you.

Yeah, me neither, but play along.

Lucian: I can't.

You will. For me.

Lucian: Anything for you . . . so maybe you get a haircut with . . . a fringe, and I can't stand the look of it. (Please don't get a fringe)

You mean bangs? *Chops hair off.

Lucian: Don't you fucking dare!

I heard you say facking. LAUGH EMOJI Fine. No fringe. Well, maybe YOU develop long-term halitosis, and instead of hurting your feelings, I just stop kissing you. Or maybe you become impotent, and we both know you can't take the magic blue pill.

Lucian: Watch it, Cheeky.

And you can't perform. So now you've got halitosis, and you're impotent. Oof. CRIES EMOJI

Lucian: TOO FAR. I'm going to colour your arse the shade of a London phone booth if you keep this up.

Instantly, I'm there, in that booth, our first sober kiss deepening as he sweeps me away with the thrust of his tongue and fingers while I moan into his mouth.

Lucian: I screwed that up perfectly, didn't I? I swear to God, I felt your moan, felt you on my fingers the second I typed that.

I felt it, too.

Lucian: The absolute worst timing as well. I have to scrub in, and I'm hard.

His admission gives me pause.

You're working?

Bubbles start and stop.

Lucian: I meant to tell you I had my privileges reinstated

**temporarily to use for more Razor surgeries. The journals are all asking for articles. I'm to be published soon.**

I stare at his text. This is it. This is where he starts thriving and where I lose him. It has nothing to do with a loss of affection for me but everything to do with the fact that not only is he claiming the life he abandoned back—it's offering itself to be better than what it was before he left. A better relationship with his family, a success against the ailment that took his brother. A promise of a much brighter future than the endless numbness that he succumbed to before he left. I was never going to lose Lucian because he didn't love me back. I'm going to lose him because he doesn't need me anymore—not to survive or get by. He would have to want me enough to give up a better life than the one he left in London and the miserable existence he lived here. There's nothing in Boston for him but me.

**Lucian: I was going to tell you the next time we spoke. Please don't be upset. I needed a way to pass the time in between sorting this mess with my family, and it will help more patients like Alexander.**

Swallowing as tears line my cheeks, I inhale the scent of the roses deep before texting my reply.

**I understand. Completely. I do. I'm so happy about that. For the families of the patients and brothers like you. For you and your family. Don't worry about me another second. I'm smiling.**

**Lucian: Why don't I believe you?**

"Because you know me," I say out loud. "Because you know me like no other man ever has or will. Because I let you. Because I gave you my whole heart, knowing you would break it. Because the whole time I wanted you, you needed me. Now I need you."

**Lucian: I have to scrub in, Cheeky, but please believe me. I'll ring you later.**

I break apart as the bubbles start and stop once more before he signs off. I know why. Things feel off now; the only thing that would make them right is if we were together. There's no way out of this—just through it. We agreed on our first call that we had to be a part of the other's life no matter what his long-term plans turn out to be. We both sincerely meant it, and neither of us wants time to pass before we do. This is the process of 'getting on with it,' and I hate every fucking second.

But if he's strong enough to do it, I can, too. Especially if he still needs me. For Lucian, I have no limits. He owns me. Something I always knew would be the case if I let him touch me—let him in.

It takes two hours of me staring at the roses and a bucket of silent tears to continue the process—but I manage, even if his next text doesn't come for two days. But it's on day two when I get my first envelope that I know why I got a delay in texts, and it's by way of a letter, postmarked from England in old-fashioned, vintage stationery outlined with blue and red piping. Opening it, I frown in slight disappointment when I see what little is written.

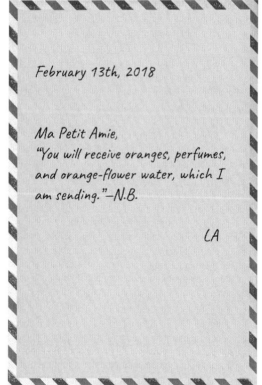

February 13th, 2018

Ma Petit Amie,
"You will receive oranges, perfumes, and orange-flower water, which I am sending."—N.B.

LA

Grinning—but a little confused—it's cleared up not long after when FedEx delivers a package. Its contents? Our hardback of Napoleon's letters to Josephine and a lifetime supply of the bath soap, shampoo, conditioner, and lotions that I drenched myself in during our stay in our London hotel. Sniffing the bottles brings instant tears to my eyes, all the while fueling my heart. The next day, I sent a reply letter in the envelope Lucian thoughtfully provided with his return address, saddened that he's resumed his residence there. A flat he told me held no personal significance for him and that he referred to as a 'former tomb.' The fact that he's living there again feels damning, but I push past it to respond, focusing on his gesture instead.

February 18th, 2018
My love,

As I ponder in thy fragrant bath water, which I have great fear will prune me beyond repair before I lay my eyes upon thee again. I continue wishing thou was with me as I urge this day forward as I have each day in your absence. Though I will gladly suffer in this scented haven until I hear from thee again! I pray thou doth make haste, doctor. For I will surely wither here in remembrance of you until I again lay my eyes on words written by thou wicked pen!

J.C . . . Not Jesus.

March 5, 2018

Ma Petit Amie,
A thousand kisses on your eyes,
your lips, your tongue, your
heart.—N.B.

You lost this, love.
LA . . . not the city

PS. This one mum gave me.

Inside this package is another love ball from Harrods that he stole initially for me on Christmas Eve. It was the most expensive, most valuable thing in either of my stolen suitcases taken at the Paris station, and I never told him about it—but had mourned the loss of it. I guess he'd looked for it and found it missing.

March 6th, 2018

My love!

You have truly outdone thyself with such an extravagant gift. I can't wait to hang this on my tree, insteadith of a headith. Your charms are as abundant as your prick, Doctor, and both are desperately missed.

A thousand lashes of my wicked tongue against yours, a thousand kisses to your chest, and more so to the heart that lies beneath. A thousand days it feels since I saw you last.

I love thee,
J.C.

March 17th

> **Lucian: How are you, Cheeky?**
>
> **Good. Drinking a green beer.**
>
> **Lucian: Highly ironic.**
>
> **Oh, why is that?**

Lucian has shared a photo.
Clicking on it, I get a better view of the pint in Lucian's hand

and stare at it for far too long, noting the faint hair on his knuckles as my eyes threaten to water.

> **Nice. But do you find it odd that neither of us are drinkers, and we're both drinking?**
>
> **Lucian: Which begs me to repeat the question. How are you, really?**
>
> **I'm great. Things are the usual, predictable. The floor is pretty boring. The new surgeon is nice enough.**

I swallow down the fact that Lucian's hiatus has lasted long enough that they've replaced him with a more permanent member of staff. If Lucian opts to come back, he no longer has a job waiting to come back to. Not that any hospital in Boston wouldn't jump at the chance of having him—which might include St. James. We haven't discussed it. Neither of us is eager for that conversation—at least I'm not and avoid it often.

> **Lucian: Is he good-looking?**
>
> **Of course you'd ask that. Yes, he's very good-looking. Older.**
>
> **Lucian: Truly? You're not just putting me on?**

"I love it when you use my own words against me," I tell him, though he can't hear me. "I can hear you saying it," I relay as I type.

> **Yes, he's good-looking, but rumor is, he's got a thing for Nurse Rogers.**
>
> **Lucian: The blonde?**
>
> **That was an awfully fast recollection.**
>
> **Lucian: Because everything from her chest up is fabricated. Is he blind?**
>
> **Now you want him to carry a torch for me?**
>
> **Lucian: Absolutely fucking not. And 'carrying a torch?' you know that expression is ancient, right?**
>
> **Heard you old-timers are into that sort of speak. I'm learning to speak fluent geezer so we can communicate better in the future.**

Lucian: Your arse, my hand. A reckoning is coming, and best believe I'm keeping tally.

Are you now? Well, as it stands, my ass is perfectly safe because last time I checked, there is an ocean between us.

Bubbles . . . then no bubbles, so I intercept, kicking myself in the ass.

I'm sorry. I didn't mean to dampen the mood.

Lucian: No. It's all fine.

I bite my lip, hating the text—hating myself for going there.

Are you being polite, Doc? Don't do that.

Lucian: I'm being personable. You'd be proud in that respect. I had lunch with my co-workers today. Told them about my best American mate.

Did you? BLUSHES EMOJI

Lucian: Yes. I told them you had an appetite for dog treats.

YOU SWORE YOU WOULD NEVER TELL!

Lucian: They laughed for five minutes, so it was worth breaking the promise, Cheeky. I might've also mentioned your sidewalk splatters.

You bastard!

Lucian: Well, they were boring me. I have to run. I'm meeting my brother for dinner.

Oh? That's good news!

Lucian: Yes, it is. Thanks to you.

Have fun.

Lucian: I hope we do. It's been a long time since we have acted like brothers.

Remember, don't hold back.

Lucian: Never again.

Bubbles. More bubbles. My heart drops when I feel like I've lost him, but five minutes later the text appears, and a sickening relief overtakes me.

I miss you, Cheeky.

**I miss you, too, Lucian. Please text it until you don't mean it anymore. My heart was breaking.**

**Lucian: I will never stop, but are you sure you want that?**

**Jane?**

**Jane?**

*Getting 'on with the process'* took a whole *week* after that text.

*April 28th*

**Lucian: I'm going to ask a question, and I need honesty.**

**Not a problem.**

**Lucian: Are you seeing anyone?**

My heart fucking stops.

**No. Are you? You can be honest. Please be honest.**

Panic seizes me as I type out the next part to be fair to him.

**If you're entertaining or thinking about it, don't worry about my reply, Lucian.**

His texts pop up in rapid succession before I hit send.

**Lucian: No.**

**Lucian: No.**

**Lucian: No. How fucking could I? I'm madly in love with a mad American woman who takes up all of my thoughts.**

As I come down from that near stroke, another text pops up.

**Jane, if we keep things as is . . . how will we get on with it?**

Feeling as if I've been struck again by the wrecking ball, I type furiously.

**I don't want to fucking get on with it. I want to love you, and that should be okay with you.**

I can't even pretend how pathetic it feels to know just how much power he has over me, of how helpless I feel hanging on his every word. I swore to myself that I would never do this again. Never hang on to a relationship that's over. Never to wait for a man who's done with me in any capacity. Never to debase myself to be loved ever again. But Lucian's different. He's not toying with me or lying to me. He's not making promises he can't keep. He's not trying to hurt me. He's simply asking if I'm entertaining dating.

To what end though? He swore he wasn't considering it, but is he thinking of moving on? Should I? We're so undefined at this point due to indecision—it's paralyzing. Cupping my mouth where I sit at the lunchroom table, all eyes float my way.

Tammy, my ever-faithful work wife, threatens to follow me when I stand, and I hold up my hand to stop her. Hauling ass toward the bathroom, I type the only reply I can manage.

**I have to go, I'm at work.**

**Lucian: I'm sorry. I'm so sorry. I was just having thoughts this morning. Fuck. Please don't misinterpret that as a quest for permission. I just want to be fair to you. It was my decision to stay, so I have no right to ask nor beg you to remain faithful, but I want to ask. I want to fucking demand it. I'm not seeing anyone. I swear to you. I can't.**

**Jane?**

**Jane.**

*1 Missed call from Lucian.*

*4 missed calls from Lucian.*

**Lucian: You can't avoid this talk forever.**

**Watch me.**

**Lucian: I love you, Jane.**

**Then DON'T ask me to stop loving you. I'm okay. In fact, I'm great. You're okay, too. So let it be.**

*June 15th*

Waking to a pounding on my door that matches the one in my head, I fumble to open it and see Charlie standing on the other side, holding her phone up as she speaks.

"I really don't want to hate him, but I'm starting to," she says as I remember the message I left in a wine haze last night—but I ask the question anyway.

"What are you doing here?"

"You know damn well why I'm here," she counters testily, pushing past me.

"Where's Elijah?"

"With his father, he's not seeing you like this. You look like absolute hell," she snaps, pulling me into her.

It's then that I finally allow the rest of myself to shatter.

"Say it again," I command as Charlie peers back at me after eyeing the mess in my kitchen for the umpteenth time. Her focus flitting between the ignored pile of dishes and the ridiculous number of takeout containers currently littering my coffee table. A Jeopardy rerun filters between our current conversation, one she's trying to refuse.

"Say it, Charlie," I order for the second time.

"No."

"I need you with me on this," I plea as she sits on an ottoman I got at the thrift store that looks as ancient as the brownstone I'm renting.

"I am, that's why I'm not helping you with this stupid mantra shit. He's made a lot of effort—the letters, the gifts, the texts, both privately and in the group chats. He loves you, and he's a good guy. Maybe he's still trying to repair his family."

"He's not coming back," I say, the words slicing and dicing as I force myself to finally speak them aloud. "You have to help me, Charlie. Tell me the truth."

"We don't know the truth."

"I think we do," I rasp out. "I think you need to give it to me straight, sis. It's been *months*."

"Fine, he's not coming back," she sighs as Alex Trebek's voice reverberates from the TV.

"This window, referred to as the 'Midday Rose,' was gifted from King Saint Louis the IX to what famous cathedral?"

"What is Notre Dame," I say, just as the buzzer rings and the contestant repeats it. "What is Notre Dame?"

"Correct," Trebek's voice echoes as Charlie's attention snaps to me, and I shrug, a single tear gliding down my cheek at the memory of that day. A day when I bared my soul, and his warmth and acceptance surrounded it—one of my favorite days.

"He's everywhere, every single day," I sniff, batting a tear from my face, "and the worst part? We didn't make a single memory *in Boston*. But he's still here. Everywhere, all the time. I've felt sick every day since I left him at that train station. I feel just as paralyzed as he did when he lost his brother. Maybe it's a selfish comparison because that's death. But that's what it feels like. I'm stuck there, reliving that day and every day before it. I swore I wouldn't do this again. I swore I wouldn't hope and pray again for a man to come back to me."

"Tell him," she demands. "Tell him how much this is hurting you."

"I can't, Charlie. I love him too much to guilt him, and that's all telling him will do. So I've been telling him I'm okay, and we're okay, but I can't keep it up anymore."

"Yeah, I noticed. Goldie Honkers and Kurt Russelfeathers are still wearing Christmas outfits," she says, snatching Poochie from the floor to nuzzle him.

"I have not resumed real living since he got on that train. I'm acting like this is my very first round of heartbreak, but I know better. I know I need to start living my life no matter what my future holds or who's in it, but my heart won't fucking cooperate this time," I swallow. "Not this time, no matter how hard my mind is fighting it. What I want, what I truly want, is for him to feel the way I do. And he can't. He doesn't. Because if he did, he couldn't stay away from me this long or be okay with this separation."

"Then end it or move to England. What's keeping you here anyway?"

"Because I've been there, done that. I've moved for men before. I changed myself, shaped my personality, and changed things about who I was for every man I fell for—and you see how that turned out. I'm not doing that again, no matter how perfect the man."

"I get that, Jane. But what if he's the guy?"

"He is. I'm certain of it. But at one time, *they all were*, right? I refuse to be the only one who is convinced of it. What if I do move, my job, my career, leave you and Elijah and everything I've ever known that keeps me stable, and Lucian and I burn out in a few months? Spoiler alert—I'll be the fucking fool *again*."

"Or you could get your man?"

"How about for once my man comes for me? How in the hell do I keep getting this so wrong? And Lucian, I can't be wrong about—I can't. Do you know what he did on my birthday?"

"Kissed you—"

"Twenty-seven times. One for every year of my life. Every single time it got better and better, it was one of the most romantic days of my existence," I say, swatting another tear. "All of them were. How did I get this one wrong?"

"Tell him," she urges me.

"Says you, who won't marry a man you're clearly fucking in love with and have been in a relationship with for over a decade. Most marriages don't even last that long anymore, Charlie."

Her backlash is instant. "That's your *one pass* for putting me under fire."

"Marry him, have more of his babies. There's always divorce," I say. "He found you and never let you out of his sight a day after. I can't seem to find a single man who wants to fucking keep me. What's stopping you already?"

"You've said your piece," she clips out in warning.

"But you can tell *me* what to do?"

"I'm not the one calling my sister at two am, crying her eyes out, looking like hammered shit, and letting herself go to hell. So yeah, sorry. Focus is on you, kid. Deal."

"Whatever," I grumble.

"Great come back," she mutters.

"I'll be here all night," I snap.

"Fine, he's not coming back."

It's like a sledgehammer to the chest, but I take it and ask for another.

"Again."

"He's not coming back for you."

Standing, I start to pace in front of her as Trebek reads out more questions I know the man I love can answer on any given day.

"Why isn't he coming back?" I prompt her.

"Because if he was, he would've by now. He's in London. He's thriving. He's made amends with his family. They're in a good place. If he was coming, he would have by now."

"Right," I nod. Her reasons are mine. I rehearsed them all with her a dozen times or more.

"So the next time he texts, you're going to tell him it's time to break up," she orders.

"No," I shake my head. "I'm not."

"Because?"

"Because we're not exactly together, but we want to be in each other's lives."

Charlie nods toward my destroyed kitchen. "See how that's working out? Jane, you look like shit, your house is a wreck, and you look like shit."

"You've mentioned that."

"Go to him."

"No, and he hasn't mentioned it again."

Well, not since our first and last fight. Or rather, my fight to drop it when he still couldn't answer whether the move was permanent or not. I made him leave it there because he still has an apartment in Boston. His clothes and possessions are still here, but he shot some of my hope down one night in a casual conversation when he mentioned a packing service. Apparently, rich people have a solution for pesky things like moving their lives overseas.

It never once occurred to me that he could have "people" pack the rest of his life here and ship it to him.

It was my last ray of hope. At the very least, I would see him again as he collected his things, but apparently, those aren't important enough for him to return for either.

For the last few weeks, I've been trying my best to bat away the

resentment I'm starting to feel about his indecision and our direc-
tionless relationship. It would be one thing if we had made a clean
break, but he continues to assure me otherwise.

Was he as gentle with Gwen when he left her?

Do his texts, calls, letters, gifts, and gestures stem more from
guilt than anything?

God, I would hate it if that were the reason. It would ruin our
relationship for me completely. It would have me questioning its
authenticity and tarnish the weeks I continually replay in my head
over and over.

It's been four and a half months, and as it seems, there's no getting fucking on with it.

At this point, I've answered my own question.

How in the hell do you get over a man like Lucian Aston?

You don't.

Especially not when you get constant texts and calls—though
it's becoming more apparent by the day that neither of us is being
honest anymore. He's made his decision to stay and hasn't voiced it,
and I'm lying about being okay with it.

Not guilting him means I've stopped being brutally honest.

But staying in this state, accepting this as the permanent norm,
is starting to mean settling for less *than him*, and my heart and mind
aren't okay with that anymore. Hence the torture I'm forcing myself
to endure.

"This is horrible," Charlie says after repeating another one of
my rehearsed reasons why I have to stop this. "I can't do this, Jane."

"Charlie," I warn.

"Because Boston was temporary," she recites with a bite.
"England is his true home."

"Right," I say, staring at the suitcase I brought home, which still
sits in the corner of my hallway—a suitcase I still haven't brought
myself to unpack. I know what's in there, and if and when the time
comes, it will become a time capsule. A luggage-sized ex-boyfriend
box that I'll never be able to toss out—at least as far as I can see
into the future. Just next to it sits a case of Louis Latour, a red wine

I loved and couldn't remember the name of, that Lucian recently had delivered with his last note. On top of it sits a box of silky gloves in every color with another letter attached that says they are to keep my hands warm until he can warm them himself—as well as a London snow globe and a few tubs of Pringles. All things big and small that only remind me of a reality and presence that's now absent and slowly withering my heart.

"Because maybe what you had was meant to be your fairytale moment, nothing more . . . though I don't agree with that one."

"Charlie," I scorn as my sister watches me pace.

"Because you can't live this way anymore. It's making you fucking sick."

"That wasn't on the list," I tell her.

"No, that's real-life dialogue because we're in a real fucking conversation, and I'm worried."

I pause my footing, look over at her, and see the concern etched on her face and the sting in her eyes. Where I used to be more tough and a lot less watery, Charlie rarely, if ever, cries. The fact that her eyes are welling now is enough to jar me.

Swallowing, I inhale deeply, knowing it's time. I made a promise to myself the last time my heart broke to avoid this very situation, and I need to start keeping it. "Okay, sis. Then help me clean my house, get back to looking somewhat ladylike, and I'll break up with him."

"Seriously?" she asks.

"Yeah, I'm not moving to England. That decision is on me, and I can't wait on his anymore, so I'm choosing home over him, too. It's over."

"But—"

"But what?" I ask, looking for hope where I know there is none.

"In the group chat, I can just tell he's not going anywhere."

"Well, he's not coming here. So that's that, right?"

She bites her lip and shakes her head. "I don't know, Jane. This guy, I don't know."

"Then it's time. The snow's thawed, and he's not here. He's

staying, and he's tearing my heart out by being nice about it. It's time."

"Okay," she dips her chin as my phone goes off in my hand, and I walk over to her as we both eye the message.

**Lucian: How are you today, Cheeky?**

"Fuck," I mutter, biting my lip as my eyes instantly water.

Charlie pulls me into her arms. "I love you, but yeah, this isn't healthy. I can't stand seeing you like this. You're not surviving long distance, sis. I mean, I hate saying it, but it's the perfect time. I'm here to catch your fall, and I want to be, for this, Jane—for this, I want to be here."

"Okay," I say as she gives me one of her brief hugs and stands.

"Okay. I'll start the dishes."

Pressing send on the FaceTime request, I'm struck sideways when Lucian appears. Instantly I'm reminded of why I've been against screen time as I grapple with the sight of him. His warm, sparkling honey eyes scour me just as thoroughly before his smile quickly turns into a frown. "You're so pale, Cheeky."

"Yeah, I've already been told I look like shit today. Are you busy, Doc? Can we talk?"

"I didn't say that. You're beautiful—you're always beautiful. I was going to call tonight, so yes, now is as good as time as any."

"What were you going to say when you called?" I ask, curious. Curious and stalling because the sight of him has me aching everywhere.

"I was going to see if you'd let me fly you over." His swallow is visible as his eyes drill into me, and he seems to find what he's looking for. "But that's not why you called me, is it Jane?"

We stare off for long seconds before he darts his gaze away and curses. "Cheeky," he whispers roughly before slowly bringing his eyes back to mine. "You're ending this, aren't you? I'm too late?"

"We dated for five weeks and broke up months ago. It was your decision to stay—"

"But I wanted you here—"

"It's my decision to stay in Boston."

"And that's final?" He asks as I bite my lip and nod.

"You never told me your choice was permanent," I counter.

"Well, I was still sorting myself out until recently," he whispers roughly.

"And what happened recently?"

"I took my nephews out on the pitch days ago. It was a remarkable day."

"And this changed things for you?" I ask, confused.

"Very much so, yes," he draws out.

"What are you leaving out?"

"I hardly think it matters now if . . . if," his voice falters. "Is there someone else?"

"No, and I can't make space for anyone if I'm talking to you," I cut myself off because I'd rather bite my tongue off than guilt him. "Not that I want to make space for anyone. Fuck." I shake my head adamantly, feeling my heart threaten to leave me altogether. "I can't do this."

"Jane, I don't blame you for being upset with me, but please listen—"

"No, I mean, I can't fucking do this. I can't and won't say goodbye to you. But will you tell me something?" I ask, my eyes filling. "Why haven't you come for your shit? You just left it here."

"My shit or you?"

"Both!" I shake away a few tears. "Never mind. I'm fine. I didn't mean that. You have a packing service. You mentioned that. If you're fine, so am I. I'm sorry."

"Come to me, Jane. I still want *us*. I still want Boston."

"Boston is here," I croak, and his eyes glaze over.

"Tell me what to do to keep you in my life, Cheeky," he pleads.

"Nothing," I reply. "You look well. Really, you look so good. I'm nothing but happy for you, Lucian. I'm just having a really bad day. You know how I get on these days. I-I'll call you another time. Just give me a few to get on with it, okay?"

"A few what, Jane? Days, weeks, months? You continue to tell me that you love me, too. That you're *fine* with things as they are, all the while refusing to discuss *us*. I just asked you to come here again, and you back away *again*. What am I to believe?"

"I don't know what I am to you."

"The woman I love," he declares adamantly.

I nod, and nod, and nod. "Okay. I have to go. I need to go."

"Please don't," he rasps out. "As selfish as it is to ask, please don't. I want to talk to you, to see you, Jane."

"Do you remember what you wore the first day on our floor?" I ask him, ignoring his pleas while concentrating on the devastation in my voice, knowing I can't break myself against my love for him any longer.

A short silence follows as I keep my eyes down before he answers.

"Not that I can recall. No."

"I do," I swallow. "You wore a black suit and dark purple tie. One that matches the dress I wore the day we left for Europe."

"Jane—"

"I was already in love with you before that plane left the ground," I admit, lifting my eyes to his. "As crazy as it may seem, I already knew it was you, Lucian, and no one on earth will ever convince me otherwise—not even you."

"Jane, please don't do this."

"I just told you I won't," I sniff. "I can't and won't say goodbye to you. Maybe I'll come."

"Yeah?" His smile beams through the phone and I drop my gaze, unable to handle the sight of him any longer, the pain stretching my chest unbearably.

"Yeah. But before I do, you have to tell me if your move is permanent."

"Jane, please look at me."

"I can't. You're . . ." *everything I've ever wanted, ever hoped for, and you're not coming back. You're not coming back. I have my answer.*

"Can you look at me anyway? We need to have this talk."

The plea in his voice is what breaks me, but there's nothing left to say.

"Jane, look at me."

"I can't," I say, sliding my thumb along the screen to end the call.

Seconds later, his text appears, as I finally accept the truth of it.

**Lucian: I love you, Jane.**

He's not coming back.

*June 30th*

**Lucian: Cheeky.**

**Doc.**

**Lucian: You haven't been answering my texts or calls.**

**I'm sorry. I've been working around the clock. I have student loans to pay.**

**Lucian: Understandable, but is there something more?**

**No. Why do you ask?**

**Lucian: Because it feels as if there is.**

**Nothing new to report, I'm afraid. Life is as predictable as ever. How is the family?**

**Lucian: All fine and well. Can we talk?**

**About?**

**Lucian: Us.**

**What about us?**

**Lucian: FaceTime.**

**I can't now. I have a shift at the bar.**

**Lucian: Jane, I need to speak with you. Make time.**

**I can't now. We can talk later.**

**Lucian: When later?**

**I don't know. I'll let you know.**

**Lucian: Christ, could you be any more evasive?**

"Could you be any more in LONDON?" I snap.

**Just let me work my shift, and I'll get back to you.**

**Lucian: Promise me, Cheeky.**

**We don't get to make those, Lucian.**

**Lucian: I miss you. I love you, Jane.**

For the second time since we left each other—I don't text it back.

*JULY 4th*

"Excuse me," I repeat for the umpteenth time, passing yet another person on my bustling street and dodging another sitting on my stoop steps. Balancing my groceries in one hand, I struggle to see over my brown bag enough to keep my footing while handling my phone in the other to slide it open.

"What Charlie?! I texted I would call you later. I have to get these groceries in, so I can get to my hot date."

"Well up yours, lady, and happy Fourth to you, too."

"Sorry, it's just that I'm melting. It's a hundred degrees out here, and I feel like I'm swimming in an armpit. I need both my hands right now."

"I was just going to tell you I'm pregnant, but I'll call you back."

"What?!" I immediately drop my grocery bag. "Oh shit," I frown at the wreckage. "My eggs are toast. Worth it. God, Charlie!" I can only make out a tiny portion of her profile as the sunlight glares on my cell screen. "Just let me get inside and get the sun out of my damned eyes, and I'll dial you back."

"K."

I narrow my eyes on what I can make out of her smile. "Are you really pregnant?"

"Yes," she boasts, "and I'm getting married."

"No bullshit?" I gasp while gathering my scattered groceries. "Barrett didn't ask my permission!"

"Does he need it?"

"Absolutely not! Oh, Charlie, I'm so happy for you." Tears

spring to my eyes, and I let them break free. "Let me get in and salvage what's left of my food, and I'll call you right back. Promise."

"Okay."

"I love you, sister," I say, pausing to appreciate the moment. "I'm so happy for you."

"Really? I didn't . . . know if I should tell you."

"How could this not make me happy, Charlie?"

Her voice is full of nerves as she speaks again. "We've got this, right?"

"Damn right we do," I say. "Five minutes."

"K."

She hangs up as I fumble with my tattered bag and keys, excitement running through me as a voice sounds at my back.

"Have I lost you then?"

I freeze and turn, shielding my eyes from the blinding sun by saluting it with my hand. Standing in the middle of a high beam is Lucian, in scrubs.

"Yeah, right," I dismiss. "Absinthe flashback."

"What?"

Snapping back to earth when he replies, I take a step forward and attempt to shake the sun out of my eyes. "Lucian?"

"Yes, of course, Jane. What in the hell? Have you been drinking?"

"Lucian," I repeat, my throat burning as I take the three steps down to get to where he stands. "You're here."

"Yes, and you passed right by me like I wasn't anyone of significance." It's then I see it—the anger in his eyes, resting bastard face fully restored. "Have I lost you, Jane?"

"Lost me?" I ask, shocked at the sight of him standing in front of me—in Boston. His eyes search me the way they always do just before they connect, his thick hair a little longer and curling at his neck.

"You said you had a hot date to Charlie, is that," he swallows and closes his eyes, "is that the true case?"

Unable to help myself, I drink him in, and it's no surprise

he's more devastating than ever. His skin is lightly tanned, his hair lighter, as if tinted further by the sun. It's the way he's dressed that gives me pause.

"What are you doing here . . . in scrubs?"

"I'm here because I know what I said to you on Christmas Eve."

"You remembered?"

"Sadly, no. But I know *you*, Jane, and I know your heart because I spent six weeks memorizing it. The more I thought about it in our time apart, the more I realized it had to be something substantial to hurt you so badly the next morning. So I could only assume I blurted the truth—which was that I was half in love with you already. Mike confirmed on the ride to the airport that that's exactly what I confessed—which you should now know is the truth. I'll easily admit that my mind took some time to catch up with my heart, and you should forgive me for that. But considering it was maybe a day or two in between, I won't beg forgiveness so easily." His stare hardens. "But you've been denying our feelings this whole time, denying that this relationship is real and taking away any merit it might have—to the point you obviously haven't taken enough of anything I've confessed to heart."

"That's not true."

"That's not the way you're behaving," he snaps, his face granite. "At all. In fact. It's not the way you behaved nearly our whole time together."

Scrutinizing him further, I see he's utterly disheveled, and there are deep purple circles under his eyes as he demands an answer from me. "Answer me this instant, Jane. Have I lost you?"

"Where is this coming from?"

"Don't play ignorant. You've been lying to me," he snaps, and I jerk back at his sudden venom.

"Lying to you how? Why are you so pissed?"

He extends his cell phone toward me before tapping the screen. A second later, my tear-soaked voice blares through.

"Charlie, I just. I need to talk. Can you call me back? I-I I'm . . . I feel like I'm dying," I croak out tearfully as realization dawns and

Lucian's unrelenting gaze bores into mine, fury in his eyes as the recording continues.

It was the night before Charlie came two weeks ago. It's the night I lost hope we'd ever be together again.

". . . what was I thinking going around and listing my insecurities off to my dream man for six weeks and thinking I could *keep him* that way? He knows everything—my flaws, my fears, little things too. Things that make me weird and are not at all endearing. Did I really think I would get to keep a man like that by being brutally honest? Hell . . . he was probably looking for an excuse to escape me when he decided to stay . . . and I love him so much, Charlie. I've never felt like this before. I can't move on. Hell, I can't even fucking move," I sob hysterically into the phone. "All the other men who broke my heart, or I thought did," my voice cracks as another sob sounds, and Lucian's guard slips slightly as I break in a recording between us. "It's never felt like this. I'm just . . . I'm at my wit's end, and I can't stop crying. I can't shake this, not even a little. I feel like I've lost my heart," I weep again over the line as Lucian bites his lip, eyes drilling into me as I go on and on.

". . . I'm depressed because I feel like I lost the love of my life. Hell, I know I have, and he doesn't feel the same. He can't, or he would be with me. He would need me as much as I do him. Why, why can't I get this fucking right? Why can't I be the *one* to a man I love with everything in me? I swore I wouldn't do this again—turn myself inside out for someone who doesn't feel the same. I'm trying to let go. I wanted him to be happy when he does finally cut the cord, so I started telling him I was okay. That I'm doing well, but I'm not, Charlie. I can't let go. Just for once, just for fucking once, I want to be selfish. I want to get my damned man—this man. Just this one. I want his Boston future, and . . . he's not coming back. I'm a *fool*, I'm the fool again . . . I believed him. I thought . . . God. How long does this damn thing record messages? . . . Okay. This voicemail will self-destruct in forty-five seconds," I half laugh, half sob before it cuts off.

My heart bottoms out while, at the same time, I come up with a number of ways to torture my sister for this betrayal. Clearing my throat as tears stream down my cheeks, I speak up. "Is death by a thousand paper cuts a real thing? Because if so—"

"Jane," he snaps.

"I was at my lowest, okay. You weren't supposed to ever hear that. Like ever."

"Wrong, you were there for me at my lowest and denied me the chance to do my best and be a friend to you."

"That's not how this works," I sniff.

"That's exactly *how we work*," he counters, his eyes cutting. "Or did work until you froze me out and started lying to me. Tell me immediately about this date you have?" He demands.

I nod. "Okay, I'm supposed to make deviled eggs."

"So, you are seeing someone?"

"Yeah, my fifty-two-year-old neighbor and dog minder, *Agatha*."

His eyes flit briefly with relief before they re-light with fury. "So, not only have you been lying about the toll our separation has taken, but we've *both* been suffering because you couldn't admit it to me. Do you think I can't feel and haven't felt the distance you've purposely imposed between us? I know I'm at fault for not being decisive enough, but now so are you. But so that you know, I was already on my damned way to you when she sent this fucking text."

He extends his phone for me to see the text sent along with the voicemail stamped nearly four hours ago.

**Charlie: Now or never, Doctor. Time is up.**

"I was halfway here," he says, "but Charlie said you left this message two weeks ago when I called her from the taxi on my way to your door. You were trying to break it off with me then and have been avoiding me since. Had you told me I was losing you, I would have boarded a lot fucking sooner!"

"But you didn't board."

"Because I didn't want to lie to you about *the when*, and you refused to discuss us!"

"Stop yelling at me!"

"It's necessary because this is life or death!" He shouts before taking a step back and palming his forehead in exasperation.

"Wait . . ." I ask. "How *are* you *yelling at me* right now? You never yell . . . this well."

It's as if it's dawned on him, too, and his eyes spark a little. "I've been going to a therapist."

*"What?"*

"Or rather, a grief counselor to sort myself out—because I truly wanted to. It's mostly what's kept me in London. With the shape my family was in, it was more than obvious that we needed help in sorting out our issues. It's helped Byron and I strengthen our relationship some . . . I did it for me, but I did it for you, too. In my mind, you deserved a partner who's as whole as possible, and my thinking was that if we were to resume our relationship—which was my true hope—I wanted to be a man capable of expressing himself fully. Because you deserve that partner and just that man."

My eyes instantly water. "I was happy with you as you were."

"I know, but I wasn't. I wanted to find a better way to deal with my grief, along with changing some of my instilled habits that were frankly rather unhealthy." His eyes flare with more anger. "Counseling and my family are the only things that truly kept me from coming to you sooner. And I did have plans to tell you, but you would hardly give me the fucking chance to discuss us. Something I will never allow again. So, we're sorting that right here and now," he says, his eyes challenging me to object before he continues.

"I've never lied to you, Jane. Not once. Our whole relationship has been based on honesty, and *unlike you*, I've been completely forthcoming with my feelings as they've progressed. Where you held back in both London and Paris—even after I knew and felt you loved me, and you did as well—you refused to admit it or discuss us. In fact, in retrospect, I only remember a handful of weeks in which you fully allowed yourself to love me back freely, and those were the last two before we parted in that station. Tell me I'm not speaking the truth."

"Because I knew this would happen. I knew you would break my heart!"

"It's what I've done everything to avoid, and in turn, you're breaking mine!"

"I've been the friend you needed me to be," I defend. "That I promised to be, first and foremost, and I can't apologize for that."

"Well, you aren't my friend anymore, Jane," he shakes his head, my words only angering him more. "I'm here to tell you that the entire time I've been trying to restore a relationship or rather establish a real one for the first time with my family, I've been absolutely fucking mortified about the possibility of losing you—and not as a *friend* Jane. As my *person*, as the woman I love. The woman meant for me because that's who you became for me. There were maybe a handful of days in the time I've been there where I considered that I might again be able to resume my life in London—and *none* of them were consecutive. Not one, and for one reason."

"H-hey, Jane?" Agatha pipes from behind me just outside our shared front door. I turn to see her standing with yesterday's mail in her hand. "I heard you out here, and shit, I'm sorry to interrupt," she looks between me and Lucian. "But I wanted to catch you because I know how anxious you were for this, well, both letters," she says.

Ever the gentleman, Lucian steps forward. "Agatha, I presume? I'm Lucian."

Her smile is instant. "It's nice to finally meet you, Lucian. I've heard so much about you."

"A pleasure," Lucian says in the politest tone he can muster as she turns to me.

"If you can't make it to the barbecue, I can save you both a plate."

"Thanks, Agatha. I'll let you know," I whisper, my eyes again glued to the gorgeous and furious man standing feet away, heart aching because I don't know if I still have the right to touch him with how angry he is with me.

Because I don't move to retrieve them, Lucian takes both

envelopes from Agatha as I remain frozen at the idea that we might not have ended in that train station—but my fear might have cost us our relationship.

Agatha closes the door behind her as Lucian stands before me, two envelopes in his hand, one with the now familiar blue and red piping and another thicker envelope. My heart jumps at the sight of it.

"Ah, well, there is some clarity for me. I see my letter has *finally* arrived," he grumbles as he eyes the second envelope. "So, what's this then?" He asks before scanning the return UMASS address, or rather, The Connell School of Nursing.

"I applied for the DNP program," I explain. "If I got accepted, I planned to start this fall."

Hurt covers his expression, a pained exhale leaving him. My lips tremble as I start with my excuse. "Lucian, I was going to tell you—"

"Well, it's obvious you were *never coming to me*, and I think it's even more apparent now what future you decided on without me," he says, his tone defeated as he opens the envelope. Despite our current state, pride shines clear in his eyes as he turns the letter toward me, and I'm able to make out the "congratulations" through my blurred vision.

"Congratulations, Nurse Cartwright, and so well deserved. You're going to be an incredible doctor, and I can't think of anyone else more fitting for the job."

The emotions between us and the fact that he's here make it all the more bittersweet as I attempt to explain myself.

"Being with you, not just that, watching you work inspired me," I expel in a pained breath, "I don't know. I've always thought about it, but I think seeing the doctor you are, and believe it or not, the badass Gwen is, made me want it more. I didn't know if it was worth taking on more debt, but I decided to toss the dice, and I do want it."

"As you should, and you will get everything you deserve, Jane. As much as it pains me you didn't share this with me—and it fucking does, so much," he whispers hoarsely. "I'm nothing but happy for you."

He swallows and pins me with more intensity. "I think it's only fair since I've come all this way, that I see you open this," he steps forward, extending his letter toward me. "Read it, Jane."

"Right now?"

"I would say the timing couldn't be more perfect." His expression is unreadable, and I curse the fact that he'll always be a master at that when he chooses to shield himself or his emotions. He's punishing me for the moment—and honestly—I kind of deserve it.

"Just tell me what it says," I hear the panic in my voice as I bat the tears away, and in turn, his anger dissipates as he traces my features with the softness I've missed so much—in only the way he can.

Warmth fills me at its appearance as I stare back at him, memories of us swarming my head as his gaze covers me. We're only feet away, but I feel the distance I put between us and know I'm guilty of everything he accused me of. I let fear and doubt take turns at the wheel when we parted at that train station instead of taking his words and his gestures as truth.

"I'm sorry, Lucian. Please," I rasp out, "this hurts so bad. Please just tell me what it says."

"Maybe I haven't been as transparent with you as I had hoped, Jane. In that, we're both wrong. Open it."

He's made another decision—it's evident in his posture, and fear sweeps through me at the sight of it. As much as I know this man, as much as I've memorized him, he's not giving anything away.

Carefully opening the letter, I see his beautiful writing and that it's dated two weeks ago—the day of our last FaceTime.

June 15th

Jane,

Days ago, I spent time with Jasper and Ben in the park in effort to appease my conscience—so I felt I wasn't such a disappointment as an uncle. The truth behind that being I didn't really have an interest in entertaining twin boys that I have nothing in common with. It's one of the truths you're not supposed to admit to anyone because of the total arsehole it makes you. But to you, I can admit anything without feeling as though I'm even more so for it. I love that about us. It's my favourite thing about us.

I've always been a sort of selfish man with my time, but things shifted during our time there. I can't exactly pinpoint why, but I started to appreciate them for simply being young boys.

I truly wanted to get to know them better and made my first conscious effort to do so. Now that I have, oddly enough, I'm looking forward to our next day at the park and have planned something special.

Some of my effort has to do with my lingering fondness for my past relationship with Byron—when he and I had a relationship similar to yours and mine. When we acted like true family, as genuine brothers, and shared all the details of our lives behind closed doors where my father couldn't hear of our true nature.

That's what it felt like every day with you.

True living, without hiding myself behind doors or barriers and expectations.

The more time I spent with them, the more my own idea of family started to shift. You rebuked your parents and made your family with only Charlie, and I believe that is the direction Byron and I are headed, and we've made great inroads in doing so.

But I genuinely believe it was your words to my father that slapped Byron awake, and for that, I'm forever thankful you gave my brother back to me.

With my mother's added attendance, I feel the first inkling and sense of family since Alexander left us. Time will tell if what remains of the Astons will ever resemble a real family again.

However, as I reflect tonight, I realize I have already started choosing the family I want.

A family of my own, and that could only start with you.

So, I'm writing to let you know that I'm coming to you in the hope that together, we can create an idea of what that future might be—no matter the postcode.

I choose you, Jane, no matter what family I have remaining or may again leave in England.

You are the love of my life and my true new beginning.

You are the family I choose.

Please grant me the short time I need to be the doctor I became, the doctor you've helped me become, to the patients who are counting on me here until I can get to you. I assure you, I'll appear on your doorstep and beg your forgiveness for thinking for a second that any future I would want excludes you. I'll do my best to give you whatever life we dream of together because it could never be a clear vision without you.

I love you, Jane.

Heart and soul.

I belong with you, and it only becomes even more startingly clear with every day that passes with your absence.

Until then, I'll be holding my every breath until I receive your reply.

Now and forever yours,

Lucian

The last page is filled with the lyrics of *She Is His Only Need* by Wynonna. I cough out an incredulous sob to see he wrote every line of it as hope floods my veins. My eyes spill as I rattle with all the love I feel. Unable to speak, I gape at him as his eyes beg me to do the opposite.

"I know how you sometimes think of me, how you regard me as if I'm something special, some remarkable, unattainable man, and I've always hated that. As confident as you are—which is one of the things I love so much about you—I know that my absence has made you d-doubt your worth to me. But if you think I don't love you with every f-fiber of my being, t-that you're not the most precious, m-most important person in my life, you couldn't be more mistaken. But look where allowing you to block that admission has gotten us."

"Lucian—"

"I just flew seven hours after being on for forty-five to get the say you've denied me, Jane. So I'll have it."

"I'm sorry," I whisper.

"So, in addition to all of that," Lucian continues, eyes watering, guard completely gone, emotion flooding his voice. "I've come to the conclusion that I've solved your mystery of why men aren't the same in matters of the heart as women are—at least where you're concerned."

"And?" I ask as I melt into a puddle before his eyes, tears uncontrollably falling.

"The brutal truth is that they didn't love you, Jane. Not in the way you desired, deserved, or needed to be loved. They didn't love you in a way that they couldn't function properly or live without you. I should know because—in your absence—I've become the man that can't."

He steps forward, eyes earnest as my heart explodes.

"But I do love you in that way, Jane. I'm the man who can't imagine a day or fathom a future without you in it any longer. You see, as much as you convinced yourself I did, I *never left you*, not truly, so I *never had to look back*. All this time we've been apart, I've done my best to remind you of that—of my love, of my devotion and affection for you—and I have refused any possibility of goodbye. I never left you, Jane. It was *you* who started to *leave me*."

I cup my mouth, paralyzed by his words and shaken.

"I love you in a way that utterly terrifies me, and my true happiness lies with your reply, so please don't make me wait a second longer. I want a new deal."

He swats a tear from his cheek as if I'm breaking his heart in real time.

Holy shit.

I'm the *asshole* again, and this asshole almost *assumed* her way out of being with the love of her life.

"I want a new deal," he repeats in a pained rush, "with the same terms but no expiration date unless it's *forever*."

Filled with the dire need to touch him and close the space, I blow out a breath, unable to help my quip. "Lucian, you are aware the Fourth of July is the day the Americans celebrate their *independence* from the *British*, right?"

"For Christ's sake," he tugs at his hair.

"Sorry, sorry," I step into him and wrap as much of myself as I can around him, and he grips me tightly to him, eyes settling when he finds what he searches for.

"Fat chance of losing me, Dr. Prick. Of course I still love you and want to be with you, and there's absolutely no expiration date for that." I sniff. "Sadly, never was a chance or could be, and I was intent on going old maid. I'm still so very much in love with you. I'm so sorry. I just didn't want to guilt you into coming to me or for you to give up your life for me if that was in London—a life you just got back."

"Cheeky," he rasps out as he scoops me from my feet, locking his forearms under my ass so I'm propped above him. I stare down at him, our eyes watering for a different reason entirely than the last time we were together. "As you are now fully aware, you are my future."

"Geesh, I hope you know you just gave me an impossibly tall order to fill."

He shakes his head as I thrust my fingers into his hair. "Jane, you're already the woman I want, with categorically *no modifications.*"

"I know, but your *every happiness?*" I bulge my eyes.

"I simply meant that I'm the version of myself I'm most proud of when I'm with you," his eyes soften on me in an unmistakable way, "and I want to be that version with you—indefinitely."

"Meh," I shrug, my words coming out in a croak. "It'll do."

His beautiful lips lift at the corners. "I see you're still tough company to impress. But what if I sweeten this new deal with an addendum?"

"Yeah. How's that possible?" I ask, as his eyes glitter up at me.

"With the eventual change of your surname," he says before crushing my mouth with his kiss.

Seconds later, we crash through my front door—me wrapped around Lucian and mercilessly sucking on his neck.

"Kurt Russelfeathers and Goldie Honkers, I presume?" Lucian says, eyeing the couple's festive Fourth garb just outside my door.

"Mmm," I say, all amusement leaving him as I grip his cock. Lucian tosses my ruined bag of groceries as he shuts us in, and our tongues tangle furiously as he sets me down seconds before our clothes start to fly.

Lucian grips my ass with one hand as I plaster myself against him, making progress harder to manage.

"Fuck it all," Lucian says, separating us just enough to unbutton my shorts and yank them down as I undo my bra and toss it somewhere behind me on the floor where our shirts are.

"You are so bloody beautiful," he rasps as he untucks his cock, and at the sight of it, I hit my knees. "I've missed you, Sir, something awful."

"Jane," Lucian grits out as I eagerly pump him, licking my lips and staring up at him.

"Anxious, Dr. Aston?"

He wraps my hair into his fist as I look forward to the future punishment promised in his fiery-lit eyes. Without any other objection, I waste no time taking him as far back as I can go. His groan vibrates throughout my entryway as I eagerly suck him in, making a mess and salivating all over him. His eyes flare in appreciation as he lovingly cradles my cheek, hardening further in my mouth, so much so it becomes a tight fit. When I start to struggle, he grips me and pulls me to stand, taking my mouth until we're both gasping for air.

"Jane, now," he orders as he scans the space and makes his decision. In seconds, I'm positioned on my knees on my oversized ottoman. One of his hands is on my hip, and the other glides along my spine until he locks his fingers around my neck. Aching one second, I gasp as he presses an inch into me and begins working to fit inside.

"Do you know why I have to align myself perfectly to fit inside you, Jane?"

"Lucian," I moan at the arrival of his tone.

"Because our bodies are lock and key once they connect. You were made for me. Only me. As I was for you."

"Yours," I murmur as he presses in further, and we both call out. By the time he's snugly inside me, we're both losing our minds. A few heartbeats later, he's thrusting like a madman as I hang onto the battered ottoman for dear life.

"Lucian," I hiss as my climax starts to build, my body humming as he thrusts in, again and again, swiveling his hips to run his perfect, thick dick along my G-spot.

"I've missed you—this—so fucking much," he whispers, his tone melancholy and tender.

"Me," thrust, thrust, thrust, thrust, "too."

He stops suddenly, and I go to crane my neck as he lifts my upper body to his chest. Thumb on my cheek, he turns my neck to accept his kiss, and he kisses me and kisses me until I'm forced to part from him. In the next stolen breath, I'm on my back, my thigh wrapped around his waist as he again presses in. Chest to chest, heart to pounding heart, he stares down at me as if I'm the only thing that matters, his brows pinching and his voice hoarse with emotion as he speaks. "I never left you, my cheeky girl. I never left you, and I never will."

"I'm so sorry," tears of relief glide down my temples. "I'm so sorry, baby. I was so blind."

"I love you, every fucking thing about you. Your fears, your weird tics, it's all perfection, Jane. I will never tire of you and only want your happiness more than my own."

"And that's all I wanted for you, Lucian. I love you the exact same way. Please believe me."

He kisses me then, turning his hungry fucking into lovemaking of the most incredible kind. Our hands slow as we explore the other, getting reacquainted as he slowly pushes into me and pulls back, watching himself disappear inside me again and again. Eyes watering, it starts to set in.

I got the guy.

He's speaking of our future and a love he can't shake—of both wanting and needing me—of a life together. It's with his next thrust that I feel the click as we lock ourselves back together. A click I've only ever felt with him as I cup the back of his head and fall apart against him.

I got the guy.

I got him by holding out, by refusing to settle for anything less than the unconditional and selfless love that he himself knew that I needed.

My dream man is mine. In his eyes, I see my worth to him, and it matches my own.

So yeah, I got the guy. But most importantly—I got *the man I deserve.*

*One week later . . .*

Lucian tucks my roller case in the overhead bin before taking his pod seat. Reaching over the partition, he grips and kisses the back of my hand as my nerves start to fray. After a week of discussion on which postcode to reside in, we're on our way back to London for two weeks. I took the paid time off—which, honestly, I desperately needed. While in London, Lucian will resume the rest of his scheduled surgeries on a few more Razor patients before moving back to Boston.

Neither of us could bear to be apart another day during this transition, even if we have spent months apart. I didn't want to, so I decided to make the trip home with him and rearrange my life temporarily in order to be with the man I love—which was no sacrifice. I also wanted to be there for him for the last session with his mother and brother. Especially after he breaks it to them that he'll be leaving again on another semi-permanent basis.

Our decision was made when we both realized that, in truth, I'm more grounded and tied in Boston than he is—especially now as I seek to obtain my doctorate in nursing. Meanwhile, Lucian can still operate anywhere and fly back to London every month or so to see his family. So, for the time being, home will be Boston for both of us.

Happy with ideas of that future, I lean forward and peek over the partition of the pod to find the most gorgeous, brilliant man I've ever laid eyes on, peering right back at me.

"Ready, Cheeky?"

"Oh, yeah. I'm . . . this is great."

"Terrible liar," he says as the plane starts to speed down the runway. My chest begins to rise and fall as Lucian keeps our hands locked, and my heart thunders as images of the horrors we endured during our last trip start to race through my mind on a loop.

*Please, God. Be merciful, and this time, no bully cats.*

Lucian calls my name softly, his soothing voice bringing my focus back to him. "Do you remember the FedEx delivery driver?"

"Vaguely," I tell him, sweat beading my brow as I think back to that day. "He seemed a little pissed, right? He was kind of yelling at you, and you practically had to slam the door shut on him."

"Actually, no. He was concerned and rapidly shouting warnings to you, which, thankfully, you couldn't interpret."

"What?" I lean forward to see more of him. "What about?"

"Well, only that we were staying in a building that was set to be condemned," he drops casually as my jaw unhinges.

"Please tell me you are joking," I say.

"I suspected as much, what with the way the electricity was wired on the rooftop and the fact that we had absolutely no neighbors.

Also, the WIFI kept kicking us off with French theft warnings. It wasn't just the Airbnb, Jane—the *entire building* was a tourist trap."

I gawk at him. "But there was . . . no tape. There were no signs on any of the doors and no chains on the gate!"

"Chains can be cut. I found a few crumpled signs in the rubbish when I took it out the day we left. Apparently, someone had been running that scheme for some time. But to validate your initial booking, I did investigate and find it was at one time a legitimate Airbnb, and the scammers must have used the old advertisement profile to lure the unsuspecting in."

"Oh, my frickin' God," I rasp out before burying my face in my hands.

Lucian laughs loudly, pulling my hands from my face. "I didn't say it to make you feel guilty or embarrass you, Cheeky. I'm revealing this to you because if we can endure a twenty-year storm during an episode of God's Rapture Survivor Frantartica, all the while falling in love, then we've got this—"

"Even if we don't," I finish, palming his jaw and hating the restraint of the seatbelt. "God, you really do love me and never even acted upset about it."

"How could I be?" he asks, measuring my hand against his over the space between us. "I fell even more madly in love with my future wife in that building."

We stare off as I shake my head, incredulous.

"So . . . feeling better?" he asks.

"Tell me, Doc. Did you save that tidbit on the off chance I ever got back on a plane and started to rethink booking a ticket?"

"Absolutely, my cheeky girl. Because I told you I want no other travel companion."

"I love you, Lucian, so fucking much," I whisper. "And yes, I'm so much better."

As soon as the light goes off, we reach for the other and begin to full-on make out across the partition with absolutely no f's to give—even as our kiss deepens close to indecent until we're finally forced to pull away.

Minutes later, as he cracks open his hardback, his hand still clasped in mine over the nuisance between us, I sit dazed by his confession along with the past week's events—as well as the fact that I'm on another plane back overseas, which I thought would definitely not be happening anytime soon. But this time, it's in an entirely different capacity.

We're starting our future.

This isn't a daydream or a conjured hope of the life I want. This is now the life I have and the future made up of my dreams—dreams that have come to fruition. And instead of holding on to the man I love, the object of my affection to the point I crack, I don't have to break myself to try to keep him. He's in love with me equally—if not more so—so with a long exhale, I rest in that. Confident his hold is enough to keep us both because he's not letting me go.

The truth he gave me outside on my steps a week ago, though a little sad—and for a split second—a little painful, is a thousand percent truth.

The men who left me, who were careless with my heart and discarded my affection, whom I fought with to give me the same respect and love as I gave them, *didn't love* me.

It's the absolute truth.

As I stare over at my forever man, it doesn't hurt at all to have that answer or truth because of the man who *does love* me. Who's never made his return affection some mystery or hidden it. Who's never made me jump through hoops or question his love past the day he fell.

It was *me* who couldn't embrace that it was possible or believe that it was so damned simple. Especially with how I complicated that truth in giving my heart away in trial and error—and all I'd endured in the aftermath. I picked my broken heart up and glued it back together in expectation for another to come along and break it again. It took unrequited love to skew my perception, though I find myself thankful for that now because it took being in requited love with the right man to clearly see the truth for what it is.

Love doesn't have to be chased, or battered, or begged for, or bought, or demanded, or put through some horrific gauntlet to be real.

Love shouldn't have to be stolen, or abused, or hard-won to be considered genuine.

It simply has to *exist* and be accepted from one open heart to another to be both *real and lasting*.

That's the simple truth about love.

Lucian's love for me exists. It's real—as real as the love I have for him.

With him, I'll never have to go through any of those things to seek that answer, and that's the most beautiful, simplistic imaginable reality he could ever give me.

# EPILOGUE

## LUCIAN

*December 24, 2023*
*Five years later . . .*

A fucking pandemic that shut down the globe . . . inconceivable. Notre Dame catching fire . . . tragic in every sense of the word.

The world is in a state of complete unrest as conflicts of old come to a head again, leaving us on the brink of war . . . unthinkable and also fucking terrifying.

Never in my wildest imagination could I have seen this coming. That common perils—similar to those I read of to Jane during Napolean and Josephine's relationship and time—would mimic our current world in any way. But as it is right now, here we are.

As hard as it's been, Jane and I have endured . . . in fact, we've thrived.

Years of turmoil in the medical field have ensued because of the Covid outbreak, which had us losing colleagues and friends.

Even with so much uncertainty—as well as the state of things as they are—I'm certain we will continue to thrive.

My current nervousness having everything to do with my own little corner of the universe.

I still write to my wife at least once a month to tell her of my innermost thoughts and fears, such as these. But mostly of my devotion to her, my need for her, and my gratitude for our walk through time together.

She writes back, just as devoted, just as scared in uncertain times, but forever steadfast, showing her vulnerability, strength, and confidence.

Our history might not match that of the late emperor and his true love, but our world is starting to replicate more of the old-world behaviors and come what may—with certainty—I know Jane and I will continue to endure.

Sadly, for both our explorative hearts and minds, our globe is no longer a safe place to venture freely. Though discouraging, I can only be thankful for the adventures Jane, and I took before March of 2020, when the world seemed to stop altogether.

Not only has that changed since our first adventure five years ago, but it seems the very definition and essence of living has as well.

Gratitude for each day isn't just a yoga prayer anymore. It's something on the mind of every global citizen. World peace isn't a rehearsed answer for beauty contestants—it is the hope of all who seek it as reality.

Because we didn't know how thankful we should have been before March of 2020, and sadly, it feels as though we can never go back. As bleak as that realization may be, in appreciating each day and being grateful now, Jane and I are way ahead of the curve—and have been since we started our lives together.

We're forever grateful for the fact we found the other, to have shown the other our true selves, our true nature, and what our hearts consisted of—because in doing so, we found our match.

It hasn't been an easy road, but as I walk toward home—the home and family that we made together, and I continue to choose—I know we'll endure as many years as we're granted, even with all the uncertainty of living.

We will have to postpone any travel plans we have for the future—a sacrifice we'll happily make for an entirely different reason.

If someone had asked me who I was five years ago, my answer would have been simple—a one-word summation.

Today, I know I'm a man who likes to take long walks. Who looks forward to the first few snow flurries of the season but who decidedly hates winter in the middle of it.

Who salivates over a good lasagna and a slice of my wife's homemade chocolate pie. Who hates TV but loves a good film.

Who enjoys working with his hands on occasion and gets satisfaction from a good shave. I'm a man who has regrets about the way he's lived and who knows his needs and also his limits. I'm a husband who loves his wife with every beat of his heart, who loves making love to her, as well as making her come, and makes a spectacle of kissing her in public when she least expects it. I'm also a son, brother, and uncle to four nephews, with a fifth coming, thanks to Charlie.

Sometime in the next week, I'll add father to that roster. The pecking order of what I am and to whom will flip alongside my world when I hold my twin sons in my arms for the first time.

At the end of it, I'm also a heart surgeon, and a damned good one.

Taking the steps up to our newly renovated brownstone, I take note of the rustle of snow-covered trees lining our street and follow the descent of the drift—briefly getting lost in it.

*Shrugging off my coat, I walk into the hospital room to find Alexander scrambling to put his oxygen tube in. Closing the door, I lay my coat and scarf on the chair as he resumes with the controller for his game.*

*"Oxygen is essential, Alexander," I remind him.*

*"So is beating this game, doctor," he retorts dryly.*

*"I see we're not in the mood to take our treatment seriously today."*

*"That's your job, grump dick," he says, giving me a cheeky grin as I note the ill fit of his new pajamas.*

"So very crass, brother," I manage past the lump in my throat. "Seems you've forgotten your etiquette as well."

He lifts his chin and pauses his game. "So forget it with me and live a little. God knows you need it."

"And you need a bath," I say, scanning him, "desperately. I hope you realize you're ruining your chances of getting a date with that stench."

"Can't miss something you've never had, and girls seem high maintenance, and I'm high maintenance enough as it is." He gestures to the medical equipment beside him as I eye the stack of books he's recently collected on religion. The latest addition adding to the searing ache in my chest. He knows, or at least he is partially aware. Eyeing the snow drift out of his window his tone turns distant and contemplative.

"Maybe I'll come back as a snowflake, falling glorious seconds to earth, and I'll land on a tree and water it. And live in it far longer than this stupid body allows me," he turns back to me. "Longer than you, big brother," he snarks, his eyes alight.

A car horn sounds next to me, breaking my remembrance. My eyes sting with the memory as I again trace the snowfall. I've never told my wife about the true reason why I get so lost in the drift. Because if I'm a man capable of having a cosmic secret—this is mine and my brothers to keep. After all, it was the drift behind her in the cab that had me truly turning in her direction before my eyes finally focused on her. From then on, there were drifts almost every day of our start, as if Alexander was telling me *this way—this girl.*

The drift started within an hour of us landing in London, and continued to fall damned near every day after for the duration of our trip. I swear Alex was purposely being cheeky with the amount of snow for a few points in time—as if it was within his power. But my fascination with the drift itself fell away as my wife continually came into view before my eyes, awakening me.

Even now, I can picture Jane's porcelain smile as she raised her face to it in welcome years ago on a London street. I spend a few minutes appreciating the strength of that memory, the moment we were in with a grateful heart.

Where I used to take walks to help my anxieties—and still do—I now often take them to remember my blessings, which are many. I hope Alexander is aware of it, somehow.

On days like today, it feels like he's aware—and everywhere.

Taking the steps up to our home, I note the blinking lights of the twin wreaths Jane recently made during her 'nesting' phase. I can't help but smile at just how ostentatious they are. Just short of the front door stands a tuxedo-clad Kurt Russelfeathers and his ever-faithful companion Goldie Honkers, who tonight is wearing a glittering dark purple dress. But that's my wife, and I wouldn't modify a damned thing about how over the top she can be when decorating—or doing anything else for that matter.

Opening the door, I step inside and kick my wellie's heels to get the snow off, and I am met by the smell of mulberry and other welcoming spices as the sight of utter chaos greets me. My wife, nine months pregnant, belly overflowing with twins, chases Charlie's youngest toddler, Elliot, around the living room in her dinosaur costume. Ungracefully wobbling, she stomps after him as he squeals in delight and gives chase, feigning his fear. My smile grows exponentially as my grateful heart is again replenished. Turning one last time to glimpse the peace and tranquility of the silently cascading snow, I shut the door and lock myself inside with the chaos, thankful for whatever comes next with the family I chose.

THE END

Curious about Tyler AKA Big Bird? Start The international best-selling Ravenhood Trilogy now.

Want some more Romantic Dramedy? Read *The Guy on the Right*

# ABOUT THE AUTHOR

*USA Today* bestselling author and Texas native, Kate Stewart, lives in North Carolina with her husband, Nick. Nestled within the Blue Ridge Mountains, Kate pens messy, sexy, angst-filled contemporary romance, as well as romantic comedy and erotic suspense.

Kate's title, *Drive*, was named one of the best romances of 2017 by The New York Daily News and Huffington Post. *Drive* was also a finalist in the Goodreads Choice awards for best contemporary romance of 2017. The Ravenhood Trilogy, consisting of *Flock, Exodus*, and *The Finish Line*, has become an international bestseller and reader favorite. Her holiday release, *The Plight Before Christmas*, ranked #6 on Amazon's Top 100. Kate's works have been featured in *USA TODAY, BuzzFeed, The New York Daily News, Huffington Post* and translated into a dozen languages.

Kate is a lover of all things '80s and '90s, especially John Hughes films and rap. She dabbles a little in photography, can knit a simple stitch scarf for necessity, and on occasion, does very well at whiskey.

# Other titles available now by Kate

## Romantic Suspense

*The Ravenhood Series*
*Flock*
*Exodus*
*The Finish Line*

*The Ravenhood Legacy*
*One Last Rainy Day: The Legacy of a Prince*

*Lust & Lies Series*
*Sexual Awakenings*
*Excess*
*Predator and Prey*

## Contemporary Romance

In Reading Order

*Room 212*
*Never Me (Companion to Room 212 and The Reluctant Romantic Series)*
*The Reluctant Romantics Series*
*The Fall*
*The Mind*
*The Heart*
*The Reluctant Romantics Box Set: The Fall, The Heart, The Mind*
*Loving the White Liar*

*The Bittersweet Symphony*
*Drive*
*Reverse*
*Bittersweet Melody*

*The Real*
*Someone Else's Ocean*
*Heartbreak Warfare*
*Method*

**Romantic Dramedy**

*Balls in Play Series*
*Anything but Minor*
*Major Love*
*Sweeping the Series Novella*

*The Underdogs Series*
*The Guy on the Right*
*The Guy on the Left*
*The Guy in the Middle*

*The Plight Before Christmas*

Let's stay in touch!

Join my reader group - Kate Stewart's Recovery Room

Order Merch and Signed Copies - www.katestewartwrites.com

Facebook
www.facebook.com/authorkatestewart

Newsletter
www.katestewartwrites.com/contact-me.html

Twitter
twitter.com/authorklstewart

Instagram
www.instagram.com/authorkatestewart/?hl=en

Spotify
open.spotify.com/user/authorkatestewart